For D.
*—and to Kristi Gunnarshaug*

# JACOB'S FOLLY

## Rebecca Miller

**CANONGATE**
*Edinburgh · London*

Published in Great Britain in 2013 by Canongate Books Ltd,
14 High Street, Edinburgh EH1 1TE

www.canongate.tv

1

First published in the United States of America in 2013 by
Farrar, Straus and Giroux, 18 West 18th Street, New York 10011, USA

First published in Great Britain in 2013 by Canongate Books Ltd,
14 High Street, Edinburgh EH1 1TE

British Library Cataloguing-in-Publication Data
A catalogue record for this book is available on
request from the British Library

ISBN 978 0 85786 896 1
Export ISBN 978 0 85786 897 8

Designed by Abby Kagan

Printed and bound by CPI Group (UK) Ltd, Croydon CR0 4YY

*This book is printed on FSC certified paper*

# JACOB'S FOLLY

Also by Rebecca Miller

*Personal Velocity*
*The Private Lives of Pippa Lee*

Wild things leave skins behind them, they leave clean skins and teeth and white bones behind them, and these are tokens passed from one to another, so that the fugitive kind can always follow their kind . . .

–Tennesee Williams, Orpheus Descending

Evil is the chair of the good.

–Israel ben Eliezer, the Ba'al Shem Tov

## ∞ 1

I, the being in question, having spent nearly three hundred years lost as a pomegranate pip in a lake of aspic, amnesiac, bodiless, and comatose, a nugget of spirit but nothing else, found myself quickening, gaining form, weight, and, finally, consciousness. I did not remember dying, so my first thoughts were confused, and a little desperate.

As the blinding layer of black cloud I was enshrouded in dissipated, I saw the moon: opalescent, crater-pocked, impassive; frighteningly close. Indifferent stars carved up the firmament with their dazzling, ancient patterns. There was an echoing sound, like huge air bubbles escaping flatulently from an enormous wide-mouthed bottle underwater in a Turkish bath with a domed roof, but there was also a tearing—a continuous ripping, as if a universe-sized sheet of canvas were being torn asunder. I now know this was the fabric of time. I felt intensely alone and cried out, but my shriek sounded submerged. Instinctively, I beat the wings I didn't know I had, and rose. I could fly! Was I dreaming? The black air was surprisingly viscous. My wings outstretched, I let myself descend, circling slowly through the thick stuff, passing through roiling, wispy clouds that felt cool on my skin. I was definitely awake. Could I be an angel? Euphoria and disbelief gathered in me. I reveled at having been chosen, against all odds, to be part of the heavenly host. I yearned to admire myself—or better, to be admired. I knew I must be very beautiful. I flapped my wings, spreading them wide, banking, making a slow round, wending my way down through the night. Below me, a web of lights, like a spume of stars, spilled out into a great darkness. As I neared, I saw the blackness churning, cresting: the sea. I was looking down on the earth! But what were all those lights?

Descending more rapidly as old rosy-fingers passed her bright hand over the ocean, washing it with light, I could now make out a crust of houses, built up on the twinkling island below like a skin malady. The massive grid of roofs rose to meet me vertiginously.

Swirling through the atmosphere, I had no idea where I was, but I knew I'd been gone a long time. Smooth-hipped, humpish carriages gleamed at the doors of the toylike dwellings; streetlamps spilled pools of steady light on ruled streets as smooth as stretched toffee: it was the future, I knew it. The last tool of illumination I had seen was a porcelain candelabrum beside my bed in Paris, in 1773. It was encrusted with light green leaves, tiny pink roses, and cherubim.

Still in the meat of my youth, I lay shivering with fever, my chest tight, sweat trickling down my sides. Now and then Solange would look in on me, the silk of her dress whispering as she moved about the room, replacing my water jug or plumping my pillow. Her gardenia perfume was too pungent for my strangled breath and I turned away as she leaned over me, yet I never took my eyes from the candelabrum. I found it a little garish—but what did I know? I was an ex-peddler, born in a tenement. I was lucky to even be next to this six-branched, delicately fluted masterpiece with twelve naked winged babies crawling over its glazed surface. Cascades of hardened beeswax spilled from each candle and all along the porcelain base, mingling with the cupids and tangling with the roses—the result of a week-long bacchanal, my meager staff too exhausted from entertaining the guests to scrape wax off candlesticks in the morning.

I watched, fascinated, my eyes dry, breath short, as each drip was formed: at the base of the flame, a little pool of molten wax glistened, plump as a tear on the rim of a woman's eye; when the pool grew too great, it breached the worn edge of the candle, trickling freely along the shaft and finding its crooked path down the petrified waterfall. Moving farther and farther away from the source of heat, the cooling wax became hesitant, cloudy, until it froze entirely, fusing itself to the spillage.

I stared at the wax dripping down the candles for hours and hours, until, at dawn, I died. Sunday, the seventh of February, 1773. I was thirty-one. After that, nothing. And now I was an angel! I imagined myself as a fully formed Christian seraph, a Viking with blond hair, a beautiful chiseled torso, hairless feet, and eyes the color of whiskey. When I was alive, I was dark haired, short, slight, with light eyes, strong teeth, and a thick, long sex that I scented and coiled inside my britches daily with great care and pride, an aspect of my physicality which I hoped had been duplicated by the Almighty; but whenever I tried to look down at myself I could not move my neck, and my arms felt very weak. I assumed this stiffness was due to the long period of being dead.

Something amazing had happened to my sight: it was as if the top of my head had been removed and replaced with an enormous eye. I could see jagged purple clouds drifting above me, the streets stretching away at either side, and the houses below. *This is how angels see*, I marveled.

I noticed a gigantic figure stride out of one of the shiny carriages. Trying to focus on him and ignore the rest of the nearly 360-degree view, I descended cautiously, not yet in full command of my wings, afraid that the man might see me, yet half hoping he would. The thought of bringing this Titan to his knees with astonishment and awe was attractive to me. I imagined myself as an angel in a painting, my chiton frozen mid-billow as I reached my delicate hands out expressively, the object of my communication falling to the ground with awe and wonder, his eyes rolling up in his head.

Yet, as I hovered above him, I had an alarming double vision: I saw the man, and I *knew* him.

Reliable, true Leslie Senzatimore stood on his square of new-mown grass at the cusp of dawn, planted his feet far apart, leaned back, and aimed a glistening arc of piss straight over the fading moon. The heavenly body glowed, lassoed by his steaming ribbon, and maybe even claimed by a man who, at forty-four, had every reason to be content.

Unlike most of the residents of this tree-lined Long Island street, Leslie owned his house outright; a split-level ranch-style home presently stuffed with three sleeping children, one au pair, a splendid wife, two cats, a daughter-in-law, and an aging cocker spaniel. A vintage motorboat, totem of the family's well-earned leisure, gleamed beneath a tarp; four cars, of varying sizes and prices, from his wife's toy-strewn Ford Explorer to his stepson's dusty Slovakian compact, were evidence of busy, work-filled lives. A smaller house to one side was also Leslie's, and contained his hard-drinking in-laws, the most voluble of a spate of dependents that Leslie had welcomed onto his back throughout his adult life like a cheerful Sisyphus. Leslie was a natural hero, and had been ever since the day he had rescued the kittens from under the Bobiks' roof when he was thirteen years old, back in 1981.

On that day, Mrs. Bobik had come puffing into the Senzatimore kitchen and dropped onto the comfy chair by the window, her flowered housedress darkened with sweat between enormous low-slung breasts, the pale flesh under her arms ruffled like the fat on a plucked chicken. This act immediately claimed the solemn attention of Leslie and his four siblings, who were at that moment eating cereal at the kitchen table, because that overstuffed armchair had belonged to their father— their father had recently hanged himself—and nobody got to sit in that chair. Evelyn Senzatimore, however, stifled an urge to flush the woman out of her house and waited stoically for Mrs. Bobik to unburden herself, as she had nearly every day since Mr. Bobik disappeared, leaving her childless and confused, seven years earlier. A hopeless alcoholic, he had last been seen staggering outside the Woolworth's in Las Vegas by a local honeymooning couple who recognized him as their former school bus driver. This unfortunate sighting did nothing to calm Mrs. Bobik's nerves; the woman subsequently lost pretty much all hold on what most of us would call reality. So, when she charged into the Senzatimore household yelling that there were cats in her ceiling, her claim was met by six pairs of pitying eyes.

"They were mewing all night," she moaned.

Leslie's mother sighed and looked at Leslie, as if to say, *You deal with this.* This was something Mrs. Senzatimore did a lot these days, whenever life's demands became too much for her. Leslie was the oldest boy, and she knew her child was flattered by, maybe even craved, her dependence on him. It made up, in some tiny way, for the violent loss of a mild-mannered father who had gradually faded out of the family over the past few years. An undiagnosed depressive, Charlie Senzatimore became more and more of a cipher, said less and less, until at last he simply decided to become a real ghost instead of a ghost that sat in an armchair and read the local paper. It wasn't that his children didn't miss him; they just couldn't fix on any one thing to miss, seeing as they'd had virtually no relationship with the man, apart from the one their mother had created for them. "Your father will be furious," she would threaten, even though they knew that all Charlie would do was shake his head sadly or stalk out of the house, banging the door behind him. "Your father is so proud!" she would exclaim, as the slender puppet propped up beside her attempted a lopsided smile. Poor Evelyn Senzatimore. Every day she had to get up and paint a vivid portrait of a father and husband who didn't fully exist. Yet when he truly ceased to, when she saw him dangling lifeless in the shed, the strength and volume of her grief amazed her. Whom was she mourning—a work of her own imagination, or the shade she'd shared her life with? Either way, now she had no one to create on a daily basis; she was left with herself, her children, the reality of her life. She missed him unbearably. At last, in death, Charlie had become real to her. Evelyn suddenly felt acutely vulnerable, and so she turned to Leslie, her solid boy.

So it was no surprise to anyone when Leslie, dressed for school in a short-sleeved collared shirt and khakis, his strong frame already taking on muscle, reddish brown hair ("Had the Vikings been to Sicily?" people often asked his mother, forgetting she was Irish) slicked to one side, stood up and said, "I'll take a look for you, Mrs. Bobik."

"Good boy," said his mother. "Take your books. You can go to school from there."

The smell in the Bobik house was suffocating. It wasn't filth— Mrs. Bobik was a scrupulously clean woman—but rather an indistinct, stale sub-odor that Leslie thought must be the smell of abandonment. The place was rank with it. It scared and disgusted him. Looking back, I think it possible that Leslie created his whole adult life as a defense against that smell.

He followed Mrs. Bobik up her narrow staircase, trying not to stare at her massive rump toiling beneath her housedress, then down the cramped hallway, past closed doors masking unused rooms of unborn children, to the tiny master bedroom, a virtual cathedral of religious iconography. The Virgin Mary took center stage in Mrs. Bobik's Catholicism, leaving Jesus to fend for himself on a minuscule cross tacked between two windows. In full color above the bed, framed on the bedside table, in statue form on the dresser, it was Mary all the way.

"Do you hear them?" asked Mrs. Bobik urgently, still out of breath from the stairs, her huge bust heaving, short legs spread wide like a bulldog's. She was shorter than Leslie, and her watery blue protruding eyes were fixed on his with an expression of questioning surrender. This was, he began to realize with a kind of horror, the final test of Mrs. Bobik's sanity. If he didn't hear these cats, she was officially off her rocker, just like everyone thought she was. He felt himself endowed with sudden, alarming authority, as though he were the doctor who was about to tell her if her cancer was operable. Her coffee breath reached him in nauseating waves. He could hear the blood pounding in his ears as embarrassment and confusion washed over him. He started looking around the room, as if for an escape route. What should he say if he didn't hear the cats? Should he lie? And if he lied, and there were no cats, then what? Should he find a stray cat and plant it in her closet and take it out and then maybe she would stop hearing cats? Was he already late for school? His thoughts were coming so thick and fast that he forgot to listen, but when his wandering gaze found Mrs. Bobik's, her beseeching expression brought him back to his task. He heard the barking of a dog outside, the sound of children calling to one another on the way to school, a bird stubbornly repeating the same flat phrase over and over again. And then, like the faraway cry of a baby, a sinew of sound drifted through the room, barely audible. It was a cat. Leslie was overcome with relief. "I hear it!" he said joyfully.

"You do?" cried out Mrs. Bobik, clasping her plump hands.

"Yes—it's—" His eyes wandered around the room, trying to follow the sound. Now that he had heard the one mewing, he could hear others. There was more than one cat. She was right! But where was the sound coming from? It seemed to be emanating from the air in the center of the room. He opened the closet, looked under the bed, under the dresser. No cats. Then he stood up on a chair and put a glass up to the low ceiling, just like he'd seen Columbo do on TV. Like an eerie secret, the sound unfurled into his ear; the plaintive mewing of weakened cats.

"Do you have an attic?" he asked.

"Naw, just a little crawl space under the roof. What do I need an attic for? I just had it resealed, as a matter of fact. A board on the side of the house was rotten."

"When was it fixed?"

"Three days ago," she said.

"I think you trapped those cats," said Leslie.

"How did cats . . . ," began Mrs. Bobik. But Lesie was already on his way back home. His mother and all the other Senzatimore children followed him back up the block, his brother Will helping him carry the tall ladder, which, Leslie knew, had last been used by their father to reach his final destination.

Other neighborhood kids, on their way to school, began to follow him too. "What are you doin', Les?" "What's goin' on?" Leslie said nothing. He just marched up to the Bobik house, ladder under one arm, the strap of his father's heavy tool bag digging painfully into the fingers of his free hand.

With brother Will's small-handed help, he expanded the ladder, set it so the top rested just under Mrs. Bobik's bedroom window. Then, his already prominent jaw set, Leslie climbed the rungs. Just as he reached the top, Mrs. Bobik popped her head out.

"You gonna damage my house?" she asked hoarsely.

"I have to take a board off if you want me to get the cats out," Leslie explained, holding a hammer out expressively.

"Jesus, Mary, and Joseph," said Mrs. Bobik, retracting her head back inside.

Leslie gently eased the back of the hammer under the new, unpainted board, a few inches above Mrs. Bobik's window, and pulled with a rocking motion, trying to wrest it free. After a few seconds there was a splintering sound and the nails gave way. Leslie pried the remaining nails out of the new wood, set the board down on the slanted roof. He put his face up to the gap. A sharp, angry hiss emanated from the darkness and Leslie realized for the first time that these cats might not want to be rescued. He looked down at his mother. "It's hissing," he said.

"Tell Mrs. Bobik—a dish of milk." Leslie took his mother's advice. Mrs. Bobik handed Leslie a dish of milk. He left it above the dormer window, just outside the opening, and called to the cat.

It took a long while, and he lost part of his audience down on the ground—kids being called away by their mothers to go to school—but eventually a scrawny gray cat walked unsteadily out into the sunshine, like a hostage freed after a month in a cave. She sniffed the milk and began to lap it. Leslie was afraid to move lest he scare the animal, yet he knew he needed to get to the next step in the proceeding. The mewing inside was so thin and high it could only be kittens. The stray had crept up Mrs. Bobik's lattice and along the roof to nestle in a private birthing room.

There were actual cheers as Leslie reached in and pulled out the first frail, mewing creature curled over his hand, a tiny orange tabby, and the exhilaration he felt was total. To be so high up, watched by all, and executing such a good deed—he was hooked to rescue for life.

The sun was high in the sky and Leslie had missed both math and science classes by the time he handed the last kitten down into the crowd of mothers, tiny children, his siblings, and the few kids his own age who had ducked their parents and played truant for the sake of this spectacle. Each kitten handed down—there were eight of them— got a new home that day—and thus began a line of cats that even now, twenty-six years later, populated the town of Patchogue, Long Island. As for Leslie and his family, they adopted a fine tom kitten they named Bob. Mrs. Bobik kept the mother, a fellow victim of abandonment, and slept with her every night, which seemed to do wonders for the poor woman's nerves. The damage to her house was fixed for free that very afternoon by a divorcé with jug ears and a thin mustache,

Vincent McCaffrey, who cannily used the event to court Leslie's winsome mother. Ten months later, McCaffrey legally lifted from her the great name of Senzatimore (*Senza-timoray*, meaning, Leslie's timorous father had told him wistfully many times, "fearless" in Italian) and became Leslie's stepfather. McCaffrey wasn't a bad man, but it was too late to start loving another father, and Leslie felt forced into the world. What he really wanted to do was become a fireman, but his mother begged him not to. Her father—a fireman—had died in a fire, and the thought of losing her son as well as her husband gave the poor woman hives. So that was out. But, determined to make something of himself in spite of his father's voluntary demise and the shadow of doom it had cast on his children, Leslie joined the Navy at seventeen and earned a college diploma while sailing around the world. Returning home, he took out a loan and revived his father's boat repair business, Senzatimore Marine. At twenty-nine, Leslie began to volunteer in the Patchogue Fire Department. He was on his way.

I perceived all this in a futuristic gush as I hovered over the big man: images of his past and inner workings batted at my vision in a vomitous stream of moving pictures, a cacophony of sounds and thoughts. It was an empathic overload, a strain to organize coherently, overwhelming in scope. I imagined what it must be for the Creator himself, who saw and heard the entire world, every thought and action, every tear and fart. I wondered if God was a madman by now, having hallucinated like this twenty-four hours a day for millions of years.

This new, angelic awareness had left me with a distinct sense of unease. I saw into this man so easily, like a hot knife piercing a tub of chicken fat; he seemed good through and through. What did he need an angel for? Very good men irritated and embarrassed me; I had always tried to avoid them. My heart (I felt I had a heart) pumping in my chest, I lowered myself gradually, both craving an encounter and dreading it. As I came closer to Leslie, I felt a warm tide of air swirl around my body. I felt naked. Lowering myself still more, I found the air around him was nearly hot, and thick as honey. This man stank of woodsmoke. He was still pissing, his face and pallid member both turned toward the dawn sky. I felt he was looking right at me. I waited for him to see me, for the terrible encounter to occur. I assumed that when it did I would know what to say, and I would understand why I had been sent back to earth. Yet Leslie was not reacting. His big jaw set, light blue eyes focused at a point just beyond my head, he zipped up his trousers, turned, and walked away from me, toward one of the box houses. Was I invisible? Suddenly frightened to be left alone outside, I flew behind him, arms outstretched, determined to follow him to shelter. I beat my wings as hard as I could, but the air resisted me. My flight felt turgid. I was floating as much as flying. Before I could reach him, Leslie had opened the door to his house and closed it gently, shutting me out. I set down on the hard, shiny leaf of a bush by the door, folding my wings petulantly as I realized that, on top of everything else, I was tiny—one of those angels that fits on the head of a pin!

With my man gone, the air went cool. Cold, scared, baffled, I focused my mind on Leslie, and was astonished to find myself as good as in his bedroom, staring down at his big-boned, comely wife—even as I shivered outside.

## 3

Hearing her husband come in, Deirdre Senzatimore shifted under the dense duvet, opened one eye, and looked at the crack between the curtains. Electric blue. Almost morning. *So many fires in the night*, she thought, drifting. *Why?* . . . In her sinking mind, her deaf five-year-old son, Stevie, was starting a small fire in her bedroom, and as it grew, the heat became unbearable. "Where did you find those matches?" she asked him, unable to pry her head from the pillow. But the little blond boy was laughing, lighting one match after another, tossing them around the floor as if throwing crumbs to pigeons. Just then, Leslie walked in wearing his full fireman's gear. He had a swollen canvas hose in one hand and doused Stevie with a fat jet of water. Deirdre cried out for him to stop, but he kept the stream of water on the little boy, as if it were the child that was on fire. The water turned off as if controlled by a tap somewhere; Deirdre ran to her dripping son to find that Stevie was covered in shimmering, translucent stones. Deirdre picked one off and held it between thumb and forefinger. It was a diamond.

Feeling her husband in the room now, and waking, Deirdre turned inside her thin cotton nightgown, twisting the fabric as she peered at him, then let her head fall back on the pillow. Hair wet from bathing, and naked, Leslie climbed under the bedding, pulling his wife into his chest, encircling her in his big arms, feeling her soft belly, her full breasts, all that strong flesh somewhat collapsed beneath the thin fabric. He brushed her heavy hair from the back of her neck and pressed his face to it. Her skin was very warm, nearly hot.

"How was it?" she murmured.

"Basement fire," he said. "Wiring." Within seconds, they both fell into a pit of sleep.

Leslie had first spotted Deirdre at the Stop & Shop in Patchogue, when they were both nearly thirty. She was pushing a large cart filled with groceries, her young son walking by her side. Bud was a skinny six-year-old with large dark eyes. He sang quietly to himself as he walked, one finger hooked over a wire in the metal cart. As Leslie passed him, Bud looked up and grinned mirthlessly with one side of his mouth. Leslie raised his eyebrows, but he didn't say anything; you couldn't talk to children you didn't know anymore. Then he looked up and saw the mother. Deirdre was close to six feet tall, with a strong-boned face, shiny brown hair, and a heavy, tight-clad bust. Even her hands were large. As she scanned the many choices for canned beans and tomatoes, she had a dreamy, contemplative way of moving that hinted at an inner depth, some secret sadness; it touched him. She wore no ring.

In the parking lot he noticed her again, her thick hair glinting as she and the boy with the crooked smile deftly, silently loaded the shopping bags into the trunk of a dented hatchback, parked a fateful two cars away from Leslie's truck. The competent, self-contained way the two of them moved made him wonder if they had anyone to help at the other end. Once the boy was buckled into the backseat, Deirdre stopped and hesitated, one hand on the empty cart, looking around her.

Leslie called out, "I'll put that back for you."

She squinted over at him, confused. "What?"

"I'll put the cart back for you."

"Oh. Thanks." He walked over to her, embarrassed by her gaze. It felt like it was taking forever to reach her. Leslie was reminded of a useless explanation a teacher had given him, of infinity: when crossing a room, first you need to walk halfway across, then half of that half, then half of that half. So you traverse an infinite set of halves, never reaching your destination. But you did, Leslie remembered thinking, always get to the other side of a room. Reaching Deirdre at last, he took the cart from her and rolled it away a little so there was nothing between them.

"I know, you want to do the right thing and put them back, but it's a pain," he said, gesturing vaguely with an enormous arm. She smiled. He flung out his hand as if reaching out to catch a falling glass. "Les Senzatimore," he said.

"That's a mouthful," she said with a laugh, taking his hand. Hers was dry and strong, but still dwarfed by his mitt. "I'm Deirdre."

"Nice to meet you," he said. In the car, Bud swiveled around in his seat to spot his mother.

"I need to get to work," she said, hesitating for a split second and glancing, Leslie noticed, at his naked ring finger. "Thanks again." Leslie felt an impulse to skip the introductory scenario, squeeze into the driver's seat of her pathetic little car, and drive the three of them away. Neither of them moved. Sexual tension eddied into the ensuing pause like seawater filling a cleft in the sand.

"Mom?" Bud called, curious.

"Okay hon," Deirdre called lightly to the boy, taking a step.

"Where do you work?" asked Leslie. He didn't want to lose her, but he couldn't ask her out, not yet.

"Um . . . Trumbull Interiors? On Main Street."

"I know it. I—I've actually been thinking of going in there." Compulsively, Leslie's tongue traced a cross along the roof of his mouth in penance for this slender lie.

"Oh, yeah?" Deirdre said, looking up at him skeptically, a hint of a smile on her face. There were little baby wrinkles around her amber eyes already. The suffering behind that cynical look of hers daunted him slightly. He felt she could see through him and beyond, far, far down. He wasn't sure he was up to the challenge. Yet he continued.

"I need to do something about my apartment," he confided, picturing his randomly furnished rental, not a hint of love in the place. Just a few pressed-plywood chairs, a brown leatherette couch, a stereo, a TV: a place to hate yourself in. Suddenly, a pang of mourning for his dead father, something he hadn't felt in years, ambushed him: tears sprang to his eyes. He rubbed them as if against the glare, took his sunglasses from where they hung on his T-shirt pocket, and put them on. Deirdre was dipped in sepia now, and lovely, filtered in this way; her high cheekbones and generous mouth, the prominent nose, wise eyes, all appeared as if in a film still.

"Well, Trumbull's pricey, but they're good, if you want drapes, or—you know, color consultation and whatnot," she said, looking down at her large sandals. Her toenails were painted coral. "I wouldn't go to them for furniture."

"If I come in, will you help me?" he asked.

"Sure. Ask for me. Deirdre Jenkins."

When he bedded her, three weeks from that day, her strength exhilarated him. They wrestled on the bed like titans, their bodies laced with shadows cast by the new, possibly slightly too feminine curtains Deirdre had chosen for Leslie in her redecoration scheme. Leslie relished Deirdre's springy thighs, her firm arms, the wide, powerful armature of her pelvis. Most of all, Leslie was afraid of living a puny life. His father had been a pusillanimous stump of a man. Leslie would live an honest, brave life, in the light of day, with this healthy animal of a woman. Her skin was always hot.

As Leslie slept with Deirdre, I, Leslie's invisible angel, clung to my swaying leaf outside the Senzatimore house, Leslie's past flushing through me like a fever, and listened to him breathe. I could hear Deirdre's breath too, the whir of heat coming on in their bedroom, the hiss of a limb gliding on sheets. I strained to see his dream, as well, but all I could make out was the shape of a very long ship.

Walking down the stairs, Deirdre saw their two cats—one white and one tiger stripe—making boneless figure eights below her as they milled like sharks impatient for a feed. What creeped her out about cats, Deirdre realized as she spooned shiny chunks of meat in a gelatinous sauce from a can, was the fact that their feet made no sound. From above, they seemed to glide. They were sneaky, parasitic, indifferent. But the Senzatimore cats were legend; every other meow in the neighborhood was somehow related to Leslie's original rescue. They would always have cats, whether she liked it or not. Their sleek pelts brushing her ankles, Deirdre opened the door and set the bowls outside. The felines sped out. Taking my chance, I zoomed in before Deirdre slammed the door.

The house was decorated on a large scale, with a hefty pine side table in the front hall, massive blue and yellow tiles on the floor. The kitchen was roomy, sunny, and neat, with an enormous metal box in the corner and a wooden butcher's table with huge pans hanging on a black iron circle above it, attended by four extra-high wooden stools. The wooden cabinets were painted a gleaming, creamy white. Everything seemed to have been built for giants. This made sense in light of the size of Leslie and Deirdre Senzatimore.

Floating into the living room, I saw slablike soft couches, shapeless chairs. This furniture was spine-deforming. The thought of how ugly a person would look slumped in it filled me with dismay. In my day, furniture helped a person move in an attractive, precise manner. I was not yet aquainted with the concept of casual that is the modern way. These flabby couches confused and disturbed me. Saddened by the furnishings, I wafted up the stairs. Through an open door down the hall, I glimpsed walls painted with fluffy clouds, and Deirdre, leaning over the huddled little form of her son.

Stevie was still sleeping, his narrow chest rising and falling, mouth shut, eyes roving under thin lids, the light curls at his neck damp with sweat from too many blankets. Deirdre wanted to take one off, but she hated to wake her little boy up, to disturb his sleep, and dreams wherein, who knew, maybe he could hear stuff. There had been no promise of operations or cures; Stevie was deaf, and that was that. I felt embarrassed, hovering there, and flew downstairs. Deirdre walked back in after a few minutes and measured out some coffee beans. Leslie appeared then, followed by the spaniel. The old dog's nails scrabbled along the tile floor with sweeping little clicks.

"You already up?" Deirdre asked.

"I got a lot to do," said Leslie. He smelled deliciously of eau de cologne. His mint-green shirt was ironed and tucked into his jeans, his short hair brushed back. Deirdre set some coffee and toast on the table.

"You want eggs?" she asked, too late, she knew, to be a practicable offer. The toast would be cold.

He smiled. "No, honey. You working today?"

"Yeah, I have a client . . . she's coming here later, after I get back from dropping Stevie."

"It's Saturday."

"I know, I'm bringing him in for a half day," she said.

"I can drop Stevie," said Leslie. "I'm going in to work later today."

"Okay," she said.

"You all right?" he asked.

"I'm okay," she said. He kissed her and left the room, a piece of toast in his hand. The dog followed.

Deirdre stood, bent over, her strong wrists resting on the edge of the butcher's table. Her Valkyrie's behind was encased in tight-fitting stiff blue trousers that descended to a pair of pointed boots of tooled leather. Intrigued by her healthy frame, I settled on the rim of a porcelain bowl and listened for her thoughts.

The quiet of the house whirred in Deirdre's ears. She saw the sound as a red circle going around and around—the pulse of silence. She wondered if this was what Stevie heard, or if it was truly nothing. Deirdre and Leslie had begun to learn sign language the day after they were told the baby was deaf. They were doing all they could for him. Yet a sense of lack, of having been robbed, seemed innate in Stevie. He lurched between angelic inwardness and fearsome, demanding rages. Deirdre couldn't stand up to him. Strong as she was, the guilt she felt about his impairment stopped her from putting her foot down. She looked up at the clock: eight-fifteen. The au pair had already gone to English class in the city. She didn't want Stevie to wake up till the last minute; if he was in a bad frame of mind, it could be hell. Some days he came downstairs filled with light, smiling, a miracle of happiness. Other mornings, anger scrabbled at him from the inside, pulling at his moods. He became suspicious, resentful, confused. She heard a sound on the stairs. It was Stevie.

"Hi, honey," she signed. A fair, fragile boy, Stevie walked up to his mother and clung to her leg, blinking his pale eyes sleepily. She took him up in her arms and rocked him back and forth, burrowing her face into his soft neck. How could she have dreaded seeing him? Her own little boy.

Outside the window a large orange tabby cat Deirdre had never seen before hopped onto the sill, fixed a furious gaze on her, and meowed emphatically, its yellow eyes boring into her. She could hear its indignant complaints through the window. That cat seemed to be trying to say something. She set Stevie down in a chair, walked to the door, and opened it a crack. The animal hopped off the windowsill, landing with a thud, and approached the open door agressively, trying to press its head through.

"What are you doing?" said Deirdre, shoving it away with her boot. "Go away. Go." The last thing they needed was another cat. She edged out the door, closing it behind her, and stamped her foot. The orange tabby hopped away, but then it stopped and sat down, its brow furrowed, and looked at her.

"What?" said Deirdre. "Go." She took a pebble from the ground and threw it a few inches from the cat. The cat skittered off, yet at the edge of the lawn it stretched itself luxuriously, almost insolently. Deirdre went back inside. Her heart was pounding. Stevie was looking at her, his eyes wide open as if to trap any information they could.

"A cat," Deirdre signed. "He needs to go back to his own house."

Satisfied, the boy became distracted by a toy left on the table, touched it with inquisitive grasping fingers. Deirdre watched her son play, relieved that he was busy. Sometimes she felt his little fingers clawing at her like insistent animals, tearing at her concentration, her mind, her spirit. She had hit him once—slapped his little hand. It made her sick to think of it.

I watched her thoughful face and remembered Solange. She used to disappear into herself like this. Oh, Solange—dear lost friend! I wonder how long you lived. Even if you became an old woman, you've been dead two hundred years.

## 4

The first time I saw Solange I was sixteen, lugging my box of *clinquaillerie*—knives, saltcellars, snuffboxes, hammers—anything I could sell—through the Faubourg Saint-Honoré, calling out my wares as loud as I could. The box hung from a leather strap that was slung around my neck and cut into the skin painfully.

A thickset bitch of a servant in a blood-stippled apron, her hands ruddy, fine red veins threaded through her nose, started pawing through my knives, checking the blades and then tossing them back into the drawer as though she wished she could slice me with them. I stood stock-still, calmly watching this ransacking. When she chose a knife at last and asked me roughly for the price, I bowed slightly.

"Normally I would charge thirty sous, but from you, *chère madame*, I ask only twenty-five." She seemed disgruntled by this offer of a bargain and snorted. An involuntary smile twisted her mouth as she dropped the coins into my hand, careful not to touch me. Imagine, a Jew giving anyone a bargain! She took the knife, turned swiftly, and waddled off, eager to forget about the whole incident. I began to make order in my knife drawer again, basking in my pathetic triumph, when

I glimpsed the blue-green silk of a fine dress and caught the dark, insistent scent of gardenia perfume.

"Do you have any snuffboxes?" The voice was musical, playful.

"*Oui, mademoiselle,*" I answered, opening the highest drawer in my box and removing three painted snuffboxes.

"*Madame,*" she corrected me.

"Excuse me," I said, my eyes flicking up to her face. She was young, maybe twenty, with a long, mournful Spanish face, small chocolate eyes. Her neck was speckled with a scatter of tiny birthmarks. Her features weren't nearly as pretty as she was. She took one of the snuffboxes and turned it in her narrow fingertips.

"How much for this one?" she asked.

"Thirty-two sous," I said.

"How can you possibly make a living like this?" she asked, replacing the snuffbox and setting a small, strong hand on top of my peddler's box. "You are a Jew, am I right?"

"Yes, madame."

"My master has a job for you if you would like it," she said. "You'll make more in a morning than if you sold this whole box of junk."

"Who is your master?" I asked.

"The Comte de Villars—this is his house," she said, gesturing to the mansion behind her, enclosed by a high wall. "It's only a few little errands. You can leave your peddler's box in the coach house; it will be safe. And then, after you are done, come to the kitchen, we'll feed you some soup and bread." She had a light, sunny way of talking that made everything she described seem enticing.

"What will he pay?"

"One louis," she said. My father often didn't make that much in a month. I imagined the suspicion that would spread over the old man's face when I brought home the golden coin.

"I can't accept that," I said.

"Why not?"

"I am sorry, madame."

"I think it's quite generous!" she said.

"It's too generous. It's . . . absurd," I said, looking down at my box.

"Absurd!" She laughed. "Are you angry with me? All right. Don't be so upset. Good Lord. What is not absurd, for a morning's work making deliveries?"

"Forty sous," I answered softly.

"My name is Solange," she said. "What are you called?"

"Jacob Cerf," I answered.

She led me into the carriage house, a well-swept, tidy room with a gleaming crimson carriage standing at its center, a family crest with two golden lions rampant decorating the door. A larger carriage was parked to one side, covered in a tarp. I dragged the leather yoke of my box over my head and set it down. Now Solange disappeared for a few moments and returned carrying several filled leather pouches, accompanied by addressed letters.

I made the deliveries. Though the shopkeepers looked at me curiously when I arrived, asking, "From the Comte de Villars?" and peeked into the pouches, when they counted the coins inside they were happy enough. I guessed that it had been some time since my employer had paid his bills.

When I returned, Solange was waiting for me outside the great house. She walked me into the kitchen and instructed the cook to serve me soup, cold meat, and bread. The cook was not happy, but she did what she was told, setting the plates down hard before me. I was very hungry, but I didn't dare eat in a gentile's house, for fear of breaking our dietary laws. I sat stupidly before the tempting meal, hands in my lap, nearly weeping with embarrassment.

"You think there's something wrong with it?" laughed the cook.

"Never mind," said Solange. "Maybe you will be hungry tomorrow. Come back, we have work for you." I returned to the count's house the next morning. After that, every day but the Sabbath, Solange found errands for me to execute: dropping a coat off at the tailor's to be mended, buying a skein of thread, a few buttons, or buckles for a pair of shoes. Solange always gave me considerably more money than I needed for my messages, but I brought back the correct change every time. I wasn't a thief.

Eventually, I convinced myself it was acceptable to eat the soup and bread they offered me, as long as I ate no meat. Each day when I was finished I came back to the kitchen and sat at the long wooden table, sipping soup, tearing at the fine white bread. I spent the rest of the day selling my wares, then put the money I had made from the Jew's box into the tin my mother kept above the stove, for food and other household expenses. The count's money I pocketed, thinking that one day I would put it to use and show my father that I was a savvy businessman.

One chilly afternoon, when I had finished the count's errands and sat gratefully spooning pea-and-mint potage into my mouth, I heard the cook whisper to Solange, "Look how handsome." My throat closed up with embarrassment and I had to leave before I had finished my soup, which I regretted later as I lay hungry in my bed.

After five weeks, Solange said, "Would you like to meet the master of the house?"

She asked me to strap my box back on. I did so. She led me down a long parquet corridor and up a marble staircase, along a strip of Persian carpet, pistachio-green walls trimmed with gold, light spilling through high windows.

"I have brought you what you wanted," I heard Solange say proudly, standing before me, partially blocking the room I faced. Her silk skirts were so wide, set on an armature the shape of an oblong hen cage, that she could not enter straight through the doorway, but had to turn sideways and sidle through it. She stood half in the room, half out, her face turned toward her master, elbows resting on the wide frame that held up her dress.

"My dear Solange," said a high, youthful voice, "you never disappoint me." Solange slipped into the room fully now, and gestured for me to follow. The count was sitting down. He was younger than I expected, maybe thirty. His short, plump legs were encased in tight apricot silk britches; as he crossed them, they made the sound of two palms sliding across each other. His neck was fat, his nose wide, his lips fleshy. He had the eyes of a basset hound. My first impression was that this man had too much face.

He looked up at me with interest. "Come in, young sir," he said, taking a pinch of snuff from an enamel snuffbox, laying it into the hollow between two tendons where his wrist met his thumb bone. He then leaned over, blocked one nostril, and sniffed.

"It might be quite impossible, you know," said Solange.

"Of course," said the count, sniffing. "That's the point, isn't it?"

Standing dumb a few feet from the door, I ogled the room: the count's study was both intimate and grand, with gilt-edged chairs, marigold silk walls, a pale blue desk on bowed and spindly legs, four sleek paintings of neat-headed horses in profile set against emerald fields, and one of a fleshy nude reclining on a red silk divan. I turned my eyes from the painted figure, the first naked woman I had seen in my life; my gaze landed heavily on an identical red divan, before which Solange stood in her red-and-white-striped dress. Her young face was serious; she stared into the middle distance, thinking. The blood-red silk covering of the divan was embossed with little pelicans and glowed richly in the cool morning light filtering through a tall window. On the opposite side of the room, among various other luscious pictures, a narrow painting of a raggedy Jewish peddler boy framed with swirls of gold hung in the center of the wall. His clothes, though more or less in imitation of the fashion of the day, were shabby and patched; his three-cornered hat shone with wear. His Jew's box hung heavily from his thin neck. In an instant I saw my mistake: it was a mirror. I took in my black, shabby, shapeless coat, red vest, baggy black trousers, the peddler's box with its many drawers dangling from my neck. Seeing myself as if for the first time, in this magnificent gilded room, I was filled with disappointment and disgust. I felt my face grow hot.

The count cleared his throat. "May I call you Jacob?"

I nodded.

"Solange is right, you are a Jew?"

"Yes, monsieur," I whispered.

"In that case," he said, jumping from his chair and standing, his back swayed, padded behind jutting out, "I have a proposal for you. Solange has been telling me that you are a very reliable young man. Really extremely reliable and . . . agreeable. As a man, quite apart from your . . . heritage. I know that you have been trained from an early age to think you cannot really mix with people like us, to fear us and to pity us, I have a feeling. Is that right?"

Fear constricted my throat.

"You may be right," he continued. "Your people are amazingly loyal to their traditions. But . . . I want to make you a proposition, something for you to think about. A new future. I need a second valet. I would like to offer you the position. In order to take it you will have to leave your family and your previous life, and in exchange I will pay you handsomely. Three louis a week. You will live here, and in my other houses whenever we go there. You will accompany me on all my personal outings and help me in all of my affairs. You will be treated absolutely without prejudice, if you choose to join my household. You will see the world. " He said this last with a grand gesture, opening both his arms and widening his eyes. His manner was so foreign to me—I didn't know how to read it. He was slightly ridiculous, with his tubby dancer's posture, his splayed feet, his enthusiasm—and yet he was encased in such finery, and spoke such beautiful French.

I felt perplexed and embarrassed—for the count as well as for myself. I turned to Solange, who was now looking at me expectantly.

"Please excuse me, monsieur," I said. Then I backed out of the room and escaped down the hall, my wares skidding and crashing about inside my Jew's box. I rushed down the marble stairs, through the kitchen, out the door, and away from that great house.

I returned to my old life, determined never to set foot in the count's voluptuous home again. The master had asked too quickly.

## 5

Now I must describe the nauseating experience of my first ride in a horseless carriage. I clung to the shoulder seam of Leslie's chemise, terrified by the spinning landscape to either side of me—blurred buildings, other carriages careening by us, pulled magically it seemed, their thick wheels spinning on the black road. With each passing behemoth I imagined the flash of metal as the great thing capsized and swirled toward us. I tried to close my eyes, but my lids seemed glued open. Unable to bear the view, I focused on Leslie's hand clamped to the steering wheel. With my new, hyperlucid vision, I noticed the cross-hatched weave of his skin. He had dry, rawboned knuckles, swollen veins: a worker's hand. I stared at the fascinating map of his epidermis until I was able to calm myself and forget my frantic body.

Leslie tilted the rearview mirror down so he could see what Stevie was up to in the backseat. The boy was wan, his hair the color of putty. He was holding a rubber dog bone, running his fingers back and forth over its nubbly surface. Leslie wondered if it was unsanitary to let the boy play with something the dog had slobbered over. He hated taking things away from the child. He had had so much taken away already. Deafness was not so very bad. Not as bad as blindness. Yet, maybe worse. Not to hear words. Was that worse? Were you set further apart? Were we really word people, or picture people? When he thought about it, blindness made Leslie panic more. Yet a blind man could sound normal on the phone. He could order lumber or a pizza, he could call a girl for a date. A deaf man sounded like an idiot. His little boy. He was so small, small for five, smaller than a lot of dogs, even, Leslie mused as he pulled up to the Sunshine Center for the Hearing Impaired. There were a lot of deaf kids, he thought. Deafness still happened. Why it had happened to Stevie, though, was the thing that tormented him. He realized that bad things had to happen to somebody, but his father's suicide seemed enough for his personal allotment of blows. He took the boy in his arms, then remembered the teacher's admonishment to allow him his independence. He put him down, gently removing the dog toy from his grip. The boy whimpered, held the bone close to his chest. Leslie tightened his fingers around the toy. He felt Stevie's body go rigid. Immediately Leslie let go of the rubber bone, but it was too late; hoarse shrieks were pumping out of the child, who was huddled over the bone, his body stiff.

"Okay, okay you can have it," Leslie said, rubbing Stevie's back, trying to relax his muscles. "Look at me, Stevie." He knelt down and took the boy's face in his hands. Stevie's mouth was downturned like a clown's, eyes clamped shut. He began shrieking in short animal bursts. His fingers had frozen around the dog toy.

"Calm down," Leslie said in a level voice, looking the boy in the face. He tried signing: "It's okay. Look," he signed. "It's okay. You can keep the toy." Finally, he scooped the sobbing boy up in his arms and walked him to the school.

Stepping into Stevie's classroom made Leslie feel like a giant. The top of his head brushed the ceiling. The children came up to his knee-caps. Ms. Parr, the teacher, wasn't too tall either, yet she surprised him every time he saw her with the extreme breadth of her hips. She wore her long fuzzy hair parted in the middle, had droopy eyes with thick straight lashes. A tiny mouth. And she smelled of wood fires, at all times of year. Leslie found Ms. Parr disturbingly, inexplicably attractive.

"Hello, Stevie," she said as Leslie tried to set the boy down. Stevie, his chest still shuddering with emotion, clung to the fabric of Leslie's trousers like a little monkey. Ms. Parr knelt down and gestured a request to him with nimble sign language. Stevie shook his head, clasping the dog toy. Ms. Parr stood and said to Leslie, still signing, "Hi, Mr. Senzatimore, how are you?" She looked directly up at him as she asked the question, earnestly waiting for an answer. She came up to his armpit. Leslie suddenly felt desiccated, as though his sternum and the backs of his eyes were stuffed with cotton wool.

"Do you have any water?" he croaked.

Ms. Parr hesitated a split second. "Sure, there's a water fountain over there." Leslie walked to the Lilliputian water fountain, his son clamped to his calf, knelt down and drank his fill. He then sat down at the miniature art table to wait for Stevie to calm down. Drawing always soothed him. Leslie put a red pencil in the little hand and watched the line, so pure and clear, arc across the page. A boat. In moments the boy was absorbed.

When Leslie was about to leave, Ms. Parr gestured to him to join her in a corner of the room. He felt afraid. Maybe Stevie was no longer wanted in the school. Too emotional. In need of special care.

"Is everything okay?" he asked, folding his arms and slumping to reduce the distance between their two heads.

"Fine, it's just that Stevie's mommy has asked me to come and spend a little extra tutoring time with him at your house, a couple of times a week after school?" Ms. Parr said, enunciating her words with care.

"Oh, right," said Leslie, his washed-out blue eyes scanning the room. This was the first he was hearing about this arrangement. Deirdre always seemed to be hiring more people to be with Stevie. "Great," he added.

"Anyway," she said, her mouth chewing the words, as if he too were hearing impaired. "I had said I could do Tuesday and Thursday but I realize I would have to say Monday and Friday, because of a conflict on Tuesday afternoons? I was going to ask her when she came today. Unless Thursday is better, but I think it's probably not ideal to do one day after another? Stevie might get frustrated." Leslie couldn't take his eyes off the woman's interrogatory mouth. "So will you ask Deirdre if that's okay?" she asked, gazing up at him expectantly.

"Just say it one more time."

"Monday and Friday, is that okay?" Ms. Parr said, smiling. "I could start this coming Monday."

"Yes, I can handle that," he said.

"Or I can just text her," said Ms. Parr, walking away and squatting to help with a little girl's puzzle. Leslie walked out into the cold sunshine.

Leslie was on his way to the hospital, to visit the old man he'd saved from the fire last night. He wouldn't normally visit someone he'd rescued, it made it all too personal—but he knew this man's family: his son, Chuck, had been Leslie's best friend growing up, until he drunk-drove his father's Mercury off a bridge in Freeport, senior year of high school. Leslie felt he should sit down with the man for a few minutes. As he drove, he went over the find—his second ever of a living victim: the apartment had been choked with black smoke. Blinded, Leslie felt his way through the bedroom on all fours, the hiss of the air tank in his ears with every breath. As he patted his gloved hand across the bed, he touched a slender arm, and the thrill of a find went through him. He grabbed for the body, lifted. It was light as a girl's, limp. It seemed like evil magic when he got to the window and saw the face like a rotten apple, slack jaw, sunken eyes. Leslie was ashamed by his disappointment. Still, he had saved him.

A violent, jangling rhythm erupted in the car, sending me flying in frantic loops, bumping against the cloth ceiling. I felt I was screaming, but no sound came out. With a push of a button, Leslie stopped the cacophony.

"Hello?" he called into the air. A plaintive, disembodied voice answered him.

"It's Evie, my whole—my whole—there's a leak in my kitchen, there's water coming down everywhere. Down the wall."

"So call a plumber."

"It's not a plumbing situation, necessarily. Come on, Les, just look at it and tell me who I have to call."

Leslie sighed and started a U-turn. "Be right over."

His older sister, Evie, was always calling him, panicked. It was her way, Deirdre told him, of letting him know she was still helpless. As if he needed a reminder. He drove up to a flat white brick building and parked. I was amazed to see a blond woman opening a door on the ground floor in nothing but a short multicolored shift that barely covered her pudendum, and a puffed-up red jacket. The flesh on her long thighs, Leslie noticed as he got out, was going spongy, melting slightly above the knee. This made her single status all the more worrying to him.

"Thanks, Les," she said, tucking her snarled blond hair behind an ear.

"So where's the problem?" asked Leslie, walking into the appalling apartment. Clothes were strewn on the couch, over the umbrella stand. A purple mat was rolled out onto the floor. On the walls, several primitive paintings, all of bare, moonlit fields, hung unframed.

"Over the sink," she said. "Look, the wall is bulging."

Leslie put his palm against the wall. It was wet. "The people upstairs have a leak, maybe a burst pipe. Do you know them?"

"Why?"

"Because if you knew what room was above this, it might be clearer what the problem is. Probably the kitchen," he said. "You need a plumber. Like I said."

"I don't have a good plumber. Who do you use?"

Leslie took out his phone and started looking up a name. "John Green," he said.

"Can you call them?" she asked, chewing on her thumb. Leslie made the call, his eyes roving over the chaos of his sister's sink: coffee-splotched cups, a plate with half a piece of cake on it, an empty canister of yogurt. His voice sounded friendly, cajoling as he arranged for the plumber to come at three that afternoon, even though he felt like weeping.

"No—I can't be here then," whispered Evie.

"When can you be here?" he asked.

"Between now and two, or between four and whenever," she said. He made the arrangements, conscious of a tightening in his chest.

"You should go upstairs and make sure they turn off their water," Leslie said.

"This is why I hate this condo, there's no real super," she whined.

"What about the—there's gotta be at least a handyman," said Leslie.

"He's useless," said Evie, pouring herself a glass of juice. "You want something to drink?"

"Nah," said Leslie. "I got things I gotta do. How's the job search going?"

"You know," said Evie, "I thought I had something in graphic design, but it didn't work out. I'm working on a children's book."

Just then I heard the sound of rushing water, and a topless man with a tanned, fleshy torso slumped into the room.

"Oh," said Evie, as if just now recollecting his presence in the apartment. "Alan, this is my brother, Leslie."

"Good to meet you," said Alan, offering his palm. Leslie shook his loose-knit hand. Beneath the sweatpants, Alan wore no underwear.

"How'd you two meet?" Leslie asked.

Alan chuckled. "We're, ah—"

"New friends," said Evie.

"Okay," said Leslie, blinking hard. "I'm late."

Evie followed him to his car, shuffling in fluffy white slippers.

"Sorry about that," she said, leaning into his open window.

"So you met him last night?" Leslie said.

"Yeah," said Evie. "He took me home."

"Did you forget he was in there, or what?"

"No, I . . ."

"Next time you're too smashed to get yourself home, call me," said Leslie. "Call me or call a cab."

"He seems nice, though," said Evie, looking back at the condo. "Doesn't he?"

Leslie didn't know what to say. He just waved at her and backed up the truck.

Of all his siblings, Evie was the most dependent on Leslie. The younger Senzatimore children's postpaternal normality was their mother's masterpiece. She and the slightly paranoid Vince McCaffrey became a bulwark of solidity, raising the three younger children with great love and many rules, dictated by the church. It was Leslie and Evie, the two eldest, for whom it had all been too late. Their childhoods were already almost over by the time Charlie de-selfed. Evie moved seamlessly toward badly chosen friends and substance abuse. Leslie created his life by using force of will.

His next stop was the firehouse. The Patchogue, Long Island, Fire Department was a large sand-colored building with gleaming red fire trucks parked in its tidy, cavernous garage. I rode on my host's back as he entered, greeting the other men, who were wearing dark blue

T-shirts with a white crest reading PFD on the pocket. Their hair was shorn, like Leslie's. There was a resounding back slap, which nearly killed me, but I jinked to the left just in time. The men seemed to be congratulating Leslie on his rescue of the night before.

"And you know what, it turns out I know the guy," said Leslie. "Mr. Tolan. He was my best friend's father growing up. I gotta say he was an unpleasant man back then. But they all mellow out."

Tony, a short, burly man holding a mug of steaming coffee, quipped, "Too bad you can't do a quick character reference before you heave 'em outta the smoke." He leaned down as if to a victim and mimed removing an air mask. "Excuse me, sir. Are you an asshole, by any chance? Because if you are, I think I'll just leave you here." Everybody laughed.

"This from the Fireman of the Year," said Leslie. "I'm goin' out to the hospital to see this guy now."

"Yeah?" said Tony, surprised.

"I wouldn't if I didn't know him. But—I figure, he's got nobody else. His son died in a stupid accident in high school, his wife is gone. You know."

"I never go," said Tony, flattening one palm emphatically. He was a professional fireman, worked in the city. He couldn't afford to be sentimental.

Leslie shrugged. "I came by to find out who's cooking tonight," he said. "If it's me I gotta shop on my way back."

"What are you makin'?" asked Tony.

"I'm thinking spaghetti carbonara, Caesar salad. Maybe a Caprese."

"Dessert?"

"You know it," said Leslie.

"Better be good. Yelding's still way ahead after that chocolate soufflé last week."

Hiding under Leslie's shirt collar on the ride to the hospital, comforted by the darkness, I wondered what my purpose as an angel here could possibly be. What could I help with? I already saw that Leslie was a noble soul overwhelmed with duty, visited by occasional odd little lustings he would never act on. He saved bitter old men who were about to die anyway from a little peaceful smoke inhalation, then went to visit them in the hospital to make up for the fact that he wished they had been children or young women. I worried that I would die all over again, this time of boredom. Confident that I wouldn't miss anything important at this rate, I allowed myself a short nap.

## ∽ 6

Having fled the great house of the Comte de Villars and his bizarre offer of employment, I had returned gratefully to the routine of my days: my mother woke me tenderly at five o'clock each morning, bringing a basin of water to my bed. I performed my ablutions, washing my hands of the unclean spirits that might have settled on my body during the night, and said my morning prayer of thanks. I put on my tzitzit, a fringed protective garment, like a prayer shawl with a slit cut in the middle for the head to go through. Over this I wore what I hoped was a French-looking chemise, a red vest with silver buttons, and a black coat. I hid my yarmulke beneath a black felt three-cornered hat.

I scurried to morning prayer with my brother and my father at one of several places of worship set up in various houses in our section of Paris—we did not have a synagogue—then my father and I yoked up our peddler's boxes and set off to make a little money, calling out hoarsely, "Watch fobs! Knives! Snuffboxes!" etc. The streets of Paris were cacophonous with the cries of peddlers selling everything from baked apples to firewood to water pumped from the Seine. Each peddler had his or her own cry, and we milled through the streets, across the bridges, baskets and boxes strapped to us, crying out our wares.

My brother Shlomo was exempt from this work; the treasured scholar of the family, he stayed back to study all day. I didn't envy him. In the afternoons I played skittles with other boys in the courtyard, or ran wild through the neighborhood with my gang of friends. I had no inclination to study the holy texts in my free time as I was meant to—nor did I have any great interest in business. I just wanted to enjoy myself as much as possible. My father, a serious, even doleful man, thought I was a ruffian in the making. His selling was punctuated by prayer morning, afternoon, and night: Shacharis, Mincha, and Ma'ariv. He was also one of a group of stalwart men who volunteered to prepare the dead of our community in the traditional manner. His attitude toward me, his blithe eldest son, was one of resigned disappointment, occasionally peppered with disgust. I avoided him as much as I could.

In addition to selling, I loaned small sums to the gentiles in the area—trifling amounts, really; I was no banker. People often needed a little something to tide them over to the next month, and usury was forbidden to Catholics. My father, brother, and I lent money at reasonable interest, collecting the pledges when they were due. Within our own community, we lent to one another without charging interest. That was our custom.

Our world of German and North European Jews took up about four cramped and winding streets of Paris, branching off the rue Saint-Martin, on the Right Bank of the Seine. The Portuguese Jews lived on the Left Bank, near the rue des Grands Augustins. They traded in silks and chocolate, and received passports for twice the time we did.

There had once been a much larger Jewish community in Paris. But in 1306, Philippe IV, in need of income for the bankrupt French state, had a brilliant idea: he simply arrested all the Jews in France, confiscated our money and property, and deported us. This initiated a series of expulsions that were revoked and reinstated several times during the coming centuries. We were let in or kicked out, depending on how important for business we were seen to be. Luckily for me, Louis XV was a tolerant king; in the past fifty years or so, we Jews had been allowed to slink into Paris in dribs and drabs, like rats trickling back into a house once the catcher has left the premises.

My young life pattered on in its usual way for several months until I got the jolting news that I was to be married. I was seventeen. My betrothed had been selected for me out of the meager handful of Jewish girls in Paris by the local matchmaker in collusion with my parents; the marriage contract was hammered out through a marriage broker. Hodel Mendel was just fourteen. As my parents saw it, Hodel was a catch: her father, Mayer Mendel, was the only ritual slaughterer on the Right Bank. The ritual slaughterer was an important man in our community. On top of that, the Mendels offered a substantial dowry, plus room and board for three years. Who could resist? As for me, I was dying to sleep with a woman, and Hodel was not a bad-looking girl.

I thought of marriage as a sort of Eden where you could pluck sensual—and sanctified—delight from every *fruitier* in the garden. I couldn't wait. The day before my wedding, my scholarly uncle Yitzak sat with me, breathing thickly through the dense hairs in his nose, and explained that what I was about to do had been done by Abraham, Isaac, and Jacob, and there was nothing to be nervous about. He gave me a brief layout of the geography of my future wife, and myself in relation to her, causing me to nearly faint with embarrassment, but teaching me nothing I didn't already know from having once witnessed two stray dogs humping, and my habit of idling inside bookshops where *livres philosophiques*, with their carefully illustrated descriptions of persons in flagrante delicto, were clandestinely sold. Having fulfilled his duty, Uncle Yitzak stood up stiffly, kissed my head, and walked out of the room. My mother, to my surprise, stormed in the minute he left, weeping, and clasped me violently against her breast.

When I saw little Hodel on the evening of our wedding, she was hanging by her elbows between her tall mother and her squat father, being guided through the courtyard of her family building like a blind person. Her face was entirely whited out by an opaque veil that fell to her waist, giving me the curious impression that her head was on backward. I stood with my parents beneath the wedding canopy, trembling in my white coat, waistcoat, and britches, over which I wore a kittel—a white linen robe, white for mourning, to remind me of my own death. Yet in truth my kittel could have been my own burial shroud, given what my marriage would turn out to be.

Hodel looked very small and rigid beside her pantherlike, black-browed mother, who was maneuvering her toward me with a firm grip. Her little badger of a father had to raise the girl's elbow in order to keep her level. It looked as if they were heaving a draped statue across the courtyard. Hodel seemed to be making no effort to walk; in fact, she was quite stiff. I wondered if her feet were being dragged along the ground beneath her wedding gown. The four candle-bearing matrons walking before this coercive procession lent the ceremony an eerie air of sacrifice. At last Hodel was beside me, perfectly hidden behind the thick white silk. After my father pronounced the seven blessings, when Hodel's veil was raised, a corner lifted by each parent, I saw that her eyes were inflamed and swollen from weeping. Her round cheeks had tear tracks on them. Her breath shuddered and caught like that of a tiny child who has been bawling. I crushed the glass beneath my heel with a sudden rush of anger.

## 7

I awoke from my nap and crawled out from under my cotton tent. I was in a sterile chamber buzzing with greenish light. Mr. Tolan, the old man whom Leslie had saved in the fire, was sitting up in bed, his skinny, shriveled arm connected to a shiny tube. Rheumy, helpless eyes glistened in the dry landscape of his face like shallow ponds. With striking vanity, he wore a ratty brown toupée that seemed to hover over his scalp. Leslie couldn't reconcile this pathetic figure with the powerhouse he had known as a child. Mr. Tolan's rages were legend in the neighborhood; you could hear him halfway down the block, screaming at his kid, wife, dog.

"If there's anything Deirdre or I can do for you, Mr. Tolan . . . you let us know," Leslie said. Ugh. Leslie was perfect! I felt so low in his presence, so unworthy. Was this what I was supposed to feel? Was this why I had been sent down here, to follow this exemplary man around day and night until I couldn't stand it anymore and had no more will to live? Could angels commit suicide? I felt a sudden, acute dislike for Leslie Senzatimore. He reminded me, I realized, of my father, a man whose damning rectitude could scorch your eyebrows if you got too close to him.

I spread my wings, jumped, and took off, circling the room as Les-

lie listened to the old man, nodding, his blue eyes wide with understanding, big jaw set. I was depressed—numbed by boredom and a
sense of worthlessness. And then it occurred to me: maybe angels had
free will. I had always been told that they did not, that it was only
humans who were distinguished with that feature, that angels were
bound to praise Him day and night for all ages. But here I was, on
"Long Island," whatever that was, not singing or praising, but floating
around useless and invisible. What if I left? I decided to try it. I flew
out the door and down the shiny hallway. My trajectory was interrupted by the sudden disappearance of the wall to my left. It dis-
solved, revealing a box full of expressionless people. I hung in the air,
staring at this phenomenon, when the wall began to close up again. A
woman rushed by me, stepping into the secret room. I was sucked into
her wake, and hovered over the deanimated passengers, observing
them with interest.

All the people, dressed in strange, ill-fitting garments, the wom-
ens' limbs exposed, hair disheveled, as though they had left their beds
in a rush, stared dumbly at the doors, which glided shut magically,
sealing us in. I now felt a sickening lurch in my stomach as the room
plummeted through space. I was forced toward the ceiling, listening
to the whoosh of the thing as it fell, then came to a soft halt. The
doors opened again. All the people walked out. I followed, grateful to
be free.

I found myself in the mezzanine, assaulted by violent, inexplicable
light. Many people walked back and forth, entering and exiting
through a bank of glass doors that slid open and shut constantly of
their own accord and led outside. The women were stripped down like
Deirdre, with tight trousers, or short skirts. There was no modesty
about them, no elegance. I noticed one such vision with white wires
coming out of her ears, talking to herself emphatically. The nails on
her fingers and toes had been lacquered to perfection and shone like
black Chinese boxes. I wondered if this might be a lunatic asylum.
Then I heard a tinny voice, crying out from within the wires: "You can

fucking pick him up for once, but no, obviously not, your mother's imaginary infection—" Was I reading the woman's thoughts? A man seated on a low couch, his enormous feet splayed in a pair of egregious blunt-toed shoes, his neck bent over a tiny keyboard, played a fast-paced tune with his thumbs, but no sound emitted from the shiny ebony instrument. I hovered over him and saw minuscule words forming in a glowing rectangle: *Get bucket of chicken am starving.* Some of these people looked unwell, others merely unhappy. The women wore no white powder on their skin or hair, yet many of them had dipped their locks in yellow dye, and their eyes and lips were daubed liberally with glistening colors. You can imagine how confusing all this was to me, innocent as I was of the customs and mechanics of this new world with which I am now so deeply familiar.

A shop selling bright flowers caught my eye. Inside, a woman with orange, greasy skin leaned on the counter, flipping the pages of a broadsheet. I flew closer to see what she was looking at: an amazingly rendered color image, so lifelike it seemed impossible to create with paint or the printer's gravure, shiny with varnish. It was a portrait of a dark-haired woman and a blond man. They were smiling. I flew to a rack of other such publications. Here I saw the same set of handsome Viking faces, alone or together or in a pair, smiling down from each of the glossy covers in different poses, with different words beneath them. Sometimes a third female joined them in the images. They all three had strong teeth and bony, flat faces. They looked Nordic. Or perhaps they were Austrians? Stamped beneath them were a series of proclamations: "Brangelina's secret wedding!" "Jen's phone call to Brad's weeping mother." "Nanny tells all in Brangelina shocker." I assumed Brangelina must be the name of the current monarch of this land, or perhaps his courtesan. In my time, we had libelous books whirling around town, depicting Mme de Pompadour, and, later, Mme du Barry, the king's mistresses, in all sorts of licentious poses with men and women of the court. It was our entertainment.

After reading as much of the libelous literature as I could without opening the pamphlets, weak angel that I was, I became bored. Determined to find new stimulation in this panorama of ugliness, I decided to take a risk and reenter the secret room that plummeted, see where it burped me up this time. I retraced my flight path out of the shop, diagonally across the room of abominably dressed humans talking into their magic shining voice boxes, and waited in front of the metal doors of the plummeting room. Eventually they opened, and I flew in, joining a young woman pushing a small, half-naked child in a low, open buggy. The young woman was chewing the inside of her lip, one bare leg flung away, the opposite hip jutting out. With that posture, I assumed she was a prostitute. But why the child? The metal doors shut, sealing us in. With a terrible feeling of being buried alive, I felt the box ascend. When the doors opened again, a warm stream of air reached through the open doors and caressed my face. Tantalized, I followed the heat, out the secret room and down the hallway. Whenever I veered away from its path, the air went frigid. Careful to avoid parting with the delicious warmth, I swam it midstream, veering sharply as it led me through an open door.

I flew high, skimming the rough panels in the ceiling, and looked down at two narrow beds separated by a cloth curtain. The shades were drawn; the room was fairly dark. Two young women were lying on the two beds. One was asleep. Her body lay jagged, as if broken, under the thin blanket. Her hand swiped her face as she slept. I floated down and had a look at her, hovering so close that I could see her eyeballs scanning beneath the lids as she dreamed. Her skin was slick. Her hair, unwashed, clung to her forehead. I was reminded of prison; the women had been so shockingly unkempt there. Hair frayed and dull, skin sallow, lips cracked. It made me realize how important a woman's toilette was to her appearance. In a state of nature, most women are hideous—even the beauties. I was so close to this one I could smell her metallic breath. Still giddy with my ability to fly, I sucked up my abdomen, pumped my wings a couple of times, and banked to the right, over the top of the curtain, toward the other girl's bed. This one was awake, looking up at a luminous box clamped to the ceiling with a metal device. I flew up to the box and looked inside it. Within, tiny figures moved around in a most lifelike way. One of them was a fair-haired woman. She removed a red wrap to reveal a slender torso barely covered in a chemise. I tried to fly into that luminous world, but was repelled by a wall of warm glass. Slightly stunned by the collision, I looped up to the top of the box and perched at the edge, feeling its heat and vibrations as I gazed down at the girl in the bed. She was propped up on several pillows, staring upward with an expression of amazed fascination. Her intent face, bathed in the cerulean glow of the box, was captivating: very large onyx eyes, padded lips drifting open to reveal an insolent gap between strong front teeth. Her long, thick hair was dark, almost navy in the half-light. Her flimsy green gown hung open, and I glimpsed a patch of naked skin. Habitually curious about all breasts, I dove down to get a better look and hung in the air, wings beating, peering into the folds of the gown. I was just able to make out the curve of a plump, high tit. As with Leslie, the air near this girl felt as hot as dipping into a bath. I wondered if she was the warm tide's source. Boldly, I landed on the nipple. Tiny as I was, I seemed to be crawling up the face of a cratered red mountain. Strange, I thought, that I was unable to stand upright. I strained my mind for examples in painting or sculpture of crawling angels, and could only think of the thick-limbed cherubim gamboling through frozen cascades of wax on the candelabrum I was staring at as I died. Was I a cherub? An invisible, fat toddler with wings? I remembered myself alive: clear blue-green eyes, a somewhat lupine yet delicate nose, a chiseled mouth. My hair was jet-black and fell in shining ringlets to my shoulders. I looked quite angelic, though somewhat too shrewd, intense.

Instinctively, I flicked out my tongue to glance the ridged mound of rose-colored flesh beneath me. I tasted salt and smelled the aroma of young, unwashed flesh—a pleasant, milky bouquet—with a faint undertone of sweat. Without warning, I felt a solid wall sweeping my body over the fleshy hill. I rolled over several times and was propelled into the air, my wings beating frantically to keep me up. A hand rose up huge before me, still in the act of brushing me off. She had felt me. I had substance! That was good. Invisible, but extant. I floated in the air, enjoying the weightlessness, the giddy feeling of power that flight brought to me. I had always hated the heaviness of life. Senseless obligation, the strictures of time—I had made my life an affront to these killjoys. True, I had only had thirteen years of freedom, but better to die beautiful, with a bacchanal taking place downstairs where certain people are actually missing your presence, than in unlusted-after old age, your day a round of senseless tasks, no pleasure in sight. Pleasure, oh! To manifest myself!

Flying in neat circles in the light of the luminous box, I was enlivened by my memories. What a joyous time a handsome young angel could have with this lush girl, as that sickly rag doll snored behind the curtain. I felt my sex so keenly it was a torture not to be able to touch it, to reassure myself it was still there, but my withered angel arms were too short, I could only wave them miserably. What if, as an angel, I had no sex, only desire? That would be a tailored hell. I had to know what I was!

I landed on a smooth, cool vertical plane. *I am so light*, I thought, *I can grasp a wall*. I rested there for a moment, gathering my thoughts. Perhaps this was only a phase of being. Corporeal manifestation might come in time. I looked at the smooth, unrippled surface before me. Reflected in it was the luminous box with its tantalizing, unreachable images. I was standing on a mirror. I stared into it, yearning to see an image of myself, but, where my form should have been, all was dark. Was I casting a shadow? Filled with hope, I took off, my wings propelling me back slightly before I rose, circling the mirror and looking into it. All I could see was the luminous box, the girl's profile, the ceiling with its gray square tiles, and a fly, zigzagging back and forth through the air. I was still invisible. I yearned to see myself. I looked into mirrors compulsively when I was alive—I never passed one without checking the state of my beauty, and I passed many lustful moments with others and alone staring at my own reflection in ornate mirrors belonging to aristocrats or the cracked, stippled rounds hanging in brothels. Now, with no reflection to confirm my existence, I felt claustrophobic, suffocated, erased. Desperate, I beat my wings and rose up; flight soothed me. The fly in the mirror rose. I let myself sink a bit; so did the fly. I landed on the mirror and watched the glass go dark, felt the cool of it on my feet. I was a fly! I wept with rage and helplessness.

## 8

Masha stared into the TV, her breathing shallow. The pillows had sunk beneath her back; without thinking, she turned to plump them. A pain, sharp, yet old, like a wound that had been poked at a thousand times, jabbed at her heart with each beat, echoing out through her chest, into her throat. She stopped as if caught red-handed, cursing herself for forgetting. Extremely slowly, like a sloth, she turned back to the TV and lay gingerly back on the pillow, waiting for her heart to slow down, the pain that bloomed inside her with each beat to subside. She took little sips of breath, her body rigid, and stared up at the screen. The only way to be free of the pain was to stay perfectly still. She couldn't lean back, she couldn't laugh, she couldn't cough. She had a quarter of an inch to move and that was it.

Masha had never watched so much television before. Through windows she had glimpsed images here and there, bright colors, flashes of expression on the actors' faces. Her mother had recently bought a portable DVD player for once-weekly use, but the only movie allowed on it so far was *The Lion King*. That was the one complete movie she had ever seen. But this night in the hospital Masha had gorged herself. She had watched *Top Gun*, *Mystic Pizza*, and several episodes of *Sex and the City*. Her eyes ached, yet she couldn't bring herself to switch the thing off. She might never be able to watch this much again. Now, on the screen, an award ceremony: a girl Masha's age was smiling. A young man beside her was wearing a tuxedo. The girl had bare arms, loose red hair. Her skin seemed very smooth. A person off-screen put a microphone up to her face and asked her what designer she was wearing. She smiled and called out a name. She said she was proud to be there. She seemed so happy. Masha looked up at the girl. A longing was taking shape in her, a charged notion that had been gathering all night. Those girls, she thought. Those girls in the movies, in the shows. They were just people. They had all come from someplace. They hadn't been born inside those stories. And the thought of getting there, the amazing getting there, to the point where you were allowed to live inside those multiple worlds, that kaleidoscopic, endless story machine, tugged at her, prying her away from all the certainty she'd had only the day before. Masha had appeared in many all-female shows in school, and for charity events, which were performed for an audience of women only. She had been, all the women said, astonishingly good. She always got the lead. But her fame was confined to the women in her community; women were not allowed to perform in front of men. Masha had always accepted this prohibition as simply as she accepted the weather. Hashem did not want her to act or sing in front of men, so she could not. Disobeying Him was out of the question. Yet today, for the first time, an alternate future glimmered in the corner of her eye. It was absurd to her, this thinking—as if she had suddenly denied the fact of gravity and insisted that one day she could float in the air like a speck of dust. She wondered if it was her *yetzer hara* talking—everyone had an evil inclination, the self-serving part of you that tempted you to disobey the commandments, or to talk gossip, or be bad in general. She tried to squelch the thought. I heard her innocent cravings in my head as if they were my own. They interrupted my despair. Masha shut her eyes. Her eyelids were pale and pure as a baby's. For a moment she drifted into sleep. Then, woken by pain, she said her morning prayer of thanks at being returned to her body: *Modah ani lifanecha, melech chai v'kayam sheh-hechezarta bi nish-mati b'chemlah rabbah emunatecha.*

For a long moment Masha and I stayed perfectly still, she in her pain and I in mine. I wished I could give her what she wanted.

A knock at the door interrupted our contemplation. Reflexively, Masha reached for the remote to turn off the TV, and her heart sped up. The pain radiated through her chest with each heartbeat, like ripples of water after a rock plunks in. She lay still, waiting for the ripples to subside.

"Hello, Masha," the doctor said. Masha turned off the television.

"Hi," said Masha, strangling the end of even that short word.

"I am Dr. Heptulla. How's the chest?"

"Not so good," she whispered. The doctor sat down. He had flawless dark terra-cotta skin, a thin nose with a little bulb at the end of it, and a smiling, generous mouth.

"We have the results of your EKG and X-ray now, Masha. I'll have to go over them with your parents. Do you have any idea when they might be here?"

"Could take them a long time," she whispered. "They'll have to walk." The doctor looked perplexed. "It's Shabbos," she explained. "We're not allowed to take the train or drive or . . ." She shrugged, embarrassed.

"Where do you live?" asked the doctor.

"Far Rockaway," she said huskily, closing up her hospital gown with a slow, old-lady motion.

"That's a long walk."

"So what do I have?" asked Masha.

"The chest pain is being caused by pericarditis, which is an inflammation around the heart. Did you have a cold, a virus, recently?"

"A sore throat," Masha said.

"Do you still have that?"

"No." He took out a tongue depressor and stood up, walking toward her. She shrank back.

51

"Open your mouth, say aahh." Reluctantly, she did so. He peered down her gullet.

"And you are twenty?" he said.

"Twenty-one," she whispered.

"All the same, I'm going to have the nurses page me when your parents get here. In the meantime you should sleep."

He pushed the red paging button and a fresh-faced nurse appeared. "Can you set Masha up so she can sleep?" asked Dr. Heptulla. There was a hint of irritation in his voice. He knew, Masha thought, that she'd been watching TV all night.

"Please don't tell my parents," she murmured.

"What?" asked Dr. Heptulla.

"That I've been watching TV."

"Don't worry, I won't," he said, perplexed. "But now you really do need to sleep." The young nurse had arranged the pillows high, and held Masha gently as she slowly rested her head on the cool pillow-case. She was so tired. Her pure eyelids closed. Within seconds, Masha was asleep.

I gaped at her sleeping there. I had run away from Jewish women for most of my adult life. Yet I couldn't stop the emotion that was building up in me. The girl was so touching: in pain, very sick, it seemed—yet with that ambition, planted in her that night, and growing, ineluctable as a healthy fetus, in the womb of her spirit. My love for her hurt; I felt it as a catch in my chest, a lump of feeling.

I marched back and forth along the metal window frame, feeling the morning sun on my wings, the steel gathering heat under my feet, a powdery smell of dust in my nostrils. Through the dirty glass I could see, far below, a man and a woman holding a small child by the hands. The living—how ignorant they were of the hoax that was being pulled on them! What indignities they had in store. I had never known such despair. Wrenched from a death that was after all not so bad, in that there was no consciousness involved, in order to become a lovesick fly, I felt hoodwinked and abused. After a lout's career of joyous disconnection in affairs of the body, I had finally fallen in love, even if it was with a Jewess—and I was dead—worse than dead: I was an insect! I hated God, that prankster, and vowed to dedicate my fly's life to his debasement. *Oh, where are the dark angels?* I thought loftily, *that I might join ranks with them to overthrow the old despot!*

I turned and looked over at Masha, who was sleeping now, having guzzled from the box of light and its world of temptations all night long. Her beauty was a torture. I noticed another fly, smaller than me, and, I intuited, a female, drinking from a droplet of orange juice on the rim of Masha's glass, just at the place where my girl's lips had left a perfect impression. I took off and alighted on the edge of the glass, just behind the female, a petite, glossy fly, recently hatched. Her smell was delicious—a cocktail of candy, orange juice, and excrement that filled me with straightforward lust. Never having done this before, I felt somewhat insecure, yet I needed above all to conquer something, someone, today of all days. Without thinking, I assertively leapt on the female. She took off. Terrified, I held on desperately, my forelegs clasping her face, as she looped through the air trying to shake me off. I was amazed to feel my penis emerge from within my body like a turtle's head and craftily enter her as she bucked and twirled beneath me, my little legs clamped around her hairy trunk. The wind whipping at my eyes, I stared at Masha's sleeping face. Masha woke now, as if stirred by my desire, and blinked slowly. She smiled, curious, mildly entertained at the sight of two copulating flies looping randomly through the air like a pricked balloon. The fact of my beloved girl watching me as I fucked was so erotic to me that pleasure infused me without warning and I ejaculated violently, my whole tiny body racked with what felt like a life-threatening explosion of sweetness inside me. The female, unlocked, buzzed off as I, barely able to beat my wings, landed heavily on the windowsill, dizzy and slightly nauseous. In all my years of sensual excess, I had never had an experience close to this. I felt a tightness in my abdomen and at the end of my back. For the first time since my arrival in the sublunar world, I relieved my bowels, dropping a string of feculae along the window ledge, infinitesimal dots aligned like the three periods used to open up a sentence to a chasm of uncertainty . . .

Some time later, I was spitting on a crumb of Masha's toast, softening it for my long tongue to slurp up. My beloved was breathing softly through her nostrils. I felt calmer. The door opened. In walked Mordecai Edelman. I froze in confused amazement. He was dressed almost exactly as I once had been, in the eighteenth century. For a moment I thought I had stumbled on a wrinkle in the fabric of time. Surely this man did not belong to the present. I wondered if this was part of the mystical hoax being played on me.

Mordecai Edelman was a big, shaggy man with a gleaming beard and small, smiling eyes. A large fur hat was set upon his head like a crown. I recognized this as the Shabbos hat of the most pious. He wore his sidelocks short, however, and tucked them behind his ears. His coat was long and black. Behind him, his wife, Pearl, walked in. Pearl was small, with a voluptuous physique and a pleasant, smiling face. She wore a glossy auburn wig that came down to her shoulders, and she was dressed in a bright blue coat that ended below the knee to reveal a pair of thick beige stockings. I watched the family reunion warily, reminding myself that I was a fly, and could not be found out or judged by these devout people. The parents hugged their daughter, and she, not wishing to disappoint them, made an enormous effort to circle her shapely arms around their necks, her heart searing the flesh in her chest with every beat. Having greeted them both, the sweet girl fell back on the pillow, her face very pale and pinched with pain. Her eyes glittered like black jewels in her ashen face.

Dr. Heptulla came in soon after and arranged three chairs so they could all have a chat.

"You had quite a journey to get here today," intoned the doctor with elegant, clipped English.

"Yes," said Mordecai, wiping his brow under the fur hat with a cotton handkercheif. "Sixty-four stairs just to get to this floor!" Pearl laughed, but there were tears in her eyes. She sat beside her daughter, squeezing her hand.

"It took us an hour and a half, door to door," she said. The doctor shook his head, smiling.

"Mr. and Mrs. Edelman, we have done an EKG, and a sonogram, and a chest X-ray," the doctor intoned, one long-fingered hand in the air as if dispensing a benediction. "Masha has an acute case of pericarditis, an inflammation around the heart, which in a healthy young woman like her we treat with bed rest and Tylenol. These cases are generally triggered by a virus. I can find nothing organically wrong with the heart itself." Pearl nodded, smiling, the tears in her eyes trembling. She had known for days that there was something wrong. Masha had said her chest hurt, she couldn't breathe properly. She should have brought her in sooner.

"If the pericarditis doesn't recede within a week, or if it recurs, there are other tests we can do," said Dr. Heptulla. "Other medications. But for now I think we should go with a gentle approach."

## 9

My wedding night was a disaster. Though fourteen, Hodel had the mentality of a small child; her submission to my clumsy fingers seemed obscenely forced by the unseen hands of our parents and tradition. She whimpered and shrank away from my caresses. Her newly shorn hair, cut after the wedding, as was our tradition, made her look even younger, and confused me terribly. I persevered, mumbling encouragements that it would soon be over. All I could think of was the examination our sheets would be submitted to by Mme Mendel in the morning. With no blood, the marriage would not be real and I would not be a man. As it turned out, I had to prick my own finger and wipe it on the sheet in the morning, having given up my entreaties by dawn. My bride had a week of relief after that first night; the blood of my finger was accepted as Hodel's, and so she was "unclean" for a week and we had to sleep in separate beds. But on the eighth day, my efforts continued. To be fair, Hodel wanted to become a woman and do her duty, but she was terrified. It took a full month to actually deflower her; her plump little body seemed to have no natural ingress. I felt I was trying to puncture a thigh, or a belly, so resiliently did her flesh resist my poor prick. Night after night I came to a crisis without actually entering my own wife, her rubbery body repelling me again and again. At last I convinced her to straddle me, and I impaled her, though my sense of triumph was dulled by her whimpering as I finally burst the dam.

I fluctuated between guilt and despair in our first months together as I realized that I had been saddled with a hysteric. Hodel spent most of her time in my presence crying for her mother.

The terrible Mme Mendel lived upstairs from us (as per our marriage contract we had been allotted one large, drafty room previously occupied by the recently deceased paternal grandparents of my Hodel), but she insisted from the first day that we live on our own as husband and wife, not as her children. A good head taller than her husband and all but one of her six sons, Mme Mendel had black eyes and swarthy, wind-lashed skin. She had an intimidating, predatory slowness about her; she never rushed, yet she was prone to sudden surges of dislike and irritation, and lashed out at her endless progeny with a whip of a tongue in the fastest Yiddish I had ever heard. Having come from a tiny town in Poland when her first few children were young, she still had the mind of a provincial woman. Her superstitions were elaborate and terrifying: a pregnant woman stepping on fingernail clippings meant certain miscarriage; a hair in the milk meant a demon had been in the house. She never entered a room without kissing the mezuzah. She had even gone so far as to avoid giving her children grand names, so as not to make the demons jealous. She chose Hodel, Leib, Sheindl—no Esthers or Abrahams for this canny lady! She never paid anyone a compliment, for the same reason. If anyone complimented her, she spat on the floor to ward off the evil eye. When her children were babies, she made tiny tears in their garments. Demons were of a lower order than humans, and they were always jealous of us, she explained. No one should be too beautiful or too lucky. She sensed countless evil spirits and sprites swirling around her, just waiting for her to slip up. Still, I was grateful that she allowed us to eat our evening meal upstairs with her and the rest of the family, as Hodel seemed to be genuinely afraid of boiling water or hot liquid of any kind.

Every evening at six o'clock I would report upstairs to the family apartment. My child-wife, having already been basking in her mother's indifference for several hours, always looked up at me from the dreaded bubbling stew she'd been forced to stir, standing as far away as possible from the pot, lest the liquid boil over and scald her—with a frightened, surprised smile, her shiny cheeks the purplish color of turnips, a few cropped ginger hairs peeking out of her matron's bonnet, as though she had forgotten all about me and our marriage and then, with my entrance, was compelled to remember.

Only eight people could sit at the Mendel table at a time, so there were three sittings a night. Mme Mendel stood until the last child was served, languorously scooping meat stew out of the enormous, dented, seemingly bottomless pot. Hodel and I were allowed to attend the first seating, because we were married. Also in attendance was Hodel's badgerlike father, Moishe, her idolized oldest brother, Leib, who, at sixteen, was the only one of the other Mendel children to be married, and his cunning wife, Leah. Leib had already impregnated his wife twice in two years. I could tell from the way the hugely pregnant Leah asked Mme Mendel, lisping, how old she was when each of her babies was born, that she planned on outdoing her. Mme Mendel, however, was not out of the running yet. Her fourteenth child was only two; she could easily drop another litter. She answered Leah's questions with deliberate vagueness, as if the age she was when she bore her eighth or twelfth child were a secret akin to Kabbalah. I was always seated next to the silent and shrunken mother of Mme Mendel, who had skin the texture of dried beef. She spent much of each meal glowering at me as I ate my stew, as if every mouthful I took were an affront to her finer manners.

Dinner inevitably began with Mme Mendel asking me in a sort of offhand way how much money I had made that day. I always told her, to the last sou. She then asked me exactly what I had sold. I had to describe each object in great detail: one painted enamel snuffbox, twenty sous; one pair of feather-lined men's kid gloves, four livres; one collapsible walking stick with an engraved tin handle, five livres; one iron teapot, ten sous. After each description, Mme Mendel would squint her eyes, as if visualizing the object and matching it with the price. Then she would either nod, frowning appreciatively, her eyebrows up, or shake her head and smile derisively at my lack of business acumen. M. Mendel, with his two badger's streaks of white down the center of his reddish hair, and his long, pointy nose, would chuckle and then suddenly gasp for air. The first time Mme Mendel asked me for my inventory, I tried padding my list with a couple of items I had not actually sold. But at the end of the meal she demanded to see the money; I was humiliated and had to confess I had made a mistake. She looked at me and smiled, as if to say, *That's just what I expected.*

Mme Mendel's disdain for me was conjugated throughout the family: male, female, plural and singular, from the wizened grannie to the petulant toddler, they all thought of me as beneath them. Only Hodel, the irregular one, did not judge me in this way. My low status was due in part to my family of peddlers being far humbler than the Mendels, and in part because I had been duped into a marriage with Hodel, a child they all knew was not right in the head. The main reason I had no status in the family, though, was that Mme Mendel had decided I was a nudnik with no head for business. If she had fallen in love with me, I would have been a demigod. Her power in the clan was absolute.

## 10

It was Monday. Vibrating in the back of the now-allowable Edelman van, I crouched in the fuzzy folds of Masha's woolen cap, near the crest of her forehead, and breathed in her scent: almond-scented soap, milk. Through the thick woolen hairs that blurred my view like tree trunks, I could see Mordecai Edelman's everyday black felt hat brushing the ceiling of the car as he drove. His peltlike beard was etched against the blare of light pouring through the windshield, the cloth of his coat bunched up at the elbows whenever he turned the steering wheel. Pearl was twisted around in the passenger seat, one arm stretched back so she could hold Masha's hand. Masha held her mother's hand loosely in her own, playing with the fingers.

The lurching of the vehicle was making me feel queasy. Backing into the dense copse of mohair, I was made to see, in my mind's eye, Leslie Senzatimore parked in his white truck by the side of the road, his big arm hanging out the side, his thumb and middle finger tapping out an impatient rhythm on the door of the cab: di-di-di-BA-di-di-di-BA-di-di-di-BA. Parked just behind him was a car, red and blue lights flashing ominously from its roof.

Dennis Doyle had some very irritating characteristics. He had stopped Leslie for speeding three times since he was stationed six months ago on this flat stretch of the Montauk Highway, which Leslie had to take to get to work and had an absurdly low speed limit. Each time Dennis had stopped him, he'd asked to see his license, then took the laminated rectangle between fore- and middle fingers and walked leisurely, bowlegged, back to his squad car, leaving Leslie cooling his balls while Dennis ran a check on him to make sure he wasn't a terrorist or wanted by the police in some other state or possibly a scofflaw with outstanding moving violations, even though he and Dennis lived three streets away from one another, had shared teachers from the first through the twelfth grade, and were both on the same Neighborhood Watch Committee. Dennis went by the book. Yet Leslie couldn't help chuckling as he watched his old buddy in his side mirror, cropped curly hair obscured by the police cap, legs stiff from too much gym work, belly swollen under the tight blue shirt, waddling up to him, pad in hand, like he was going to take his order at a drive-in hamburger place.

"Everything okay with my record?" Leslie asked him, sunglasses still on just like Dennis's were. He knew a cop was meant to ask you to remove your sunglasses and he wanted to make Dennis Doyle ask a man he had smoked his first joint with to please remove his eyewear so he could compare the photo on the license with his actual visage. Dennis declined to take the bait. "If you don't like being checked, don't speed," he said.

"Okay, officer," said Leslie. Doyle stalked back to his car with a straight-backed, offended air. Leslie wondered if this man could still be classified as his friend.

It was already quarter to nine; as a rule, Leslie liked to be at work by eight-thirty. It set the tone for his guys. The large sign reading

SENZATIMORE MARINE was visible from the highway. Whenever Leslie saw it, his chest warmed with pride and a glimmer of surprise that he had amounted to anything.

The great rolling door was open as he drove up. Leslie walked in, scanning three boats on blocks for signs of progress. The men waved to him as they caught sight of him. He greeted them with the usual good cheer. Once he got his coffee, he would talk the day through with his team and get to work. Leslie did most of the fine woodwork himself. He looked through the glass windows of his office and saw that the coffee machine was fully loaded. Vera, his secretary of the last thirteen years, was sitting at her desk, her curved back to him. Leslie found Vera comforting. He walked into the office and poured himself a cup.

"Hiya," said Vera.

"Dennis Doyle gave me a speeding ticket," said Leslie.

"Who's Dennis Doyle?" asked Vera in a nasal whine, swiveling toward him in her seat. About sixty, wizened, with whipped-up gray hair and manicured arthritic hands, she was a model of efficiency.

"A guy I went to school with," Leslie said, taking a sip.

"Well, if you knew what I know, you wouldn't have been in such a hurry to get here," she answered, turning back to her desk.

"Why?"

"I have bad news."

Leslie sat down at his desk. "Shoot," he said.

"Remember how I've been chasing down a final payment from that Mr. Croft, for the job you did on his speedboat last December?"

"Yeah."

"He's filed for bankruptcy. I don't know when—if ever—we're getting paid for that job."

Leslie took this in quietly. "How much did he owe?"

"Ten thousand. So that makes twenty K in owed bills I can't get people to pay. They all blame the banks for not lending. Who knows? We can get a collection agency onto them, but some of these people are good customers. Like Mr. Clancy."

"Clancy?"

"He just closed his store up. Says nobody's buying high-end furniture."

Leslie leaned back in his chair. It made a squeal.

"What you need is some blue-chip clients," said Vera, turning to him, her skinny arms waving in the air. "Truly wealthy people don't feel the pinch; they keep spending."

"Okay," said Leslie. "So find me some truly wealthy people with leaky boats."

"You think I'm kidding," said Vera, arching her plucked brows. "I'm not. You're in the wrong niche. I'm telling you. You need to cater to the very rich."

"Vera," said Leslie, chuckling in spite of his worry, "I'm glad you have it all worked out. Because it's looking pretty dire at the moment." He rubbed his eyes, thinking of Stevie. There was a private elementary school they had found for him, but it cost thousands. His parents-in-law, his stepson, stepdaughter-in-law, step-grandchild, wife—they all depended on him. Leslie had to find a way of making more money. As often happened when he felt cornered, and for reasons he could not understand, Leslie escaped into the worst memory he had.

On the Saturday his father killed himself, Leslie had finished his pancakes and dumped the plate in the sink. He was late to meet his buddies down the block. Evelyn, his mother, was buttering the two-year-old's toast. His sisters were putting each other's hair in a bun for ballet class. His brother was attempting to tie his own shoes. No one was talking. Everyone in the room seemed to be indifferent to one another, yet if you walked in as a stranger you would get the feeling that they were all doing something as a team, so thick was their complicity, despite their silence and focus on their own activities. Even the slap Evie gave Martha was a little percussive ping in the calm symphony of Saturday morning in the Senzatimore home. Leslie wanted to get his bike out before his little brother Will looked up from the wit-twisting activity of learning to tie his own shoes and demanded to tag along.

He walked outside, head down, whistling randomly. There was a chill in the air for the first time all summer. He'd be back in school in two days. The shed had the light on in it, he noticed; his dad must be in there. Charlie Senzatimore repaired boats for a living, mostly holes in fiberglass and ripped upholstery, but when he wasn't at work he fiddled with wood. He loved to spend time in the shed outside his house where he had his table saw, band saw, lathe, hammers, glue, nails, screws, clamps, sawhorses. He could make bookshelves, tables, jewelry boxes—almost anything. He always made the kids a present on their birthday, and gave it to them as a side dish to whatever bought toy Evelyn wrapped up for them. It was in fact hard to get Dad out of the shed at all when he wasn't at work or in his armchair reading the paper. Charlie wasn't a sociable guy. If anyone came over to visit unexpectedly, he'd slip out the back door and stay in the shed till they had left. He couldn't even stand to have people who weren't his wife or kids see him eating. If he was at the table and the doorbell rang, he'd just take his plate and finish his meal in the shed.

Over the last few months, Leslie's father had been working on a secret surprise. He didn't want anyone to see it and kept it covered with a tarp. He worked on it through the night sometimes. His mother joked she thought maybe Charlie had a woman tucked under that tarp, he spent so much time there these days. When she said this, Charlie would let a little air escape from his mouth, smile, and look down shyly. He was still a very slender man, no taller than Leslie at thirteen. He had dark hair, swarthy skin, and brownish circles all the way around his eyes, which made him look Italian and exhausted. The thing he was building in the shed must have been important to him; a couple of times Leslie had started to open the door and his Dad had shouted to him to wait a minute. Charlie almost never raised his voice; when he did, it made an impression. After a couple of these incidents,

Leslie had taken to knocking on the door of the shed to see if his Dad was in there working on his secret project.

This particular morning, Leslie knocked on the rickety little door, but there was no answer, so he figured it was safe to walk in. The first thing he noticed when he opened the door was the canvas tarp his dad used to cover the secret thing, crumpled on the floor, and the thing itself, displayed on a sheet of plywood resting between two sawhorses. It was a wooden replica of a battleship, about four feet long. Leslie walked up to it, awed. Every gun turret, miniature helicopters, everything but the two aluminum propellers and the helicopter blades, had been constructed out of wood. The hull of the ship had been made with interlocking pieces of wood. Somehow Charlie had cut each piece for the body of the boat with just the right curve, and he had joined them all like a huge puzzle. The wood was raw, sanded, except for the words USS NEW JERSEY carefully lettered on the side with red paint. It occurred to Leslie that this must be his birthday present. Guilt at having seen it months ahead of time, twinned with amazement at the mind-boggling love it would have taken his father to produce such a marvel, overpowered him, and he made ready to leave the room and pretend he hadn't seen it.

As he turned, a little explosion of light, like a flashbulb, bounced off an aluminum ladder in the corner of the room. The A-frame ladder was on its side, and open, like an arrow pointing toward Leslie. Above it, in the deep shadow of the corner, among several of his father's old coveralls that hung like deflated figures from hooks in the low ceiling, the face of his father turned toward him, eyes wide and glassy. His father was flying. That's what Leslie thought for a quarter of a second. Then he realized the man was hanging by his neck from an orange rope that had been looped over one of the rafters, the body pivoting lazily, like a Christmas ornament that twists this way and that way on its branch. Leslie spotted his dragonfly-green Schwinn leaning on the wall behind his dangling progenitor. He inched up to it, grabbed it by the smooth plastic handles, backed it up a foot, then rolled it in an acute semicircle, just avoiding his father's feet. He walked it, freewheel ticking, across the room, kicked the door open, swung his leg over the saddle, pedaled it as hard as he could out the driveway, sped down the street to Dennis Doyle's house, and screeched to a halt at the gaggle of kids already assembled at the base of the cul-de-sac. He spent the day with Dennis, Chuck Tolan, and Danny Morano playing James Bond and fighter pilots, every second expecting his mother to arrive in a state of hysteria. He didn't go home for lunch. He didn't care if he never ate again. If he could have made the day last forever, he would have. He considered running away. He stayed with his friends till evening sucked all the light out of the little cul-de-sac and the mothers started hollering. His mother called Mrs. Doyle on the phone to tell him to come home for dinner, but there was nothing in the woman's facial expression to indicate that his mother had mentioned finding her husband hanging in the shed. Leslie rode home and walked into the house, his belly leaden. Dinner was on the table and the girls were already sitting down. Will was washing his hands.

"Where's Dad?" Leslie found himself asking.

"In the shed," said his mother curtly.

"Don't you think he's hungry?" asked Leslie. He had to get her in there somehow. He couldn't tell her, not now that he'd waited all day.

"I don't want to disturb him when he's working on his project," his mother said bitterly. "He'll come in when he feels up to it." Leslie tried to eat. He chewed every mouthful until the food was like sludge. The crickets outside seemed to be screaming. He realized the poor man would be stiffening up in that shed all night, plus on top of that he'd be in the doghouse with his wife for staying in there, when really he was just dead.

"Want me to take him a plate?" he asked in desperation. Evelyn made up a plate in silence and handed it to him, adding dryly, "Make sure to give him our best regards."

Leslie walked to the shed, closed his eyes, and prayed. "Please let it not be true," he murmured. Then he opened the door, shut it, and walked back across the lawn and into the kitchen, still holding the plate of food.

"Mom," he said. "You need to go in there."

After Evelyn's shrieks; after the children had come storming into the shed; after Leslie had pushed the children out of the shed; after he had called the police, the ambulance, the relatives; after he'd put the other kids to bed, having magically become the oldest child, unofficially but permanently superseding his older sister Evie, who started sucking her thumb that night and never stopped, her ongoing pupa status manifested by an endless changing of careers into her forties accompanied by serial dating of stunted and puerile men who tended to either have strange sniggering laughs or be married, doughy, and unavailable; after mad Mrs. Bobik had come in wielding a coffee cake which she cut up and ate three pieces of, talking all the while in whining, breathless tones about how mysterious men could be; after he had sat up nearly all night with his grieving, furious mother, transformed from a fairly normal thirteen-year-old kid into the head of a family eviscerated by a man who jumped at his own shadow—Leslie lay in his bed and thought about his birthday present. He knew quite a bit about woodworking, having been trained for years in Senzatimore Marine, helping put the boats back together with his dad on weekends or sometimes after school. Occasionally there was woodwork involved, especially on the older boats, and those were Charlie's favorites. Leslie knew that you wouldn't make a model of a battleship like that, with all those interlocking pieces, unless you intended to have it taken apart. The boat was a puzzle.

Leslie got dressed very quietly and padded out of the house in his slippers. The crickets had gone quiet, though there was a silvery, hissing insect sound rising from the trees. He walked to the shed and turned on the light switch just inside the door. The bare bulb screwed into the ceiling shed a cone of cold blue light on the reshrouded USS *New Jersey*, leaving the rest of the room in a reddish black penumbra that seemed to radiate menace. The battleship cast a pointed shadow on the concrete floor. Leslie stood in the doorway, unable to move. The familiar little shed now felt electric with dread. Something palpable, like a massive Jell-O cube of negative energy, repelled the boy as he tried to walk into the room. He had to press his way into this force field, conquering his terror step by step. He made himself look only at the boat, avoiding the corner where he had seen his father's livid face swinging around at him hours earlier. Leslie lifted off the canvas tarp gently and laid it on the ground. The boat was as long as his arm span. From above, it had the shape of a very elegant pointed shoe. Its lines were refined, elongated. The gun turrets and bridge had been made of quarter-inch plywood, glued and sanded. Four helicopters with little metal blades stood at the ready on the flight deck. He imagined all those seconds flowing through his father's fingertips into this ship, all that time he didn't spend with his son poured into something that turned out to be for Leslie after all. Leslie felt so bad for resenting his old man.

The gunwales and the deck all seemed to be glued together, of a piece. He gently pulled at the top of the ship and it came away. Looking inside was a little shocking: the upper floor of the interior was a fully realized replica of a battleship: panels with switches, wheels and gears, all meticulously constructed out of wood. To see the rest of the interior, he dislodged the first interlocking piece of wood on the exterior using his fingers and laid it gently onto the worktable under the window. He decided to only take apart one side of the ship to begin with, and tried to lay all the pieces out in an order that would make sense to him later, so he could put the boat back together. It took him about forty minutes to disassemble the thing. Inside, in mad detail, were three stories of a miniature battleship. A crew of men with hand-sewn uniforms worked in the four engine rooms, lay on gray-blanketed bunks reading tiny whittled books, manned the intricate control panels, ate painted plaster dollhouse food, played chess on minuscule chessboards; still others cooked and cut up little replica vegetables. Leslie noticed a magnifying glass resting amid the debris on his father's worktable.

Only one of the rooms had a number on it: 753. Inside, a whittled blond man lay sleeping on the upper bunk. His fair hair was real, and could only have come from the head of Leslie's baby sister Martha. The blond man's arm, which was made of wire, dangled in sleep over the side of the top bunk. The seaman in the bunk below, a smaller, dark-haired man, was reaching for the blond, sleeping man's hand with his own wire arms and hands. Beneath the bottom bunk, Leslie noticed strands of coarse, black hair, a patch of muslin. He drew out a little doll, a tiny woman with painted-on lips, a white face, and real, long, black hair. There was a trickle of red paint drawn down the side of her mouth. Swiftly, fingers shaking, Leslie stuffed the little replica of the woman back under the bottom bunk. He hurriedly replaced every interlocking wooden piece that made up his father's masterwork, rebuilt the whole boat as quickly as he could. Light was streaming through the windows by the time he was done. He felt something bad had been released by opening the boat. The feeling of menace, which had dissipated while he was working, had returned. He felt his father's secret in the room without knowing what the secret was.

Leslie's slipper dragged a piece of paper along the floor. He bent and picked it up. It was folded over neatly. On the outside was written, *Please read*, in his father's careful writing. He didn't understand how he hadn't noticed this before. Maybe it had been tucked under the ship and fluttered down to the floor as he removed the pieces. He sat down on the cool concrete and unfolded the piece of paper. His father would explain the secret to him, maybe. He read: *Please pack this model with care and send to Hutch Sonderson, 14 Humbolt Street, Dayle, Iowa.* And then, inches beneath that, like an afterthought, was scrawled *This pains me.* Leslie sat as though he had been hit on the head, unable to form a thought, for a long time. Then he heard his mother calling him. He stood up and left the shed.

Later that morning, he nailed together a sturdy box out of scrap wood left around the shed, lowered the boat into it, and stuffed the box with newspaper to keep the boat steady. He wrote a note with a flat pencil his father had once used to mark measurements on wood: *Dear Hutch Sonderson, My father made this for you and then he hanged himself. Sincerely, Leslie Senzatimore.* He laid the note on the ship and nailed the box shut. Then he and Chuck Tolan wheeled it to the post office on a flatbed hand truck borrowed from Chuck's grumpy dad, who was in the moving business. Once they were there, Chuck Tolan helped him lift the box off the hand truck and waited outside while Leslie stood in line, the box at his feet, shoving it forward with his foot as the line grew shorter. When his turn came, he heaved the box up on the counter, paid the considerable postage with his own allowance, left the post office with Chuck Tolan, the two of them riding the hand truck along the sidewalks like a big scooter in total defiance of the menacing Mr. Tolan's strict admonishments, and tried to forget the thing had ever existed. He managed, for the most part. But now and then, as he grew up, Leslie imagined finding Charlie while he was still alive, wriggling in his noose. He always cut the poor man down, then, with his penknife.

Leslie never opened the door of the shed again. Nobody did, until Vince McCaffrey married his mother and they turned it into a canned food storage area. McCaffrey was a suburban survivalist, and kept enough canned stew, bottled water, and beans to last several lifetimes in that shed, convinced that once the big war started and all government was a thing of the past, the McCaffreys would need a lot of stew.

I crouched on Masha's hat, awash, by some olfactory miracle, in the scent of Leslie's coffee, and gazed at his recollection. That was a betrayal you wouldn't get over too fast. Yet there he was, so cheerful, capable, reliable, helpful—I didn't believe it. There was a gash under all that exemplary maleness, a sucking crater of a wound, like his head had been ripped off and he'd just sewn on a new head. All I wanted to do was introduce him to himself.

Leslie sat still, arms folded, his deep-set blue-glass eyes staring down at the desk, as the memory evaporated and he returned, slowly, as if drugged, to the present. Segundo, stocky, phlegmatic, knocked on the door. Reflexively, Leslie's expression changed to interested curiosity, a hint of a smile. He was knee-jerk affable, in the main. Could never stick to a bad mood.

"Segundo!" he exclaimed, his voice lifted, expectant.

"I need to show you this joint," said Segundo softly. Leslie got up and followed Segundo out the door. As he checked the hull of the repaired speedboat in the cavernous hangar, leaving his pathetic memory behind him, I found myself following another chain of occurrence, one unavailable to my strong-jawed host but suddenly, fleetingly, visible to me. Eager for knowledge in all its forms, I hurried down this wormhole and emerged in a battleship, on the Mediterranean, in September 1955.

Hutch Sonderson sat shirtless, nipples fatly convex from the heat, his chest smooth as a girl's, strong arms lank at his sides, wheat-colored buzz cut damp with sweat, limpid Caribbean-blue eyes unfocused on the tilting horizon. Charlie Senzatimore, dark, quick-limbed, a fast-talking urban shrimp in comparison to Sonderson's milky, farm-boy laconism, had fallen in love with Hutch some weeks earlier, but he didn't know it yet. The tightness in his chest as he watched Hutch space out, the feeling of embarrassed happiness whenever they spoke, he put down to a strangeness that had come over him from being off-shore for so long. Three months on the USS *New Jersey*. The nights were the worst. Lying below Hutch, watching one big, limp hand dangling over the side of the top bunk, long, strong fingers open as if inviting him to hold it—he would never forget the nightly sight of that unattainable hand. For the rest of his life, when Charlie Senzatimore looked back on the disaster that those days were to become for him, he remembered three things: Hutch Sonderson's hand floating above him, black in the half-light, like an ink stamp; the girl's round, puffy face dusted with pale powder, her childlike lips tinted red; the body, so small and limp on the bed, limbs twisted randomly like some abandoned doll, strands of dark wet hair stuck to her forehead, her cheeks still hectic, though she had stopped her labored breathing some time before. It had been an accident; there was no doubt about that.

When she walked him into the room, a breeze puffed out the white muslin curtains like sails, then turned tail and sucked them back out again. A fan circled in the ceiling lazily. The bed was made up with what looked like clean pink sheets. Charlie lay down. The girl sat down beside him. He could hear the wheezing in her chest from where he lay. "You need a doctor," he said. She smiled at him, uncomprehending. He thought, *She's probably doing this because she needs a doctor.* The thought of leaving her some money and running down the stairs crossed his mind. He felt no desire. He was agitated, and fidgeted on the crisp sheets, looking up at the winding fan, trying to think of something that would stimulate his imagination. He didn't have much experience to review. There had been a few awkward, tooth-clanging kisses with one brush-haired girl at the movies, the tentative cupping of her heavy breast. None of this made him even slightly aroused. Ironically, the only thing that made him interested in sex at that moment was Hutch Sonderson, when the whole point of being in this room with this very young, sick girl was so that he could lose his virginity and stop thinking about Hutch Sonderson. It was a simple equation and one that Charlie felt would work. It had to. If it didn't he would throw himself into the sea. The girl said something in a whining tone, clawing weakly, insistently, at his T-shirt. She was in a hurry. Her fingers irritated him. She wore a loose-fitting robe. Her hair was long and black. He took a handful of the hair and smelled it, eyes closed. He imagined smelling Hutch's skin, smooth, salty, warm, sun-baked. The pitch of his desire tossed him at the girl, whose thin, weak frame collapsed beneath him. He could hear her phlegmy breaths as he toiled to maintain his desire. Losing an internal battle, he flipped her over. She cried out, protesting, because perhaps she had not had that done to her, that particular thing, or it wasn't in her contract, or it cost extra—anyway, she cried out and he muffled her cry, his hand over her mouth, only for a moment it seemed, just long enough, the breath in her lungs gurgling liquidly, like the sound of a straw sucking up the last drops of milk in a glass. The curtains kept puffing into the room and then being sucked out again, as though an enormous being the size of a house were breathing steadily outside the room. When he was done, Charlie took his hand away and she was still. He sat up and she didn't move. He turned her over. Her mouth looked bruised. She wasn't breathing. He prodded her, slapped her lightly. He listened to her heart. Nothing. He opened her little wet lips and puffed her full of air. He pounded her narrow, bony chest. He wept in panicked disbelief, kneeling over her. He prayed. But she was gone. It had taken so little to end her life.

He climbed out the window, shimmied down a drain, made his way through the lane, passing two stylish women laughing, then out onto the Istanbul street, walking as fast as he could without looking suspicious, his U.S. Navy uniform attracting the stares of passersby as it was, until he came to the harbor and the battleship, as long as a city, it seemed. When he got to his berth, there was big, smooth-limbed Sonderson sitting on Charlie's bottom bunk, his bare feet flat against the lockers opposite, all golden hair and skin, glowing like Apollo, polishing his boots. His presence dwarfed the cabin. He grinned at Charlie, his teeth white as a picket fence.

"How was it?" he drawled. Sonderson had declined to come along to the whorehouse; he had a fiancée in Iowa and was going to go straight home and fill her to the brim with his gleaming seed the minute his tour of duty was done. Charlie crawled past Sonderson to lie down on his bunk, inching as close to the wall as possible, his stocking feet nevertheless inches from his bunkmate's rock-hard ass. Sonderson continued his polishing. He didn't notice—or didn't mention—the tears that were coursing from the corners of Charlie's eyes, past his temples, and wetting the pillow. Hours later, they set out to sea again. Charlie imagined the girl growing cold alone in that room.

Though Charlie Senzatimore was too frightened to commit suicide that night, cowed by the church's famous threats of hell meted out to all self-killers, he did manage an internal death. He never told anyone about the little whore's accidental asphyxiation, or his love for Hutch Sonderson. He served out his time in the Navy, walked off the ship, took eight befuddled years to meet the very tall Evelyn Bresnihan, and started living the life he was supposed to.

Leslie knew none of this, of course, yet somehow he'd grokked it all.

In the bleached, impeccable Edelman bathroom, perched on a soap dispenser near the sink, I watched Pearl Edelman help Masha undress for her bath. Pearl, her wig exchanged for a snood, a terry-cloth head covering with a little sack in the back to catch her hair, lowered the straps of Masha's floor-length jersey dress; it crumpled airily to the floor, followed by her long-sleeved gray shirt, bandage-white brassiere, and cotton child's underwear. I gazed at her perfect imperfection: rounded, graceful arms, full breasts that grew upward like buds and culminated in rosy nipples. Her hips were smooth, her legs strong, lean, and a little bowlegged. I no longer know if she was beautiful. Probably not—but she had a fluid, animal grace. Her black hair fell down her back in glossy waves. Her great, glittering eyes seemed to take up two-thirds of her face, and made her seem like a tremulous creature, vulnerable and fierce.

Tearful with longing, I turned toward the mirror, pivoting on the slick pump of the soap dispenser clumsily, still unused to all my legs, and surveyed my ugliness. My enormous convex eyes were the color of persimmons; their surface looked like the fine mesh on a fencing mask. My cranium was translucent, shiny. Yet I was prevented, mercifully, from looking into my own brains. There was perhaps some sort of skeleton holding up the structure of my head—there must be. My mouth was permanently agape. I could not bring my lips together. In my open gob, a hairy tongue lurked. I stretched it out, and a thing, like a furry cock with a flat pad at the end of it, emerged and reached all the way to the counter. It tasted something bitter and retracted, as if it had a mind of its own. My gray-and-black-striped trunk was covered by long, sparse hairs, as were my fragile, threadlike legs. Only my delicate wings held a shred of beauty. Other than that, I looked like one of the devil's minions. And yet I was a part of creation. The Old Bastard had fashioned this monstrosity and decided, *It is good*. What an egomaniac. At least I was never a maggot, but emerged fully formed like Athena, breached from the head of Zeus armed and ready for battle.

It was not astonishing to me that I had been cosmically revamped, though I found my form insulting; my cousin Gimpel, a Hasid, had told me all about *gilgul neshamot*, the transmigration of errant Jewish souls in order to atone for their sins. Some came back as Jews, or animals; but the spirits of the wicked returned as demons. Was I a demon? That at least would be interesting, because demons can converse with humans. In fact, their main purpose, aside from stealing the breath of infants and the seed of sleeping men, was to derail the righteous and lead them into various temptations. That seemed like a perfect job for me. I decided to test myself. I took off and flew across the bathroom, landing on the rounded edge of the porcelain tub, inches from Masha's face. She was leaning back in the water now, watching a narrow column of hot water flow, amazingly to me, from the tap. Tiny beads of sweat had appeared on her upper lip. She licked them off with her tongue. I could taste the salt! Her eyes shifted. I saw what she saw: the soap. She needed it. She sat up to get it. Too fast. The pain, again. Each heartbeat rang with pain that echoed into the base of her throat.

Dong . . . Dong . . . Dong . . . Dong . . . she waited for the tolling to grow faint. She sat perfectly still, taking little sips of breath and staring at the shiny lozenge of soap. She glanced at the door. Pearl was gone to tend to the other children. Masha had to do this on her own. Once the pain had subsided, she began to move very slowly through the water, millimeter by millimeter. It was hard to tell she was moving at all. She reached the soap, clutched it, then sat back again, keeping her mouth shut tight, breathing through her nose. I waited for the pain to recede until I tried speaking in her head.

*Scratch your head*, I commanded. Masha's head inched to one side, as if she were listening. *Scratch!* I said. Then I heard her thought, a feathery voice in my ear: *I wish I could just sleep in here* . . .

*Scratch!* I implored. At last, miraculous to me as the parting of the Red Sea, a plague of frogs, a burning bush: Masha's strong, slender arm rose slowly from the water. Her tapered fingers reached into her hair, and . . . she scratched!

I perched at the edge of the tub, stunned by my capabilities. I simply couldn't believe it. Chills were going down my spine—if I had a spine. I felt flushed with power. It might take a long time, I vowed, but I would raise this girl up and out of her sanctified sleep of self-abnegation, raise her to fame. I would put her in that luminous story box she wasn't allowed to watch; I would destroy her obedience to the old Tyrant, Humorist, Soul Recycler, Spy. And, somehow, I would bring Leslie Senzatimore, that pillar of goodness, down. Maybe Masha could even help me. I smelled the truth in these people; I needed to scratch until I found it. Two wounds, like a snakebite in the white thigh of Hashem.

## 11

Aside from the evening meal, every aspect of my married home life was to be maintained by Hodel. She prepared my ablutions in the morning, washed my linen, cleaned our room, and laid herself out on the bed for me each evening like a nightdress. Yet I had the impression, when we coupled, that she was holding her breath. The only time she seemed happy was when she took out her dolls and induced me to play house with them. It was a pathetic image: a young man and his bride feeding invisible porridge to a couple of rag babies. I was being sucked into her little world of the imagination, and actually began to feel paternal toward these poppets. We slept with them between us at night, made them speak in baby language, moving their heads and arms in a lifelike way. When we had intercourse, they lay with us, their bored button eyes fixed on the ceiling as if waiting for us to finish up.

After a few weeks of marriage, Hodel began to have attacks of an explosive intestinal nature. Mornings were spent almost entirely in the latrine. Her gas smelled like rotten meat. She lost weight. Her skin became pale, her face gaunt. I was increasingly repulsed by her. I hawked my merchandise through the city day after day, spending extra hours working in order to stay away. At night I bundled myself at my side of the bed and shut my eyes, conjuring delights of the flesh with plump, healthy women I had seen on the streets, and trying to ignore my wife's toxic night flatulence. When I overcame my revulsion and mounted her, I kept imagining necrotic stalactites of excrement clinging to the inflamed lining of her intestines. Her fits of homesick weeping rained down on my ears like needles. When I managed to fall unconscious, I slept fitfully in a slick of erotic dreams oozing one after another into my head. Often I woke sticky with nocturnal emissions. I would wash myself off and try to cheer up poor tearstained Hodel by feeding her dolls their breakfast. Given the state my life was in, it's no wonder that I turned to religion.

My cousin, Gimpel Cerf, had come to Paris from Mezritch, in Poland, to try to make a little money selling merchandise with my father and me, and in order to raise awareness of a radical new type of Judaism. They called themselves the Hasidim, the holy ones. They were known for their dancing and singing, a joyous form of worship. They put less emphasis on learning than we Talmudic Jews. For them, the simple were most beloved by God. I first met Gimpel in my parents' apartment one Saturday. My mother liked me to come to eat the last Shabbat meal with her, my father, and my brother every few weeks. I was grateful for a respite from dinners at the Mendel household, and walked up the rickety stairs of our tenement the first Saturday of every month without fail. Hodel rarely accompanied me on these visits; either her bowels were liquefying, confining her to the latrine, or she said she needed to help her mother—who of course would have liked nothing better than to be rid of her for a day.

The first person I saw when I walked into the room was my little dumpling of a mother, the crisp lace of her Shabbat bonnet framing her scrubbed, full face, her small, upturned mouth and pointed nose giving her the look of a cheerful fox. I hugged her, drinking in her intoxicating aroma until my sinuses were filled to the brim. My mother worked in a bakery. The nooks and crannies of her head—the soft cartilage valleys behind her ears; the neat crease where the solid flesh under her chin joined her neck; the downy nape—smelled of challah, every day of the week. It was her perfume. When I was a boy, I imagined that my mother was originally made of challah dough. Instead of being born like everybody else, she had been baked in the oven until she was the perfect mother. Anyway, I released my hold on her, and was very embarrassed to see a shambolic young man in a stained black caftan beaming at me from the kitchen table with a smile of benevolence and understanding, a fur hat set back on his head, plump hands open, palms down, on the table. One brown eye wandered in its socket; the other gazed at me with burning affection. His beard was sparse, his side curls long. When he saw me loosen my grip on my mother, he stood, opening his short arms, and exclaimed, "Jacob! At last!"

Reluctantly, I walked up to him. I felt the shock of his hug deep in my rib cage. His breath was hot and smelled rather pleasantly like a pond. The hug went on far longer than I had anticipated. There was rocking back and forth involved. My arms dangled crookedly, splayed out by the force of his embrace. I looked imploringly at my mother, whose hands were clasped at her breast as she watched, her neatly frilled head cocked.

"And this, of course, is your cousin Gimpel, who has come to visit all the way from Mezritch," said my mother, who then walked over to the hearth, lit that afternoon by a gentile woman my parents hired for every Shabbat, and began to serve the stew that hung in a pot over the fire. Shlomo, my scholarly younger brother, walked in, shuffling his feet, a book under his arm. I noticed he was developing a faint dark mustache, like a smudge of dirt on his upper lip. He would be fifteen soon. I felt for him, thinking they would try to marry him off any minute. Then his life would be over, just as mine was.

Watching Cousin Gimpel eat was a diverting experience. He took ravenous bites, hunkering low over his bowl, then hummed as he chewed, gazing up at the ceiling, entranced. My parents ignored him as he did this, though the muscles in my father's jaw were standing out like cables as he chewed, and my brother shook his head in disapproval several times. At one point Gimpel stopped humming, looked down from the ceiling, and saw me staring at him. He smiled, half-chewed noodles peeking out from between his teeth.

"I am releasing the sparks," he explained, his *s*'s spraying a little shower of kugel across the table at me. "From the food."

"The sparks?" I asked.

"The spiritual life in the food," he said. "That's what produces the taste." I looked at my father. Impassive, he took a helping of cabbage. "'And they saw God and they ate and drank,'" continued Gimpel, smiling, holding up his small wineglass. "Exodus 24:10. The rebbe says that when a man eats he should free his mind so that it can soar to think on God while each mouthful is being swallowed. This is how we will right the universe and bring on Moshiach. Bit by bit." He took a gulp of his wine, then started humming again.

"By eating?" I asked.

Gimpel stopped humming and looked at me. He seemed shocked. I wondered if I had angered him. But he laughed, his open mouth packed with chewed noodles, his belly shaking. He laughed so hard his eyes were watering, and he dried them with his napkin. "By eating!" he kept repeating to himself hoarsely. Finally, when he had recovered, he looked at me with a serious, loving gaze.

"In time, I'll tell you all about it," he said.

The following day, Gimpel followed me on my rounds as I lugged my peddler's box up and down the streets energetically trumpeting my wares, the leather strap cutting into my neck. As I chanted the contents of my box in a singsong voice, my bearded cousin followed silently, his beaver-fur hat gleaming atop his head, sidelocks drooping, caftan fluttering behind him like a black sail, the gaggle of iron pots and kettles slung over his arm clanging with his every step. Walking ahead of him in my elegant pointed shoes, I imagined I was leading a couple of heifers to market, such was the bell-like ringing of his merchandise. Gusts of his pond breath enveloped me whenever my pace lagged. Mortified by his absurd getup, I tried to keep a few paces ahead, proclaiming up into the balconies, "Ladies' lace collars! Pocketknives! Snuffboxes! Wonderful prices!" I sold nothing. By noon, sheer fatigue forced me to sit down on the step of an equestrian statue. Gimpel sat beside me, swiveling my peddler's box to face him and opening each of the smooth-action drawers with the intent curiosity of a chimpanzee.

My box was a mobile shop, meticuously organized. I had bought it cheap from a man in dire need of funds, about to be deported from Paris on charges of selling without a passport. Made of rosewood, it had four drawers. Arrayed in the first and thinnest of my drawers were small personal items: snuffboxes, shoe and belt buckles, watch fobs, and other trinkets, depending on what I had come across in the markets or fairs. In the next drawer down I kept gloves, napkins, lace collars, handkerchiefs, epaulets, and leather portfolios. In the third, I kept razors, hunting knives, and charming little pocketknives. In the bottom, largest drawer, I kept chisels, kitchen knives, small axes, inkstands, and other bulky items.

"You are not strong enough to carry all this," said Gimpel, after his long, simian examination.

"I do it every day," I said breezily.

"You will ruin your back," he exclaimed. "You should let me carry it."

My neck and shoulders were permanently sore; it was a tempting offer. Yet he was driving my business away just walking behind me.

"Thank you," I said. "But I think it's better if, after today, we sell separately. You might do better in our neighborhood."

Gimpel nodded, smiling, his good eye on my face. I felt suffused with shame.

"On the other hand," I stammered, "if you really don't mind, I would be relieved if you—just for an hour—" Gimpel's face brightened. He stood, took off his hat, revealing a yarmulke embedded in a greasy mop of hair, and heaved the heavy box up, drawing the yoke around his neck. He then replaced the beaver-fur hat delicately, as if it were his crown.

"I will take your things," I said.

"No," he said, reaching for a kettle. "Today you will walk free. You do the yelling and the selling. I will be your ox." We set off. I couldn't help feeling he looked better carrying a Jew's box, oxlike figure that he was, his untamed beard and sidelocks drooping, than I with my slim hips, pale hands, and tethered hair.

In the coming weeks, we became companions. We shared the weight of my peddler's box, and some of my profits. Gimpel loved Paris, and kept exclaiming about the proportions of the buildings, gesturing broadly with his free arm.

Due, I think, to Gimpel's flamboyant appreciation of the Pont Notre-Dame, coupled with his super-Semitic attire, Inspector Buhot, the police inspector in charge of the Jews, stopped us on the bridge one morning. Buhot was a gaunt man with a chapped face who carried a notebook everywhere, jotting down the comings and goings of each Jew in Paris with persnickety attention to detail. Buhot knew us all, and had us individually pegged, good or bad, honest or dishonest. He arranged to have us deported and imprisoned regularly, like a stern mother sending her child to sit in the corner, then welcomed us back after a few months with a cool smile.

"Good morning, Jacob," Buhot exclaimed with edgy affability, the skin beneath his eyebrows red and flaky, his lips chapped. "Who is your friend? I don't recognize him."

"This is my cousin, Gimpel Cerf," I said. "Gimpel, may I present to you Inspector Buhot."

"*Beau—beau!*" exclaimed Gimpel in what was perhaps the only French word he knew, his unruly eye floating upward, his free arm sweeping wide to include the bridge built up on either side with shops

and houses, the clusters of ragamuffins, peddlers, nobility, and trades-
men swarming by us, the glittering Seine below. Inspector Buhot
assessed him warily. Gimpel's caftan, wild beard, and long sidelocks
were of interest to him.

"Gimpel doesn't speak much French," I explained. "He is here
from Poland. Mezritch."

"Ah—Poland. Is this how they look in Poland these days?" he
asked me. I blushed. "You are always so tidy, Jacob," said Buhot. "You
should teach your friend how to present himself. He will make a lot
more money that way. Parisians aren't used to shaggy Jews. And teach
him some French," said Buhot.

"We will teach him." I said. "Give him your papers," I instructed
Gimpel in Yiddish. The penalty for being a Jew without a valid passport was deportation or imprisonment. Smiling like an idiot, Gimpel
handed the tall, bony Buhot a wrinkled paper covered in florid script.
Buhot squinted, attempting to read the tiny writing. I noticed a faint
tremor in his fingers.

"It's in Polish," I said helpfully.

"He should have reported to me when he got here," said Buhot,
handing the paper back to Gimpel. "He's here illegally."

"He only just arrived. We were going to pay a visit to you this
afternoon."

"What is your business in Paris?" Buhot asked Gimpel, his eyes
two crystalline points of inquisition. I translated his question into
Yiddish.

"I have some pots, some pans . . . ," said Gimpel with a shrug. "I
would like to sell them."

"How long do you intend to stay?" asked Buhot.

"That depends on you," said Gimpel, with a servile bow. "I must
return to Poland within the year, anyway."

"You'll be back in Mezritch a good deal sooner than that, my man,"
said Buhot with a fatuous smile. Then, turning to me, he announced,
"I will be in my office at the Châtelet in two hours. Bring him in, I'll

give him three months. Your father is a pillar of the community, Jacob. It's for him I am being so lenient. Normally I would send this fellow back out of the city tonight." I nodded, proud of my swift translation. My French was better than I'd realized.

When the inspector left, Gimpel chuckled and poked me in the ribs.

"You were ashamed of me," he said without rancor.

"No, I wasn't," I said, irritated.

"It's true what he said," Gimpel said, looking over at me. "You don't look like a Jew. You look like a Frenchman. That's the problem with the Jews in Paris. They all want to be French. How many—two hundred and fifty males in the whole city, your father said? In Mezritch we have more than a thousand people! We have schools. We have a synagogue. You don't even have a synagogue. It isn't right."

"They only let a few of us into the city at a time," I whined, "to lend them money and sell them what they need. They love to borrow money from us but then they blame us for lending them money. What are we supposed to do? We aren't allowed in the guilds, we have to carry everything around all day on our backs. We can't own land. The Portuguese Jews, they do better. I don't know why. . ."

Gimpel wagged his head. I wondered if he was a simpleton.

One morning I woke up in a puddle of cold, sticky semen. Hodel's hand passed through it as she stirred to wake and she sat up in bed with a start, wiping her palm on the sheet with a disgusted expression.

"I told my mother about that," she said, looking down at my sodden long johns. I lay waiting for what she would say next, bathed in humiliation. It was no use admonishing Hodel for betraying me to that black-eyed bitch. She would only cry.

"Mama says it's a succubus, coming to steal your seed and make baby demons with it," said Hodel, opening her clear blue eyes in credulous wonder, her little bud of a mouth puckered like a nursling's. "She says we have to have relations every night I'm clean, otherwise the baby demons that the succubus made with your seed will kill our babies when we have them. They'll suffocate them in their sleep." My child-wife's eyes were filled with tears—whether at the thought of dead infants or nightly encounters with her husband's prong, I could not tell. I lay there in a cold, congealed puddle of my own spunk and imagined a female succubus hunched, squatting over me, wild-haired, naked, with wine-dark nipples and a fleshy mouth, shuddering as she stole my seed for her evil progeny. I found the image intensely erotic and had to lie on my stomach to hide my condition from my wife. What was wrong with me?

I discharged my worries into Gimpel's willing ear that afternoon as we walked single-file along a narrow, muddy street. In the middle of my speech, a carriage passed; I flattened myself against a building. "Mme Mendel thinks it's succubi, coming to steal my seed," I said, wiping specks of mud from my face.

Gimpel chuckled, lumbering in front of me, kettles clanging, his broad back slightly bent. "The Besht says that's just a natural occurrence."

"So you don't believe in demons?"

"I didn't say that! Demons were created by Hashem. In fact, Cain's wife, Lilith, may have been a demon! But the body—the body is basically good," he shouted over his shoulder, stopping to let a clutch of Cistercian nuns rush by. The sisters held up their starched white and black habits as they leapt over a stream of sewage that coursed down the center of the street. Paris stank in those days. "The act of love between man and wife is a holy thing," Gimpel continued loudly. "There is even a belief that it can help heal the universe, which was torn when the vessels were broken!" Gimpel turned then and smiled at me, his anchored eye twinkling, the other, disconnected one rotating freely in its socket.

"Shsh," I begged. "The world doesn't need to know my problems."

"The world doesn't speak Yiddish," he said.

Once we had reached our destination and sat organizing our wares on the Place Louis XV, I went on: "What if I am no good? No good at all? I can't stop myself from thinking about carnal matters. I mean, even succubi don't sound so terrible to me. My wife—being with my wife is—like being with a sick child. She holds no appeal. Yet I am tormented by lust."

"The Besht says it is possible that even sin is from Hashem," Gimpel pronounced sagely, biting into an apple. "When you have strange thoughts, during prayer, for example about women, think about the origin of those thoughts—the origin is divine love. If everything is Hashem, and Hashem is in everything, then He is in badness too. If you were destined to think bad thoughts, you will think them. Even sin has an element of destiny. There may not be such a thing as evil in the world. I admit, I don't know much about any of this—I am at the beginning of my studies. But I get to eat the crumbs that fall from the rebbe's table, and I have learned a lot that way, believe me. You mustn't turn away from your wife, Jacob. When a man couples with his wife, the Shekinah couples with Hashem in heaven."

"What do you mean?" I asked.

"The heavenly spheres reflect our sublunar world," he answered. "Our acts—good and bad—have the power to shift heaven. The more good we do, the faster Moshiach comes. Simple."

"But the Shekinah—"

"The Shekinah is Hashem in the world. She is female. She is the part of Him we can touch down here. She reunites with Hashem." He clasped his hands together, whitening the knuckles. I stared at this simple elucidation of what I imagined as a hermaphrodite God, my mind drawn to the mystery without understanding. Gimpel's simple authority was irresistible. I took him that day as my model and my leader. I grew my sidelocks and curled them. I grew my little goat's beard as long as I was able. When Gimpel and I walked through the streets in our caftans, Jews and French people alike stared at us. Every morning when I prayed, I wound the leather strands of the tefillin around my left arm: thrice around the upper arm, seven times around the forearm, with the little leather box containing tiny scrolls from the Torah nestled at the biceps, pointing toward my heart. I wore the head tefillin strapped to my forehead. I rocked back and forth as I prayed beside Gimpel, the enthusiast. Gimpel never missed a chance to pray. Every morning he rushed off to a home where a makeshift shul had been set up—these moved from week to week, to keep ahead of the police, who sometimes raided places of worship—and I tagged along. When we set off with our wares, he brought along his striped prayer shawl, which he folded up and tucked into a little velvet pouch. Wherever we were in late afternoon, Gimpel managed to find eight more men so we could pray, even if he had to run out in the street collaring Jews for a minyan. In the evening it was the same. He never missed a prayer. He even prayed spontaneously at non-prescribed times, to my father's irritation. He began to be known in the neighborhood as Holy Gimpel, or, behind his back, "That crazy Hasid from Mezritch."

Though in normal life I often skipped the afternoon prayer, when I was with Gimpel, I always prayed at Mincha. I even bought myself a little velvet tallis bag, like Gimpel's. We threw our striped prayer shawls over our heads and rocked back and forth fervently three times a day, chanting our prayers like clockwork. I have to admit that there were moments, as I recited the prayers and read the Hebrew letters of the Torah, when I discerned the edge of something, like the fluttering hem of an infinite garment—something too vast to describe. In those moments I felt a wave swelling inside of me, carrying me up with it as it rose. But I was always washed up at the shore of my own mind, brought down, perhaps, by the instinctive irony that one day was to take over my whole spirit like a crazed vine. Gimpel, though—he was swept away daily. He cried out to Hashem, he wept, he implored. He prayed to become worthy. To stop being such a lousy sinner.

To Gimpel, worship didn't end when you removed the prayer shawl. On the contrary, he was in a virtually constant state of joyous worship. It was a new way of being a Jew, he explained. He was a Hasid. To them, depression was sin. Happiness was good. Gimpel even said a prayer after he took a dump. I started saying it, too, when I left the latrine: "Creator, who formed man with many openings and hollow spaces . . . if one of them would be opened or sealed it would be impossible to survive and stand before you . . ." God was everywhere for this man, and everything was joyous. I tried hard to emulate him—I wanted so much to live ecstatically at one with the Creator, to escape the reality of my life—but I couldn't avoid Hodel, weeping in our conjugal bed night after night. I couldn't squelch the lustful thoughts that multiplied in my head like maggots.

I kept the extremity of my sadness from Gimpel for as long as I could. Finally, one afternoon as we sat by the Seine to rest, I unburdened myself, weeping: my wife was half mad, hated the sexual act. Her farts smelled like a dead rat. Gimpel nodded and sighed. "It's hard to know what the answer is," he said. A young water carrier trudged by, a curved stick balanced on his shoulders, two full buckets weighing him down, spilling every few feet. Gimpel watched the water sloshing around in the buckets until the boy had passed us. At last he asked, "Has this girl been given an amulet against the evil eye? She's obviously sick."

I shook my head.

"Well, she needs something," he warned.

Gimpel continued to stay with my parents, taking my place in the bed I shared with Shlomo before I was married. Every Friday he used my mother's kitchen to prepare huge pots of pea soup, which he and I heaved down our staircase just before sunset in order to feed the poor a Shabbat meal. The widow Morel, our landlady, was a branchlike, bent, red-faced woman who always seemed to be searching for her cat. She had a merciful heart and allowed us to set up a long wooden table and chairs in her courtyard. There were some desperately poor people in the few streets where the Jews lived, and Gimpel endeavored to touch each of them with his ladle. He had a kind word for every arthritic crone, every barefoot urchin, every failed peddler. He knew all their names. Occasionally a starving gentile joined us; Gimpel welcomed them all. Tucked by his joyful side, I ladled thick green soup into chipped bowls held out between dirty, cracked hands, and I enjoyed doing it—or did I enjoy looking as if I were enjoying it? No, I honestly think I was becoming good by doing good. If Gimpel had stayed in Paris, I am sure my life would not have progressed the way it did.

Once the soup was all served up, Gimpel would say a blessing over the five or six loaves of challah my mother had convinced the baker to donate to the poor. He then presided over the table as the people ate their Shabbat meal, doling out thick slices of the sweet bread, along with stories of the Rabbi ben Eliezer, also known as the Ba'al Shem Tov, founder of Hasidism—and unorthodox servings of Kabbalah. Cold as it often was in the widow's courtyard, we were warmed by Gimpel's impromptu and often shocking statements.

His mystical cosmology was foreign but compelling: when Hashem set out to make the world, pouring infinite light like molten bronze into vessels meant to contain it, there was a terrible accident. Hashem blundered! He poured too much light into the vessels; they shattered. Sparks of Divine Light fell onto the earth and are now trapped in every mundane created thing, with or without breath in its nostrils. The reason for the exile of the Jews is the gradual release of the sparks trapped in the world. Through the performance of our daily duties, through fervent prayer, through the sanctified marital bed, through concentrating on the Divine while eating—through all of the hundreds of mitzvot performed each day by Jews, each of whom have a certain number of sparks they are destined to release in their lifetime, the sparks will all be returned to the Almighty and Moshiach will come. I wondered at the paradox: Hashem, perfect, spilled the light. Yet clearly it was His intention. Even evil, which was the result of the accident, was in His mysterious plan. There was nothing He hadn't thought of.

One Friday about six months after Gimpel had moved in with my family, my mother was waiting for me, smelling of challah. After sunset, she hid her eyes with her ravaged hands and prayed over the lit candles. As always there was a hush in the room as she made her wish to the Creator, the mother's gift every Shabbat—to make her wish. During the meal, Gimpel was humming and looking at the ceiling, as usual, when he stopped and said:

"A wandering soul may have been punished for its sins by being made to inhabit food. Only by being eaten by a tzaddik—a true spiritual master—in a spirit of holiness can the wandering soul be released from this torment."

"Does the soul know that it is a piece of food?" I asked.

"I don't know, I'm no tzaddik," shrugged Gimpel, and went back to his humming. Out of nowhere, it seemed, my father brought his fist down on the table so hard that it sounded like a chandelier had fallen. Everyone but Gimpel looked at him, terrified.

"What is this about wandering souls?" my father said. He was really angry. His blue eyes were sharp, intense, and fixed on Gimpel, who smiled back at him warmly.

"Wandering souls? You know," Gimpel said helpfully, "those who go through *gilgul* and keep being incarnated until their sins are redeemed. It's all in the Kabbalah, of course. And did you know that my teacher can look at the forehead of a man and tell from what source his soul came, and the process of *gilgul* through which it had passed, and what its present mission is here on earth?"

There was an ominous pause.

"Your teacher . . . ," said my father.

"Rav Dov Ber. He is the disciple of the Ba'al Shem Tov. The Besht, as we call him, tells of a soul who was incarnated in a fish and the soul was redeemed when it was eaten by a holy man!"

"Gimpel," said my father, "you are my blood. But you can't live here anymore. This muck you are wallowing in is very dangerous."

"But we are the same, you and I," said Gimpel. "A Jew is a Jew. It's all written—"

"No, we are not the same. Those Hasidim over there in Poland are crazy people and I don't want you infecting my sons with those ideas. I'm as Jewish as the next Jew, but I want my children to have a chance at a good life in this country! I don't want them dancing around all the time in ecstasy! In this house we have the Torah and the Talmud and that's the end of it! Do you want them to kill us all? Is that what you want?" My father's cheeks were flushed; flecks of spittle marred his fine beard.

"Do you believe Moshiach is even coming?" asked Gimpel gently.

My father sighed, averting his eyes. "I believe he's taking his time," he said sadly, a depressive film coating his eyes. It was then that I realized that my father had given up on Hashem. He only believed in rules now. As much as I had resented his rigid system of behavior and belief, I despised the cynicism concealed beneath it.

The room was silent for a long time.

"This too is *beshert*," Gimpel said to me as he got up from the table. I could tell that my father felt sick from his outburst. He pushed his dish away half eaten. My mother had tears shivering in her eyes, but she made no move to stop Gimpel from leaving. His mysticism and my sidelocks frightened her.

I watched as Gimpel made a bundle of his few possessions in the room where I once slept.

"I should be getting back to the rebbe soon anyway," he said. "It's so difficult being away from him. Paris is impossible for the Hasidim. The Besht's work will never take root here. It is too late."

"What did you mean when you said, 'This too is *beshert*'?" I asked him.

"Destiny unfolding," he stated, tying the bundle fast.

"I just don't see how we can have free will, as the Torah says we do, if God knows everything beforehand."

"That's the mystery," said Gimpel, sitting down on my old bed and leaning back on the wall, his belly shivering like a bowl of pudding beneath his stained caftan. He smiled, looking relaxed, satisfied. "For example, I came to Paris to make money for the Hasidim in Poland, but I didn't make any money. I came to see if we could bring the work of the Ba'al Shem Tov. But they're all waiting to become Frenchmen. So why did I come to Paris?"

"I don't know," I said.

"I came to Paris to meet you," he said. "That's what I'm guessing. Come with me to Mezritch, Jacob. For a time. You must meet my rebbe. Eat at his table. If your wife is too sick to come, return to her when you have learned something. I'm worried that if I leave you, you will be lost. You are still so soft, everything you lean against makes an impression. I don't want your soul tossed back and forth in Gehenna for all eternity."

Clearly, I should have gone with him.

## 12

Deirdre Senzatimore strode over to the "parent trap," as she called the smaller house beside her own, to be sure everything was in order for her appointment with Mrs. Drexler. She used part of the house—the living room and foyer, to be exact—as a showroom for her decorating business. Everything in that area of the house was for sale, right down to the candy dishes. Her parents, Don and Libby Jenkins, had the run of the rest of the place. This deal seemed pretty sweet to Deirdre. Her father, Don Jenkins, was appalled by the vulgarity of living in a showroom, but, as his wife Libby reminded him frequently, he didn't have much to say about it, seeing as he was between jobs and had been for the past seventeen years, having lost his position at First National Bank at the age of forty-nine for being intolerably discouraging to loan applicants. He couldn't help himself; he just had to be honest, and most of the ideas these people wanted loans for were asinine. Don would open the conversation by saying, "Let's just go over this," and proceed to eviscerate the applicant's business plan, even as he approved their loan, often as an afterthought. People left his desk feeling they had lost the battle already, that, though they had the money they needed to accomplish their goals, they were doomed to failure. Don didn't mind lending them the bank's money—he just hated to see them weave such idiotic dreams. There was even a physical attack by one Jeff Wyant, who, though normally a patient man, simply couldn't stand listening to Don Jenkins's condescending theory on why a fish farm could never succeed in eastern Connecticut. Wyant punched him in the face, broke his nose. The police were called, but the culprit walked free the next day cleared of aggravated assault, maybe because the particular policeman who answered the call had fantasized about smacking Don Jenkins over the head for years, having endured one of his lectures about the stupidity of opening a cat kennel. Don was a dream masher.

Deirdre walked into the foyer and was pleased to see that everything was still in place: silk orchids in a Chinese ceramic vase, a large photograph of a lily pond on the wall, peach silk-upholstered bamboo couch beneath it. She lit a vanilla-scented candle on the hall table and stopped, hearing the ominous, high tinkling of ice landing in a glass. She walked into the kitchen. There was her father, Don Jenkins, bent over the freezer drawer, a bottle of vodka on the counter.

"Dad," Deirdre said, packing as much patience, exasperation, disappointment, and love into that one word as any daughter possibly could.

"Don't ask me if I know what time it is, lovely," Don said, unfolding himself to an impressive height. His fingers were wet from refreshing the ice tray, the one domestic chore he always undertook without being asked, and he flicked his hands to dispel droplets of water from his elegant fingers with an impatient gesture. Don had a long, squared-off head, and his face was a mass of wrinkles. His once-aquiline nose, diverted by the Wyant attack, listed to one side. Don wore a cherry-red cashmere sweater, a gray silk cravat tied in a loose knot at the base of his thin neck, and hadn't shaved for several days.

"I assume your mother has let you in on her latest fiasco-in-the-making," he said, pouring an inch of vodka into the tall glass and rooting around in the chaotic fridge, removing a half-eaten container of yogurt, some mold-furred strawberries in dented plastic, a glass jar with a smear of Marshmallow Fluff left in it. "This refrigerator is exactly like her mind, by the way. Filled with sweet, rotting substances of no use to anyone, least of all herself."

"I have someone coming in half an hour, Dad," Deirdre pleaded. "I'm going to need you to stay upstairs for a little while."

"Stay upstairs?" he asked her with a show of magnanimous agreement. "Of course I'll stay upstairs! I'll stay in the closet. She wants a divorce."

Deirdre's seventy-year-old mother, Libby, slipped in at that moment wearing a diaphanous pouf of a turquoise nightgown that just covered her matching panties. Her short blond hair was tousled. Mascara seemed to have been applied with feathery brushmarks all around her eyes. She was very tanned.

"That's right, you old shit," she snarled, leaning back against the wall. "I've had it."

Don, having cleared the first tier of the fridge, found a bottle of tomato juice in the very back, then theatrically checked the expiration date, squinting, a vaudevillian expression of disgust on his face.

"He can't even see," said Libby in a voice hoarse from shouting. "You can't read that without glasses," she called out to him. "Stop showing off!"

"I'll clean out the fridge later, Dad," said Deirdre.

Breathing heavily through his nose, Don filled the tumbler with tomato juice, seasoning it without haste.

"Guys," said Deirdre. "This woman is coming in twenty minutes. Can you please stay married that long?"

"Sweetheart," whimpered Libby, tiptoeing up to Deirdre. She only came up to her daughter's chin. "He's killing me. I mean literally. I am dying. I am suffocating. He is so fucking pretentious. I have to save myself."

"Mom," said Deirdre, "look. You come to the house. Okay? Just walk over there. Put a coat on. You can take a shower over there. Or I'll treat you to the beauty parlor. How's that? And Dad, you go to your den and read, and when the woman leaves, we'll talk it through. Okay?"

Deirdre rushed her mother over to the big house, holding a yellow slicker around her narrow shoulders. Libby, still in her aqua-blue cloud of a shortie and rain boots, veiny legs kicking out through the open jacket and revealing a streaky orange fake tan, was uncharacteristically silent; Deirdre wondered if this time her parents really would split up. They had only started drinking heavily in the past five years, since they had moved into the parent trap. At first getting sloshed together had bonded them, but it had gotten rapidly ugly.

Deirdre called the beauty parlor in town, made an appointment for her mother, ran back to the parent trap to find her something to wear, then drove her downtown, trying to ignore the tears that were running down Libby's cheeks and staining her fuchsia velour sweat suit. She made it back to the parent trap just as Mrs. Drexler, her client, drove up.

"Call me Mimi," said Mrs. Drexler, craning her short neck, standing on tiptoe, and giving Deirdre an awkward hug. They had only met once before. Mrs. Drexler was pinched and petite. She made Deirdre feel enormous. In the living room, Deirdre opened the book of samples she had prepared for the Drexler home, casting a critical eye on her own large hand.

"I just love this beige for the sofa," said Mrs. Drexler, fingering a swatch with slender digits.

"It's linen," said Deirdre.

When she picked Libby up from the beauty parlor, Deirdre found her mother's spirits had been lifted, along with her hair color. She was chatty on the way home, twice mentioning the possibility of getting breast implants. "Why not?" Libby said breezily, looking out the window, her snub nose in the air, wrinkled little hands with their bitten-down nails limp in her velour lap. As often happened to Deirdre, she found herself wondering how this could possibly be her mother. She

seemed more like a girl. It had always been this way. A typical school
day in Deirdre's childhood would start with her mother harrumph-
ing into the kitchen, red pillow lines stamped into her cheek like a
road map. Furious that she had to get up early, she'd slam the door
open and start frying food: bacon, sausage, eggs. Nothing could keep
Libby from her frying pan in the morning. She woke up and reached
for the pan. Deirdre always watched her mother's performance with
quiet interest each morning as she ate her cornflakes. This was a kind
of statement she was making to her husband and child. She was saying, *I'm cooking you a real breakfast, how many mothers do that anymore?*
*Now leave me alone.* But once she'd had her coffee, put on her face, and
found a cute outfit, maybe a pair of high-heeled boots, she could be
kittenish and loving, embracing her daughter and flirting with her
husband. Libby's moods shifted fast. Not that she was an ignorant
woman. She had gone to Connecticut College, majoring in American
literature. Deirdre used to pore over scrapbooks of her mother's college
days, when she was sloppily sexy, with oversized sweaters, no bra, tousled brown hair, and the same petulant little pout of a mouth she had
now. Her eyes were small, downturned, intelligent, and suspicious.
Even now, at seventy, she had a kind of puffy charm. Yet over the
years—probably because she was married to Don, the most pretentious
man on the planet—Libby had come to hate intellectual ambition of
any kind. She watched crap TV, read books she bought in the drugstore, and derided anyone who even tried to hold a scrap of an elevated
conversation. Yet Libby had, Deirdre knew, a far subtler mind than
Don, the Yale man. Don had gone to college on scholarship to study
economics. The fact that he had gotten nowhere in life was almost
entirely due to his pathological negativity—that and the fact that his
parents weren't socially connected. If she parsed it out, Deirdre could
see how her mother had come to be the way she was, and in a way she
even respected her for choosing a way to be, rather than blindly becoming. Yet Libby's childishness riled her, and she found herself get-

ting more and more dour in her mother's presence, as if to discipline her, or water down her tastelessness. The more time she spent around Libby, the older Deirdre felt.

For Deirdre, there had never been any question of not going to college. Don wouldn't hear of it. In the end, she chose Duke. She liked the pace of the South, she liked the way the men talked, and she loved being away from her parents. After college, she stayed in Chapel Hill and got pregnant by a nervy business major two years her junior by the name of Armand. Once he graduated, the two of them came back to the Northeast armed with a baby and very little else; they were running out of money—and interest in each other. Armand was a Long Island native and had ambitions to open a restaurant in Westhampton. Within a month of their arrival, however, they were separated. Deirdre was on her own with little Bud.

Having grown up in Connecticut, Deirdre didn't know people in Long Island. Yet she didn't want to move back home. The idea of living near her parents, who had driven her nearly crazy before she left for college, was depressing. She couldn't afford to move to Manhattan, or even Brooklyn, where a couple of her college friends had ended up. So she found an apartment above a dry-cleaning store on Patchogue, Long Island, Main Street, and decided to enjoy it. She relished her weird, disconnected existence shared only with her serious little baby. Deirdre and Bud slept in the same bed every night, curled up like lost puppies. She worked on her short stories whenever he took a nap, got a job eventually, and went out recreationally with the occasional fellow, but the dates were futureless. Bud and Deirdre had twinned, and moved through their days in unspoken complicity. It was as if Deirdre had extended the skin of her self, stretched it over her head like a thin membrane to include her child. As Bud grew up, the two of them coexisted inside that invisible fiber, unreachable, peaceful, until Leslie rescued them back into the world.

Leslie came home from work early to do some paperwork. He had forgotten about Ms. Parr bringing Stevie home. Yet there she was in the living room, leaning over his willowy son. Shivering, leaf-shadowed afternoon sunshine blasted through the plate-glass window, silhouetting the two of them. Leslie watched the boy in profile. His pale irises, suffused with light, shone translucent as two drops of water. Neck bent like a drooping stalk, he was poised, immobile, over a pristine page of paper. Abruptly, his arm flared out, causing an unbroken line to arc from one end of the paper to the other, his hand one with the pencil. The child's mark was pure, unhurried, confident. Drawing was his solace. Ms. Parr noticed Leslie and smiled.

"Ms. Parr. I forgot you were coming," he said.

"That's okay, Jenny let us in," she said. Leslie walked into the kitchen.

Jenny, his daughter-in-law, was making a cheese sandwich in the kitchen, her baby on her hip.

"Where's Deirdre?" he asked.

"I don't know." She shrugged. "She just called and asked me to let Stevie and his teacher in." Jenny's hair was in braids. She was wearing a gingham dress. The old spaniel was licking up crumbs at her feet, like Toto's understudy.

Leslie walked back to the living room. He stood at the doorway and watched his son drawing, the tendrils of Ms. Parr's hair floating above the paper. He could smell the woodsmoke wafting off her from where he was standing. He saw the hint of a bleached mustache on her upper lip, glinting in the sun.

"Can I ask you a question?" he asked her softly. She looked up at him, straightened, smoothing her long cotton dress over those prodigious hips.

"Yes?" she said. He backed up a few steps from the room, nearly to the front door. She followed him, an expectant look on her face.

"Mentally," he said, barely audibly, though the boy was deaf, in the other room, and engrossed in his drawing, "do you think there's something?"

"In what way?" said Ms. Parr in a small voice.

"At home, he . . . he's unpredictable. You never know. He gets real angry sometimes. Or . . . sad. Screaming. He hits. I'm not sure how he is at school . . ."

Ms. Parr looked up at him with a solemn, level gaze. Her humorless honesty had a shriveling effect on him. "I think it would be prudent to have him assessed," she whispered. "All the behavior you describe is normal, to a point, for a deaf child. They get frustrated. But see? How he is when he draws. Maybe that's the key."

Deirdre decided to bring her mother to the main house rather than leave her at the parent trap and risk a big blowout with Don. She was surprised, then, to see her father, shaved and showered, playing with Stevie in the living room. When Don turned and saw his wife, he grabbed his heart. "Who is this glorious woman?" he exclaimed. Libby giggled and sashayed over to the bar.

"Mom," said Deirdre, "it's three o'clock."

"I need a drink after all the emotion," said Libby, one bitten-down hand already strangling a bottle of vermouth.

Deirdre sighed, blinking slowly. In a langorous show of defeat, she tossed off her shoes and fell onto the couch. Stevie ran over, nuzzled up to her. She held the frail boy tight, her eyes shut. Leslie watched them lying there. Every day with Stevie was a struggle for her, Leslie knew. He wished it were otherwise. He wasn't proud of her, in that way. He wished he could be proud.

———

That night Leslie kissed naked Deirdre in the dark. A crack of light from the bathroom they shared with Stevie, eternally illuminated for his sake, limned the outlines of her cheek, her arm, the rounded pitch of her hip, with silvery strokes of light. He swept the hair back from her face with his rough palm. She lay on her side, slid her hand over his massive shoulder, down his back. "You're the only man in the world who can make me feel small," she whispered.

"You are small," he said. "You're my tiny little wife." As she smiled, a glistening thread ran along her temple. Leslie wiped the tear away with his thumb.

"What is it?" he asked.

"Nothing," she said. "I just . . . I don't want anything to happen to you."

"What's going to happen to me?" he asked.

"Sometimes I get scared," she whispered.

"Of what?"

"How much I need you." He took her in his arms, her full, warm flesh relaxed against his taut belly. He nestled his face into her neck, felt her heart beating at the base of her throat, the skin vibrating against his lips.

## ∞ 13

I sat basking on a warm windowsill recently scrubbed by one of Masha's many sisters, or possibly the housekeeper, in preparation for the coming Shabbat. I had realized some time ago that I didn't need to go anywhere in order to keep up with Leslie or Masha. I couldn't escape them. Their two stories were switched back and forth in my mind ruthlessly. The only thing that prevented me from going mad during this period was the sensual delight of sublunary existence. I had, in the past days, become fat from the nano-scraps unwittingly left around by the scores of children, cousins, friends, and neighbors bouncing around in that house on any given day. It was a fly's Eden. Not that it was dirty—Pearl spent much of her time sucking up dust with her vacuum, wiping up or sweeping crumbs, spraying sterilizing sprays all over every ceramic or glass surface—and yet still the specks fell from the food. For me, one iota was a feast. And I was not the only fly attracted by this bonanza. Other samples of my species—largely female, I am happy to announce—were born in the Edelman house every day of the year. I had achieved a bit of a reputation among the girls by now, and the virgins tended to congregate coquettishly around me, gathering like, well, flies, hoping I would inseminate them.

I never realized it before, but there is a charming little mating ritual for houseflies: the male, having spotted the female (there were, I admit, occasional encounters with male flies, but these were flirtations, I assure you), begins to follow her, occasionally beating his wings very quickly and making a distinct buzzing noise. The female, if a virgin, might slow down at this (female flies only like to mate once). The male continues to follow. The female pretends she doesn't know what's going on and walks along, nonchalantly licking up stray drops of food or excrement. Then—this is my favorite part, and I have to say I take my hat off to the Creator for being so generous to even the lowly fly—the male sneaks up behind the female and gives her vagina a little lick. He didn't have to give us that, but he did. The female is then often somewhat more interested, opens her wings, and the male strikes, leaping onto her while curving his abdomen forward and entering her, stroking her face. We could remain in this happy position for up to two hours. Though I am not one hundred percent sure I was fertile, being a demon, I did fuck a lot of flies that spring, and, whatever their paternity, a generation of them bashed their way out of maggots—so many that mother Pearl was forced to buy a selection of fly swatters, and I nearly lost my life on a number of occasions. Pearl Edelman had a vicious swat and surprisingly good coordination. I did not give much thought as to whether these new flies—very possibly my own children—were incarnated souls, or just flies. To be honest, I was so incapacitated by the stories of my two humans as they flashed through my poor brain that I was barely able to think at all. My only recreational activity was lust. Its satisfaction brought me a blissful, fleeting respite from the stories of Leslie and Masha.

I did, however, try to remain in Masha's presence as much as possible. Her animal beauty soothed me; her pain saddened me. I had accepted the fact that I could not have her and that my love for her was an absurdity. All I wanted now was to change her destiny.

Masha woke from a nap but kept her eyes shut, alert for the pain. She took in a breath that swept through her chest, searching for a catch, a dig, an impediment. She sat up carefully. Nothing hurt! She swiftly said her morning prayer of thanks for being returned to her body, reached under the bed to draw out the water-filled red plastic bowl and pitcher, performed her ablutions, dried her hands on a towel that was crumpled near the bed. She stood up, tentatively at first, then, pain-free, she bounded past the tidily made beds of her two younger sisters, Suri and Yehudis. She passed the desk the three of them shared, covered with Suri's earnest homework, out the door, along the hall, passing the petite Sri Lankan housekeeper, Trina, who was vacuuming, and clattered down the stairs. Pearl, who was in the kitchen making challah, looked up at Masha, worried.

"What's the matter?" she asked.

"It doesn't hurt anymore," Masha announced, automatically touching the mezuzah screwed into the wall by the door, then kissing her hand.

"*Baruch Hashem,*" said her mother. "You still need to take it easy." Masha took an apple from a basket and bit into it with gusto.

"Wash the apple," said Pearl.

"Can I help?" asked Masha, holding the apple under the tap.

"You sit down," said Pearl, using her wrist to wipe a stray hair from her flushed face, then retying her headscarf good and tight with dough-covered fingers. Eighteen-year-old Yehudis, who looked much like Masha, only rounder, with smaller eyes, her prettiness lacking the haunted fierceness of her sister's, smiled sympathetically.

"You want some tea?" she asked.

"I'm okay," answered Masha, yawning luxuriously and sitting on a bench beside the long Formica table, drawing her knees up to her chest, pulling her long dress down to her ankles. "Where is everybody?"

"The baby's sleeping, and I let the little ones take out the portable DVD thing because it's Friday," said Pearl.

"They're watching *The Lion King* again," said Yehudis in a teasing tone.

"Mommy," said Masha, laughing, "you gotta get 'em another DVD, they know it by heart."

"We did fine without it, and we will again, if anyone else complains," Pearl warned. "I probably shoulda never got it anyway."

"Okay, okay, Mommy," said Yehudis, kissing her mother on the cheek.

Six days had passed since I had gotten Masha to scratch her head. I had since convinced her to eat two pieces of chocolate cake in one sitting and use her mother's lipstick without permission. I also tried suggesting she drink a glass of milk only five hours after eating meat, instead of the usual six, but she berated herself for even thinking such a thing. I would have to tread carefully on the religious habits, I realized.

Suri, fourteen, with a waxy complexion and fine wavy hair, walked in carrying Pearl's eleventh and probably final baby, Leah. "Hi, sweetie," cooed Pearl, her fists deep in the challah dough. Suri strapped the red-headed mite into her high chair and the baby started screaming, bashing the plastic apron of the high chair with her fat mitts.

"Where's Trina?" asked Pearl.

"Vacuuming upstairs, she didn't hear the baby," said Suri.

"Give the milk!" said Masha, holding her ears. Yehudis dumped a measure of white powder into a baby bottle, filled it with water from the water cooler in the corner, shook the bottle, and handed it to the shrieking baby, who snatched it from her and sucked at the nipple desperately, breathing loudly through her nose as she guzzled like a nursing calf. There was, I noticed, a touch of animalism in some of the females in this household.

"Mommy, what can I do?" asked Suri.

"Help Yehudis cut the fruit," said Pearl, working the dough. There was a moment of quiet. Then Masha, lying back on a few pillows that had been left on the bench, closed her eyes and began to sing. Her voice was eerie, raw. The song was in Hebrew. It had a winding Eastern melody, like an incantation. The other two girls joined in, creating a complex harmony. These girls could really sing. Pearl smiled, tipping the pot and rolling out the yellowish challah dough. I hovered over her, enduring the occasional swat from her flour-crusted hands, and watched, riddled with nostalgia, as she divided the moist, shiny orb into three separate balls, one for each loaf she was going to make, then cut each ball into three parts, rolling the sections into thick strands and braiding them swiftly. She cut off the ends of the three loaves to burn in the oven, just the way my mother had done, but, unlike my mother, she placed each loaf in a disposable tinfoil container, brushed them with egg, and slid them all into the electric oven. I loved Pearl. She didn't smell of challah all week long, as my mother had, but she had a delicious concentration when she worked, the younger children weaving in and out of the room whining for chocolate ice cream (they got some), and reporting various bite marks that the wildest of all the children, Estie, had made with her little otter teeth. The serene Yehudis drew ferocious little Estie, a petulant child with badly tangled dark hair, onto her hip and rocked her while singing placidly. I remembered that my mother-in-law, Mme Mendel, had always said that matted hair was caused by demons snarling it in the night, and that one should never cut the knots out for fear of angering the demons. Eventually the little girl relaxed and rested her head on her sister's shoulder, her eyelids fluttering. Suri sang like a good student, hands clasped, hitting all the right notes. Masha sang with abandon. Leaning back on the pillows, eyes closed, throat arched, she seemed posessed by the song.

As the women worked and sang, I clung to the ceiling with exhilarating ease, my feathery feet somehow fastening me to the plaster. My orb eyes were panoramic: I could see the white expanse of ceiling around me, the women moving around below, a blur of green out the kitchen windows. I could even glimpse a sliver of the hallway, and the unlocked front door, which opened and shut incessantly as a stream of purposeful Edelmans pumped in and out of the house all day.

The men—Masha's bony, pallid sixteen-year-old twin brothers, Dovid and Simchee, her father, Mordecai, and various brothers-in-law, wore their black hats set back from their heads as they returned from work, went off to pray, came back for a bite to eat, went out to study Torah, popped in for a cup of coffee, dashed off to pray again. Dovid and Simchee kept to themselves, reading Torah or the commentaries every single spare moment they had, arguing fine points in twin fuzzy beards, long fingers waving emphatically. Dovid had started growing his sidelocks long, Hasidic-style, as a gesture of extra piety, and wound them around the arms of his eyeglasses. The bearlike patriarch, Mordecai, always seemed to have a baby in his arms when he was home—his own, or one of Miriam's. Miriam, the oldest of the Edelman children, already had four children under five. She was twenty-eight. The Edelmans procreated very nearly as efficiently as the flies in the house did.

Miriam arrived, bossy, breathless, holding a Bundt cake in one hand and a heavy plastic bag in the other. Two identical little girls slipped past her and ran to the playroom, where Miriam's youngest siblings, along with two of her own tiny kids, were still watching the movie.

"Didn't you hear about the asparagus?" Miriam asked, her eyes falling on two dozen bundled spears lined up on the counter.

"What about them?" asked Pearl.

"We're not allowed to eat them this year. Too many bugs."

"Since when?"

"It was in the paper. It's an infestation. You can't get them out even by soaking," said Miriam officiously, holding up a bunch of asparagus and waving it regretfully. Bugs, I knew, were not kosher, so we always had to check fruit and vegetables carefully, even in my less observant home long ago.

"Not even by soaking?"

"No."

"Oh. Well," sighed Pearl. "We'll be one vegetable short, then. But you brought a Bundt cake!"

"I only got back from work at two so I couldn't let it cool enough," said Miriam. "There are big chunks missing where it stuck to the mold." Pearl patted her arm.

Now the door opened again. Another daughter. This one was Alyshaya, a petite twenty-two-year-old princess with a very long, thick brown wig that came down to her waist. She pushed a baby in a carriage. "Could somebody get the soup? It's in the back of the car," she said. Yehudis dashed out. "I forgot to season it," said Alyshaya. "I forget everything now." She cast a loving, baleful eye on her baby, asleep in the carriage. "Honestly, Mommy, I don't know how you did it with all of us. I can't begin to imagine it. I would die," she said. Yehudis appeared with a heavy tureen of what I guessed was matzoh ball soup.

"What are you talking about?" said Pearl, laughing. "You get used to it. You expand."

"I'll say," said Miriam, smoothing her curvaceous hips. Her waist, still small, was cinched with a stylish wide belt.

"I meant spiritually," said Pearl, chuckling. "But isn't it worth gaining a few pounds to have all these lovely babies?"

"Of course it is," said Miriam. "But I still wish my hips weren't so wide."

"I can't wait to have babies," said Yehudis. "I don't care what I look like."

"Your husband will," said petite Alyshaya, shaking salt into the soup.

"Babies happen soon enough," said Pearl.

"I don't really want to," said Masha, her chin on her knees. Everyone turned in her direction, as if they had forgotten she was there.

"How could you not want to have a baby?" asked Alyshaya.

"Dunno, I just don't," she said, lying back on the pillows drowsily. Pearl looked at Miriam anxiously. Miriam widened her eyes at her mother.

"Okay," Miriam said to Masha, shrugging. "You can take care of mine, then."

I remained on the ceiling for hours, mesmerized by the workings of the clan, as the light through the windows faded. New to my celestial and corporeal powers, I was still trying to work out how to read the layers of my demon perception. Whereas Masha was transparent to me (as was Leslie), the rest of the Edelman family—the secondary selves—emitted a wavering frequency, confusing me with stray images, yearnings, and memories. A compulsive observer, I was gluttonous for every scrap I could glean. Stilling my thoughts, I became nothing but a pair of eyes, a recording mind. In this meditative state, I imagined God's head as a great sac lined with millions of red fly eyes. In my vision, the earth floated within this eyeball-lined sac as if in a womb; the lidless domes stared, taking in all acts, each thought, tallying the blemishes on every soul. The Old Bastard was watching me too, I thought nervously, my fly feet shifting on the ceiling. He was watching me watch.

After sunset, we all assembled for the Shabbos feast, the men in their black hats and suits seated beside their wives, the unmarried children clustered at the end of the table. A chubby, fresh-faced young student from South Africa named Aron was staying with the family over Shabbos. He was seated between Dovid and Simchee. My beloved Masha had been placed at the head of the table opposite her father this evening, possibly because of her illness. She was wearing her long gray jersey dress, her arms covered with a long-sleeved white shirt, her black hair falling around her face a bit wildly. Her eyes were glazed and puffy. She looked ill.

Mother Pearl had changed into a flowered top and black skirt, and tugged her faded auburn wig over her auburn hair, checking her reflection in the mirror in her room as I danced on her powder compact. With her peaches-and-cream complexion and her generous figure, she looked quite fetching. The other girls had tidied up as well. The little children had all been masterfully put to bed by Pearl, Yehudis, and the now-on-the-bus-to-Brooklyn housekeeper—all but the sour-tempered Ezra, seven, who was allowed to stay up, and the anarchic Estie, who had wandered back downstairs in her pajamas and hung from the back of her mother's chair like a little monkey. The long table—actually several folding tables put together—was covered in a white-and-gray paper tablecloth, bunches of hydrangeas nestled into four squat vases set along its center line, disposable yet elegant square plastic plates and cutlery for twenty-two arranged by Miriam with characteristic perfection. The table had been set up in the Edelman living room, a bare space normally furnished with a couch and two chairs that were permanently pushed to the edges of the room, the bare floor wide open, as if the place were a public hall. There were few ornaments on the light green walls, no paintings. Photos of the many children were placed on shelves and hung on one wall. The books were all religious, leather-bound volumes, exegeses of the Torah and the Talmud.

The shaggy, fur-hatted Mordecai stood up at the tip of his beauti-fully set table, twenty-one heads turned in his direction, and chanted the Kiddush, a brimming silver cup of wine in his hand. Once he had finished, he took a careful sip of wine, then poured a few drops, sadly cut with apple juice, into everyone's glass. I realized grimly that I had landed in a family of teetotalers. They all took a gulp of the pathetic concoction, then Pearl and the girls got up briskly to set out the feast: French roast beef, pistachio-stuffed chicken breasts, salmon roulade, gefilte fish with horseradish, quinoa salad, fruit and lettuce salad, potatoes in mustard sauce, roasted garlic, hummus, baba gha-noush, blueberry cobbler. Two of Pearl's sweet loaves of challah were nestled beneath their embroidered crimson velvet coverlet like dew-covered manna. It was paradise. With a shudder of pleasure and surprise, I stepped into a droplet of gravy and tasted the rich, salty fat through the pads in my feet! In a trance of sensory overload, I strolled from one luscious crumb to another, sometimes even flying to a serv-ing dish to drink from the rim, knowing full well that my hosts were forbidden to kill anything—even flies—on the Sabbath. These peo-ple were not even allowed to wash lettuce after Friday sundown, lest they kill the bugs hidden in the leaves. I was completely safe. They shooed me away several times, of course, but nobody dared swat me. Alyshaya's husband, Yitzak, a humorist, even quipped, "He's a Jewish fly; he knows we can't kill him today." I laughed at that joke along with the rest of the party.

The men sang a hymn with strong voices, rocking their heads, tapping the table with their fingers. While the men sang, the women, forbidden to sing in front of men they were not related to, lowered their eyes and mouthed the words silently. *The singing of a woman is akin to nakedness.* I remembered that from the old days.

Eventually the ladies let the men keep singing and engaged in conversation.

"Mommy, have you ever tried rice kugel?" Miriam asked.

"No, but I heard about it."

"Dr. Cohen told me about it while she was sewing me up from my last cesarean."

"What are you talking about?" Pearl said with a laugh.

"You know how I always manage to have my babies on a Friday, right? So she's delivered the baby and she's sewing me up and she's telling me about this great new recipe for rice kugel she's trying and she had to leave it half done because I went into labor. I'm lying there trying to act interested, with my belly open like somebody's purse."

"Miriam!" said Pearl. "We're eating."

"How many cesareans you had?" asked Suri, "Two, right?"

"The last three. I told Dr. Cohen she should just put in a zipper."

"You shouldn't do more than three, I thought," said Alyshaya.

"We'll see," said Miriam. The men finished their hymn, unfazed by the women's lack of attention.

Masha, meanwhile, was silent. Her stare was inward, intense. Pearl looked over at her several times, but she didn't want to fuss over her too much. The girl worried her so. I decided to try a little something. Flying behind her shoulder, I noticed she was working the paper napkin in her lap, twisting it with her fingers.

*Tear it*, I said. I knew she wasn't allowed to tear on the Sabbath.

Not even toilet paper. They had to use Kleenex. Her fingers kept working the paper, but she wouldn't rip it.

*Tear it*, I said, forcing my voice into her head, looping through the air. *Tear, tear, tear.* And then, with a calm, intent face, my beloved tore a single layer of the paper napkin under the table, her heart whomping against its boundary like a carpet beater. The thin layer of paper seemed to take a fortnight to rip asunder. Just one steady tear, on and on, as the men started in on another hymn.

Masha, whom I was now watching from the back of mother Pearl's chair, raised her eyes and watched them sing, all the while secretly tearing the napkin. I tried to listen to her thoughts, but all I got was her voice, singing the same haunting song as the men. They were singing K'vakoras, a prayer generally reserved for Rosh Hashannah and Yom Kippur, only occasionally dusted off for more ordinary occasions due to its extreme beauty and holiness. Masha was singing very loud inside her head, watching them, eyebrows raised, her lips mouthing the words. And then, to my astonishment, she began to actually *sing*. At first she didn't realize what she was doing. She had forgotten herself. But then, she knew. Her voice became clear, strong, defiant. It drowned out the men's voices. One by one, the men stopped singing and stared at her. She sang with all her heart, her pure eyelids shut. The party looked at her, stunned. Dovid, Simchee, and the young visitor Aron looked down at their plates, rigid with embarrassment, as though she were performing a striptease. Even I was shocked. When the song ended at last, blood came to Masha's cheeks. She opened her eyes and smiled, embarrassed.

Mordecai spoke softly, with disappointment and astonishment. "*Masha*," he said.

Masha shook her head, looking at her hands. Pearl stood and walked over to Masha's place, gently held her by the elbow. Masha stood. Tears glistened in her great black eyes. The two women walked out of the room, Pearl's arm around her daughter's narrow shoulders. Weakened with joy and pride, I was unable to move at all.

Once they had gone, Miriam exhaled. "What's wrong with her? Is she going crazy or something?"

"Don't say that," said Mordecai. "She's had a shock. She was in a lot of pain." Then, turning to the guest, Aron, he said, "I apologize for my daughter's behavior. She has been very sick."

"She hasn't been the same since she got back from the hospital," said Suri, wide-eyed, her cheeks flushed and shiny as a fall apple. "Like, remember, she said she never wanted to have kids?"

"But that's Masha," said Alyshaya. "She likes to say things to get a reaction."

"Anything for attention." Miriam sighed.

"Shah! Don't talk like that," said Mordecai.

"She'll be the one with ten babies," said Yehudis brightly.

"No way," said Alyshaya, "*you* will."

"Daddy," said Yehudis, turning her face to her father expectantly. "If I had a boyfriend, what would you say?"

"Get married," Mordecai said, shrugging.

"I wanna get married so bad . . ."

"You have someone specific in mind?" asked Mordecai.

"No . . ."

"She's always getting crushes," said Suri.

Yehudis smiled. "No one will set me up on a date 'cause I'm not nineteen yet."

"And that's the way it should be," said Mordecai.

"You need to go to college for a couple years, get some kind of an education," said Miriam.

"That's what I want to do, I want to study graphic design, I told you, but I want to do everything together, with my husband! By the Sephardic, they get married at sixteen, seventeen."

"You're not Sephardic," said Mordecai. "You'll wait till you're nineteen to start dating, like everybody else. It's only, what, three months?" His gaze drifted in the direction of the doorway where his wife and daughter had disappeared.

"I just feel like I'm wasting so much time," whispered Yehudis.

Upstairs, Pearl was sitting at the edge of Masha's bed. Masha was sitting under the covers, staring at her hands, which rested, palms up, in her lap. "I just did it," said Masha. "I don't know why."

"But you have to know why," Pearl said. "You know you can't do that, all your life you haven't sung in front of the men, suddenly you do it?" She stood now, trying to hide her anger. "I think you should rest a little. You got up too soon, maybe." She tucked Masha in and walked out of the room, flashing her an encouraging smile as she shut the door. But, once in the hallway, she slumped against the wall. Masha's transgression was a major affront, deep disobedience, demonstrating a total lack of respect. Pearl was so thankful that, up until now, all her children had grown up innocent, protected, and observant.

The next evening, as Pearl walked the few peaceful blocks to the ritual bath, the three-quarter-full moon looked melted away, like a sucked-on candy. Pearl had known for a long time there was something wrong with Masha. The girl had been sickly, intense, oddly, unconciously seductive all her life. Now Masha was twenty-one, the perfect age to find a husband. But who would marry a sick girl, a rebellious girl? No parent would allow it.

Pearl slipped off her robe and walked naked down the steps to the mikveh. If Masha didn't marry by the time she was twenty-four, twenty-five at the most, her chances dwindled, she thought as she submerged herself in the water, feet hovering a few inches from the floor of the tank, her long red hair floating around her, then rising, taking a breath, and going under again. The competition to find a man and start having babies was enormous. The men didn't start dating till they were twenty-five, as a rule, and then they wanted the young ones. Rising once more, Pearl saw the kindly bath attendant, a tiny old woman in a headscarf, observing her to see she was cleansing herself properly. The woman was nodding with approval. Pearl Edelman was a model mother. She had eleven children, a loving husband, and she knew the depth of happiness family life could bring. Her purpose, the purpose of her children, was to bring good Jews into the world, and teach them the Torah.

*I have to get Masha married as quickly as possible*, she thought as she went under one more time. *That's what I have to do.*

Later that night, when Pearl sat at the edge of her bed combing out her long, wet hair, Mordecai walked in, shutting the door behind him quietly. Pearl's pale skin was luminous. Her full arms emerged from the puffed sleeves of her prettiest cotton nightgown, legs crossed. Peeking up, nearly shy, she smiled at him. They would make love. It is written in the Shulchan Aruch, the legal code:

*Every man must lie with his wife on the night of her immersion.*

# 14

The day my fate was to change, the sky was a seamless vivid blue, the air a frigid claw. I had made my usual tense, skittering way across the courtyard to the latrine clutching a wad of rags, my hands chapped and ruddy from the cold. Inside the stinking privy at the base of the stairwell, my pants down, I felt colder than I had outside. At least the smell of crap—largely Hodel's, I guessed—was dulled by the freezing air. Sitting on the rough wooden seat, I gazed up at a circle of cobalt sky through a high round window. When I left, I could not bring my-self to say the bathroom prayer of thanks for my crevices.

On my way to morning prayer, the wind sliced through my thin trousers, ran up my sleeves like trickles of freezing water. As I prayed in Rabbi Noé's house, my prayer shawl over my head, I could not keep my thoughts still. I was singing hymns along with the other men, but my mind was on the coming day of lugging my peddler's box through the glacial streets of Paris, hoping to sell a pair of gloves to a man who already had fifty pairs when my own hands were numb, or perhaps a lace collar to a woman who owned a hundred almost exactly the same as what she was buying from me. I sold useless objects to people who didn't need what I sold, in order to support a wife I didn't love, whom I had come to fear in a way. I rocked back and forth, back and forth, and it suddenly occurred to me that I might ask God to help me. I prayed: "Please, Hashem, Great One, please, change my life." That's what I said, over and over. I was interrupted by the man to my right. He was whispering my name. At first I wasn't sure, but then I realized that, yes, he was speaking to me.

"Jacob," he whispered. "Jacob Cerf." I looked up and saw the cheery face of Blond Nathan, a man I occasionally bought merchandise from. He must have sidled up to me when I wasn't looking. Nathan was an affable fellow with a shady reputation. My father would never go near him because some of his merchandise was stolen. I tried as much as I could to avoid fenced items when I bought stock, and for the most part I think I succeeded. Today, however, I was very vulnerable, low, and frankly I was capable of much more serious crimes than buying a knife that had been lifted from some powdered little turd. Nathan gestured for me to come outside after the morning prayer had ended. I did so, and we both stood outside stamping our feet and breathing into our hands.

"I have a wonderful haul of knives, straight from Thiers, in the Auvergne, I just got back to Paris yesterday," said Nathan urgently. His front teeth were very prominent, and brown at the tips, as if they had been dipped in tannin. His eyes were round and gray. "I'll give you an excellent price."

"Bought wholesale?" I asked doubtfully.

He nodded, pulling up his lapels to protect his neck from the wind. "I rode all the way to the Auvergne and back in a cart with a load of onions, just to get the best blades. You know those poor French fellows in Thiers who grind the blades, do you know how they do it? They have to lie down all day on their bellies. They look like dybbuks, pale as death—they lie there right over the gorge, on freezing slabs of stone, holding out the blades against the grindstones, with big shaggy dogs curled up on their backs like living blankets, to prevent them from getting pleurisy! I'm not joking! What a way to live, eh? It's like something you'd expect in Gehenna . . ."

We were already halfway to Nathan's rented room. The narrow, muddy street was crowded with men, women, and children, nearly all dressed in black. The women sold firewood, the men sold rags, bagels, teakettles, pots, the boys walked dutifully behind their tutors, going off to study Torah, or, if they were urchins, they scampered about looking for pockets to pick or a hunk of bread to make off with. The occasional shop window boasted paltry items: a couple of salted herring, some seedcakes, a barrel of pickled cucumbers, cuts of meat, candy, all displayed side by side. People talked fast and loud; there was a marketplace atmosphere to the neighborhood, which was, in fact, only a few blocks away from where I lived. I was anxious to get inside again; in spite of the rags I had stuffed down my undershirt, I was shivering from the cold.

Nathan, checking left and right, led me through a door into the courtyard of his building, where two barefoot children, a girl and a boy, were chasing a bedraggled chicken, and up a set of cramped stairs. We plodded, shuffling. Dust swirled in a parabola of light let in by a tiny high window. After a three-flight ascent, Nathan stopped at a heavy oak door. Squinting in the low light, he picked out three keys, and tumbled a trio of corresponding locks.

"Now," he said. Turning to me and smiling with his tea-dipped overbite, he heaved himself, shoulder-first, into the massive door, which gave way grudgingly. I stepped inside behind him. The only furniture in the murky room was a small desk with a few papers fanned out on it, a high-backed chair, and a double bed. I glanced at the papers and noticed that Nathan had written out his accounts in neat Hebrew. On the floor were three large trunks with flat tops.

Nathan took his key ring out again and unlocked the first trunk, flinging it open. Without much interest, I observed the dull steel of many knives neatly arrayed in rows on velvet. There were clearly several tiers of cutlery in each trunk. Nathan took out each tray and set it onto the bed, then lit a meager fire in the grate. This hint of warmth relaxed me; I was suddenly overcome by sleepiness and wished I could lie down for a few minutes. I did not want to look at knives. Nathan opened the last of the trunks, set all the trays of knives and cutlery onto the bed, sat on the chair by his desk, and lit a small pipe with a bell-shaped bowl he carried in his inside pocket.

"Just knives for me," I said. "I don't have room for the full sets in my box." Nathan nodded and frowned down at his accounts, puffing on his pipe. As I watched him, his fair hair was suddenly rimmed with golden light. The sun must have come out from behind a cloud at that instant, because the room was transformed. A rectangle of light threaded through with white veins trembled on the wall to my right, thrown through the warped glass of the window. The lifeless gray knives on the bed had become smears of blazing silver. The illuminated smoke from Nathan's pipe rose liquidly through the air like a sinuous dragon. I felt the warmth of the sun on my face and was suffused with a strange, almost ecstatic joy. Then, as though a great fist had closed itself over the sun, everything went dark again. My doldrums returned. So sad and bored I could have wept, I approached the first of the trays on the bed and listlessly thumbed a few blades. Pocketknives. I could sell these. The blades were sharp, tapered, shining. They had been hinged into simple bone handles, for the most part. A few of them had a bit more detail on them and could fetch a higher price. Very slowly, as though drugged with valerian, I selected eight knives, placing them on Nathan's desk. And then, as I shuffled toward the bed again, an extraordinary object caught my eye, tossed in among knives. It was a pistol dagger—a long knife with a little pistol built into the blade. The handle was a finely carved ivory horse's head. I had never seen a weapon like this before. I picked it up and turned it in my hands. It was as long as my forearm. The blade was very sharp. The barrel of the little gun was burnished steel. The trigger guard of the pistol was shaped like a shell. I took it to the window to examine it more closely. The horse's head had been carved in great detail; it looked alive, the nostrils flared as if in mid-gallop, the mane flowing.

"I was wondering if you would sniff that out," said Nathan with a smile.

"Where did you get it?" I asked.

"An old woman in the Auvergne sold off her whole estate. Her husband had died and left her nothing but debts. She had great stuff, I wish I could have bought more." He puffed on his pipe, looking over at me benignly. I tried to lay the weapon back on the bed and feign a lack of interest, but I couldn't relinquish it. The initials DV were engraved under the horse's chin.

"What was the name of the man it belonged to?"

"No idea," said Nathan.

"Well, what was the widow's name?"

"We didn't exactly have a personal relationship. I bought her stuff by the pound. She was desperate to get rid of it."

"Where are the other things you bought?" I asked.

"Hm?" asked Nathan.

"The other things you bought from the widow."

"Jacob, I would love to let you browse all day but I have another client who wants to see this stock." Nathan had grown as serious as a man who can't cover his front teeth with his upper lip can look.

"How much for the eight pocketknives?"

"Three livres."

I forced myself to replace the pistol dagger on the tray and pretended to forget about it.

"I'll give you two livres for the knives," I said.

"Two livres ten sous," he countered.

"Two livres five sous."

"Forty-eight sous. My final offer," he said, looking down at his accounts.

"You're robbing me." I paid out the money.

"And the widow's weapon? Not interested?" Nathan asked as he wrote me out a receipt for the knives.

"Oh, I don't know," I said, shrugging. "How much do you want for it?"

"Fifty livres."

"What?"

"It's a rare piece."

"You said you bought the stuff by the pound!"

"You'll sell it for much more than I'm asking."

"Forget it," I said.

"Forty-five," he snapped. I looked down at him. His clear round eyes were glacial pools.

"Is this going to bring me trouble, Nathan?"

"Not unless you fire it."

I paid him the money, all I had. He threw in a tooled leather sheath, made in Spain, he said. "It's not the original, of course, but it fits very nicely."

I rushed home, breathless, as if to a tryst. There was no one at home. Unable to wait another moment, fingers trembling, I unwrapped the dagger from the square of wrinkled linen Blond Nathan had swaddled it in. The weapon gleamed in my hands, the tiny pistol tucked so neatly against the flank of the long blade. The carved ivory horse's head had been rendered by a master; I tried to imagine the tiny chisel he had used to pick out the flared nostrils, the widened eyes. Gazing at that perfect object balanced on my fingers, I felt an intense longing, something like love, rise up in me.

It occurred to me that it might be nice to offer a bit of gunpowder and a few bullets along with it, as an incentive to buy.

Old Aaron Mayer, who provided armor and munitions for the French soldiers, had his shop a few streets away. Locking the weapon in my peddler's box and yoking up, I dashed down the street and walked into Mayer's shop. The room was paneled with dark wood. Glass-fronted cases filled with gleaming muskets and swords lined the walls. Old Aaron, his back badly bent, his gray beard fine as a sprig of baby's breath, was helping a young aristocrat choose his equipment. The young man stood very straight, chest out, one foot splayed. He wore a powdered wig and was dressed in an exquisite yellow-and-sky-blue-striped coat with matching britches. As was the custom in those days, he was armed with a long, sheathed sword that hung from a fine leather belt around his waist. The young man's face was powdered very white, and he wore a little black dot above his lip. He watched me enter in the neutral, slightly irritated way one observes a wet dog slinking in through an open door. Aaron turned. Seeing me, he gestured for me to sit down in a corner till he was finished. The young man was holding a musket in clean, tapered fingers.

"There is really no reason to begin with the finest gun you can buy," Aaron said, taking the gun. "It's wisest to begin with something solid but economical, like this." He held up another, seemingly identical musket. The young man stood there for a moment, one long finger on his chin, thinking. Then he pointed at the more expensive of the two muskets. He told Aaron to put it aside for him for a couple of hours, along with the ammunition. He would be back very soon. "Of course," said Aaron. The young man walked out, leaving me in a cloud of intoxicating perfume.

"And off he goes to borrow money from Loeb Hildesheim, and so the trouble begins," Aaron said in Yiddish, shaking his old head. "Not one of them lives within his means. When they go into the army, they all need to buy the fanciest gear. And so they borrow from us, and then their parents get furious at us for lending." Aaron shrugged. "I'm not complaining. So, Jacob, what can I do for you?"

"I need some bullets and gunpowder. For a pistol dagger I want to sell, but I have never sold such a thing, and I thought it would be nice to have the *accoutrements*."

"Listen to your accent! You sound almost French."

"We all have to try, a bit," I said.

"Of course. Now. You're not wearing the weapon, of course."

"Are you mad? It's in the box." Jews in Paris were not allowed to bear arms of any kind on our persons; swords, guns, even hunting knives, were forbidden to us.

"Well, I better show you how it functions. So you can demonstrate for the customer. Always a good idea to know how your merchandise works."

Tenderly, I removed the wrapped weapon from the bottom drawer of my peddler's box, laid it on a table, and revealed it. Aaron looked at it somberly for a long moment. "Where did you get this, Jacob?" he asked me quietly.

"I bought it along with a load of other knives from Thiers," I answered casually. Aaron lifted it, examining the carved handle.

"You must have paid a great deal for it," he said.

"It was a part of an estate. A widow. I did think it was particularly nice," I said fatuously.

"It's signed," Aaron said, passing his thumb over a tiny scrawl embedded in the bottom of the handle. "Le Page. You see? Pierre Le Page is commissioned by the finest families in France. You'll need to be careful how you sell this. I can't believe . . . Who sold it to you?" Sensing my hesitation, he looked up at me from under his wiry gray brows. "All right. Well, first you put a measure of gunpowder down the barrel like this." He took what looked like a silver hip flask in his crooked fingers, removed a pointed silver measure affixed to its top, then unscrewed its cap. Carefully, he tipped a measure of gunpowder into the pointed silver cap, then emptied the powder into the barrel of the gun.

"Here's a bullet. You wrap it in a little piece of rag, like this." He enfolded a round lead bullet neatly into a square of cloth, then stuffed it into the barrel. He snapped a little metal rod from a clip under the barrel of the gun. "Use it to push the bullet all the way to the bottom of the gun, like this." I nodded, absorbed in the demonstration.

"Now," he said. "When they are ready to fire, they should simply tip a tiny amount of gunpowder into the pan here, cock the gun like this, and pull the trigger. The flint ignites the bit of powder in the pan, then the spark travels through the little hole, and—boom—there's an explosion behind the bullet, and it flies out. But you can't fire from too far away with this pistol. A few feet at most. This is for close range. Better to just stab them, really," said Aaron with a wry smile. "Then shoot them for good measure."

"How much for the powder flask?" I asked.

"Oh, I'll give you that as a wedding present. Just pay me for the bullets. Ten sous for a dozen, and a bit of powder. You don't need to give more than that with a pistol dagger like this. They're very popular with my set these days," he said, gesturing toward the young man who had returned with funds for his musket.

"Ah—monsieur, back so soon!" exclaimed the old man. I nodded to Aaron and left.

That night I had a dream. Hodel was sleeping with her nightgown bunched up around her breasts. I could see her naked belly, the red hair of her sex. Her skin was very pale. An eerie, animal growling was coming from somewhere in the room. It veered into a high whine. It was coming from her gut. The skin of her belly began to ripple and undulate; something sinuous was writhing under her skin. The whining got higher, louder. I became frightened. In the dream, Hodel sat up suddenly, her eyes wide, her red hair a mass of serpentine curls around her head. She opened her mouth as if to vomit. I saw with horror that she had no teeth. Her mouth was a shiny pit. Something was moving around inside her throat. I couldn't stop myself from leaning in to see what it was. A black eel with round yellow eyes lunged out of her mouth and clamped its needle teeth onto my forehead, undulating as it injected poison into my brain. I woke in a state of terror.

Beside me, Hodel slept, her stomach growling. I leapt out of the bed. The floor felt icy against my naked feet. I searched in the dark for a pair of wool stockings, but I couldn't find any. The bare window was a black square. Within it, the young moon shone. Panicked, I lit a candle beside my bed. As the flame grew, huge shadows leapt onto the walls. The bars of our iron bed became enormous stripes from floor to ceiling. My own shadow was a giant. The air in the room felt hectic with malign power. The sounds coming out of Hodel's belly were inhuman. I was filled with panic. My Jew's box was in the hall near the door. I carried it into the middle of the bedroom so I could see. I unlocked the bottom drawer where my pistol dagger was. Holding the weapon in my hand, I loaded it as Aaron had taught me, my hands shaking. I was so afraid. I kept thinking of what my cousin Gimpel had said, about Hodel needing an amulet against the evil eye. What was wrong with her? I sat down on the rocking chair in the corner of the room and watched her sleeping, the long knife in my hand, its loaded pistol resting in my palm. Every time she moved, I gripped the weapon, expecting her to fly out of the bed and attack me.

After several hours, the terror receded, I got cold and sleepy, and, convincing myself that the worst Hodel was going to do to me that night was infect the air around me with her carrion farts, I went to bed, sliding my weapon under my pillow. In the morning, I swallowed my bread quickly, while she was still sleeping. I had a terrible urge to wear the pistol dagger on my hip in that thick, tooled Spanish sheath. I imagined how wonderful it would be to walk through Paris armed like any Frenchman. If I hid it with my coat, who would know? Maybe I should just wear it around the house. I threaded the sheath onto my own belt and slid the still-loaded pistol dagger into it. It felt so good to be wearing it. So powerful. Hodel stirred and rubbed her eyes like a little child. I swiftly drew on my coat and skullcap. She sat up in bed and smiled at me. She had dark circles around her eyes. My heart went out to her.

"I am going to work," I said, lighting a fire in the hearth to make her some tea. I noticed that my hand was shaking.

"So early?" she asked.

"I'll go to prayers first," I said, grabbing my prayer shawl bag. I served my little wife tea in bed, feeling guilty for the murderous night I had spent ready to stab her in the heart. Then I left, armed.

## 15

Masha meandered down her leafy block, her own private fly perched on her shoulder. Her chest was still clear of pain, but she felt altered. The oddest thoughts had been filtering through her head since she sang in front of the men last night. It had been humiliating, yet she couldn't help wanting to do it again. It was like an itch you weren't allowed to scratch. Why had Hashem given her a nice voice if she wasn't allowed to use it freely? She knew asking why was a fruitless undertaking. There were so many rules, likes and dislikes the Creator simply had, the way some men don't like blueberry muffins. And, if you love that man, you don't serve him blueberry muffins. It was simple. And yet.

As for me, I was thrilled. My girl had made an enormous leap by singing in front of the men and breaking the Law of Torah. As I saw it, she had crossed over to my side. The sky was the limit now. She wandered up Beach Nineteenth Street past Kitov Hebrew Bookstore, Kosher World Supermarket, Chapines Bakery, the library. She had never been inside the public library, with its panoply of secular novels, and wondered what it was like in there. Who went. She kept walking, past the nursing home, past Heddie's Dry Cleaning, the last outpost of her own turf. There she paused. The next neighborhood was a ring of uncertainty. She had never walked it before, though she had passed through in a car many times.

It was a beautiful day. The shining sun made her feel brave. She walked on. Here, the strangers stood around chatting, or sat on front steps in aimless lassitude, devoid of her neighborhood's bustle. Uneasy but determined, Masha walked close to the side of the buildings, past a sign advertising live chickens. Two tall men in colorful knit caps loped by her, laughing in shrieks, as if the street were their living room. They turned their eyes to Masha with disinterested curiosity as she passed them, their minds on the joke. Her throat constricting, Masha lowered her eyes and kept walking. Pearl would have died to see her walking down this block. The smell of fried meat, sweet and fatty, seemed to ooze from a graffitied doorway. A young woman in a red leather jacket, short caramel-dyed hair, big hoop earrings, tight jeans on wide hips, marched by, holding two tiny children by the hand. The woman's eyes traveled down Masha's long black dress. A few blocks later, a yellow Volvo marked the beginning of yuppie territory. That was where she saw it, next to the pharmacy: Bridget Mooney School of Acting. The building also housed a tuxedo rental place and a podiatrist, both on the second floor. Masha stopped and peered into the plate-glass front of the acting school. A young girl with a flame-shaped thatch of white hair was manning a large wooden desk. Masha pushed the door open and entered.

"Hi," said the white-haired girl.

"Hi," said Masha. "I . . . was interested in maybe . . . taking a class."

"Sure. We have a new term starting next week. Here's a schedule." The girl stood up, sliding a folded orange pamphlet across the desk. Her torso was very long and narrow. Masha thought she looked like a Q-tip.

As Masha perused the schedule, she heard a door shut. She looked up and saw a woman traveling down the hall thoughtfully, her head down. She walked with a slight limp and used a cane. Her free hand hung loose by her side; it was in the shape of a claw. Thick-waisted, immaculately coiffed, wearing high-heeled boots and a fitted skirt, a pair of reading glasses hanging from a chain around her neck, she looked up, saw Masha, and stopped. The skin around the woman's eyes was swollen up like puff pastry. She peered out from under the doughy lids, her gaze curious, penetrating, covetous maybe. Then she turned and stalked into one of the rooms off the hallway.

"That's Bridget Mooney," said the Q-tip girl. "This is her school. My name is Shelley."

"Hi. Can I keep this?" Masha asked, holding up the brochure.

"Sure," said Shelley. "You should come. She's a fantastic teacher. She'll change your life."

Outside, Masha sat down on a bench in the weak sunshine and read the schedule. I settled on the splintered wood behind her and tried a little internal ventriloquism.

Masha: *The classes are at six p.m. on a Tuesday, and at eleven a.m. on Saturdays . . . I definitely couldn't do it on Shabbos.*

Me: *That leaves Tuesday nights.*

Masha: *No way could I tell Mommy and Daddy.*

Me: *But why not just take the class, who would it hurt?*

Masha: *I'd be with guys all the time . . . and performing in front of men . . .*

Me: *There's nothing wrong with just taking the class. It wouldn't be performing, it would be learning.*

Masha: *But there would be guys there. They'll think I'm weird 'cause I won't shake their hands . . .*

Me: *Or just shy . . .*

Masha: *How could I possibly get out of the house at night?*

Me: *What about a job that goes till eight or nine at night, and get Tuesdays off?*

Masha: *But what kind of job goes till eight o'clock?*

Me: *A pizzeria!*

Masha: *No way would Mommy let me work in a pizzeria.*

Me: *But if it's Jewish?*

I remembered having passed Mendel's Pizza on the way over. We walked over there and peeked in. Everyone behind the counter was male, wearing a yarmulke. No way would they hire a girl. Then, as we passed the Jewish Care Nursing Home, Masha stopped. The nursing home! She could get a few shifts there. They were always looking for volunteers or low-paid staff. She walked over there and asked the lady behind the desk if they needed anybody to work the evening shift, from four to nine. They did! It was all arranged in a heartbeat. I was horrified at the idea of having to spend time with smelly old people, but Masha didn't seem to mind at all. She ran home to tell her mother. But when she had almost reached the house, she stopped. Where would she get the money for the class? It cost three hundred dollars a term! She had a hundred and fifty saved up from babysitting. I suggested maybe they would let her man the desk at the school, like the fluff-haired girl, who was clearly a student. Maybe she got free lessons.

Pearl was delighted by the idea of Masha volunteering, and maybe eventually working for pay at the nursing home. It was a mitzvah to do volunteer work, and also she was convinced that Masha needed structure in her life, to keep her from being so moody until she could get her married. Then she would be too busy to be moody.

The next day, Masha walked over to the Bridget Mooney School of Acting and asked to speak to Bridget Mooney. It took a while, but eventually Bridget limped out in her high boots, leaning on her cane. She had the look of a grizzled demimondaine.

"What can I do for you, honey?" she rasped.

"Well, um . . . ," Masha began. Shelley was looking up at Masha curiously. When she met Masha's gaze, she winked.

"Come into my office," said Bridget in a low, smoky voice. She turned and walked with her unhurried, hip-swinging limp down the hall and through a doorway. Masha followed. Bridget's snug office was cluttered with memorabilia. The walls were covered in photographs of theatrical productions and individuals. Bridget as a voluptuous younger woman figured in many of them.

"Sit down," said Bridget, her chair creaking. Masha sat. Bridget scrutinized Masha, her head cocked, blinking her reptilian eyes.

"Are your eyes dark purple? Or am I seeing things?" she asked.

"They change in different light," said Masha, feeling her cheeks go hot.

"You're an amazing-looking girl. So. What is it?"

"I wanna join your class this term, on Tuesday nights, but I only have a hundred and fifty dollars. I plan to make more, but I, ah, I was wondering if you ever let people work for classes, or is that irritating? Like, I thought maybe that girl out there . . ." Bridget's claw hand was resting ominously on the mahogany desktop. The nails, Masha noticed, were polished light pink.

"Have you ever done any acting?"

"I did all the productions in high school. I always got the lead . . . I dropped out of college after a year, so I didn't get to act there."

"Where did you go to high school?"

"The Torah Academy."

Bridget paused, taking this in.

"Aren't those productions all girls?"

"Yeah," said Masha. "But they're very good."

"I'm sure," said Bridget. "But . . . how would you feel about having a male scene partner? You'd have to rehearse, and . . ."

"It's okay, I could . . ."

"I have a feeling for who you should be paired up with, but I don't want to give him to you if you're not going to be willing to do the work," said Bridget.

"I'll work," said Masha.

"That's not what I mean. I mean . . . how can I say this? I'll be frank. From your outfit, I'm guessing . . . are you Hasidic?"

"No," said Masha. "I mean, it's similar, we're Torah Jews, but we don't, we don't have a rebbe, we don't speak Yiddish. We don't, like, have a town in Europe we're associated with, but we basically follow all the same rules—it's less strict . . . I have cousins who are Hasidic. It's hard to explain. "

"But you can't, for example, wear pants?"

"No," said Masha.

"Or be alone with a man who isn't your relative?"

"I could do it if the door is open, like for work. Women work all the time, we manage."

"Do your parents know you're here?"

"No." Masha blushed.

"Would they approve if they did?"

"I'm twenty-one. I'm allowed, right?"

"Okay," said Bridget. "You've got me curious. Come here at six on Tuesday. We'll work out the details down the line."

## 16

The morning after I bought the pistol dagger from Blond Nathan, the sky liquefied. It rained hard for days, then weeks. Paris was sodden. The Seine was engorged. Drains overflowed; tangles of earthworms writhed in crumbling logs of shit. Mme Mendel guided Hodel through this chaos one evening, firmly insistent that her daughter purify herself after the two-week period of being unclean, whatever the weather.

Throughout Hodel's menses, and for seven days afterward, I had been forbidden to touch her. We slept in separate beds. She was not even allowed to hand me a glass of water. No contact whatsoever was permitted until she had been ritually cleansed, after which copulation was a must.

Had we lived in Metz, or indeed any town with a decent Jewish population, Hodel could have gone to the ritual bathhouse and been cleansed in a vessel of immersion filled with water fed from a living spring. But we did not have a mikveh in Paris. Much like the country women who lowered themselves into rivers, our women had to cleanse themselves in the water of the Seine. There were, however, several *bateaux de bain* stationed along the Seine, and one of these was available for use by the Jews.

As she always did, Hodel began the ritual by washing in our wooden tub at home. Every bit of her had to be scrubbed clean. There could be nothing—not one particle of dirt—between her skin and the purifying water. Once she had scrubbed herself, washed her hair, cut her toenails and fingernails (making sure to burn the nails lest her sister-in-law step on them and lose the baby), and removed her jewelry, she waited for the sun to set, then walked the winding streets to the Seine, her mother's arm clamped firmly through her own.

On an average day, the water of the Seine is gentle enough to swim in; after three solid weeks of heavy rain, the river was a torrent; you couldn't hear your own voice over the rushing water. Yet there was business to be done, and the boatman, his skiff modified for Jewish patronage, was on the lookout for ladies in need. When he spotted little Hodel and her freakishly tall mother waving their white handkerchiefs in the darkness, the man dispatched his wife in a rowboat. Battling the current with her single oar, the woman managed to keep the little boat level long enough for Hodel and Mme Mendel to jump into it from the riverbank. The next few minutes were treacherous; the boat nearly capsized several times, and Hodel, terrified, was soaked in river water and rain by the time she climbed onto the lurching deck of the bathing boat. A Jewish lady, Mme Zimmerman, acting as attendant that evening, dutifully pulled my little wife to a standing position, and they staggered about trying to enter the tentlike screen that covered the deck for modesty's sake. In lieu of a vessel of immersion, a barrel with holes in the bottom had been nailed to the side of the hull. This was so that the Jewish women could lower themselves into the water in the barrel safely and modestly, dunk under, and return via the ladder.

As Mme Mendel told the story to us later that night, weeping with rage: once inside the protective tent, Hodel disrobed and stepped from the tent out into the darkness, her arms held by Mmes Zimmerman and Mendel. Naked, shivering, my child-wife walked down the few slimy steps into the barrel filled with frigid, churning water. Halfway down, the women released her. But Hodel slipped! She fell in a diagonal, hitting a rotten board in the side of the barrel. The thing gave way, and Hodel disappeared under the water. Mme Mendel screamed at the boatman furiously, to no avail. She watched as her daughter popped up several yards away and whirled limp, like a belly-up dead frog, pale skin glazed by the roiling water as a clump of orange peels and a stiff dead cat sped by her. A few more seconds, and Hodel was swallowed by the darkness.

I imagine my little wife waking up just as she was passing under the Pont Notre-Dame; struggling and choking by the Pont au Change; fainting again—probably from shame at her nakedness—somewhere around the Pont Neuf, and ending her journey snagged among the many narrow, tethered skiffs that lined the Seine. This is all I know for certain: a washerwoman abed in her laundry boat—plying her darker trade, as so many of them did when not bleaching clothes—woke to find a naked Hodel clutching her starboard side. She pulled the bleeding girl out of the water, dressed her in clean linens, and brought her to her family apartment.

Hodel spent two full days in the washerwoman's crowded home, unable to remember where she lived, as all the men in our community, a quarter of a mile up the Seine, searched the river for her body. Even the Paris police lent a hand.

At last Hodel's address dawned on her. She arrived at our doorstep one afternoon in an immodest décolleté, her face a blank. Beside her was a woman with a large, firm bust and lined face—the laundress, who, I suspected, used her hands for more than just soaping underwear. I handed the louche rescuer a livre for her trouble. She seemed pleased, though she was clearly shocked when she saw from my mode of dress and our interior decoration, which included a menorah, that Hodel was a Jewess.

The next morning, Hodel woke up and asked for some meat. Her mother fed her a bowl of beef broth. Hodel drank that, but she wanted flesh, too. Mme Mendel brought some beef left over from the Shabbat. Hodel ate it ravenously, then went to sleep. When she woke up, she said she was hungry again. I brought her a chicken leg. The color began to return to her cheeks. Her intestinal problems seemed to be healing, as well. No extra trips to the latrine. What's more, she arranged her dolls on a bench by the window and didn't take them into bed with us that night. I almost reminded her, but thought better of it. Once we were settled in bed, with the candles blown out, I jumped in surprise when I felt her little hand on my belly.

Minutes later, as I was taking my pleasure on top of her, Hodel began to breathe strangely, and cried out as if in pain. I stopped moving, searching her face for an expression in the near dark. She writhed beneath me, her back arching. I realized with a shock of pleasure that these were the hoarse cries of ecstasy. Once that happened, there was no stopping her. Hodel wanted to couple every day—morning, evening, afternoon if I was available. It was fantastic. This was the married life I had been hoping for! I went to sell my wares whistling with joy, and hurried home at day's end to my little lustwagon. I was no sooner through the door than she pounced on me, tearing off my coat, ripping her frilled bonnet from her head, and letting the curly red locks spring up around her young face.

## 17

Mrs. Cohen, the matchmaker, had over five hundred names in her computer, each of them individualized: likes, dislikes, talents, and family histories were all entered in on Mrs. Cohen's master file, a genetic gold mine, promise of the future, *shidduch* machine. Mrs. Cohen would stay up late into the night shuffling and reshuffling the names, matching this one with that one, that one with the other one, playing with the kids' futures like a novelist thinking up different twists a tale could take. This would have been a nerve-racking business if it were not for the fact that Mrs. Cohen believed that really all these matches were *beshert*, destined, anyway—Mrs. Cohen was just the facilitator for the divine. Still, she worked hard to find the voluble girl to draw out the studious boy, the levelheaded oldest sister to bring a dreamy baby of the family to heel. Mrs. Cohen made a lot of good matches. This was, of course, all on a free-will basis, and if the kids didn't hit it off with each other, this too was *beshert*! As long as they married somebody. Mrs. Cohen believed in marriage above all things, because Jewish marriage meant Jewish babies. Her whole family—seven people—had been murdered by the Nazis within a month of one another in 1943. Only one ten-year-old boy, her grandfather, survived the camps, though he nearly died from the Hershey bar an American soldier gave him to buck him up on the day they liberated Dachau. When he came to America he married a girl who lived on Hester Street and they had thirteen children. Mrs. Cohen's work was a continual joy.

When her second cousin by marriage, Pearl Edelman, called and asked her to find a match for her daughter Masha as soon as possible, Mrs. Cohen needed to take a breath and think. Masha Edelman was a good catch in some ways: she came from a wonderful family. She was FFB: *frum* from birth, meaning she came from an observant family and was not one of those girls who turned to Torah Judaism from the outside. A lot of those women were lovely, but they tended to try too hard, and they weren't as desirable in the marriage market as the FFB girls. The Edelmans, though—they were an exemplary family. On the downside, Masha wasn't sturdy, healthwise, much as the mother tried to hide it. Mrs. Cohen had done her homework. She was a bewitching girl, what's more, and allure was only good in moderation. Even wearing a skirt five inches below her knee and old lady shoes, this girl managed to look immodest. The wrong man—an overly sympathetic or weak man—could end up being the girl's servant. An overly lustful man would never leave her alone, or become crazed with jealousy. Too much appeal, Mrs. Cohen had learned over the years, was almost always a curse. And what about the relentless strains of child-rearing? There were no sick days for mothers. Mrs. Cohen tried to imagine Masha helming a brood of three, four, five, eight children. It didn't seem right. Yet the girl had to marry someone.

Late one night, Mrs. Cohen sat in her housecoat and slippers, a steaming cup of tea on the desk, and stared at Masha's file on the computer. The letters of her name were displayed in capital letters in red, like all the other names, yet for some reason this name seemed different. One by one Mrs. Cohen tried matching Masha with each boy on her list. As she always did, she imagined their children, what they would look like, which characteristics from each of their parents they might inherit. Each of the young men on the list had something special: this one would make a good businessman, this one a scholar, that one would be a great father. The girls, having all been raised to be mothers—though many of them would work all their lives as store clerks, teachers, doctors, therapists—could be various types: harsh, hotheaded, resourceful, loving. But for Masha, all Mrs. Cohen could come up with were qualities of no use to anyone: charismatic, laconic, possibly canny, with an odd power over people. Mrs. Cohen kept up the game of matching men with Masha until she had three believable alternatives. One of these men would work. She knew it.

Seth Allen was courtly. Masha liked the way he opened her car door and flared his nostrils slightly, allowing her to settle herself fully before clicking the door shut with just the right amount of oomph and then walking, unhurried, over to his own side. Opening the door, he whooshed into the leather seat deftly for such a husky guy, and started talking about himself.

Seth was twenty-eight, a successful businessman. He had lived in Israel for several years but, he said, "I came back home to find a wife. The women over there—they're beautiful, but—I don't know, they're different. I couldn't bring myself to propose to anyone. A great Jewish woman is a tall order," he said. There was something about the way he said it that made Masha want to climb out of the car at the next stoplight.

When they arrived at Delgano's, he opened the restaurant door for her, pulled out her chair, reached around her, unfolded her napkin, and dropped it into her lap, careful not to come too close, then glided around to his seat, asking the Italian-looking waiter for the kosher menu, and perused it earnestly.

"You'll have the chicken cutlet," Seth announced, nodding to himself.

"How do you know?" Masha asked.

"I know what's good here." *You also know what's the cheapest thing on the menu*, thought Masha. "With a green salad," added Seth. "You're watching that figure, I assume. Good habits start early." He then ordered spaghetti bolognese for himself.

Seth had a way of talking straight through his nose, with no break between the words. The boneless-looking hands he flapped in front of his face to make his points actually reminded Masha of chicken cutlets.

"My kids are going to the Lubavitcher preschools, they're the best," he droned. "And I want the boys in *kollel* to study for at least three years once they finish yeshiva. I don't care if they're married—a good wife deals with these things, she'll be happy anyway, who doesn't like a scholar for a husband? Do you agree about the Lubavitcher preschools?"

Masha shrugged. "My sister Miriam, one of hers goes to the Chabad preschool, the other ones went to the one in her neighborhood. They all seem pretty happy."

"School is not all about happiness," said Seth. "But on the other hand, pleasure has its place." He smiled at her, his lips shining with oil from the pasta. There were specks of tomato sauce on his jacket. "It's simple: to have a harmonious home, a couple needs to think things through and be on the same page from the outset, because that's where the misunderstandings come in." He glanced at the menu. "How about a scoop of sorbet?" he asked.

"Great," said Masha glumly.

## 18

A strange thing happened one Friday afternoon, a month after Hodel fell into the Seine. I was downstairs, having come home early, as was my custom on a Friday, to help with Shabbat preparations and go to afternoon prayer. The delicious smell of boiling meat pervaded our rooms. As I removed the yoke of my box from over my head, I heard Mme Mendel screaming upstairs. I ran up the rickety staircase, opened the door to my in-laws' apartment, and found my mother-in-law looking outraged and alarmed. I took a few steps into the room to see what she was yelling about. There was Hodel, her hair uncovered, gravy on her lips, her hands dripping. She had been eating stew out of the cholent pot with her hands. When I approached her, I saw with alarm that a strange, incongruous smile was lurking on her greasy mouth.

"Who are you?" asked Mme Mendel.

"I'm Hodel," said Hodel simply.

"No, you're not," said Mme Mendel. Then she turned to me. "I have known about her for days, but I didn't think anyone would believe me." I just stood there, baffled. Then, turning back to the girl, she yelled, "Where is my Hodel?"

"I don't know what you are talking about, Mother," said Hodel, wiping her mouth with the back of her hand. "I was just so hungry."

She took a step toward her mother, but Mme Mendel shrieked, "Away! Get away!" And she slapped her. Hodel was always very meek with her mother, but not today. She grabbed the woman's hair beneath her matron's bonnet and pulled. The older woman punched her daughter in the side of the face.

"Please, Mother!" I cried feebly, trying to pry these two maniacs apart. "This is your daughter, Hodel. I mean, look at her! Who else could she be?"

"*You*," said Mme Mendel darkly, glaring down at me. Then she stalked out of the room, slamming the door of her bedroom behind her. Hodel washed her swollen face and gravy-stained hands in silence. Then she followed me downstairs. I watched the nape of her neck as she tidied our room, and appreciated her newly rounded buttocks as she bent to make our bed. Yet I didn't leap on her. Something about that smile upstairs stopped me. She turned, as if feeling my gaze, then grimaced.

"What is it?" I asked.

"I am unclean!" she pronounced furiously, jerking open our chest and pulling out a few cotton rags.

During the first Shabbat meal, after Friday sundown, Mme Mendel watched Hodel with the eyes of an eagle expecting a rabbit to emerge from under a rock any second. Yet the girl did nothing unusual. It's true, she ate much more than the old Hodel would have done—mostly meat—but that was a blessing. I was so much happier to have a healthy, plump, lusty wife than the diarrheal moper I'd married.

That night I slipped reluctantly into the cold sheets of the extra bed we kept in our room for the periods when my wife was unclean. It was difficult to separate from Hodel. Over the past weeks I had become used to sleeping with her, our limbs entwined. I closed my eyes sadly, my member stiff. Yet there was nothing that would induce me to touch my wife. The punishment for lying with your wife while she was unclean was excision from the community: *karet*. Children born of such a union were cursed. It was out of the question.

I was deeply asleep when I felt the pleasure spreading into my thighs. I woke and was shocked to see Hodel hunched over me, rocking back and forth, her eyes shut. I tried to push her off me, but just at that moment she was racked with a sudden, jerky climax, causing a terrible chord of sweetness to pass through my body, draining my will. I was powerless. Afterward, she slipped off me without a word and slunk back to her bed. I sat up, horrified, covered in her blood.

"What have you done? Hodel! What have you done!"

But the form of my wife huddled in the dark didn't move. She had gone to sleep. Had she been sleepwalking? I wondered if the sin was as grave, in this case. But I—I could have thrown her off me, and I didn't! Oh, Hashem, Hashem, what was I to do? Tell no one. That was all. Perhaps she wouldn't even remember. I would give money to the poor. I would atone. I washed my poor bloody member with the cold water stowed under my bed, water meant for the ritual washing of hands in the morning. I knew this was desecration, but, given the sin I had just committed, it seemed like a minor crime. I sat up through the night, shivering with cold and fear.

The next morning, Hodel sat up and rubbed her eyes in her usual girlish way, yawning and stretching. She pulled the basin from under her bed and poured a cup of water three times over one hand, then the other. She closed her eyes and said her prayer. Then she got up and started a fire in the hearth, not looking once in my direction, though I was sitting up in the spare bed observing her. She scooped up some water from the covered wooden keg in the corner, filled an iron pot with it, and hung it on the hook in the hearth. When the water was warm to the touch, she filled a shallow basin, set it on a stool, squatted over it, hiking up her nightgown, and began washing her sex. Then she looked up at me. Her smile was cold and blank, as it had been when she ate her mother's Shabbat food with her hands. The look she gave me was terrifying. She knew. She knew what she had done!

That morning I did not go to morning prayers. I couldn't bring myself to speak holy words, or wind the tefillin around my arm and head. I could not wear a prayer shawl. I felt cut off from God. The pistol dagger hung, loaded, in its tooled sheath at my hip. I meandered through Paris in a daze, walking brazenly into a café, my box of goodies hanging from my neck. We weren't meant to solicit in cafés, yet many of us did. There was a lot of money to be earned that way. I didn't care if I was stopped.

I stayed out until well after dark. When I came home, dried out with exhaustion, freezing and hungry, I found my room filled with people: the eldest few of the Mendel children, the pantheresque Mme Mendel, and her fat-sack husband all sat on chairs lined up against the walls, staring at our bed, which had been dragged into the center of the room. Hodel lay on the bed in her petticoats, feet splayed, palms upturned. She was breathing very quickly, eyes shut tight.

A white chalk circle had been drawn on the floor around the bed. Within it, a young, heavy man was walking, talking to himself very quietly. He turned. It was my cousin Gimpel! I was overjoyed to see him, and began to cry out, but the look he gave me shut me up. It was a look of total concentration, mastery. I approached Mme Mendel, utterly confused. I wondered if someone had discovered what we had done the night before, if this was some sort of punishment.

"What is happening?" I whispered.

"I heard the maggid was back in Paris. We had to call for him. She ate my Shabbat food with her hands again, like an animal. She attacked one of her brothers. Broke his arm!"

"But what is Gimpel doing?" I exclaimed.

"When Hodel fell into the water, a river demon took her place," whispered Mme Mendel factually, her eyes on her daughter. "It's exactly as I thought."

"What do you mean?" I asked, my sternum rigid with fear.

"It's an exorcism," hissed Mme Mendel, turning her black eyes on me fiercely. I walked to the corner of the room and watched my gentle cousin Gimpel wave his small hands over the body of my wife, muttering words no one in the room could hear. I had been told of holy men who knew the sacred words to make demons exit the bodies of human beings. I never dreamed that Cousin Gimpel was such a man. He had hidden his identity well behind that bumbling exterior. As I watched him, I swear I saw a blue flame flare up around the perimeter of the circle. I staggered forward, overwhelmed, tears streaming down my cheeks. Then I lost consciousness.

When I woke on our extra bed, Gimpel and the others were gone. The room was back in order. The chalk circle had been scrubbed off the floor. Hodel was standing by the stove, her back to me. Horror overtook me. I couldn't move.

Yet when she did turn, it was just Hodel, as she had always been, before the accident. She seemed years younger than the creature I had been sharing my bed with. She smiled at me bashfully, and set a pot of tea on the table near the extra bed where I lay. As she leaned over me, I noticed a red string tied around her neck, from which swung a narrow leather pouch—a protective amulet. Gimpel had written the magic names on the scroll inside that pouch to guard her against possession. I couldn't speak. My heart was hammering in my chest. There was sweat trickling down from my temples. Hodel modestly put her nightdress on over her head, disrobing beneath it. She put her clothes away in the cupboard and got into bed. I was mute with confusion and dread. I did not move. Eventually Hodel fell asleep. In the morning, at dawn, I went out to peddle my wares.

Skipping prayers again, I returned to the large café where I had been selling my merchandise illegally the day before. There were plenty of customers coming in and out all day. Also, the wind was cold now, and I enjoyed the warmth. A young lady had approached me to peruse my wares, and was holding a cheap brooch I had bought at Les Halles some months earlier when I felt a firm hand on my shoulder and turned. It was Inspector Buhot.

"Jacob Cerf, hello," he said, looking down at me with a tense smile. I noticed an explosion of red veins around his nostrils, flakes of dry skin on his cheeks and eyebrows. "I am surprised to see you here."

"Hello, monsieur," I said.

"Jacob, may I see your papers?" He had renewed my passport himself a few weeks earlier. I reached into the pocket of my coat carefully, trying to keep the pistol dagger hidden. Buhot's eyes flicked to my waist, but he didn't react.

"Two more months on here, is it?" he asked affably, holding up his lorgnette to read.

"Yes," I answered. He perused the paper.

"You are armed, Jacob," he said, not taking his eyes from the document.

"Not armed, sir."

"What, then?"

"I was hoping to sell it. It's a fine piece." He looked at me, his eyes twinkling with mirthless intelligence. He handed me the passport and folded the lorgnette with a deliberate snap, slipping it into his jacket pocket.

"Jacob, don't be crafty. You are armed. Disarm." I stood frozen to the spot. The large café was filled with people, yet in this corner all was silent. Two men got up and walked out swiftly, sensing a confrontation. Buhot put his veiny hand on the hilt of his sword.

"Disarm, I say."

"Why should I not carry a weapon to defend myself?" I heard myself say. "I am a human being, after all." My Jew's box hung from my neck, a barrier and an impediment.

"Remove the box," Buhot said, drawing his sword, but keeping it low. I removed the box from my neck. "Disarm."

I took my pistol dagger by its fine horse-head handle and began to draw it out from its sheath. But, instead of handing it over as I had expected to do, I found myself brandishing it, backing up. A woman screamed. Buhot pursued me into the street. Our weapons clashed absurdly. I had no idea what I was doing. I had never been in a sword fight before. Like a cornered child, I fought him. The cut he inflicted on me was deep in the flesh of my arm, above the elbow. Thoughtlessly, aiming vaguely, I cocked the loaded gun and fired. Buhot lunged at me through a dense white cloud of gun smoke, pressing the point of his blade into a button at my chest. Clearly, I had missed him.

"Drop it, you stupid Jew, before I kill you!" he yelled. I let my weapon fall gently on my shoes, not wishing to shatter it. Buhot bent down and picked up my treasure, examining it carefully. Then he looked up at me, breathing hard.

"You surprise me," he said.

I was in a cell with two Frenchmen, both thieves. They found it fascinating that I was a Jew, and asked me all sorts of questions, like whether we really mixed the blood of Christian children in with the Passover matzot, and was I in for cheating on loans. I didn't answer, but sat there listlessly, in a kind of shock. The prison nurse had bandaged the cut in my arm, but it smarted. I would be in the Bicêtre Prison for years. I didn't care. I was more afraid of Hodel than of incarceration. The world of river demons and succubi, Mme Mendel with her evil face, the terror that had moved into my body like a living spirit since my marriage, eating away at my rational mind—it was all locked away from me now. I never wanted to return to it. I began to fantasize that I would be deported; then I could begin a new life somewhere else.

The following morning, inspector Buhot arrived looking put out. A guard began to open the barred door of my cell.

"Jacob. You have a visitor."

"Who?" I asked.

"Follow me," said Buhot dryly.

I followed him down a long hallway lined with piss-stinking cells, down a worn stone stairway. The inspector took out a key and opened a heavy wooden door. I could smell rancid sweat rising from my armpits.

The room was filled with light. The rest of the prison was quite dark; I had to close my eyes to let them adjust. When my vision returned to me, I was surprised to see a man in the powdered wig and splendid clothing of an aristocrat sitting by the window.

"Here he is, Monsieur le Comte," said the inspector. "The man who stole your weapon." It took me less than a second to remember the wide nose, fleshy lips, basset-hound eyes. For the count, it was more of a struggle. When he did recognize me, he laughed shortly.

"I don't believe it," he said. "It's you, isn't it?"

"Yes, Monsieur le Comte," I whispered.

"Your name is . . . Cerf?"

"Jacob Cerf."

"That's right! This is bizarre, don't you think? When the inspector told me the man who stole my dagger was a Jew, I wanted to meet him. It took skill to swipe a weapon right out of my opera box while I was in it," he said, smiling.

"I am sorry, sir," I said. "It was not me. I only bought it to sell."

"That's disappointing," said the count with a pout. "Nevertheless. I loved the story of the duel with the inspector. Do you find it odd that we have met again, in this way?"

"Very much so," I answered. The count looked out the barred window of the visiting room. "I detest prisons," he said with a shudder. Then, standing, he placed his hands on his wide hips. "Once again, I ask you. Would you like to be my second valet? I have been looking for a Jew. You are very difficult people to convince."

"Why a Jew?" I asked.

"I have my own reasons," he answered. "Do you really think you should be questioning me at a time like this? The inspector just told me you would get years for this infraction. Inspectors don't like to be shot at. But I could write to some of my friends at court. You would be out within a month, if you decide to work for me."

You can guess my decision.

## 19

Masha opened her eyes. The room was filled with people moaning, squatting, weeping, whispering to themselves. The cinder-block walls were the color of mint ice cream, the linoleum floors grimy oatmeal. Shelley, of the long torso and dandelion-fluff hair, was kneeling beside her, stroking an invisible body. Her cheeks were slick. Snot and tears collected to form a mucus pendulum that swung fascinatingly from the end of her nose, yet she did not wipe it away, such was the anguish that she felt, stroking this invisible thing.

A man in his forties wearing a tie and pressed pants straddled a chair. He was making grunting noises and hitting the air with his fist. He kept muttering, "Oh, yeah?"

A plump girl was laughing, eyes closed, face turned up to the ceiling.

A young man in pajamas stretched, letting out yawnlike moans.

Masha sat in a corner, knees pulled up tight to her chest, arms clamped around her calves, hands cupped around an orange, fingers running over its pitted surface again and again. She had been told to memorize it with her hands.

Bridget Mooney, wearing her high-heeled brown boots and tweed skirt, sedately wove her way through this pain festival, claw hand behind her back, the other on her cane, tortoise eyes narrowed as she checked each of her students in turn, inspecting the quality of their anguish.

Masha heard the ominous click of her teacher's heels approaching, the dull rubber thud of her cane.

"How's it going, Masha?" rasped Bridget, dragging a chair over and lowering herself into it slowly.

"Okay, I think," said Masha.

"Have you tried putting down the orange?"

"No."

"Put it down." Masha put down the orange.

"Now try and feel it with your hands." Masha made a little well out of her hands. She closed her eyes. She felt the cool skin of the orange, the weight of it gathering there. It was working.

"I think so," she said. "Yes."

"Good," said Bridget. "Now. Sniff." Masha sniffed her make-believe orange. All she got was an image of the orange in her head. No odor. She shook her head.

"When you can smell the orange, you're ready to try a scene," said Bridget, easing herself off the chair.

Shelley looked over at Masha, wiping her nose at last with a paper towel. "Don't worry," she said. "Almost nobody can really smell the orange. She'll still let you do scenes."

At the end of class there was a little flurry of recognition near the door. Late twenties, tall, lanky, with a black eye, Hugh Crosby loped in like he owned the place.

"I'm back," he said in a gentle Southern drawl.

"Hugh," said Bridget, opening her arms. Masha could tell immediately: Bridget loved this guy. She felt herself lurch over a surprising hillock of jealousy. Bridget put her arm around him. "I have the perfect scene partner for you. She dropped in out of the blue."

"That so?" said Hugh. "Who's that?"

"Masha," Bridget growled. "Come here."

I dreamed of Solange wearing a yellow dress. She was standing in a square hedged garden, holding up a silver tray. On the tray was a single porcelain cup.

I woke in darkness, wanting my morning tea, wondering if the count was up yet. I stretched my limbs, expecting to feel cool sheets against my skin. Instead I was crawling through a tunnel. I saw a pinprick of light, which grew until I emerged from my burrow to see Masha's face rise up before me, gargantuan, her puffed lips in a pout, the pure, kittenish eyelids shut. Remembering my condition, I beat my wings with an ignominious buzz, rising up through the tepid thick air, landed on her puffy lip, and crawled along its dips and valleys. Disturbed by my morning constitutional, Masha turned on her back and shook her head from side to side. Strutting back and forth disgustingly on the cracked ledge of her perfect mouth, I worried about my quest.

I wasn't really getting anywhere with either of my hosts: Leslie was continuing his daily round of good deeds (he was at that moment pouring motor oil into the engine of his father-in-law's car); Masha, in spite of the clandestine acting lessons, was the object of an all-out maternal campaign to find her a good husband and set her on the right path. Her first suitor, Seth Allen, had been an absurdity, but the next one up was making me very nervous.

## 20

Eli Bloch turned out to be surprisingly cute, Masha thought. Not too tall, but fetching, with a compact, athletic body, a little dimple in his chin, five o'clock shadow. No way would he use a razor on his face, they weren't allowed. Masha thought he must use depilatory cream. Eli wore his black hat set far back on his head. No sidelocks. He took her to a deli. She ordered a roast beef sandwich.

"You're the first girl I've ever gone out with who ordered real food," he said.

"You gone out with a lot a girls?" asked Masha.

"Well, you know, not for long, but yeah, a few, to see. It's not going so well."

"No nice girls in Brooklyn?"

"No, of course, but not, ah—not *the* girl."

"How you gonna know when you see her?" asked Masha. "You could maybe get it wrong, who your *beshert* is."

"I'm not worried about it," said Eli. "I figure, Hashem'll take care of it. I just go on the dates."

"That's a relaxing attitude," said Masha, laughing.

"What's the point of getting all stressed out? She'll find me." He looked right in her eyes when he said that. Eli was a fine singer, Masha knew. He had won the big community men's singing competition, the Jewish Orthodox American Idol. Masha's brothers, Dovid and Simchee, had been to it, and they said he was really good.

"Do you ever . . . think you might sing, like, professionally?" Masha asked as they waited for their food.

Eli hooked an arm behind his chair, spreading his black jacket wide. "Nah. You go out the door into that world, you're out the door. I want to stay in the community. I wanna have kids—here in the Five Towns, or in Brooklyn, wherever—it doesn't matter. I'm okay with singing as a hobby and then I'll have a job, and—it would mess with my head to start trying to break into show business. It would be ridiculous. Certain things, they're out of the question for us, right?"

"Right," Masha admitted. The plate hit the table hard as the waiter served her. She looked down at the massive sandwich. She was going to have to do a lot of chewing to get through this one. She looked up at Eli. He smiled lazily. His relaxation was drawing her into him, making her teeter forward. Any second she might lose her footing and fall.

Masha really had to plot in order to find a time to rehearse her scene with Hugh Crosby. She didn't like to do any extra lying to her mother, beyond the whopper about Tuesday nights spent at the nursing home, but she had no choice if she was going to rehearse. The one time that Pearl was definitely out of the house was Sundays, when she taught Sunday school at the synagogue and then organized coffee and cake for the mothers afterward. She always took Suri, Ezra, Estie, and the baby with her. Typically on a Sunday afternoon, dreamy, idealistic Yehudis was out in a van delivering kosher food to Jews in hospitals all over the five boroughs. Yehudis simply shone with goodness. Some man was going to get so lucky with her, Masha mused as she pulled on her coat and hurried down the block, the slender copy of the play Bridget had suggested secreted in her pocket, her fingers fiddling with the pages. She had told her mother she was going to stay home and rest. In case someone came back early and found her missing, she would buy a few groceries she knew they needed on the way home and appear with them. She didn't like the dissemblance, but the sharp need she felt to get to this rehearsal outstripped her conscience.

Shelley let her into the school.

"Hey, Masha," she said. "Hugh's not here yet. You want some coffee? I just made some. We're allowed to use Bridget's machine when we rehearse."

"Sure," said Masha.

Shelley gave her the warm cup. "I put lots of that fake creamer in it, it's so delicious."

Masha sipped the coffee. She liked the sweet, chemical taste. "Yum," she said.

"What scene are you doing?" Shelley asked, sitting on the desk, her long, skinny legs dangling in argyle tights.

"Um . . . from *Orpheus Descending*, by . . ." She took the book out to check the cover. "Tennessee Williams."

Shelley smiled, looking at her quizzically. "You never heard of him before?"

Masha shook her head.

"Never mind. So, you're playing Carol?" asked Shelley. Masha nodded.

"Great part. And Hugh is perfect for Val," Shelley said. "He's from Mississippi. Bridget loves him. If she gave you Hugh Crosby as a scene partner, it means she has her eye on you."

"What do you mean?" Masha asked. Hugh walked in then, his face pale and tight from the cold. The bruised right eye had faded to khaki green at the cheekbone. The eye socket was outlined in blackish puce.

"Sweet Jesus, it's cold out there," he said. "Hi, Masha. Am I late?"

"You're always late," said Shelley. "Coffee?"

"Sure," said Hugh, removing his wool hat. His light brown hair stuck straight up in the air from the static.

They read the scene through, sitting on metal folding chairs in the main room of the school. Masha was nervous. She felt like she was snagging the words, gluing them together, like molasses spilled into a cup of paper clips. She kept glancing up at the closed door.

"What is it about the door?" Hugh asked.

"I'm sorry," said Masha. "I was just wondering. Do you think we could open it?"

"Sure," said Hugh. He stood up and opened the door a foot. "Okay?"

"Thanks," said Masha.

They read the scene again. This time Hugh reached over in a casual way and touched her knee. Masha stood up.

"What?" asked Hugh.

"I'm sorry," she said. "But . . . I'm not allowed to touch you."

"Come again?" he asked. She shook her head, embarrassed.

"Maybe this isn't such a good idea," she said.

"Just tell me what the problem is," said Hugh, shutting the play on his finger and looking up at her. "Here. Sit here and talk."

She sat. "I . . . I'm Jewish," she said.

"I'm Methodist," he said.

"I mean, I'm a religious Jew. Men and women don't touch each other unless we're related or married."

He looked at her for a long moment, nodding. "Okay," he said. "Ever?"

"No," she said.

"I guess we can play this scene without touching," he said with a shrug.

"And I'm not really s'posed to be with a guy alone, except if we open the door it's sort of okay."

"Does Bridget know about this?" he asked.

"Yeah," Masha said.

Hugh chuckled to himself, shaking his head. "Okay," he said. "I get it. Let's go." They read the scene again. Masha managed to get most of the words out in one piece. "It'll get easier once we know the words," Hugh said kindly. "Can you make a rehearsal this week?"

"I don't know if I can do it till next Tuesday," she said.

"I'm free most afternoons."

"Oh," she said. "I don't know if I can get away."

"Take my number."

She did get away for an hour, that Thursday. They rehearsed again. It was less awkward this time. She knew most of her lines. Hugh looked startled sometimes when she was speaking, as though she were doing something odd. She asked him once what he was staring at. He said he had just been listening.

A week later, they performed the scene for the class. Afterward, Bridget sat for a long moment scrutinizing Masha through her pro-fiterole eyelids.

"I'm trying to figure out what it is about you," she rasped. "It's like watching a cat onstage. You aren't doing anything, but you're fascinat-ing. Tell me something. Are you feeling anything when you're playing the scene?"

"I don't know," Masha said.

"Okay," said Bridget, nodding.

The next week, Masha managed to smell a make-believe orange. It happened in the cafeteria of the nursing home, during her break. She had been practicing with real oranges all week at home, sniffing and sniffing. She thought it would never happen. Smell was the hardest thing. That's what everyone told her. It was a faint whiff, but it was there, in the very back of her nose: a real smell, memory of a scent. It thrilled her.

Bridget seemed pleased when Masha told her that she'd sniffed the make-believe orange. She didn't care that she had already performed a scene. "Now you can start remembering what other things smell like and feel like, things that have associations. Like your favorite teddy bear, or the smell of your kitchen. Whatever. Sad things, happy things," she said. "You can use your senses to access emotion in the scenes. Do you see?"

Masha had a crush on Eli Bloch. That was the truth of it. When she saw him coming up her walk to pick her up for a date, her chest constricted. When he wasn't around, she missed him. They'd been on five dates. It was getting exciting. She had a conversation in her head a few times in which she told him about Bridget's class. Sometimes Eli understood. He promised to keep her secret. Other times he was disappointed with her and walked away.

## 21

Two weeks after the Comte de Villars came to see me in Bicêtre Prison, Inspector Buhot himself shook me awake roughly in the dark.

"Cerf. Get up. You're free."

Befuddled by a bare hour's sleep eked from the cold and noise of a night in jail, I sat up and followed him from my cell, down the reeking hallway, through a padlocked door opened by a pallid teenage guard, down a long, narrow set of stairs. In the courtyard, Buhot's narrow, erect form etched a peevish silhouette against the milky sky. He turned to me, framed by the arched stone entryway, the iron gates of which were, miraculously, swinging open on my account. I could hear the hoarse cries of the lunatics housed in the next courtyard. I hesitated, unable to believe I was being released.

"Jacob," he said sharply. My head pounding with fatigue, I followed my captor out the prison gates, clutching my filthy lapels around my bare throat, and saw, as if in a vision, the vermilion coach of the Comte de Villars rising from a swirl of morning fog. I recognized the family crest of two lions rampant that had so impressed me a year earlier. A driver, impeccably dressed in a light blue uniform edged with white, a powdered wig on his head, looked down at me implacably from his perch.

"Here he is," said Buhot to the coachman dryly, as if sharing a joke. The man stepped off the coach and opened the door crisply.

"Monsieur," he said, his brutish face an expressionless mask. I put one foot on the step of the coach and looked back at Buhot.

"Well, Jacob," he said. "This just goes to show that none of us can predict his fate, eh?" And then he smiled coldly, his chapped, flaky cheeks creasing. I said nothing, but stepped into the coach and flopped back in the seat, staring ahead. The driver closed the door. With a jerk, we set off.

As we clattered through Paris, sending urchins dashing out of the way and forcing peddlers to pin themselves against the buildings to avoid getting hit, I peeked out through a crack in the drawn curtains and surveyed the desperate poor looking up at the coach as I passed, some of the men touching their hats in respect for the great man who must be inside. If they had known it was an unwashed Jew, fresh from prison!

I lay back on the yellow silk bench of the coach and drifted into sleep. In what seemed like no time, my door swung open. The dead-faced driver stood at attention, waiting for me to disembark. He had small brown eyes, heavy eyebrows, a dark mouth. I stepped out onto the buffed stone floor of the count's carriage house. Solange stood at the top of a short staircase. She wore the same red-and-white-striped dress she had worn when I last saw her. I looked down at the floor, ashamed of my appearance.

"Come," she said kindly.

I followed her up the steps and into the kitchen where I had imbibed so much wonderful soup a year earlier. Solange put a plate of fried potatoes and a glass of milk in front of me. I ate ravenously, my eyes on the plate. When I had finished, she refilled it.

"Thank you," I said.

"I knew you would be hungry," she said.

When I had eaten my fill, Solange led me across a stone courtyard, through a lacquered red door, up a staircase, down a fragrant, light-drenched hallway, and into a dining room. The Comte de Villars looked up from his breakfast and smiled, looking like a benevolent frog. Beside him, a desiccated-looking man in a tightly curled wig sat frozen, a cup of coffee halfway to his puckered lips.

"Jacob Cerf," said the count, "may I present Monsieur Cabanis, the man of letters. Monsieur Cabanis, Jacob Cerf." I wasn't sure what to do at this point, so I bowed slightly. M. Cabanis put down his cup.

"Good Lord," he said.

"You can go now, Jacob," said my master. I heard Solange rustling behind me. I retreated gratefully from the room.

I followed the quick-stepped Solange up another flight of steps, down a hall, and into a room painted light green.

"Of course, it is a guest room, but the count wanted you to be most comfortable to wash and prepare yourself," said Solange. I could not bring myself to look at her.

"First of all, you can wash. It might make you feel better," she said, opening a paneled door to the bathroom.

The bath was being topped up by a heavy young maid who glanced at me curiously out of the corner of her eye as she knelt to pour the steaming water from a great tin bucket, her hands ruddy and wet, arms shaking from the weight. As I entered, I glimpsed myself in a mirror: I looked inhuman, terrifying. My sparse beard had grown wild, my side curls were frazzled, hanging at either side of my sooty face. I stood, slightly stooped, in my stained black jacket and torn trousers, trembling with fatigue, cold, and embarrassment. The muscles between my shoulders ached. Solange darted, birdlike, from one side of the bathroom to the other, pouring a few drops of lilac scent into the bath, then fetching a clean sponge, a cloth, a dressing gown. The maid had disappeared.

"I will leave you now," said Solange, folding a clean bath sheet and setting it on a chair.

"Thank you," I whispered. With a slight smile, she retreated, shutting the door.

I undressed as quickly as I could, leaving my rotten clothes, yarmulke, and protective fringes in a pile on the floor, and lowered myself gingerly into the scalding tub. Looking into the cloudy surface of the old, speckled mirror before me, I saw my sinew-and-bone body, frog-belly white, swarthy genitals framed by a silky black flame of pubic hair, disappearing into the water. Behind me, the walls were dark pink Indian silk edged with gold, the dresser painted rose, shelves of crystal bottles glinting in the cool light. I soaped my hair and beard and fashioned absurd shapes with the stiff white hair, making myself look like a crazy old man. I laughed, not realizing I would be dead before my first gray hair sprouted.

I emerged from the bathroom, fragrant, swaddled in the woolen dressing gown. Solange was sitting erect on a delicate chair, waiting for me.

"Sit down," she said, her voice musical, lilting, as she offered me her chair. My heart hammering against my chest, I sat. I had put my yarmulke on again after my bath, even though it was dirty; my people were forbidden to go bareheaded. Looking at me in the small mirror on the white dressing table, her head cocked, Solange placed her fingers on my skullcap.

"May I?" she asked. I nodded faintly. She lifted the yarmulke from my head, setting it down on the white vanity table. The little brown dome stared up at me reproachfully. I could still feel it on my head, as if it were there. Solange's sharp nails raked through my wet hair, causing a tingling bolt to branch down my spine. "Wonderful hair," she murmured. A little pair of golden scissors glinted in her hand. With two quick snips she amputated the peyos from the sides of my head. The curled black ribbons of hair lay discarded on the shiny white table. I felt unwrapped, displayed, vulnerable. Solange cut my hair, and trimmed the last few strands from around my small red ears. She soaped my beard and took a razor in her hand. "My father is a barber," she said reassuringly. I submitted, as if in a dream.

Afterward, casting a shy look at my delicate face in the glass, the blue eyes with long, thick lashes, shaved cheeks flushed, my head so naked without the peyos, I was shocked by my girlishness.

Solange laid out a set of livery on the bed: robin's-egg-blue britches and matching jacket with brass buttons, a green waistcoat, white hose, a white cotton chemise with a frill tacked to the neck. Then she left me. I drew on the clothes, savoring the dense fabric, the sturdy seams. The britches were loose at the waist, but they fit. Solange knocked softly on the door and opened it, carrying two pairs of shoes with silver buckles on them.

"Oh, look at you," she said. "Try on these shoes and see which are the best size. This pair belongs to my husband. But he works at the country estate now, he never wears them."

Once my hair was dry, Solange fitted me with a neatly coiffed horsehair wig. The hair had been powdered with white starch and drawn in a little braided ponytail at the back. I stood up awkwardly. Solange assessed me, cocking her sleek head to one side, then another, her elbows resting on the wide armature of her striped silk dress.

"You look like a different person," she said with quiet delight.

"Excuse me, madame," I ventured. "What is to be done with my old clothes?"

"We will wash them, and you can have them," she said. "If you like."

"I would like to have them burned," I said. "There is nothing that will clean those clothes. Only the vest with the fringes and the—the little hat there, I would like to keep them."

"All right," she said. "Now. Let's go and see the count."

The tubby count leapt from his chair and clapped his hands when I was led into his study. He took me in, shaking his head incredulously, then circled me.

"He looks fantastic. Solange, you are a marvel. How do you like your uniform, Jacob Cerf?" he asked me.

"Very much, Monsieur le Comte," I answered.

The count frowned, looking at Solange. "What are we going to do about the accent? He sounds like . . . maybe German? Can we say he's German? Isn't Yiddish similar to German?" he asked me, his brows knit.

"Many of the words are the same," I said. "But I don't speak real German."

"That doesn't matter at all. You'll learn German, French, English, whatever you like. We need to think of a name. How about . . . Gebeck?"

"Gebeck?"

"A tradesman's name. You come from a long line of bakers. It's believable. I like Gebeck. This is my new valet, Gebeck. From . . . Tutzing. In Bavaria. No one ever goes to Tutzing. It's perfect. And I was in Bavaria a few months ago. I can say I poached you from Vieregg's schloss. Can you read French?"

"Only a little, Monsieur le Comte."

"Well, we will begin our lessons tomorrow. Go now to Le Jumeau. He will train you."

Solange told me Le Jumeau, the first valet, was in the kitchen. I walked into the large, fried-onion-scented room, gleaming copper pots hanging from hooks in the ceiling, and saw the dark-lipped coachman who had driven me from prison, glaring at me from a low table where he was shining a pair of shoes.

"Excuse me," I said. "I was looking for Le Jumeau."

"You've found him," said the man.

I stood staring stupidly. "You're the valet?"

"Unless you've already stolen my job, yes."

"I was told that you would give me something to do."

"Here," said Le Jumeau, standing. "Shine these." I sat on the low stool he offered me, noticing, as I passed, that his cheeks were deeply scarred with pockmarks. The coachman had no such marks.

"Figured it out yet?" asked Le Jumeau, leaning back on the stove.

"You're twins," I said.

"Hence my name. The master loves renaming people. Who are you, now?"

"Gebeck," I said.

"Nice," he said, laughing. "So, Gebeck, where did you live before you were arrested? With your mother, by the looks of it."

"I lived with my wife's family."

"Married already. How old are you?"

"Almost eighteen."

"You look younger. You look like a girl. So where is the wife, then?"

"With her . . . with her mother. When the count got me out of prison, I made a bargain to leave . . ."

"Your wife."

". . . my life, before."

"And how do you feel about your bargain?"

"I don't know," I said.

"Yes, you do," he said. "You love it. Who wouldn't love being free from what came before?"

"Someone who was happy," I ventured.

"Yes, that is the question," said Le Jumeau, glancing with surprising thoughtfulness out the window. "What is preferable: freedom, or happiness?" Just then the cook, a voluptuous, bustling woman, walked in and reached up to pluck a clove of garlic from a strand that hung from the ceiling. Le Jumeau lay a pensive hand on her plump rear, charting its curve. She slapped his hand, laughing.

"Today," he said, "happiness."

I was to sleep in a small chamber off the master's bedroom, so that I could, once trained, be called at any time of night to undress him or get him what he needed. The room was tiny, but warm and dry, furnished with a bed, a chair, and a high chest of drawers that took up an entire wall. The room had two doors; one led directly to the count's bedroom, the other to the hall.

The following morning, the weak light shining through my tiny window woke me just after dawn. I said the prayer of thanks to Hashem and sat up. My first thought was my ablutions; I must rinse my hands. I drew the little bowl of water and tin cup I had provided for myself for this purpose from under my bed, and had just begun to perform the ritual washing of hands when I looked up and saw the count standing in the doorway in his dressing gown and nightcap, a small red leather notebook in his hands.

"Monsieur le Comte!" I whispered.

"Good morning, Gebeck," he said cheerfully, pulling up a chair and sitting down. "Sorry to frighten you. It's just that I am fascinated by your habits. The habits of your people. And I was anxious to know which of them you would preserve while in my employment." I lay in my narrow bed, half propped up on one elbow, and stared at him stupidly.

He continued. "Certain things you have already given up. Your head was uncovered yesterday. Though of course you could have thought of the wig as a covering . . ." I shifted in the bed.

"So," he continued. "Please tell me. What were you doing with the water?"

"Washing my hands," I said, pouring a little water thrice over one hand, thrice over the other.

"Why so urgently?"

"A little bit of death or . . . unclean spirits can settle on the body in the night," I explained. "If you wash your hands, it gets them off the whole body." The count nodded, watching carefully, and wrote in his notebook.

"Do you think you would be able to wean yourself off this practice?" he asked dryly.

"In prison I was not allowed to have a jug of water," I replied.

"This is not a prison," he said. "If you decide to continue with your rituals, your superstitions, that is your choice. If you decide to free yourself of them, that is also your choice. You are a free man, Gebeck."

"These are difficult habits to break," I said, my sentence emerging from my mouth in an ugly string of mangled French. The count winced.

"You have time," he said. "Now dress yourself, get me my breakfast, and then we will begin in the library. You have an enormous amount of work to do. What's that?" He asked, pointing to my fringed garment, the tzitzit that I always wore beneath my clothes, which was laid out over the back of my chair.

"It's my protective garment."

"You will wear it beneath your chemise?"

"Yes."

The count wrote this down in his little red book. "And your head covering?"

"You were right. I decided the wig was enough."

The count smiled and nodded.

I began my day with Le Jumeau. When I entered the kitchen, he was there eating his breakfast. The cook, Clothilde, had her broad back to me. The stiff cloth of my livery made me move differently, with a straighter back, a longer neck. My wig was a bit itchy around the temples, but otherwise I felt very well in myself.

"You're a late riser," said Le Jumeau, glancing up at me.

"Not usually," I said. I didn't want to tell him about the count's visit. It was embarrassing.

"Luckily for us, the count doesn't usually wake up until ten."

"What shall I do?" I asked.

"Do what I do. If you shadow me for a few days, you'll get the hang of my duties."

Clothilde snorted a laugh.

"But why does the count need two of us?" I asked.

"In a great house, it's normal to have more than one valet," said Le Jumeau.

A bell rang insistently. Le Jumeau stood up. "And he's conscious.

167

The day begins." Clothilde began heating water immediately. In moments she had set a silver tray with a porcelain jug of coffee, a cup, some fresh cream, bread, and a nest of freshly boiled speckled quail's eggs.

"You carry it," said Le Jumeau to me. "Hold it like this," he said, taking the breakfast tray in both hands and holding it stiffly before him, back straight, expressionless. "Your face must remain dead."

I took the heavy tray and tried the look. Both Clothilde and Le Jumeau burst out laughing. "Don't worry," he said. "You'll get it eventually."

I followed Le Jumeau as carefully as a tightrope walker, terrified to upset the delicate gold-rimmed porcelain on the silver tray. After trudging up two sets of stairs and down several hallways, we arrived at the count's high, gilt-trimmed door. Le Jumeau knocked softly. The muffled voice of the count answered. Le Jumeau opened the door and stepped back to let me in. I walked in stiffly, my face frozen. Only my eyes moved, roving over the tray to be sure nothing toppled.

"On the bed," Le Jumeau ordered softly. I placed the tray with its stand like a little bridge over the lap of the count.

"How is our neophyte doing?" asked the count.

"Very well, Monsieur le Comte," said Le Jumeau. "Soon he will be fit for every sort of demand."

"He looks French, don't you think?" asked the count, beaming at me with his bulging, myopic eyes, his ugly young face creased with sleep.

"Absolutely Gallic," said Le Jumeau.

"He looks, in fact," said the count, "more French than I do, though I come from one of the oldest houses in France."

"French, French, utterly French," sang Le Jumeau, opening the silk curtains.

"No need to overdo it, Le Jumeau," said the count, cracking an egg.

"What does Monsieur wish to wear today?" asked Le Jumeau, clicking his heels in what seemed to me to be an open parody of a military stance.

"My gray silk," said the count. "Gebeck, follow him closely. You will be dressing me soon enough." Le Jumeau was silent, but his animosity was palpable. I really didn't want to be on the bad side of the valet. He seemed dangerous. "You know, I just realized, I haven't given Gebeck a first name!" exclaimed the count.

"Haven't you?" asked the valet, folding a pair of exquisite dove-gray silk britches and vermilion stockings over the back of a chair.

"What about . . . Johann? Johann Gebeck, of Bavaria!"

"I thought you wanted him to look French," said Le Jumeau.

"The accent precludes it," snapped the count. "There are dark-haired Germans in the south. And he has blue eyes . . ."

"True," said Le Jumeau.

"Johann Gebeck, this is your new birthday," said the count. "Make a note of the date. We'll celebrate it next year."

"Will Monsieur le Comte have a bath this morning?" asked Le Jumeau.

"No, you may dress me," said the count, patting his wide mouth with a linen napkin. Le Jumeau took the tray to a side table. The count stood up by the bed and raised his arms. Le Jumeau lifted the count's chemise from him. Beneath the nightdress, the master was naked. He had a wide-hipped, tubby, knock-kneed frame. As he turned to step into the knickers Le Jumeau held out for him, I noticed his back was badly scarred with red spots.

"Oh, Gebeck," said the count, as Le Jumeau drew up his linen and fastened it around his waist.

"Monsieur le Comte?"

"If there are any rituals you feel compelled to perform throughout the day, no matter how insignificant to you, please advise me."

Le Jumeau's snigger broke over my head like a raw egg.

## 22

The phone rang cruelly in the middle of the night. Leslie felt a sharp pain in his right eye as he answered.

"It's Don," said a low, conspiratorial voice on the other end of the line.

"Don?" The sound of his father-in-law's voice at this time of the night was an automatic emergency. Leslie sat up immediately. "I'll be right over," he said.

"No, no, son," said Don in a slurred whisper. "We're not at home. We . . . just need a ride."

"Where are you?" asked Leslie.

Leslie drove along the coast to the east end of the island, where the mansions were. He looked down at the beach. Near the shore, the waves were marbled with phosphorescence. The great houses stood at the edge of the bluffs. Leslie smiled, thinking that Don had finally found his way to his kind of people. He turned down a road lined with perfectly maintained hedges.

Iron gates opened for the truck the moment he arrived at the address Don had given him. The house, at the head of a long, circular drive, was large, shingled, beetling over the crashing sea. All the windows were illuminated. Leslie recognized Don's Chrysler parked outside.

Leslie rang the bell. The door opened immediately. A small man with a mop of tong-curled brown hair, wearing what looked like a boy's blue blazer, looked up at Leslie expectantly.

"Hello, sir!" he said.

"I'm looking for Don and Libby Jenkins," said Leslie. "Don called me and said he needed a ride," he said.

"Did he mention that?" said the younger man nastily, stepping back to let Leslie into the house. Leslie noticed that his host had a very shiny face. His skin looked like ironed wax. He had tiny, dark, crescent eyes and a plump mouth.

"I'm Ross Coe," he said, offering a boy's hand for Leslie to shake.

"Leslie Senzatimore," said Leslie. He found Ross Coe distinctly alarming. "Where are Don and Libby?"

"Just down here," said Ross. He wore patent-leather loafers with no socks, Leslie noticed as he followed him down a wood spiral staircase. Leslie found himself descending sideways. His feet were too long for the steps.

Don and Libby were sitting silently among a clutch of chattering people. Don was in his usual cherry cashmere and gray cravat, his elongated, squared-off head flushed and seemingly more creased than usual. He glanced at Leslie sheepishly, but made no move to get up, and said nothing. Libby, stuffed into a low-cut leopard-print minidress, sat beside him holding a glass of green liquid between her palms. She was staring into it, as if for an answer. Ross Coe led a petite, elegantly dressed older lady across the room. She had luxuriant brown hair. "This is my wife, Helga," said Ross Coe, presenting the woman with a flourish of his small hand. Helga Coe had a fixed smile on her withered face, and big white teeth.

"Welcome to our home," said Mrs. Coe, in what sounded like a German accent.

"Good to meet you," said Leslie, then he stood at the lip of the room, arms dangling, waiting for Don and Libby to make a move. But both his parents-in-law sat immobile.

"Ready to go, Don?" Leslie asked.

"Sure, sure," Don said. But he didn't move. A youthful, elfin man in his sixties wearing a white cap, white jeans, and a crisp white shirt sprang out of what seemed to be a bathroom, singing, "Love is in the air . . ."

Ross Coe let out a high giggle, his shiny, ball-of-wax face contorting as if pushed this way and that by a sculpting hand, his eyes growing even smaller, like slits. It was impossible to tell how old he was.

"Leslie Senzatimore," said Ross Coe, "this is Derbhan Nevsky." Derbhan Nevsky ran spryly up to Leslie and took his hand between both his rigid palms, leaning forward and thereby shrinking still more. "Great to meet you," he said in a grating voice. Leslie was fighting the urge to lie down on the couch. He wanted to sleep so badly. It came to him that he was almost a foot taller than every freak in this room.

"Don, it's late, I gotta get up early," Leslie said, looking at his watch. Three o'clock in the morning. He may as well forget about sleep.

"Sure, sure, son," said Don absentmindedly. His face was livid, his eyes unfocused.

"They drank a little of the Green Fairy," Ross Coe said. "Strong stuff. Sit down for a minute." Leslie could see he wasn't getting Don and Libby off the couch anytime soon. Sighing, he sat on the slippery leather.

"What line of work are you in, Leslie?" asked Derbhan Nevsky, leaning forward in his chair with a jerk. His every movement seemed provoked by an electric zap. His clothes were bleached blue-white. Even his sneakers were white. His face beneath the cap was tanned, leathery, humorous.

"Boat repair and customizing," Leslie answered. There was a pause.

"Senzatimore Marine!" exploded Nevsky, lifting off the couch and pointing at Leslie as if he had guessed a clue at charades.

"Right," said Leslie grimly.

"Senzatimore Marine, top-of-the-line customizing of classic boats, best in the state," Nevsky said, opening up to Ross Coe to share this news. Leslie attempted a smile. "Ross! Here's your man!" Ross Coe smiled vaguely, nodding, as he sat down to a gleaming grand piano.

"That must be a sound business," said Nevsky, whipping back around to Leslie.

"It's not the worst," said Leslie.

"Probably helps to have Don here for a father-in-law." Nevsky chuckled.

"What was that?" asked Leslie, looking at Don, who gave him a strained smile. Ross Coe began to play.

"Rosco's a genius," pronounced Nevsky. Leslie noticed that Libby's eyelids were fluttering.

"What is the Green Fairy?" asked Leslie.

"It's absinthe, a kind of alcohol brewed from herbs," said Nevsky. "They'll be fine. Rosco's father was in shipping. Coe Frigates. He made billions in the eighties. Sent Rosco to Brown. As for me, I'm in entertainment," he said.

"Oh?" asked Leslie.

"Personal management. I used to be out on the West Coast. But not anymore," he continued, snapping his fingers with both hands. "I fried myself out there. Had everything I could wish for. Back in the day. Overdid it. Rising from the ashes now. Based in New York. Rosco here. Obsessed with boats." Snap. "You should get to know him." Leslie had a look at Ross Coe, playing the complex piece with ease, swaying back and forth with the music, his waxy face shining. Behind him, his aged wife stood with a patient, capped smile, reading the music and turning the pages when he needed her to.

Don and Libby were silent on the way home.

"So what was all that about?" asked Leslie, glancing at the lurid sunrise, maraschino red bleeding into the sky like it was paper toweling.

"That young man," said Don.

"Ross Coe," said Leslie.

"Yes. That young man is one of the richest residents of the state," said Don. "We happened to meet him at the Mexican restaurant in Patchogue."

A pause as Leslie thought of the place. "Ranchero's?"

"Yes."

"If I was one of the richest residents of the state I wouldn't be eating at Ranchero's."

"He and his wife like to meet people there," said Don, a bit mysteriously. Leslie nodded.

"They are sociable people who like to mix," added Don, as though in response.

"And match," said Libby from the backseat.

"So then, you mixed a little at Ranchero's, and then you went home with them," said Leslie.

"For a drink," said Don.

"Plural," said Libby.

"I developed a terrible headache," Don said. "I'm a migraineur, as you know." Libby cracked up. Her laugh was loose, hissing. She was plastered.

"So you've made some new friends, anyway," said Leslie.

"These people could be of real interest," said Don. "They are connected to avenues of intelligent risk. Of credible investment."

"Investment," repeated Leslie, hiding his concern.

"Sensible investment," said Don. "These are cultured people."

Leslie nodded. "As opposed to me," he said, without rancor.

"It's just a different sphere, Leslie," said Don.

"Oh, dry up," growled Libby.

By the time Leslie had unloaded Don and Libby into the parent trap, it was nearly five. Deirdre was sitting up in bed when he walked in.

"What the hell did they do now?"

"Oh, boy," said Leslie.

"Tell me."

"They got snared by a couple of strange people, this very rich young short person with a face like I can't even begin to describe, sort of—rubbery—he plays the piano—and his German wife, who must be seventy."

"Where did they meet—"

"At Ranchero's."

"Really?"

"This guy Coe. Coe Frigates. He has a house in East Hampton. The worst of it is, I think Don is making them think he has a lot of money. I'm too tired to talk about it. Oh, and your father's getting a migraine."

"Why do my parents have to live right next to us?" asked Deirdre. "Why can't we rent them a house someplace else? Like Arizona?"

"Can we talk about it in the morning? Please?" Leslie lay down. "I only have two hours."

It had been Leslie's idea to install her parents next door, five years ago, when he and Deirdre went to visit them in their eighteenth-century stone house in Connecticut and it was so clear that they weren't managing to live on Don's Social Security. Libby was working as an incompetent waitress in a roadside diner off Route 7, a sad little bungalow sandwiched between a McDonald's and a Wendy's. Don had been caught siphoning gas from a neighbor's tractor. Yet he insisted on taking the bus into the city once a month in his wedding tux so he could go to a concert at Carnegie Hall. It didn't matter what was playing, he just needed to be there. Leslie came home from that visit depressed. After three days of brooding, he suggested buying the house next door for the in-laws. He didn't realize they were to become his children.

Leslie turned out the light and lay on his back, trying to void his mind so he could get some sleep. He was so tired, but his heart was pumping in his chest like he'd run up a flight of stairs. Hot beneath the duvet, he flung his great leg out from under the fluff and lay there. Deirdre shifted, mute. She was clutching her sleep-rights tight.

As he waited for unconciousness, an ugly notion settled into Leslie's mind. He had humiliated himself at the Coe house. He felt obscurely ashamed—but for what? He went over the visit, but he could find nothing wrong in the way he had acted. If anything, Don and Libby had made fools of themselves. Maybe that's what it was. He was embarrassed for them? Yet it was personal, this sensation. There was fear mixed in too. Why? What harm could those weirdos do to him? He never had to see them again. Giving up on sleep, he got up and walked to the bathroom.

As he showered, Leslie concentrated on the coming day. He would begin by polishing out the scratches on the windshield of the 1968 Lyman. If that didn't work, they would have to order a new windshield; no way around it. He loved working on the old boats. He'd send the guys out on the outside jobs; he was too tired to drive all day—though he'd have to get Don back to the Coe house to pick up his car eventually. Maybe he'd let Deirdre do that. Thinking about his work, lathering his body, Leslie cleansed his mind as well as his skin. By the time he dried off, he was whistling.

# ∞ 23

Derbhan Nevsky was breakfasting at that moment, newly sixty, sporting a pair of white jeans pressed by his mother and current housemate, Silvia, along with a bleached white shirt—also octogenarianly pressed—and tumble-dried sneakers. He looked like Mr. Clean without the muscles, or the earring. He blazed with new sobriety, singleness of intent, and the remains of a West Coast tan. As much as he had wanted to get to the top when he was a young man, that ambition was nothing compared with his determination to climb back up now that he was old and toppled. He sipped his sugary black coffee, his first of twelve cups for the day. Silvia walked in, a tidy figure wearing lilac pull-on trousers and a matching blouse, the paper in one hand. She poured herself some coffee, then aimed a sprinkling of Frosted Flakes into the china cup. Lit a cigarette.

"What are you up to today?" she asked, dipping her spoon into the coffee and taking a bite of soggy cereal.

"I'm going to see Bridget," Nevsky said, in his sped up, jerky way.

"Who's Bridget?"

"Bridget Mooney. Remember her? I lived with her. Before I moved to L.A."

"Oh. The big one."

"She wasn't so big," he said. "She was curvy."

"That's not what you said at the time."

"I was an idiot."

"You're telling *me* this?"

"Okay." Nevsky got up to go, springing out of his chair as if he had just remembered he had a plane to catch.

"You marrying her now or what? She must be sixty years old," said Silvia, pointing her powdered face in his direction and raising her penciled-on eyebrows up a notch. "Just like you are."

"Forget about it. She's an old friend. She teaches in Far Rockaway now."

"That's a coincidence. You both ended up in Queens."

"I'm going to see her class. Looking for the next big thing," said Nevsky, leaping over to his mother and kissing her on the cheek.

She shooed him away, chuckling. "Okay, okay," she said. "Throw me a twenty, will ya? I'm low on cash." Nevsky unpeeled a bill from the wad in his pocket, knowing full well his mother had more money than he did; she just hated spending it. Now over eighty, Silvia had welcomed her firecracker of a son two weeks earlier with the shrug of a fellow addict, told him his dinner was in the oven, and caught the bus to Atlantic City so she could work the slot machines till dawn and return, silent and morose, the following morning, having lost yet another chunk of her husband's life insurance money, one quarter at a time. Silvia was counting on dying any minute. If she didn't, she warned Derbhan, he would have to support her completely. She didn't give a shit about reforming herself. Her addiction gave her a spiritual high, a sense of absolute, all-consuming hopefulness she defied any holy roller to replicate. She was a fatalist through and through. "If you're born to be hung, you'll never be drowned" was her favorite expression. Hence, her unending consumption of Benson & Hedges extra-long cigarettes, her breakfasts of Frosted Flakes in black coffee, and her absolute devotion to one-armed bandits. She simply didn't believe in freedom of choice. Thought it was absolute hooey. This made Silvia Nevsky a very relaxed individual.

Derbhan jittered spryly along the sidewalk in his blazing whites, snapping his fingers as he wove through the human traffic, scanning faces. Somewhere there was a girl. He needed to start with a girl, a face, a surprise. Something to build onto. There was a new movie franchise he had just found out about, an old casting agent friend of his had tipped him off. They were looking for an unknown. Someone stupendous. Derbhan needed to find some girls. Boys too, but Derbhan was better with girls. He ran down the subway steps in Woodside, feeling invigorated and intensely happy.

It had taken him some time to find Bridget Mooney. Her acting school in Manhattan wasn't in the phone book anymore, and he hadn't kept up with any of their mutual friends. It wasn't till he ran into her son, Gavin, while he was in line at the drugstore, that he caught a break.

Gavin was around thirty-five, with a big sloppy build, wearing trousers covered in smears of clay, and a rank T-shirt that Derbhan, who was himself fastidiously clean, had smelled before he recognized the kid in profile. Even though he hadn't seen him since he was a teenager, there was no forgetting that bulldog face.

"Gavin!" Derbhan had called out in his boyish, hoarse voice. Gavin turned around, his angry eyes expecting something bad.

"Derbhan Nevsky," said Derbhan.

"Whoa," said Gavin, looking him up and down. "You're back."

"Risen from the ashes."

"I'll say."

"How's your mother?" asked Derbhan.

"She had a stroke," said Gavin ruminatively.

"Oh, Christ, I didn't know," said Derbhan.

"She's okay, she still teaches."

"I looked up her school, but it was—"

"She gave that up. It was too much. She teaches in Far Rockaway now. Bought the bungalow next to us."

"You're married?"

"With two girls," said Gavin joylessly.

"And—let me guess—a sculptor?"

"Potter," said Gavin.

"Wow. Pots. Give me your mother's number, I'll give her a call," said Derbhan, shifting from one foot to the other. Gavin noticed this.

"I'm clean, by the way," Derbhan said with an embarrassed grin.

"None of my business," said Gavin, flipping open his phone. He read out Bridget's number so quickly that Nevsky barely had time to punch it into his phone.

"Let me repeat that back to you," said Nevsky, doing so.

"Yup, that's it," said Gavin, not checking.

Once he'd picked up his prescription, Gavin made an insolent little salute and ducked out of the shop, his eyes on the floor.

Derbhan Nevsky took the 7 train to Times Square, then walked to Port Authority and got on the A to Far Rockaway. He stared at the newspaper while snapping his fingers, a lifted, excited feeling in his belly. Seeing Bridget again after her stroke alarmed him somewhat—what if half her face were drooping like wet underwear hung on a line?—but still, he looked forward to seeing his old friend. Plus she might have some interesting students. She always used to. Then again, maybe she was just clinging to the idea of teaching; maybe her class was stuffed with losers, or worse, virtually empty, a sad shadow of the days when she trained some of the hottest young actors in New York.

He had to walk from the station. There was dirty snow on the sidewalk, but the sun had a hint of warmth in it for the first time in two punishingly cold post-California weeks. Nevsky breathed in deeply and wandered through the suburban streets. A lot of serious Jews out here, he noticed: men in black hats, fringes peeking from under their vests, climbing into minivans or hurrying along the sidewalk, heads down; women in snoods pushing strollers. Then all of a sudden artists, with their trademark filthy garments and jobless look, started popping around corners, lurking in cafés, riding by on bicycles. He also stumbled into a small Carribean neighborhood, where the smell of fried plantains wafted tauntingly through the air.

After asking several people and getting deeply lost, Derbhan came on the Bridget Mooney School of Acting, installed in a storefront below a tuxedo rental establishment. He pushed open the glass door and clocked a bombshell, right off the bat. She was straightening papers at the desk. Her hair was glossy, nearly black. Her eyes, when she looked up at him, seemed to be dark purple.

"Can I help you?" she said.

"I'm looking for Bridget Mooney," Derbhan said. "I'm an old friend of hers."

"She'll be here soon," said the young woman. "She's out." *This one would need diction class*, thought Nevsky.

"Oh, that's good she can get around," he said, trying to get a subtle look at the girl's body, which was well covered in a button-down checked shirt and, he noticed as she stood up, a long black skirt. The girl seemed uneasy, and walked across the room to the filing cabinet, opening the glass door a crack as she passed it, in spite of the cold outside.

"I heard she'd had a stroke," he said. The girl said nothing, but went about her business as if he weren't there. Presently another girl glided through the glass door on Rollerblades. She was built like an athlete, with short, strong legs. Her face was red from the cold.

"Hi, Ellie," said the bombshell.

"I never signed up for scene night," explained the girl on Rollerblades, grabbing a pencil from a cup on the desk and rolling across the room, where a list of names was taped up on the wall.

"There's still room," said the black-haired one, gesturing to the list with a languorous flourish.

"You're doing *Orpheus*," noticed Ellie.

"Yeah," said the girl.

"Good. See ya tonight," said Ellie, swinging the door open and gliding out onto the street. The bombshell kept the door ajar, returned to the desk, took out a copy of *Orpheus Descending*, and started reading, cheek on fist. Derbhan Nevsky sat, his hands pressed between jiggling knees, for a good five minutes. The cold seeping through the open door was beginning to irritate him.

"You mind if I close that door?" he asked. The girl hesitated. "I've been living in California for the past eight years," he explained. "Not used to the cold anymore." The girl looked up at him, impassive. Nevsky rose and pushed the door to.

"Where you from, exactly?" he asked.

"Farrackaway." She said it as one word.

"Are you one of Bridget's students?"

"Uh-huh," she said.

"I'm an old friend of hers. Derbhan Nevsky."

"Masha," she said. Nevsky whipped out his hand for her to shake, but she just looked at it.

"Hi," she said. But she wouldn't take his hand. Eventually he sat down again. The girl smiled awkwardly, then returned to her book. Nevsky was startled by the sound of the door. He looked up and there was a sixty-year-old version of the voluptuous and caustic Bridget Mooney, limping over the threshold.

"Bridge," said Nevsky, standing. Bridget didn't recognize him at first. She tucked her chin into her neck, squinting at him.

"David," she said.

"Derbhan, but yes."

"You're back."

"Very much so."

"How did you find me?"

"I ran into Gavin. He gave me your number, but I must have written it down wrong, so then I just looked you up. He said Far Rockaway."

"I'm impressed. Come on back," she purred. He followed her, casting one last look at Masha, who was studying her lines.

"I'm starting again, Bridge," said Nevsky, perched at the edge of his chair, leg shuddering.

"Are you okay, then?"

"Clean, sober, ready to go," he said.

"Where are you living?"

"Queens, for now."

"Glad to see you. Sorry I'm not much to look at these days," she said, holding up her claw. "I was struck by a little brain lightning."

"You look great," said Nevsky. "I thought you'd be all scrunched up."

"Thanks."

"Bridge, I need help finding some girls. A guy too, maybe. I'm going back into management. You know I'm the best. I just need a break."

She looked at him doubtfully, lips clamped shut.

"Okay," he said. His voice was hoarse, as if he had been yelling, though he hadn't. "Just let me see *something*—a scene night. Whatever. Let me court you. Them. If you have anyone. Do you? Have anyone? That one at the desk looks amazing, but she's a little odd. She wouldn't shake my hand."

"She's an observant Jew. She's not allowed to touch strange men."

"How's she gonna be an actress if she can't touch strange men?"

"It's a process. That girl is a long story."

"You know who she reminds me of? A young Judy Garland, but sexier . . ."

"I've thought Judy Garland too," she said. "But David. Look. No offense. You come here out of the blue, the last thing I heard, you . . . These kids aren't ready, anyway, most of them. To go out in the world. I just set up here six months ago. A few followed me out here, some are already working, but the rest are brand-new. I'm not inviting any agents out here yet. It's not just you."

"So we're both rising from the ashes! How 'bout I come as a friend? As a *friend*! To see what you're up to. I want to reconnect anyway. I missed you." And this was true. He had missed Bridget Mooney.

"Okay, okay," she said, chuckling. "Come back in two weeks."

"Can I buy you dinner tonight?"

"You don't have to do that," she said, wondering if he was good for even a meal. "Truth is, after class I'm exhausted anyway."

"Lunch tomorrow?" he asked.

"Take it easy. You live here now, right? We have all the time in the world."

Derbhan Nevsky had been Bridget Mooney's lover in the late 1970s, when he was still scrabbling his way up a pile of assistants to become a talent agent at the American Artists Agency, and Bridget was an ingénue with a Mae West twist. She had trouble getting work, was the truth of it, because she had a midcentury build—all hips and boobs and lips; the ideal woman had lost about twenty pounds over the past fifteen years, and Bridget had come of age too late: however much she starved herself she couldn't get Ali McGraw thin. Too big for the serious parts, too pretty for the funny parts, she had to content herself with playing an endless stream of next-door neighbors. They simply wouldn't employ her to do the work she'd have been great at.

She and Derbhan lived, for the most part, in Bridget's railroad apartment on Great Jones Street. Derbhan's given name was David, but he decided, while sitting on Bridget's fire escape high on acid one Friday afternoon, that his true soul's name was Derbhan. His inner self, a young man looking just like him but with huge yellow eyes and a lilac silk shirt, walked up the fire escape and told him that he would never achieve his true maximum potential unless he changed his name to Derbhan. He spelled it out and everything. Nevsky, his inner self said, he could keep. Even while he was hallucinating, Nevsky's practical ambition was turning over, like the idling engine of a getaway car: he wanted a name that no one could forget. He planned on becoming a legend. It's true, he had an eye for talent. Jane Stamp, Hal Maynard, RoSalind Jones were all to become his discoveries. He had a knack for what kind of person was fashionable, who would appeal to the crowd. Once he took someone on as a client, he worked them over, bringing them to parties and charity events, grooming them, putting them on diets, getting their hair extended, teeth straightened, their past made more or less interesting with the help of various publicity agents around town. But all this was after he and Bridget had broken up. They were really only lovers for six desperate months when neither of them had broken through and all they had for consolation was each other and the occasional bottle of Wild Turkey. But once David Nevsky became Derbhan Nevsky, his luck changed; he was promoted to agent within the month. Naturally, Bridget leaned on him to represent her. He, in turn, put so much pressure on her to lose weight, making her eat radishes and cottage cheese for lunch, boiled beef and salad for dinner, Weetabix with apple juice for breakfast, that she became violent with hunger, her rages climaxing when she broke her pitiful lunch plate over his head and ground the shards into the carpet with her platform shoe. Derbhan left then, cottage cheese in his hair, and told her he didn't represent fat actresses. He was steamed, but he wasn't bitter; he knew Bridget was a great girl—it wasn't her fault she was curvy. Bridget was hurt, but she realized the relationship had been doomed, and she really just wanted to teach anyway, and eat what she liked. So they remained friends, grabbing a bite every month or two, as Derbhan rose through the ranks of the agency and Bridget trained to become an acting teacher. They called each other regularly through Bridget's marriage, the birth of her son, her quick divorce, all the way till Derbhan moved to Los Angeles in the early eighties, when they lost touch. Bridget heard and read things over the years, of course. She saw Derbhan's feature in *Time* magazine, where he was proclaimed one of the most successful young agents in Hollywood; she also saw the article in the *Daily News* that described his sad dismissal from the agency he had helped build. The board of directors had simply fired him—albeit for good reason: he was coked up far past normal behavior patterns pretty much all day, his clients were leaving him in droves, he refused to acknowledge there was a problem, stopped sleeping, and spent all night making manic, unnecessary phone calls to producers in whatever part of the world was awake, ranting on behalf of his clients who were filming in Prague or Australia, making outrageous demands just so he didn't have to go home to his empty house and the heartbreak of coming down and feeling lousy enough to hang himself. He'd sit there, his feet up on the desk, noose of a tie hanging at an angle, eating Reese's Peanut Butter Cups and calling producers of his clients' films the way he used to make prank phone calls as a bored kid in Queens, telling women their girdles were ready to be picked up:

"Miss Gory needs a new orchid. In a pot. Every morning. Yes, a fresh orchid. And a plate of ripe mango. Never use the word 'ready' when you talk to her either, by the way. Say 'are you okay to come to set.' Never 'ready.' I'm warning you, now . . ."

He stayed awake in his office for three twenty-four-hour cycles, shaving and changing his shirt each morning so no one would suspect, which of course they did, until there was an intervention. Six talent agents, accompanied by two drug counselors and Derbhan's own therapist, swooped down on him one Thursday morning and told him he needed to take a break. Somebody who didn't like him very much must have called the papers, because there was a bank of photographers ready when he was escorted into the back of a Subaru belonging to the detox facility already booked by the agency. His fall from the golden chair was documented in all the major U.S. papers, then syndicated worldwide. Bridget Mooney read of his humiliation over her morning coffee, her shapely nails glinting in the morning light, green eyes narrowed with pain for a man she had once loved but now only pitied.

Though the Subaru brought him to a large, hushed mansion in the French Provincial style haunted by rich housewives coming off barbiturates, and, of course, celebrities, several of whom Derbhan had once represented, his stay there didn't really do the trick, because, as well as being an addict, he was having a psychic breakdown that none of the experts seemed to register, they were so focused on getting him clean. The fact that he barricaded himself in his room for much of the day when he wasn't in group therapy was considered problematic but not psychotic. He was released after three months. So Derbhan left the Waynsedale Clinic straight, but crazy. He returned to his palatial home in Beverly Hills and made it through seventy-two sober, friendless hours convinced that his neighbors had all decided to get together, tie him up, and slit his throat like a pig. Then, on the fourth day, he caved, called his old dealer, bought a little Kilimanjaro of cocaine, dumped it on his coffee table, and lived off it for a month. His savings, already thin on the ground from his extravagant habit, his sudden trips to Europe with very young women he hoped to impress, and his loyal subsidizing of his mother's gambling habit back in Queens, had wrought havoc on his finances. In short, Derbhan was broke. He had to drain his pool, sell his house, release his birds, fire his housekeeper, and move to a halfway house, where he promised not to do any drugs in exchange for a bed and a roof and the privilege of not living on the street or going back to his mother. In the end, he did go straight, and his mind eased up, but he had to move back in, at the age of sixty, with Silvia Nevsky, his alpha and omega. It would have been depressing if

Nevsky hadn't felt so maniacally happy at the moment. Finding Bridget Mooney again had given him a sense of continuity, safety, hope. Crippled as she was, that woman was solid as an oak tree. And he, shimmering and rustling in the unpredictable wind that was his destiny, would be her foliage.

## 24

I t's okay, I'll walk from here," Masha said, planting her feet on the sidewalk fifty yards from her front door. "I need to think a little."

"About me?" asked Eli, looking up at her from under the brim of his black felt hat.

"Maybe," she said, starting to smile.

"My parents . . . my parents are a little worried about you," he said.

"Yeah? How come?"

"They think you . . . I don't know, maybe they think you're too pretty or somethin'. It's okay with me, though," he said.

"Yeah?" she said.

"Yeah." He looked into her eyes.

"Thanks for lunch, Eli. I had fun," she said.

"We always have fun," he said. "I'll call you tomorrow."

"'Bye," she said.

"'Bye." He turned and walked down the block, looking down at his shoes. Once, he swung around to see her, his hands in his pockets, black hat set back on his head. Then he turned a corner and he was gone. This was it, she thought. She married him or she never saw him again. He had decided, she could feel it.

She walked to her own door, but she couldn't get herself to go in, even though it was cold out. She needed to think. She should really go home and help with Shabbat preparations. Yet she found herself meandering past her house, down the block, past the synagogue, to the railroad station, her demon hiding under her belt loop. She had never been on the train by herself. Dreamily, she walked a few steps and stood on the open-air platform.

There were only two people waiting for the train: a woman in a long down parka, and a man in a suit and coat, reading the paper. The woman looked professional. Masha wondered what her job was. The train came. The doors opened. The woman stepped into the train. Masha followed her, and sat down beside her. It took a few minutes for the woman to get settled in her window seat. She took off her parka, set it on the empty seat between herself and Masha, then took out some papers to read. She looked like she was Pearl's age. The conductor strode down the aisle, asking for tickets. The woman handed him hers.

"Change at Jamaica for Penn Station," he told her. He looked down at Masha.

"Round trip to Penn Station," she said.

"You coming back off-peak?"

"I don't know," Masha said.

"I'll sell you off-peak. You can pay the conductor the difference if you change your mind," he said. "Thirteen seventy-five." Masha gave him a twenty. She took the ticket from the conductor and stowed it in a zip pocket of her purse. It took forty minutes to get to Jamaica. Masha stared out the window, watching the houses blur by, wondering about the people who lived in there, the details of their lives. She wished she could pry the doors open and peer inside.

When they reached Jamaica, she followed the professional woman in the parka across the platform, and got onto the Manhattan-bound train. They were there in minutes. At first she tried to follow the woman out of Penn Station, but she walked so fast, she got swallowed up in the crowd.

Masha stepped onto an escalator, followed the light up to the street. She had no idea where she was going. It was almost two. She figured she had an hour before she had to start back home. It would be dark around five. She was fine. I crawled inside the lining of her coat to avoid the cold as she walked along the street. The pale, congested sky seemed very close, bearing down. She felt a raindrop prick her lip. A few people glanced at her long gray skirt peeking out from her red coat. But nobody knew what she was. She passed a few men in black hats or yarmulkes hurrying to the train station to be back in time for Shabbos. They couldn't get on a train after sundown. Neither could she. It felt odd to be moving in the other direction from them.

She walked down Sixth Avenue to Twenty-third Street. It started to snow. Dopey fat snowflakes sifted through the air, interspersed with glistening needles of rain. Masha stopped in the middle of the street and stared, taking in the strange precipitation. Snowflakes on her eyelashes blurred and magnified the flashing orange, yellow, green lights of store signs and traffic lights, made them seem like glowing jewels. People on the street rushed by her, huddled, frowning, some glancing at her curiously—a young woman with no hat on, coat open, standing in the street, her face wet, mascara running. The neon light of a bar flashed in reflection on the wet pavement at her feet. She turned to look up at it and saw warm light through a window, shadowy forms inside. She walked through the door and into the small brown-paneled place, shrugged off her coat, and scrunched it onto her lap, perching on a stool. Her muscles relaxed in the warmth. She ordered a Coke from the indifferent barman, brushing the dark wet strands of hair from her forehead, and looked around her. A longtime drinker was hunched over his glass at the end of the bar, his toothless mouth collapsed like sunken, parched ground; a group of young men in suits exploded in laughter at a table in the corner. One of them glanced at her pointedly. She turned her back to him. She liked being alone like this, nobody knowing a thing about her, in a strange neighborhood. She could be anyone. She took a sip of Coke.

"Masha?" She turned. It was Hugh Crosby. The black eye was healed. "What are you doing here?" he drawled.

"I was just moseying around Manhattan," she said.

"In this weather?"

Masha shrugged.

"I can't believe it's April." He sat on the stool beside her, setting his amber-colored drink down on the bar.

"What about you?" she asked.

"I live over on Tenth Avenue," he said.

"I thought you lived in Queens."

"No, I just go out there for Bridget's class."

"Wow."

He shrugged. "I started with her in Manhattan eight years ago. I suppose there's a kind of security in coming home to Bridget. Oh, hey, guess what?" he said, turning to her.

"What?"

"I'm gonna be a doctor."

"No way. You got it?"

"I sure did. Dr. Darling. That is the actual name."

"So they decided to go Southern," she said.

"No, I played it East Coast," he said.

"Congratulations." She raised her glass to him.

He took a sip of his drink. "So," he said. "What's new?"

"I might be getting married soon," she said. There was a breath of silence.

"I didn't know you had a fella."

"We don't date like you, we date to get married."

"Have you been dating?"

"I've gone on six dates with one man. I need to decide soon."

"How can you know so fast?"

"My sisters say you just know. But I . . . I really don't."

"Masha," he said, and then nothing.

"What?" she said. He squinted, took a breath, then shook his head and went quiet.

"What were you going to say?" she asked.

"I have met a lot of people, but I've never met any other woman with your particular combination of . . . attributes."

She looked up at him out of the corner of her glimmering onyx eyes. "No?"

"No," he said. She finished her Coke. He offered to buy her a glass of wine. "If you're gonna play Carol Cutrere, you need to know what a little wine feels like."

Hugh seemed untethered, loose on the world. Being with him in this bar, Masha felt time and the facts of her life disappear. Everything was melting into sheer, freewheeling possibility. "I can't have wine that isn't kosher," she said. He ordered her a whiskey and ginger ale. She took a sip of the drink. It burned her throat. They talked more, and they laughed. Glancing out the window, she lurched forward, checking Hugh's watch, then turned to look outside again. It was dark. Her hand flew to her mouth.

"What?"

"It's Shabbos."

"You need to be somewhere?"

"Home. I'm—I can't go on the train anymore. The sun set early," she said, as if the sun had tricked her.

"Not even if it's an emergency?"

She shook her head. "Only to save a life."

"How long does Shabbos last?"

"Tomorrow sunset," she said, her head in her hands.

"No transportation. Well, you are going to have to stay in Manhattan," he said.

"My mother will die." She slipped off the stool and stood at the door of the bar, looking helplessly into the street through the glass, her thoughts muddled by the alcohol.

He walked up to her. "You better call your family," he said.

"I can't use the phone after sunset."

"I'll call."

"They won't answer."

"If they're worried about you they will."

"But . . . they don't know about the class or anything. If you call, they'll freak out."

"How about if I dial your phone and you talk into it? Surely these are extenuating circumstances?"

"Okay," she said. They walked back to the bar and sat down. She leaned in to the phone while he held it up to her ear.

Pearl answered, hushed, after the first ring. "Where are you?"

"Mommy, I'm sorry," said Masha. "I'm in town. In Manhattan."

"What? Why? How did you get there? I've been on the phone to Eli, I— Did someone—" Pearl thought she'd been kidnapped.

"I took the train. I don't know. I just needed to think. I just . . . I got on the train and walked around and now it's too late, I can't get back."

"Okay, honey—let me ask your father what you should do. Maybe he knows someone there. Hang on." Pearl was trying for her calmest voice, the one she reserved for total inner hysteria.

Masha took a sip of her drink and whispered, "They might know someone I could stay with."

"You could stay with us," said Hugh.

Masha heard her mother's voice whispering on the other end. "How can we not know one person . . ."

"Mommy? Mommy, don't worry, there's—a lady here, a friend of—of—a lady I met here that will let me, um, stay with her. She's holding my phone, I was so worried about Shabbos and she dialed for me. I'm sorry, Mommy. But I'll be okay and I'll see you tomorrow night. Don't worry about me. I'm fine. I just made a mistake, that's all. 'Night."

"Will you pay for my Coke?" she asked as he hung up, nodding to her purse on the bar. "There's a twenty in the wallet. I can't touch money on Shabbos."

He pushed the purse back to her and paid the bill.

She stared at her bag. "Would you mind carrying it?" she asked.

Hugh couldn't help laughing. "I'd be delighted," he said.

Hugh lived in a big old building on Tenth Avenue. The elevator was broken, so they walked up five flights of stairs, Masha's purse slung over Hugh's shoulder. The stairwell smelled of Indian food. Masha was quiet on the way up. She felt a kind of compression on the top of her head as she trudged up the marble steps, her hand on the broad metal banister—as though she were being shrunk. Hugh opened the heavy door and let her in, flipping on the light.

The door opened onto a large room furnished with a Weimaraner-silver plush couch and several green reclining plastic lawn chairs. A triptych of large windows dominated the space; walls and wooden floor were painted brownish red. A galley kitchen was nestled into a nook in the wall on the right. Dishes had been washed and neatly stacked on a rack. Masha sat down on the only real chair she could see, an office chair on wheels. Hugh found a bottle with a finger of whiskey in it and poured it out for himself.

"We have another bottle, if you would like a cocktail," he said.

Masha was eyeing the shut front door. He opened it a crack.

"That better?" he asked. She nodded. "Are you worried?" he asked her.

"Yeah," she said.

"Because you're staying here, or because you feel bad you forgot to go home?"

"Because I forgot," she said softly.

"Well, it's done now, you might as well relax. You hungry?"

"A little."

"There's a Chinese restaurant on this block. They serve kosher food. You eat kosher, right?"

No real kosher restaurant would serve after sunset on Shabbos. Masha shook her head. "I'm okay," she said.

"Or how about I make pasta?"

They ate at a small card table. He found the other bottle of whiskey in a cabinet in the kitchen, poured out some in a glass of ginger ale, and drank it with his meal. She just had ginger ale.

Hugh's skin was stretched very taut over his face, Masha noticed. When he chewed, a web of muscles stood out under the skin of his jaw.

"Hey, how about we rehearse our scene?" Hugh drawled, letting his fork clatter onto the table. Masha pushed herself back in the wheeled chair, reversing a couple of feet, and turned, scuttling crab-wise, starting to negotiate the room.

"I don't feel like it." she said. "It's nice here."

"It'll be better with real furniture," said Hugh. "I'm going to change my life shortly, and that'll make all the difference."

"What's wrong with your life?" asked Masha.

Hugh walked over to the window, opened it wide, and lit a ciga-rette. Placing himself on the sill gingerly, as if worried he might fall off, he rested his forehead on the glass and looked down onto the street.

"I'm at what I'm hoping is the tail end of a long fiesta, but it just keeps going on. I have been warned of ruinous consequences to do with my liver and career. Doctors, agents, and relations are of one mind in this regard. I guess it's easy to see that people are wasting themselves when you look at them from the outside. Take you, for instance," he said, turning to her.

"What about me?" she asked.

"You want my opinion?" His voice sounded different, she noticed. Coated.

"You have an opinion?"

"Yes, I do."

"I don't know if I want it, though," she said, coasting by him on the office chair.

"I think you could be really fine, Masha, truly exceptional at your work. If you don't try you'll never know what could have happened, the work you might have done. But . . . you can't do it halfway like this. I mean, it's Friday night. You think all the theaters are closed? You think Broadway is shuttin' down 'cause it's Shabbos? And Hollywood? The TV studios? They work Friday night, they shoot Saturdays. You're gonna have to make a choice. You're one thing or the other, but you can't be both. You either stick with it, or . . . I don't know, you get married, and find another line of work." His voice shook, and he turned back to his view out the window.

"I'm sorry," he said, his forehead pressed to the glass. "It's none of my business."

Masha had stopped her game, and sat in the chair, staring at the floor. She knew what he said was true. Yet she couldn't bring herself to dwell on the contradiction. She pushed the floor away sideways with her feet, pivoting back and forth for a while. Then she looked up at him with solemn hopefulness.

"Can we watch TV?" she asked.

"You came all the way to Manhattan and you want to watch TV."

"I already broke the rules so bad . . . you'd have to turn it on."

"How about a movie?" he asked.

I had never seen anyone observe that way. She was so *alive*. She watched the film as if witnessing a close relative in a bare-knuckle fight. Every moment *counted*. Her whole body tensed up with the thrill of scary moments, her feet tucked under her. She squinted at love scenes through her fingers. And when there was a laugh, she spun around to share it with Hugh, so vital, filled with the miracle of the joke. I was painfully jealous of him. If I could have sat beside her, oh! What wouldn't I have accomplished? After a while, Hugh stopped watching the film and just watched Masha. At the end, her face wet with tears, hiccuping from the weeping, she let him shut off the box. Clearly, he was enthralled by her now. Who wouldn't be?

Hugh made up his bed fresh for her; he slept on the couch. His room was barren, but for a few books by the bed. Masha lay awake for a long time after she had said her evening prayers. Watching that movie had scooped her out, filled her with want. She yearned to be one of those people who became other people. She had to find a story to live in.

The next morning, a young woman's voice woke Masha up. She rose, still in her dress, and peeked through the door. It was Shelley, her dandelion-fluff hair lit up by the morning sunlight streaming through the dusty window. A husky, tall young man stood over her. They were laughing. Masha walked in.

"There she is!" said Shelley. "We heard about your mishap. I hope you're not in trouble."

"What are *you* doing here?" asked Masha, pleased.

"I live here," said Shelley.

"You do?"

"I thought you knew," said Hugh, who was huddled under a pile of coats on the couch. "I figured you two had talked about it."

"This is Paul," said Shelley.

"Hi," said Masha, her hands clamped behind her back. Paul looked at her somberly.

"Isn't she beguiling?" asked Shelley.

"Yes, she is." Paul smiled. Shelley's boyfriend had a pugnacious face, eyebrows puckered over a pair of intense little eyes.

"I'm so glad you got stuck in Manhattan," said Shelley. "Are you hungry?"

Masha wasn't allowed to go back home until that night at sunset, so Hugh went out and came back with bags of bagels, kosher cream cheese—and smoked salmon, which surprised Masha. Maybe he was rich? Shelley made eggs. She was wearing a light cotton dress and Mary Janes. The two men lay on the couch and talked, waiting to be fed. There was something improvised about the setup. They seemed like orphaned children, the three of them, and Shelley was playing the mother. Masha set plates onto the flimsy card table and Shelley served them all. Masha sank her teeth into the thick cream cheese, tearing at the doughy bagel with her teeth, eyes closing. She felt so satisfied here. Later, Shelley showed her the room she shared with Paul. Unlike Hugh's room, it was carefully furnished, with a wicker bedstead, a desk, a couple of chairs.

"I'm desperate to move out," Shelley whispered as Masha investigated the many photos up on the wall above the bed.

"Why?"

"It's over between me and Paul, we're like a sixty-year-old couple. Now I'm stuck; I can't afford to leave," said Shelley.

Masha craved a shower, but it was forbidden to use water heated on the Sabbath. She washed herself with cold water. For toilet paper, she used Kleenex she found in a drawer; she still felt bad about the time she tore the napkin at the Shabbos table. When she left the bathroom, she whispered the benediction *asher yatzar*, thanking Hashem for her working orifices, walked into the living room, and saw that angular Hugh was grabbing the coats he'd used for bedding off the couch. The other two were gone.

"Where did Shelley go?" she asked.

"She and Paul had to go out for an hour or so. They have an appointment with a professional," he said. "One of those rituals you perform when your relationship is dying, apparently." Masha didn't know what he meant. She picked up his copy of the play, which was on the floor, and leafed through it.

"You don't understand," she said.

"What's that?"

"To you, all the rules are weird and hard, right? You think being a real Jew is hard."

"Seems like it."

"But I know the rules like I know how to breathe, so it's easy. What's hard is living without the rules. That's hard."

"I'm sorry if I said something I shouldn't have," he said. "I do that a lot."

"Let's play the scene," she said, tossing the play on the couch.

He plucked the lawn chairs out of the way so they would have room to work. I flew onto a standing lamp and watched them. From the moment she began the scene, Masha's body changed. Barefoot, she circled her prey with a confident animal grace. Her hand came close to Hugh's arm, but it never landed. She was not allowed to touch him, and she would not. Yet the charge coming out of her was stunning. I tried to find her thoughts, but there were none of her own. She was the person she was pretending to be. She had become Carol Cutrere, lost Southern belle (albeit with a Long Island accent). Her face seemed molded to the skull in a different way; she looked older, ground down by a ten-year party, yet gloriously defiant in her chosen wildness. Poor Hugh Crosby was getting lost in her performance. Skilled as he was, he was no match for this creature.

Afterward, she flopped, spent, onto the office chair, and began to swivel it side to side again as she slowly came back to herself. Watching her, a knot of fear formed in my fly's belly. There was something inhuman in her stare. It was an expression that I recognized, but I couldn't remember why.

Afterward, still in the grips of the scene, Masha splashed water on her face in the bathroom. As her head swung up, she caught her reflection and froze there. Framed in powder-pink tiles, her pale face, with its inky frame of hair, seemed to be floating. Her dark, kohl-smudged eyes looked vast, glassy, tinged with violet. Her mouth was slightly open, and the insolent gap between her two front teeth was just visible. She looked predatory. For the first time, Masha took her own breath away. I inhabited her as she stared at herself, felt the vanity solidifying in her like cooling fat.

When night fell, Hugh walked Masha through Penn Station. She allowed herself to hold on to the edge of his down jacket, following him in her long dress as he fought through the roiling crowd to buy two tickets at a kiosk. In the train, he sat beside her, his legs crossed at the ankles. Dread was gathering in her now as she stared out the flashing window, her red wool coat sliding down her shoulders. They would be angry, maybe. Disappointed. Yes. This was so far from what was expected. It would frighten them, she knew. Oh, why? Yet she couldn't muster regret.

On the Far Rockaway platform, Hugh lit a cigarette. There was a thick, complicit silence between them. He walked her to the end of her street. She stopped then, faced him. She was frightened now.

"Thanks," she said.

"Good luck with the family," he said, his eyes flicking down to her mouth.

"Yeah."

"See you Tuesday?"

"Okay." She turned and walked down the block.

The lights were on in her house. The first person she saw was Miriam, walking out the door. Seeing her, Miriam charged down the block, grabbed Masha's arm, and pulled her toward the house, her mouth a tense red slash.

"What happened? Mommy was like dead all Shabbos, she could barely talk."

"I told her. I missed the train," Masha said.

"Yeah, but . . . were you alone?"

"Yes."

"I saw you with a guy just there."

"You were spying?"

"I caught sight of you. I was waiting for you to say goodbye. Forgive me for not screaming your name in the street."

"He's a friend."

"A friend? From where? Where did you get a friend like that? What's going on with you? I know something is going on!"

Masha tore loose of her sister and walked into the house. In the living room, the whole family was looking up at her, a nest of bafflement and reproach. She backed away from them, mute, like a hunted thing, and ran up the stairs.

She sat on the bed and took in her room. Everything was as she had left it yesterday morning, yet it seemed acutely not the same. Her chest of drawers, the forest-green rug, the green-and-blue curtains, Yehudis and Suri's tidily made beds, her hairbrush on the bedside table with a snarl of black hair in it—it was all so . . . alien. It seemed as if this were a room she was visiting for the first time in years. Something had changed, forever, in a single day. Loss swept through her.

Her mother's knock was soft. "You want something to eat?" Pearl asked.

"No, thanks, Mommy."

"You must be so tired." Pearl hugged her.

"I'm sorry I scared you," said Masha.

"It's over now," said Pearl. Masha held her mother, gripped the flesh of her arms, put her head against her soft breast, searching for the comfort she had always found here. But a protective case was forming around my beloved, like a magic spell that repelled everything familiar. Her little tear-stained face seemed so strained, so thin, it broke my heart.

Pearl stroked her head. "I am so glad to see you, sweetheart. You rest now. We'll talk tomorrow."

Pearl shut the door gently. Masha began to undress, removing first the left shoe, then the right, as she had been taught to do. She was so tired all of a sudden. The door opened. It was Estie.

"Where were you, Masha? You ran away!"

"If I ran away, how come I'm here?"

"Hashem's gonna be so mad at you."

"Why? I didn't do anything. I stayed put. He would have been mad if I'da got on the train."

"I got in trouble too," said Estie, one gangly leg up on Masha's bed.

"What else is new? Okay," said Masha. "Scram. I'm tired."

"Mashie. Could I sleep wit' you?"

"No way."

"Please?"

Masha sighed. "Just lie down with me five minutes." The little girl nestled up to her sister under the blankets, wrapping her small hand in a black lasso of Masha's hair, and gave her neck a long, satisfied sniff. "Don't cry, Mashie," Estie said.

"I'm not crying, stupid," Masha whispered.

"You *was*," said Estie drowsily. Masha held the girl's warm body close. Within seconds the two wild daughters of Pearl and Mordecai Edelman were fast asleep.

## 25

I was summoned to the library. The count was writing a letter at a round table.

"Sit down, Gebeck," he said. I sat. He slid a piece of paper, a quill, and a bottle of ink toward me. "Write your name," he said. I began to write *Jacob*, but turned it into *Johann*, then *Gebeck*. He took the paper and squinted at it.

"Do you normally write in Hebrew?" he asked.

"That's what I learned," I said. "But I do write some French."

"Your handwriting will improve," he said with a shrug. "Now. I have an undertaking for you. I wrote a little journal of my travels in Italy last year. I would like you to write me out a fair copy." I peeked up at him, confused. "Just copy what is in my journal into this clean notebook. Practice your handwriting first. Write out my first two paragraphs on this scrap piece of paper. There." He left me then.

Half an hour later I was asleep, my head on the table. I was still feeble from my time in jail. Solange led me to the settee and drew a blanket over me. I slept there for several hours. When I woke, I found a tray with soup and bread, water, and hot coffee on the library table. I ate my meal, careful not to spill a drop of soup. Refreshed, I spent the next two hours improving my script, copying out French I barely understood.

As was the count's intention, the act of copying his language made me more fluent in French. By the end of the day I had begun to understand a bit more of what I read. By the end of the month I was reading easily. The journal was, for the most part, an exhaustive description of the count's pursuit, seduction, and abandonment of various ladies of the Italian nobility. It seemed to me that he would not be very welcome in that country, should he ever wish to return.

It took me two months to make the fair copy of the Comte de Villars's Italian journal. During that time I also learned from Le Jumeau how to:

- Lay a table in three different geometric formations: chevron, oval, and rectangle, according to the design of the house steward.
- Serve all meals, both formal and quotidian.
- Address each servant according to his or her rank, and my betters according to theirs.
- Deliver a message.
- Open a door.
- Close a door.
- Bow while walking backward.
- Shine shoes.
- Brush hats.
- Dress a count.
- Shave a count.

I perfected the deadened aristocratic expression required of a servant, a chilly look they called "morgue" in those days. As I studied Le Jumeau, the count continued to study me: he might appear at any time—when I was eating, sleeping, praying, washing. I had to enunciate every blessing I said over food and drink so that he could copy it down in his little red book. I spoke out my prayers like lines in a play. The effect of all this was to make my religious habits seem more and more like performance. Whatever real feeling I had invested in my daily rituals was being sapped.

My first Friday in the Hôtel de Villars, at sunset, I lit a candle in my room and said the Shabbat prayer, then ate what dainties I had set aside during the week as a Shabbat feast. However, I was unable to devote twenty-four hours to prayer, joy, and rest, as we are prescribed to do. Close to midnight, the count arrived home from the theater and called for me to undress him. Saturday morning, Le Jumeau barked at me to light the stove, shine the shoes. Sunday morning was the servants' only time off, so that we could attend Mass, which I did not do, of course. Neither did Le Jumeau, by the way; he was busy with the comely cook, Clothilde, who had, I learned by way of the scullery maid, abandoned her husband and children to live with the irresistible valet. Now that I was installed beside the count, they shared a bedroom off the kitchen.

One morning I was performing the ritual washing of hands when the door opened. The count strode into my room, reached down, took the basin, jerked the window open, and threw the water into the courtyard. Then he turned on me, his broad, fleshy mouth turned down in an exaggerated grimace, his face red.

"Enough," he said. "I have been patient with you, Gebeck. But now you need to wake up. Meet me in the library in half an hour. Have some bread and coffee. Forget about my breakfast. Le Jumeau will bring it to me later."

I reported to the library at the prescribed time, badly shaken. The count's mood had softened.

"I am sorry to be harsh. There is a reason for my behavior. One day I believe you will be grateful for what I am about to give you. Now your French is strong enough. Never mind your duties today." He had opened the glass door of a high bookcase and was selecting various leather-bound volumes, setting them on the table. He chose one from the pile and opened it before me. "I will return in an hour or so. You can ask me anything you like then. I am no professor, but I have been taught well, by brutal teachers with great minds: the Jesuits. Your only obligation for the next few months is to educate yourself." I was overwhelmed by confusion, fear, and a rising sense of privilege. When I answered, my voice barely emerged from my throat.

*"Merci, Monsieur le Comte."*

And so began my enlightenment.

He started me on Aristotle. I felt I was drowning. I had no comprehension, nothing to cling to, no reference for this mode of thinking. The count walked me through the great ideas of classical civilization as patiently as if I were his own son. My education had been thus far exclusively religious, including only the Torah, the Talmud, and, through Gimpel, heretical whiffs of the Zohar and the Tanya. There was much wisdom in these books, but it was all predicated on faith, and tainted, for me, by the nightmare of Hodel. Logic and empirical reasoning was a relief, like a gust of fresh air after being locked in a closet. To my surprise—and the count's too, I think—I showed an aptitude for philosophy, and developed a love of language, learning adequate Latin and fairly good French, even some English. The count loved a well-turned phrase. Pleasing my master had become very important to me. I had never managed to impress my own father much. He regarded me as a dud, serious about neither selling nor studying; married me off to the first lunatic with a dowry that went on the market. What would he say now, if he saw his chump of a son in a powdered wig, speaking the language of Cicero?

The count was determined to rid me of my superstitions. He bathed me in Locke, lathered me in Voltaire, and powdered me with Diderot. The Jews were, my master contended, sealed off from civilization. Steeped in ancient custom, with a superiority complex supported by our holy text, we were permanent primitives forever linked by a pseudo-historical umbilical cord to an imagined, heroic past. Worst of all our crimes was the mothering of Christianity, which the count detested as the religion of slaves. My master imagined me up a utopia where Jews, Muhammadans, and Christians alike lived for themselves and one another, not in fear of divine retribution, not ensnared by an intricate net of laws, but free. It was a dizzying prospect, frightening and seductive.

## 26

Two weeks had passed since Derbhan Nevsky had visited the Bridget Mooney School of Acting, and he had used the time well. He had moved in on his old aquaintance, Ross Coe, the richest man he knew outside the entertainment industry. Nevsky had met Ross at the Carmel Yacht Club in the nineties. Nevsky represented a star who was deeply involved in the sailing world, and he spent a lot of time on boats because of it. He was amazed, at the time, at all that untapped money flying around, so close to Hollywood yet untouched by its itchy fingers. Sailing folk were, as a rule, conservative types who had their money tied up in bonds and property. They weren't big risk takers. Yet Nevsky had always been convinced that, with the right approach, they could be bled and not even feel it. When he met Ross Coe, who had just had a nose job, the first of many plastic surgeries he was to suffer over the years for reasons only his psychiatrist understood, Derbhan recognized a man who could be led deep into uncharted waters. Coe was young, rich, bored out of his mind, and had some very strange predilections. Most people found him repulsive. Nevsky saw him as an opportunity waiting to happen—he just couldn't figure out how to activate him at the time. Plus, luck was streaming in from all sides back then—he didn't really need any more of it. But now that the gods had turned on him and he had been washed up on the shores of New York with nothing but his wits and the clothes on his back, he had to make friends with the natives. So, on instinct, he called Ross Coe, guessing he'd be bored enough and odd enough to want Derbhan Nevsky back in his life. He was right.

The parties at the Coes' were filled with older men in bright-colored trousers, occasional women in their thirties and forties with ebbing looks and a hungry gleam in their eye, ready to snag any billionaire with most of his teeth in. Nevsky navigated his way through these grizzly affairs with his characteristic energy, limbs jerking this way and that, his shirt and jeans blindingly white, skin tanned as a well-cooked sausage. He flirted with the women and cajoled the men, made connections with people who had never heard of him before, who just thought of him as a veteran man in entertainment starting up a new company. He gradually became indispensable to the Coes, who were always desperate to entertain but lacked any real social magnetism, apart from their money, of which they had an enormous amount. The other reason they were a difficult sell socially was that Mrs. Coe, formerly Orschler, came from an old Nazi family. Her mother was the first cousin of Herta Schneider, Eva Braun's best friend. When in her cups, Mrs. Coe had an alarming tendency to get nostalgic about the lovely Eva and her flawless skin, her generosity with the staff, and the sad fate that awaited her in that damn bunker. These musings did nothing to endear her to the Jewish element in the Hamptons, nor, in fact, any thinking people, and so the Coes were socially marooned when Nevsky came into their lives, forced to cruise nearby towns looking for likely acquaintances. The Coes were both allergic to solitude, especially the type that involved spending time alone with each other, and needed to be entertaining constantly in order to feel well in themselves—or, perhaps, in order to feel at all. Nevsky relieved them of the nightly burden of having nothing to say over dinner, he regaled them with stories about Hollywood personalities, he got them all excited about the company they were going to start together, made them feel part of it. In short, he breathed new life into their stale and decadent existence. Consequently, Ross Coe asked Nevsky if he'd like to come live in the guesthouse until the company was up and running. Nevsky pretended to think about it for a couple of days, and then he arrived with a large suitcase. He was, he felt, on his way. He had been punished enough.

It was scene night at the Bridget Mooney School of Acting. Nevsky was seated on a metal chair in the second row, behind Bridget. The girl who wouldn't shake his hand came onstage, followed by a lanky young Southern guy. They were doing a scene from *Orpheus Descending*. The actor playing Val the drifter was relaxed, intense, a pro. The girl playing Carol Cutrere was kind of unbelievable. She played the part with no feminine mannerisms, yet she was intensely erotic. Her sexuality ran like dark sap through the scene. Her words, spoken with swaybacked diphthongs, sounded odd for the Southern Carol, yet every word she said sounded true. There was a moment—Nevsky had never seen anything like it—when Carol was begging Val to take a drive with her, and the girl put her hand on his arm. The man reacted as if he had been burned; the girl put her hand to her mouth, tears came to her eyes. When she said the lines *"I'm an exhibitionist!* I want to be noticed, seen, heard, felt! I want them to know I'm alive!" the words, filled with fury and pathos, seemed ripped from her soul. Nevsky got chills. This girl connected with an audience like a live electric wire.

Masha sat collapsed in the metal folding chair beside Hugh, knees together, feet pidgeon-toed, hands in her lap, waiting for the critique from Bridget and the class. She was still trying to make sense of what had happened. She had touched him; she remembered that part. She had touched him! The skin of her palm hurt when she did it, an ache she could still feel. She was forbidden to touch him, and yet she had done it. This was why she was not allowed to act. It had been inevitable. She couldn't hear what Bridget was saying. The other students were talking, but she couldn't focus. When Hugh stood up from his chair, she took her cue and followed him offstage.

"Are you all right?" he asked in his warm voice. She nodded, tears in her eyes.

"You want me to take you home?"

"I think if I just sit for a while . . . ," she said. Then she went into the bathroom and soaped her hands for a long time.

The minute Masha and Hugh left the stage, Bridget turned to Nevsky, twisting in her seat.

"Don't say anything to her until I speak to you," she said.

Back in Bridget's office, Bridget held fast: she wouldn't allow Nevsky to send Masha out on auditions for three months. She needed that time to work with her. In addition, she asked that Nevsky take on another student. Nevsky chose frazzle-haired Shelley, whose scene had come after Masha's. Shelley was funny. She could do well on TV, he thought. Nevsky wanted Hugh too, but he already had an agent. Just as well; he never got along as well with the guys.

When Masha was on her way out of class that night, Nevsky slipped her his card.

"Bridget won't let me send you out till later, but I want you to have this. I would love to represent you, when you're ready," he said.

The next day, Masha's chest began to hurt again. She couldn't sit up or laugh without pain. Pearl took care of her, kept her in bed. I never left her side, buzzing loyally around her as she swatted me away. Masha was very sad during that period. She kept thinking about walking down Sixth Avenue with the snow in her eyes, what it was like to be alone like that, and free.

She had to go to a cardiologist. She lay back as a nurse smeared her naked chest with lubricant, then fixed little suckers to her skin. Wires attached to the suckers made a picture of her heart, the nurse explained. Afterward, the young doctor came in and sat down.

"Well, we've done an EKG and an echocardiogram, and we can't find anything wrong."

"How can there not be anything wrong?" asked Pearl. "She can barely move!"

"Have a look at the echo from the hospital, when Masha was diagnosed with pericarditis," said the shiny young man, clipping two X-rays up on a light board. "Here's the one from the hospital. You can see the fluid around the heart, right? This little sort of dense sac? But in the one we took today, it's clear."

"How come I have pain, then?" asked Masha softly.

"Well, the brain is funny," said the doctor. "It can remember the recipe for a certain pain. And when something happens to the mind, like stress, the brain sometimes recreates that pain."

"But why?" asked Masha.

"We don't know," said the doctor.

"So you're saying this is psychological?" said Pearl.

"Not exactly. It's physiological pain, real pain, without a somatic cause. Sort of . . . ghost pain. A rogue symptom."

"So what do we do?" asked Pearl.

"Be happy she doesn't have pericarditis. And . . . give her Motrin."

"But if there's no inflammation, why should she take an anti-inflammatory?" asked Pearl.

The doctor shrugged. "For the pain," he said, with a wisp of a smile. "There is a lot we don't know about the brain, Mrs. Edelman."

The following Tuesday, her chest had improved, but Masha skipped class. She went straight home from the nursing home instead. Touching Hugh in the scene had frightened her. She tried to keep busy, took extra hours at the nursing home, and began to earn a salary there. They said she was wonderful with the old people.

———

One afternoon, while she was on break, her phone rang. It was Shelley.

"What the heck happened to you, Masha? Are you okay?"

"I can't come to class anymore," said Masha.

"Are you sick?

"I was, but . . . that's not why."

"You're crazy, girl, you were stupendous in that scene last time."

"I just . . . it's hard to explain."

"Listen, Mr. Nevsky—you remember, that guy who gave you his card?"

"Yeah," said Masha.

"Well, he wants to represent me too. And he said, if you and me want, there's an apartment near the Hamptons we could have rent-free all summer! They would do everything for us—pay for everything, just till we're ready to go out on auditions. Mr. Nevsky's a friend of Bridget's, he's not some weirdo. And listen, Masha, I went there and checked it out and it's amazing! The apartment is clean and pretty, and the guy's mansion in Southhampton, where we would be most of the time, it's like paradise, there's an indoor pool and an outdoor pool and a sauna and fucking Pilates machines. The owner and his wife are a little creepy, but it's a great deal. I'll do it if you do it or maybe I'll do it anyway, I need to get away. But I think they only want me if you come. Nevsky thinks you're amazing. Masha?"

Masha was quiet. Her mind was blank.

"I . . . can't," she said.

"So what am I telling Bridget? You're quitting class?"

"I guess so," said Masha. "Yeah. Sorry. 'Bye." She hung up the phone.

## ∞ 27

My master had a mistress. Her name was Antonia Giardina. Le Jumeau said she cost the count four hundred francs a month, more than my father earned in a year.

I was amazed at the elaborate toilette the count inflicted on himself in preparation for seeing her. It took him twenty minutes just to trim the hairs in his nose. I myself had to tame his ear hairs. Le Jumeau shaved him, confidently gliding the sharp blade of the razor up the tender lines of his neck.

"Le Jumeau, tonight I will take the little one," the count said through soaped lips. "He has never been to the theater."

Le Jumeau grunted. "There's a first time for everything," he said ominously. I couldn't tell if he was pleased or not. As for me, I was dying to see a woman worth so much.

When the coach arrived at the side entrance to the Hôtel de Bourgogne, where the Comédie-Italienne was housed, I hopped off the driver's bench where I had been sitting with Renard, the twin coachman, and opened the count's door. In the interest of my cultural education, he bought me a parterre ticket for two sous and then walked up the staircase to his loge. I was to dash up to him the moment the interval began.

Standing on the packed floor of the theater, I read the gilt lettering sewn into the velvet curtains: CASTIGAT RIDENDO MORES, which I translated with my newfound Latin as "Laughter Improves Morals." Delighted by my own comprehension, I looked around me, grinning, and just stopped myself from slapping the back of the man beside me. Mercifully, he did not notice my familiarity. I felt a sharp thrill. There I stood on the packed floor, elbow to elbow with every kind of Parisian, from nobles to ruffians and drunks, and I blended right in. What a relief it was to look like a Frenchman! Had I been in my former garb, I would have had to endure curious, hostile, or evasive glances, to feel, at best, apart; at worst, hated or feared. The guards who were walking around the theater with an eye out for misconduct would surely have asked me what I was doing there, and to see my passport. But as it was, I just looked like someone's valet, or possibly a coachman, in a nice crisp set of livery.

The orchestra, which had been warming up tunelessly, began to play a rousing folk song. The heavy red velvet curtains parted, revealing four characters frozen in a painterly rural tableau, washed in a warm glow of light. Slowly, the actors came to life. A young shepherdess with long braids the color of raw pine sang a jolly aria in a playful soprano. She then did a little jig, moving her arms and legs with an easy, athletic grace. This was, I guessed, the count's lover. As the performance continued, the little shepherdess fell in love with a dashing duke, and he with her. The style of the play was broadly comic. Mlle Giardina was funny and very free. The moment the curtains closed on the first act, I pushed my way through the milling crowd on the parterre, then started up the stairs to my master's box, climbing against the torrent of well-heeled box holders on their way down to the refreshment bar.

"Go out and buy three dozen lilies," said the count when I finally got to him, handing me a few coins. "Deliver them to Mlle Giardina with this note. Hurry. There is a florist in the building, just next to the entrance where we came in."

When I arrived, panting, at Mlle Giardina's door and knocked, having gotten lost on my way out of the theater and again trying to find her dressing room in the maze of back rooms, I heard a bright voice say:

"Who is it?"

"I have a message from the Comte de Villars," I called out. The door opened. Through the thicket of lilies I saw the little shepherdess. Her braids had been untied and her caramel hair was tousled around a merry young face. She parted the flowers and peered at me.

"What happened to Le Jumeau?" she asked.

"I am the second valet," I said. She eyed me carefully as she tore open the note from the count.

"Come in," she said. I walked into the small, warm room, still carrying the bunch of lilies. A fire raged in the grate. "Put them over there," she said, indicating a round table in the corner. She sat down at her dressing table looking at her reflection, then shifted her gaze to mine.

"What is your name?" she asked, rouging her cheeks.

"Gebeck," I said, my voice breaking. I was still unused to the name.

"Doesn't that mean 'baked goods' in German?" she asked, crinkling her small nose.

"I come from a long line of bakers," I answered.

She swiveled around and smiled, raising her perfect eyebrows. "Tell the count I will be happy to meet him after the show," she said.

"I shall."

"Tell him I will need twenty minutes here after the curtain goes down. Then he can collect me."

"Very well, mademoiselle," I said.

"Does he always use you as his message boy now?"

"Usually."

"That's interesting," she said, turning back to the glass.

From then on, I went to the Comédie-Italienne with the count twice a week. On occasion he visited Mlle Giardina in her dressing room during the interval. I served them their champagne before withdrawing discreetly. As a rule, however, I simply brought two armfulls of lilies and a note to the little actress, waiting at her door with a hammering heart. Her roles alternated between shepherdess, Arabian princess, chambermaid, and wood nymph, depending on which show was on that night. I preferred to be greeted by the diaphanously clad wood nymph. Once, as I handed her a note, Mlle Giardina trailed her fingers across my palm, causing me to retreat in a flurry of shy confusion.

Hanging about the foyer one night, waiting for the show to end, I learned that the ticket collector, Algrant, a slit-eyed young man with brown teeth, was Mlle Giardina's *greluchon*, the word used in those days for a courtesan's personal lover. I became seized with jealousy and couldn't take my eyes off him. Though it was utterly out of the question that I would ever touch the courtesan of my master, I didn't like the idea of this shifty-looking scoundrel pawing her for free.

The count owed a lot of money, I gathered from being by his side all the time, party to most of his conversations. He also dictated many of his letters to me, now that my French had improved. He gambled almost daily, paid a fortune for Mlle Giardina, and insisted on the finest clothes, food, and horses. The income thrown off by his inherited estates was never enough.

One day he told me to get the coach ready, we were going out. I was alarmed to hear him tell Renard to take us to the Jewish quarter.

"Why are we going there?" I asked.

"Why do you think?" he snapped. "I need money."

As I have said, it was forbidden for Catholics to lend money at interest, but it was one of the only businesses Jews were allowed to engage in. Nearly all of us lent trifling sums to the Christians, but for large sums one had to go to one of the serious bankers.

I had never met Loeb Hildesheim, though I had heard his name many times. He lived and worked on the edge of our neighborhood, in a big house on rue Saint-Denis. When the coach stopped outside this residence, I shrank back, hoping the count would let me stay behind. He got out and turned to me.

"Gebeck," he admonished. Reluctantly, I followed.

The house was well appointed. A young Jewess opened the door for us and offered to take our hats. My master let his eyes linger over her face, and handed her his hat gently. I saw that the young woman was careful not to touch my master's fingers as she took the hat. I too gave her my hat, wondering if she would guess what I was, but she took it without looking at me.

"Please wait here," she said, indicating a small, cozy sitting room furnished in the latest Parisian style. My master sat; I stood by the door.

"He's made something of himself, you have to give him that," said the count, looking around him at all the evidence of the man's wealth. "All on interest," he said, waving his arm. "This is one of the reasons the Jews are resented, Gebeck. They say you draw the innocent young sons of France into spending more than they can afford, luring us into a trap of loans and owing."

"Is that what you think?" I asked.

The count shrugged. "I suppose they make it easier to get the money so we can waste it. But the prohibition against Catholics charging interest is stupid."

Just then Loeb Hildesheim walked in. An august man in his sixties, his long gray beard divided into two points, he shook my master's hand with the barest hint of a bow. Hildesheim wore several large rings on his hand, I noticed. He then sat, spreading out the tails of his silk coat on the seat behind him. His skullcap was crimson velvet. Once he had settled himself, he turned to the count and, with kingly reserve, asked:

"What can I help you with, Monsieur Le Comte?"

"I need two hundred louis," said the count. The Jewess walked in carrying a silver tray laden with tea and a plate of small biscuits. She offered me one as well. I ate it. Loeb Hildesheim waited until she had left before he spoke again.

"That's a great deal of money," he said.

"I have always made good on my pledges to you," said the count.

"It's not that, you are a wonderful customer," said the old Jew, casting his keen eyes in my direction. My spine tingled as he looked at me quizzically. Then I realized he was simply gazing into space, calculating. "With a figure so high, we need to increase the rate of interest, you understand."

While they quibbled about interest, I practiced a look of icy contempt, echoing the disdain I knew the old man had for my master. Hildesheim thrived on libertines but despised them all the same. He himself, I was sure, barely took a glass of wine at dinner, slept only with his wife. Temperance was endemic among the Jews.

My master signed the pledge and got his money. When we left, he shook his head.

"He's a cunning one," he murmured. "Now. What do you say we use a bit of this cash?"

The first place we went was the Place des Victoires. There my diminutive master alighted from the coach. His hands shoved deep in a white lynx muff, he stood leaning against the grillwork at the base of the equestrian statue of Louis XIV, staring at a little church opposite, L'Église des Petits Pères, where Mass was just letting out. The crowd of worshippers was disgorged and went off on its way. Several women remained behind, however. They didn't seem to be in a hurry to go anywhere, and fanned out, walking back and forth in front of the church in a leisurely fashion, the colored plumes on their hats making them look like proud birds. I stood by the coach all this time, baffled. Eventually the diminutive count gestured to one of the feathered ladies. She approached him. I could not hear their conversation. She rushed over to one of the other women and whispered something in her ear, at which she too came tripping over to the count. Renard opened the coach door for the ladies, and they sat on the forward-facing bench. I sat opposite them, beside my master.

The armatures of the women's dresses were very wide, and, due to their being crammed together, puffed the skirts up to a point that we could only see slivers of their animated faces through the hedges of silk and tulle. One of the girls, I discerned, was dark and plump; the other, fair, bug-eyed, and an enthusiastic talker. The high feathers on their hats were entwined, and buckled by the roof of the coach. I could tell that my master was partial to the sloe-eyed dark one, but he was very polite to them both, inviting them to come with him to his house in Neuilly. I looked at him, surprised; I had not been aware that he had another residence so near Paris.

We arrived at a charming little house with a low fence and a gate, which the count opened gallantly for the ladies, walking up the path behind them and casting three bright knocks on the red door, which popped open immediately to reveal Le Jumeau, dressed in a pair of green silk britches, ivory stockings, and a snug navy jacket. I had never seen him out of livery on a working day.

The moment I walked inside the cramped foyer, the valet set me to making tea. I started opening cabinets and drawers, clueless as to the wherabouts of the tea things. The kitchen was well stocked, however, and I had soon set out an inviting tray. Le Jumeau handed me a box of colorful meringues, which I set out onto a gilded plate shaped like a leaf. I then served the party in the drawing room. Le Jumeau sent me back for an extra cup and saucer for him. When I poured him his tea, he nodded at me.

"Thank you, Gebeck," he said, slurping his tea noisily and crossing his legs. The count didn't seem to notice this disrespect. In fact, all the normal rules of service seemed suspended in this place. I had just re-turned to the kitchen to have my own tea when I heard Le Jumeau bellowing, "Gebeck!" I scurried back into the sitting room.

"Take Mademoiselle Charelle up," he said, indicating the plump, dark-haired girl. "First bedroom at the top of the stairs." I led the little sausage up the staircase, opened the first door I found, and was amazed to see an array of whips and canes hanging neatly on the wall. The brunette strode up to the collection and, with the air of an expert, took down a long horsewhip, raised it over her head, and flicked it in my direction, laughing. Stung on the hand, I jumped, then sucked my knuckles. In waddled the count, wearing only his chemise and rumpled red stockings, followed by Le Jumeau. The talkative bug-eyed blonde emerged from behind them carrying a length of rope. A quiet, strange atmosphere came over the party as they found their places. Intensely embarrassed, I took hold of the doorknob.

"Gebeck," said Le Jumeau sharply, bringing me up short. I stood still, the door open a sliver, looking at him imploringly. "Go, then," he said in disgust. Feeling I had failed a test of some kind, yet relieved, I spent the next hour downstairs in the cozy sitting room, chewing on the leftover meringues and reading a novel I found on the shelf. Whatever was going on upstairs, I felt frightened and repelled by it. Eventually I fell asleep curled up on the couch. I woke with a slap on the ass from the bug-eyed blonde, who was dressed only in her chemise.

"And how is our little naïf? Sleeping?" She asked, cramming herself into the space between me and the back of the sofa and cradling me like an infant. She then exposed her vast wobbling tit for me to nurse, clamping it between her fingers and causing the sausage brunette and Le Jumeau to melt into helpless laughter. The more I craned my neck to avoid her plate-sized nipple, the more hysterical they became. Finally I freed myself, vexed and humiliated, my wig askew, and stood panting in the middle of the room. Le Jumeau patted me hard on the side of the face with his palm, in a manner both brotherly and threatening.

"That's what you get for desertion," he said, swinging himself into a chair, one leg over the arm. He winked at the bug-eyed blonde, who rolled off the couch and glided over to him on her knees. The brunette plonked herself on the other sofa and lay down, sighing, her arm over her eyes.

"Where is the count?" I asked.

"Upstairs, Le Naïf. You get to clean him up," said Le Jumeau. He rested his head back, and his dark lips curled into a lazy smile as he looked at me through half-closed lids, his hand open on the blond one's bobbing head. "You'll find everything you need in the box on the chest of drawers. Go on," he said. "We need to get him home."

I found the count alone, naked, on a chair. His droopy brown eyes were unfocused, his back slick with blood. The floor was smeared with it. I gagged, and had to open the window, sticking my head into the air and taking long, desperate breaths. I would get used to it soon enough.

## 28

In the weeks that followed, when Masha was alone, or on a break in the nursing home, she would sometimes reach inside her purse and take out Derbhan Nevsky's cream-colored card. The black lettering was embossed:

PERFORMING ARTISTS MANAGEMENT
DERBHAN NEVSKY

She ran her thumb over it again and again, until it was floppy and worn. It didn't do any harm to keep the card.

Eli asked her out three more times. One night, as Masha was sitting on her bed brushing her hair, Yehudis skipped in and bounced onto her own bed, beaming across the room at her.

"Guess what?" she asked.

"What?" asked Masha.

"Mrs. Cohen just called Mommy and they talked for a long time. She told her Eli's mother is *sure* Eli's gonna propose to you. She didn't say when or anything, but she said there was no question that was his intention."

"Oh, wow," breathed Masha.

"Oh, Mashie, I'm so happy for you! You're so lucky," said Yehudis, who had leapt onto Masha's bed and was hugging her, tears in her eyes.

"He hasn't asked me yet," said Masha.

"He will, though. Mrs. Cohen said there was no question! Don't tell Mommy I told you, she doesn't think I know, I listened to her tell Daddy."

"When is Mommy planning on telling me?" asked Masha.

"In a minute. I'm going back downstairs. Oh, this is so exciting, Masha, he's so cute!" Yehudis disappeared. Happiness stole into Masha's heart and settled in, a surprise visitor.

The next day, Eli came for her. She walked out of the house in a long yellow dress. At the restaurant, she ordered fries, but she couldn't eat them. Eli sat with his black hat tipped back from his forehead, his relaxed, open face bathed in warm light from the window.

"Let's get married, Masha Edelman," he said.

"I'm worried I would maybe disappoint you," Masha said.

"I know you're delicate. I know you went to New York that time. I know all that."

"Why would you want someone like that?"

"Your health doesn't worry me. Whatever comes up . . . we'll deal with. And . . . people do crazy stuff. It doesn't mean you're a bad person. I mean, you're not gonna stop performing the mitzvahs, you're gonna honor Shabbat, you'll raise our kids Jewish, right? I'm not so by-the-book either," he said. "I'm on the Internet, I read, I know what's goin' on out there . . . it's okay, I figure, as long as you do what you need to do."

"Okay, let's do it," she said. "But it has to be soon."

"How soon?"

"As soon as possible."

When Masha came home and dropped the news, Pearl burst into tears. Then she spent an hour and a half calling family and close friends to invite them for the *l'chaim* that evening. Miriam was in charge of buying wine, Yehudis and Alyshaya made the salads. Suri and the little kids helped Trina, the housekeeper, clean the kitchen and set the table under Miriam's nervy supervision. Dovid and Simchee arrived with Mordecai at six, already armed with the news. Mordecai had moist eyes when he hugged his daughter. His beard felt silky against her cheek. That evening, bride and groom were both frozen in endless flash-whitened images, their happy smiles sweetening the memory sticks of all present. Masha was almost blinded from all the flashes going off. Her belly was filled with glad fear. She and Eli didn't touch, but their not-touching felt like something palpable; the space between them was a pillow of energy. All the girls crowded in on Masha to tell her, breathless, how cute Eli was. Which he was.

The next day, she called Hugh up and told him he would have to find another scene partner.

"I'm getting married," she said. He was quiet for a long moment.

"Well, you made a choice. That's the main thing," he said. He sounded sad.

"Yeah, 'bye, good luck," she said, snapping her phone shut. This was the way it had to be. This was good and clean and right. This way and no other. She prayed to Hashem to keep her safe from her own selfishness. I tried to talk to her, but she wouldn't listen. She executed all dissident thoughts, regardless of their origin.

Eli presented Masha with a diamond ring, a bracelet. The ring had a simple, pretty setting. The diamond was bigger than any of her sisters' rings. Eli's parents were well off. The diamond bracelet shone on her wrist, a thread of light.

Eli came to the Edelman house for Shabbos. He sang with the other men. Masha didn't think of joining in. I did what I could to make her want to, but she swatted the thoughts away. After dinner, Eli had to leave. He was staying at the Weingotts' next door. He couldn't sleep in the house; too much temptation. The family gave them a moment alone at the door as they said goodbye.

"See you tomorrow," he said to her, his voice low. There were inches between them. She felt desire flush through her body.

"Okay," she whispered.

The next morning, I rested on Mordecai's fur hat as the whole family walked to the synagogue: Pearl, holding Estie by the hand; Mordecai, pushing Leah in her stroller; Dovid and Simchee, looking at the ground; Ezra and Suri, bickering; Miriam with her teeming brood of four lively children; the still-visiting, infuriatingly handsome Eli; and, finally, Masha and Yehudis, walking behind the procession, giggling to each other. Alyshaya and her baby had stayed home, but Yitzak, her husband, ran to catch up with Eli. It was an impressive phalanx of people, I can tell you. Once inside the building, men and women of the family parted; the women and girls walked into the back room reserved for females, the men and young Ezra to the front of the shul. As the two sexes beat a path to their requisite doors, I hovered in the air, torn. Though we did not have a synagogue in Paris in my time, I had gone to services in Metz, when we went to visit my cousins. I remember feeling so important as a boy, walking to the main body of the synagogue with my brother and father, as my mother crammed herself onto the balcony with the other women, where they were corralled like wild animals. Today, though, I decided to stick with the girls. I didn't want to leave Masha. It was the end of our time together. Once she was married, I might as well croak.

The women's section in the back of the synagogue was a little cramped, but pleasant, with freshly upholstered benches and an ingenious barrier constructed of mirrored louvers the shape of venetian blinds. In this way, the women could see slivers of men in black hats and hear the service, yet the men could not see into the female enclave at all. Here, Masha was free to sing. Her eerie, low, soulful voice blended with that of Yehudis and Pearl, Miriam and Suri and Estie, and all the other women standing with their prayer books in their hands. The raw power of their voices was stunning. I could see why it would be distracting to the men, who were, after all, trying to pray with total attention, thinking only of the Creator. I flew onto one of the mirrored slats, resting for a moment between the two worlds. Then I took off to join the men for a while. Floating over the field of black, swaying hats, I lowered myself gradually, scanning faces, until I found our menfolk toward the front, near the cantor. Dovid was davening furiously, rocking back and forth like he had a spring in his waist. The others were subtler in their movements, but they were all swept up in prayer. I swung down, taking the chance to get a real close-up of my competition. Eli's eyes were closed; he didn't notice me buzzing around his face. This was the villain who was taking my girl away. Him and his dimpled chin. What would come of this union? How would Masha forget what she wanted, be reabsorbed into this world? Could she be happy with him? I had to admit, Eli was appealing. They would have laughs, sensual delight. I wanted him to die. Yet that seemed beyond my meager powers. What could one little demon do against the power of destiny? I traveled back to the women's section, landed on Pearl's handbag, and glowered.

A few weeks later, at the engagement party held in the basement of the shul, Eli was break-dancing with some of the other young men. The women danced with one another on their side of the room. Watching Eli, for the first time since she was a little child Masha thought it would be nice to have a baby.

Pearl drove her to the best wig salon in Brooklyn, the one the Hasidic ladies used, and had her fitted. Alyshaya, the hair expert, came along. Pearl made Masha come outside five times to check the color of various lustrous dark wigs against her own hair. Each time Masha lowered her head to pull another one on and flipped the hair over, she looked like a different person. The first wig had bangs; this girl was funky and independent. The next had a bob. She seemed serious and cute. She even got Pearl to let her try on a long blond one. Masha found herself shockingly pretty in it, but she didn't dare say anything.

Pearl laughed. "Honey. This is an everyday sheitel you're buying."

Alyshaya, who was busy trying on a half wig, her own splendid one flung over a chair, her fine frizzy mop in a careless ponytail, walked up to Masha's chair.

"You got the best coloring in the family, don't change it. Plus she got the best hair," she said ruefully, turning to her mother. "It doesn't even frizz up."

"Blond is more for the older women," added the wig maker, an Israeli woman with a generous, elastic mouth.

"Good idea," Pearl said with a laugh, "go blond when you're my age, you'll need to by then." Two very young women in jeans were combing out wigs in the corner. At this statement they both tittered, and one of them said something in rapid Spanish. The Edelman women looked over at them with good-natured surprise, then returned to their conversation.

"You should get a new wig, Mommy!" said Alyshaya.

"Yeah," said Masha. "Try one on."

Pearl shook her head, filled with pleasure to be with her girls. "I don't need one!"

"Are you kidding?" said Alyshaya. "This is—how old is this thing?" she asked, touching her mother's auburn head.

"I don't know, maybe . . . maybe eight? Eight years?"

"The color has totally faded! You need a new wig!" exclaimed Alyshaya.

"First we get Masha set up with everything. Then we take a look at the bank account," said Pearl firmly. "I personally loved the second one you tried on."

In the end, they decided. The hair on the wig was black, unnaturally plentiful, glossy, of unknown origin. Shorter than Masha's own hair, it was layered, stylish, and curled over her shoulders. Wearing the wig was exciting; she seemed to be another woman—someone organized, together. She couldn't wait to wear this wig.

One day Bridget called her.

"Are you all right?"

"Yeah," said Masha.

"You sure?"

"I'm just—I'm getting married."

"I know. If that's what you want, Masha, congratulations. You seem young to be getting married to me, though it's none of my business. I'll be sorry to lose you."

"I can't do both things," said Masha.

"I know," said Bridget. "I realize it's hard and I respect your choice. I just want you to know that . . . if you ever need anything, I'm here. Okay?"

"Okay," said Masha. "'Bye." She hung up. Bridget thought she was being brainwashed! Masha was pissed off. Why should her stupid, childish desire to pretend to be other people be more important than her God?

I was extremely depressed in this period. I even lost interest in sex. I just crawled around very slowly, like a dying fly, which was what I felt like. The Old Bastard was winning. My beloved was going to end up as a good Jewess, after all. Married and muzzled. I tried to get into her thoughts day after day, I pleaded with her not to waste her talent, but she derided me.

At last I was able to wring a single concession from my newly chastened queen. I told her she needed to go to the class one more time, to give Bridget the money she owed her, and to say goodbye. Why should she slink into the night as if ashamed? These people had been kind to her, they had believed in her; she owed them a final visit. It was a last-ditch effort, but it worked. Masha put on her jacket at five-fifteen and said goodbye to the nurse on duty at the nursing home. She walked the ten blocks to Bridget's school, looking up at the sky. The days were long again. Summer. She felt happy and light.

She got to the school half an hour before class and walked back to Bridget's office, the envelope of money in her pocket. Bridget was at her desk, scanning the newspaper. She looked up over her reading glasses and smiled.

"Masha," she said. "It's good to see you. Sit down."

"I came to bring you the money, what I have, it's not everything, but I'll pay you back when I can," Masha said, placing the envelope on the desk.

"That's fine," said Bridget. "Thank you. Sit down. Are you all right?"

"I'm good," said Masha, sitting and standing in one motion. "I should probably go."

"Why not stay for the scenes?" asked Bridget. "It should be fun. Hugh and Shelley are doing *Sexual Perversity in Chicago*. Ellie and Mike are doing *Summer and Smoke*, which if I never see that play again it will be too soon, but don't tell *them* that." Masha smiled, embarrassed to be confided in this way. Bridget was treating her like an equal.

"Come on," said Bridget. "You can sit with me. For old times' sake."

This was a big deal. Nobody sat next to Bridget, except for occasional guest teachers. Once, a former student, Jeff Huff, now a working actor and even a bit of a TV star, sat beside her and gave his critique of the scenes. The fact of his fame was nothing compared to being allowed to sit beside Bridget, to be sanctified by her. Now it was Masha. She felt elect. Hugh and Shelley finished setting up their scene. Hugh gave Masha a surprised thumbs-up when he saw her. Now she could hear the yawnlike sounds of his relaxation exercises, and imagined him stretching backstage, in his own world. As he and Shelley played the scene, Masha had to fight off an acute feeling of possessiveness. Hugh was *her* scene partner. He and Shelley were funny, slick; their timing was excellent. Masha's cheeks were going hot. She wanted to be up there so bad.

After the scenes were over, Masha hugged all the girls and smiled at the guys. They all congratulated her, admired her ring. They told her to come by and see them once in a while. Hugh just gave her a nod and slipped away. She could tell he was upset, maybe angry with her. As she walked down the hall into the front room, she saw Miriam standing there, clutching her large purple handbag like it was a life preserver. A bolt of fear branched through Masha's belly, flashed into her wrists.

She walked up to her sister and just stood there, her heart pounding.

"I went to the nursing home to talk to you about the wedding during your break and they told me you left, that you usually leave around five-thirty on a Tuesday," Miriam hissed, taking Masha's elbow and guiding her out the door. "Then, when I walked out, I saw you down the block. I followed you here. I've been waiting two hours."

"I was just saying goodbye," said Masha.

"Walk fast. Mommy's waiting."

"You told her?"

"Of course I called her. You expect me to lie?"

"I'm not asking you to lie."

"Not telling her would be lying."

When they got to the house, Pearl was very quiet, tense. She took Masha's jacket from her and hung it in the hall closet. Mordecai was in the living room, pacing the wooden floor, his white shirt wrinkled and half untucked from his black pants, the knots of his protective fringes dangling from his thick waist.

"I don't understand how you could be this sneaky," he said. "That's what I don't understand. You need to perform? Is that it? Is that what was happening that Shabbos? You need to perform in front of men?"

"Daddy. Please."

"Just explain to me how you got so devious. How did this happen? I don't recognize you! You aren't my Masha. Who are you?"

"Morty—" Pearl began, wiping a tear from her face.

"Don't—" The gentle Mordecai put up his hand with a rare show of firmness. "This is something that needs to be talked through. This is not a thing to gloss over and pretend it didn't happen. Masha. Sit down. Tell me. How are you paying for these acting classes?"

"With the money from the nursing home. I was just dropping a payment off. I quit the class, Daddy."

"So you got this job at the nursing home which we were all so proud of so you could sneak away to, and afford, acting classes with a bunch of—who knows who with? Boys, I assume?"

"And girls. It was nothing about the boys—it was just learning how to act. You knew I loved it, it's not a surprise."

"What's a surprise, young lady, is how willing you were to deceive your family and your husband-to-be."

"But I quit," she said miserably.

"Did you want to quit?" Mordecai asked her, his voice softening.

"I don't know," she said. "I wanted to want to. Yes."

"I think we have to tell Eli's parents," Mordecai said to Pearl.

"Please, no," Masha begged.

"I will not let you turn me into a dishonest man!" said Mordecai, his face reddening.

"At least let me tell Eli myself."

"Masha," said Mordecai. "You know I love you and I want you to be happy. This is not a trap, this way of life, this house is not a prison. I hope more than anything that all my children follow the Torah as I follow it, as your mother does. If you leave, you will break our hearts, but: we will not chain you up. This situation is not just about you, what's more. It's about Eli. I will not let you ruin a man's life. He wants a wife, not a—a snake in the grass. Or an actress. We all want you to be something, Masha, we wanted you to get an education, it was your choice to drop out, your choice not to go to Israel for a year." He looked up at Pearl gloomily. "We should never have let her leave college. It's all this sitting around, this is what it's led to."

The next morning, Eli and Masha sat at the kitchen table in silence. The house was empty, save for Pearl upstairs with the baby. Eli kept turning his tall glass around and around in his fingers. Masha watched his shivering cola: endless tiny bubbles kept breaking the surface, like feeding fish. The kitchen clock sounded so loud; she had never noticed how loud that clock was. Each tick had a tail, a little comet of sound—like a snare drum.

"I gotta be honest, I'm in a quandary here," Eli said, his voice cracking. Masha's eyes were fixed on his soda bubbles. "How long were you taking that class?"

"Three months," she said.

"So the whole time we've known each other you've been secretly going to that class, and you never mentioned it?"

"I wanted to. I just . . . couldn't get myself to say it. I didn't think you would like it."

"Well, I guess we'll never know now."

"Would you have?" she asked.

"Would I have liked you taking acting classes, with guys? No. But . . . you know I'm not so by the book . . . The thing is, you weren't just taking that class for fun, you were hoping it was gonna lead some-place, right? I don't understand how you were going in two directions at once."

"I quit because of you, though," she said softly. Even as she said it, she felt it was not true. Why had she quit? She couldn't remember. She felt stupid, fuddled.

"Is it more the class, or the not telling you?" she asked, her voice high, meek, not her own.

He was quiet for a while, turning the glass around and around. "I just feel like I don't know you like I thought I did, and it scares me," he said, looking up at her. His face was reddening, swelling, like an angry pimple coming to a head. She realized with a shock that he was about to cry.

"I'm sorry," she said.

"Me too," he said. Then he got up and left.

Masha walked upstairs slowly and lay down on her bed. She took off the diamond ring and the bracelet, set them glimmering on the bedside table. She felt leaden. Pearl came and sat beside her, stroking her hair until the door banged and the first of the kids came home. As the afternoon wore on, Masha could hear her younger siblings coming home from school in waves. The house filled up with sound. She sat up, her hair a shining cascade. She walked downstairs, touching the mezuzah screwed inside the kitchen doorjamb, then kissed her fingers where she had touched it.

"Mommy," she said, "I'm going on a little walk."

"Where?" Pearl asked. "You want Yehudis to come with you?"

"No, please. I won't go far."

She stood on the boardwalk and looked out. The sky was the color of day-old snow. The sea was camouflage green. A Styrofoam cup was embedded in the gray sand; beside it, a dirty sneaker. Shreds of torn paper napkin swirled in the breeze like frantic white birds. A heavy young jogger plodded reluctantly along the waterline in a maroon sweatshirt, his gaze on the ground, hands in his pockets.

As if a sash blind had been snapped up angrily to wake a lazy sleeper, light washed over the sea, turning it silver-white. The jogger's hoodie went luminous red, the sand a strip of yellow. Lured by the light, Masha walked down the metal steps to the beach, numbly placing one foot in front of the other, staring into the blinding water. The sand dragged at her boots. She felt suspended above her thoughts, incapable of anything but walking toward the sea. Her mind was as empty as a shiny metal bowl, containing only what was around it, in warped reflection: the blinding sea, the pale sand, the jogger's daub of red bobbing along, the sky pale blue between torn gray clouds. This light was an accident of beauty in an ugly afternoon. It felt like she had walked a long, long way to see this.

She found Derbhan Nevsky's worn business card stowed in the zipper pocket of her purse and called him. He was at Bridget's, ten minutes away. He knew just where she was. He would be right there. Fast as he could. She sat on the cool sand and waited. Once she saw him standing on the boardwalk, hopping up and down like an electrified scarecrow, she texted her mother: *I love you, Mommy. Don't look for me. Will call soon. Masha.* Then she pried off the back of the phone, took out the SIM card, and flicked it into the sea.

## 29

Leslie's stepson, Bud, was naturally deadpan, electively Buddhist, possibly a little depressed. Even as a child, he had always been somber. By the time he was ten, he was sorting Leslie's mail into piles: bills, junk, and personal. On this particular morning, he emerged from the basement carrying his baby girl, Chloe, on one skinny hip. Leslie looked up from his cereal.

"And there she is . . . ," said Leslie, opening his heavy arms. Bud handed Leslie the baby and watched with his serious face as she bobbed up and down on his stepfather's wide knee.

"She looks so much smaller on your lap," he observed, untying the plastic cover of a loaf of toast bread.

"Everything's relative," said Leslie. "Jenny still asleep?"

"No, she's just lying there staring at the ceiling," said Bud. "She had a rough night."

"You look okay, though," said Leslie, addressing the baby, who was sucking on her fist.

"Yeah, she's great. Babies are destructive forces," said Bud, grabbing his toast as it sprang from the toaster.

"Is she hungry?"

"She just ate," said Bud, ripping into the toast with his teeth and slurping a mouthful of coffee. "I gotta get to work. Can you hang on to her for ten minutes till Jenny gets up here?"

"Sure," said Leslie. "Where's the job?"

"In Quogue. The same guy as last year, remember the addition to the pool house? He's adding to that."

"An addition to the addition. Always a sound idea," said Leslie.

"I think he just likes people around. He's an old guy." Bud fastened his tool belt around his narrow hips, kissed his baby daughter on the head, and walked out the door.

Deirdre came in wearing a fluffy peach robe. "How long has she been up?" she asked, taking the baby.

"Bud just left. Jenny had a bad night."

"Okay," said Deirdre, rocking the baby and sniffing the top of her head. "We'll watch you, won't we, Chloe?"

Bud and his nineteen-year-old wife, Jenny, had moved in with Leslie and Deirdre weeks before the baby was born. They just needed a place to start out, Bud said. Leslie helped Bud fix up a little efficiency apartment in the basement for the newlyweds. It had everything they needed, minus light—but they spent most of their time upstairs with Leslie and Deirdre anyway, and out at the pool when the weather was fine. It was lovely having the baby around. But Jenny believed in large families. What's more, she and Bud both had a certain passive openness about them that, Leslie surmised, might not lend itself to the regular practice of birth control. He imagined a baseball-team-sized passel of Buddhist grandkids bubbling out of that basement in the next few years. What he couldn't quite picture was Bud supporting them all.

An hour later, Leslie was walking a slack, unconscious Chloe around on his shoulder while he talked to Vera on the phone. Little mother Jenny appeared, puffy-eyed, her hair in fraying braids, reached up and peeled her sleeping daughter from Leslie's massive shoulder. The baby's body kept a crescent shape, as though she'd been molded to Leslie's arm, her legs folded up tight. Jenny laid her down gently in a little bassinet by the couch. Unfurling, eyes shut, the baby stretched, grunting and rubbing her nose. She missed Leslie's warmth. Leslie watched as Jenny wiggled a pacifier against the baby's lips, slipped it into the tiny mouth. His granddaughter fell asleep again, her mouth working the rubber, limbs relaxing. He poured Jenny a cup of coffee and handed it to her, the phone still clamped to his ear.

"And finally, a guy just called about a big job," Vera announced. Her voice was nasal, no-nonsense, reassuringly abrupt. Leslie adored that voice. "Ross Coe. He has a boat he wants you to look at." Ross Coe. It was that weirdo shipping guy in East Hampton—the one with the rubber face.

"Oh, boy," said Leslie. "What kind of boat?"

"He says it's vintage, but he won't elaborate. 'A potential masterpiece' were his exact words."

"That guy is an unappealing character."

"It sounds like money, though," said Vera. "Vintage masterpieces take time. Remember what I said about the Very Rich."

"I better go out there," said Leslie. "Where is the boat?"

"He's had it towed down from Rhode Island. It hasn't been in the water for years."

"Hull's gonna be cracked."

"All the more work for you," said Vera cheerfully. "Around two would be ideal, he said."

Leslie sighed. "Today?"

"He said you've been out there before."

"Yeah, I know where it is," said Leslie glumly.

At the appointed hour, Leslie drove his truck over to the Coe house to have a look at that mystery yacht. He crept along the circular drive, gravel crackling beneath his tires, and parked in front of the gargantuan dwelling, which was far bigger than he had realized when he'd picked up Don and Libby on the night of the Green Fairy. It was an old-fashioned, shingled mansion, probably built in the 1920s, with quaint light green shutters pinned back against the brown shingles. Immaculately pruned roses were on parade all along the front of the house. Ross Coe himself was walking toward Leslie's truck before he'd even turned the engine off, dressed in a pair of khaki shorts, pink polo shirt with the collar flipped up, and loafers. His wavy hair was freshly brushed, and his reconstructed face, shocking at any time of day, wore the pouty smile of a socialite. Leslie realized as he stepped down from the truck that Coe had a woman's face. That's what it was: he was a youngish man, with the face of an older woman who had had a lot of plastic surgery. Leslie wanted to turn around and get right back in his truck, but instead he leaned down, put out his broad hand, and shook Coe's small, soft paw, noticing as he did so that Coe was wearing a smear of gloss on his swollen lips.

"Where's the boat?" Leslie asked, barely able to contain his disgust.

"Just around back, in the big garage," said Coe. "I can't tell you how glad I am to find you."

"How long has it been out of the water?" Leslie asked.

"Oh, I'd say three, four years," said Coe. "The guy who was going to restore her had a fatal heart attack, and the family just left her rotting in the barn."

He led Leslie around the house, following a strand of the driveway, until they reached a large garage, shingled to match the house. In the background, Leslie made out a long pool and a Palladian-style stone structure, with several columns and a domed roof. Coe noticed him looking.

"That's the nymphaeum," said Coe. "A folly of my mother's. She was always building Greek doodads. She was Greek. I'll show you around later," he offered, tugging at the sliding garage door, which rolled up with a clatter. There, gleaming inside, was a large wooden motor yacht. Its black hull glowed dull in the dark of the garage. It was a broken-down beauty. Leslie's stomach lurched at the sight of her.

"A Futura," Leslie said. "I've never seen one with a black hull."

"It's the only one they made," answered Coe, stroking the flank of the boat proudly. "It was custom-built for the son of a Chris-Craft dealer. Stayed in the family all this time. But it's been neglected for years. It's a wreck, in fact, wouldn't you say so, Mr. Senzatimore?"

Leslie ignored the question and walked around the boat. The hull was cracked, as predicted. The teak decks were buckled in places.

"You'll have to tow her outside for me to get a real idea of what we're up against," said Leslie.

"But she's a beauty, isn't she?" asked Coe.

"The Futura Sports Express is a great boat," said Leslie. "They'll last forever, if you take care of them."

"And I intend to! I want to invest in this boat. I want her to be perfect," said Coe, clasping his hands together, his Carol Channing face beaming up at the hulking craft. "Boats are in my blood, Mr. Senzatimore. Nothing gets me more thrilled than a beautiful boat that looks like a broken-down old woman. It's just so thrilling, isn't it, to bring a boat back to life?"

"Yes, it is," said Leslie. This restoration could end up costing hundreds of man-hours. He might even be able to send Stevie to that private elementary school for the deaf if he took this on. On the other hand, he would be working for Ross Coe. And that gave him a very uneasy feeling.

"Come have something to drink while I get the boat pulled out for you."

"I can come back tomorrow," said Leslie.

"If you have time I would love you to look at it today. To give me a sense of what it would be."

"I can't give you a full estimate today."

"That's all right. Take as long as you need. I would rather the boat not leave the premises, though," said Coe slyly.

"Not leave the premises?"

"No. I would like you to do the work here."

"I can't do that," said Leslie. "I don't work alone. And . . . my whole shop is set up for boat repair."

"I have the space. You will have every piece of equipment you could possibly need. Everything. I will pay for every scrap of an hour you spend setting things up here."

"I have to run my business," said Leslie.

"It's just . . . ," said Coe, looking up at the sky, as if for support, "I want the work to be done here. In my presence. I want to . . . see it transformed—with my own eyes. That's why I'm spending the money."

Leslie sighed. This man was repulsive. Taking this job was a commitment to more or less living with him for up to a year. Yet—he couldn't turn it down.

"If you have it towed outside, I'll have a look at it, and then we can talk about whether it's possible to do here," said Leslie, looking at his shoes as they followed Coe's size fives around the side of the house and up the steps to the wraparound porch. A dark-haired man in khakis and a blue polo shirt was standing at the ready with a tray of glasses and a silver pitcher. The smell of roses was dense in the back of the house. Leslie sat down in a wicker chair. It creaked, and he rose swiftly, worried it would collapse under him.

"You're all right," said Coe.

The khakied man unobtrusively poured out lemonade. Leslie looked up at him.

"Thanks," he said. The butler smiled in a self-erasing way. Leslie leaned back in the uncomfortable chair, took a reluctant sip, and glared down the length of the shimmering blue-bottomed pool. Three figures sat at the other end, in the nymphaeum. One of them was gesturing emphatically. He popped out of his seat, waving his arms around and pacing back and forth.

"That's Derbhan Nevsky," said Ross Coe. "You met him a few weeks ago, when you came by."

Leslie nodded. He didn't remember the name. Once Nevsky rose and started walking toward them, though, he recognized him. He was still talking, flanked by two very young women. One of them had a fine spray of white-blond hair, and loped along in a pair of tiny shorts, her giraffe legs unfolding and straightening with each step. The other was wearing a dress to her ankles. She had long black hair. In the rippling heat, Leslie had the sense that she was shimmering, immaterial, like a spirit. Alarm gathered in him as the young woman approached. She was looking ahead, listening to Nevsky intently. By the time she had reached the porch, Leslie was actually frightened. He had no idea why.

"Leslie Senzatimore," Ross Coe said, "you've met Derbhan Nevsky. And these are my guests, Shelley Douglas and Masha . . ."

"White," said Nevsky. Masha looked over at him. It was the first time she had heard her new name spoken out loud. Masha White. Masha White. She looked over at the big man holding a glass of lemonade between his fingers. He was mountainous. His bleached-out eyes looked up at her, squinting against the sun. When she approached him, he was doused in her shadow. He stood up, rising into the light like a swimmer emerging from a dark pond. She looked up at him and put out her hand, as Nevsky had told her to. The big hand felt rough. It was the first time she had shaken a strange man's hand. The feeling of closeness was surprisingly pleasant. She left her hand in Leslie's for a moment, a second too long.

"Good job," whispered Nevsky. She let her hand fall from Leslie's grip. He sat down, her shadow traveling up his body again.

"So, girls, what's the plan for today?" asked Coe, rubbing his palms together with relish.

"We have elocution lessons for Miss White, and a trainer coming for the two of them," said Nevsky. "Then a little lie-down. And I have to get them to Bridget's class."

"Surinder will drive you," said Coe. "Will we have a late supper afterwards?"

"Don't worry about that," said Nevsky. Then, seeing Coe's crestfallen expression: "I'll send the girls straight back. I'm hoping to have a dinner date," said Nevsky.

"Intrigue!" said Coe, pursing his lips.

Masha and Shelley followed Nevsky into a big Victorian house under renovation, just down the street from the Patchogue Boat Club. Coe happened to be turning the house into apartments, Nevsky explained. The girls would be staying in the first finished unit. They walked past several workers carrying boards and hammers, up the circular staircase, down a hall, and into the rent-free apartment. The white room was glazed with light, carved up with brilliant rectangles of sunshine, and smelled of fresh paint. A mod red couch and two black chairs cut streamlined shapes out of the back wall.

"This place is spanking new!" cried Nevsky. "No one has lived in this apartment. You're the only tenants in the building so far."

"Isn't the furniture great?" exclaimed Shelley.

"Courtesy of Helga Coe. We'll get you curtains," said Nevsky, trotting past the girls and peeking into the bedroom, then popping his head back out. "Pretty nice, eh?"

"Yeah," said Masha, walking past him into the spacious bedroom and peeking into the bathroom, which had one bare window with a view of the marina down the street, boats gleaming in the sun.

"You have the charm of a Victorian, with all the amenities of modern life," Nevsky explained as she returned to the living room, his arms whipping around as he indicated the various appliances. "Washer and dryer are downstairs in the laundry room. But you got your dishwasher, garbage disposal, coffeemaker, all that's in the kitchen. There's gonna be Wi-Fi eventually! I got you a few groceries, and later I can take you to the store so you can pick things you like, or if you have any dietary requirements, if you're vegetarian, or—"

"I'm not a vegetarian," said Shelley. "I eat whatever."

"I'm not vegetarian," said Masha.

"I don't know if you, ah—Masha, if you—"

Masha turned and looked at Derbhan Nevsky. He was asking if she was going to be eating kosher. "Don't worry about me," she said.

"Truth is," he said, nodding, Masha thought, with approval, "you'll be eating at the Coe house most of the time, or in the city between auditions." Nevsky sat on the brilliant red couch, shielding his eyes from the sun. "This is going to be a very busy few months, girls. Sit down." They each sat on a stiff black chair. Nevsky snapped the fingers of both his hands once, as if to command his own attention. Then he began.

"First off, I need to get you ready. Each as an individual. Masha, you need to tone down the accent. Shelley, you need conditioner. Just kidding, but seriously for both of you, trips to the beauty parlor. Exercise! Facials! Manicures! Shopping! I don't just want men looking at you two on the street. I want them *following* you. Bridget's class— obviously, you need to work on the technique, that's a lifelong process. Once you have your confidence up, we start meeting casting directors. General meetings. Auditions to follow. If necessary, Bridget's agreed to coach you on your auditions. All expenses paid. You understand?"

Shelley laughed. "I feel like I just won the grand prize in a game show," she said.

Masha looked at Nevsky. He was wearing his floppy white tennis hat at an angle today. She wondered if he was a legitimate person. Yet, if Bridget was letting this happen, it had to be okay.

"What do you get out of it?" she asked.

Nevsky's face brightened. "I'm glad you asked that," he said, taking two contracts out of a battered briefcase and handing Masha a pen.

"Ten percent, that's all. Ten percent of anything you girls make while I'm your manager. If you make nothing after six months, you owe nothing. I'm rebuilding an empire here. You're my first two bricks."

He took them to the grocery store. Masha chose a toothbrush, toothpaste, simple toiletries, makeup. She picked up some underwear from a sale barrel near the entrance. Then she walked down the aisles secretly looking for kosher meat products. All she could find were hot dogs. She took a couple of packets and threw them in the cart.

Nevsky dropped them off at the apartment and told them he would pick them up at five to take them to Bridget's class. They should eat a snack, then they would have dinner later, with the Coes. Masha threw two huge kosher beef hot dogs into boiling water.

"I can lend you clothes," said Shelley, "till you have time to get something. Unless you're planning on going home to pick stuff up . . ."

"No," said Masha. "If I go back, I'll never get out again." She gave a hot dog in a roll to Shelley, then, before taking a bite of her own, she whispered a blessing over it.

"What are you saying? Grace?" asked Shelley.

"Kind of. It's a *bracha*. A blessing."

"You always do that when you eat?"

"Or drink," said Masha.

"Every sip?"

"Nah, just once, then even if you're drinking out of a bottle of water for an hour, the *bracha* lasts the whole time. There's different *brachas* for meat, dairy, water, wine, whatever."

"How do you remember it all?"

Masha shrugged. "I knew most of them by the time I was five."

"My grandparents always said grace at dinner," said Shelley. "And my dad, I think, I don't exactly remember."

"Did he die?"

"No, he just relocated." Shelley looked over at Masha. "It's so weird how things happen," she said. "I mean, if it wasn't for you walking by the school, no way would you and I have ever even met. You would just—excuse me for saying this. But—you would be one of those people I stare at all the time."

"What do you mean?" asked Masha.

"Well, I mean, the men who wear the hats and the sidelocks and the women are all covered up, with the thick stockings. Those people."

"Yeah?" said Masha.

"I always want to know why. Why do they dress like that? Why do the women wear wigs and wear long sleeves in August?"

"It's something called *tznius*," said Masha. "It's just a kind of modesty. If people are staring at your legs or whatever, they won't see your *neshama*, your soul. Who you are as a person. Those people you're noticing are probably Hasidic, which I'm not, but it comes to almost the same thing. They're just more . . . more."

"But what if who you are is someone who likes to wear really short skirts?" asked Shelley. Masha laughed, shaking her head.

Shelley lent her a jean skirt that came down to her ankles and a baggy striped top, choosing a tartan miniskirt with a little white sweater and platforms for herself. As they walked out of their building they saw a light blue vintage Mercedes idling loudly at the curb. The back window glided down and Nevsky waved from the crack. He was on the phone. A slender man in a black suit and white turban emerged from the driver's side and opened the door for them.

"I am Surinder Multani," he said with a kind smile. "I am the driver of Mr. Coe."

When they arrived at the school, Masha scurried from the car into the building. She didn't feel safe so close to her own home. When she got inside, Hugh was standing there.

"Hey," he said. "I hear you moved."

"Yeah," she said.

Hugh passed his hand over his spiky hair. "Derbhan Nevsky. He's legit?"

"I guess so," she said. "I couldn't think of another way."

After class, Bridget took Masha back to her office.

"You've made a break," she rasped.

"Yeah," said Masha. "I still can't believe it."

"Your mother and your sister were here asking about you."

"They were?"

247

"I told them you were fine and that you would be in touch with them when you felt ready."

"What did they say?"

"Your sister—"

"Miriam?"

"She was pretty upset with me."

"Sorry."

"I have no problem with being a buffer, but I think you should write to them."

"I will."

"You have every right to do this, you know. You're an adult. Are you okay?"

"Yeah." Masha shrugged.

"Masha. Listen. I feel responsible for you in a way. You know I hoped that you would choose this work, to try to learn the craft of this work. And now you've chosen to, and I'm nervous as hell that it's going to mess you up."

"It was my choice," said Masha.

"I know," said Bridget. "But . . . use me. Use me as a sounding board, adviser, whatever. Talk to me whenever you need to. It's going to be a big, gradual process."

"What is?"

"Integration. I don't even think you are aware of how different you are."

"I'm not that different," said Masha.

"You don't understand," said Bridget, tucking in her chin and fixing Masha with a steady look. "You need to be rewired."

Jeans: indigo, acid-washed, boot-legged, peg-legged, high-waisted, low-waisted, rhinestoned, butt-lifting. Organized into piles, crammed onto shelves, fanned out on tables; the sheer intimidating volume of them made Masha want to curl up in her long gray dress, pull it over her feet, and weep.

Shelley had several pairs draped over her arm and was efficiently checking the size of another. "You need at least two pairs," she said. "No one has just one pair of jeans."

Masha nodded. She had been quiet all morning. She had known this would happen, that it had to happen. If she wanted to be an actress, eventually she would have to wear pants.

The dressing room was painted fuchsia; a mirror stretched mercilessly from floor to ceiling. Masha turned from it, trying to shut the curtain completely so no crack of light showed. Her back to the mirror, she pulled up her dress, clamping it under her chin, and tugged on the first pair of jeans. As she pulled the stiff material up her legs, she felt she was being bifurcated, like a mermaid having her tail cut in two.

"How're you doing in there?" asked Shelley from outside the curtain.

"Not sure," said Masha, hopping up and down as she struggled with the zip.

"Can I see?" Masha opened the curtain a crack so that Shelley could sidle in.

"Wow," said Shelley, "those look great."

"They do?" asked Masha.

"Have you even looked at them yet?"

Masha turned and faced the mirror. There was a young woman in tight blue jeans. Nothing out of the ordinary in that. Yet how was she supposed to walk out in public like this? Her sex was right behind there at the place where her legs joined. She felt naked.

Nevsky popped into the store to pay. Then they all went out to lunch.

"Thanks for the clothes," said Masha.

"Yeah," said Shelley.

"Thank Ross Coe, not me," said Nevsky, gnawing on a ham sandwich. "For him, it's an investment." He drummed his fingers on the

249

table in a brief volley of nervous taps. "He's the primary stockholder in my new management company. He wants to help me do this right." With a jerk, he turned, hailing a passing waitress. "Excuse me, miss! Could I get a cuppa coffee here?" Then, his head snapping back to them: "You girls for coffee?"

Back in the light-smeared apartment, Masha set the crinkly bag of new clothes on the chintz bedspread and flopped down beside it, gazing up at the ceiling fan batting the air in slow rounds. She felt warm, and so alone in the silence. It was strange not to have her family talking in the next room, to know that Estie wouldn't bust in any minute with a complaint about Ezra, or Yehudis, spouting a stream of enthusiasm about some boy she'd seen through the barrier in shul. She was so used to Pearl walking in and gently asking her if she'd like a piece of toast, or a bowl of soup, or ice cream. She wanted to go home. *I'm nothing but a baby*, Masha chided, tears coming to her eyes as she closed them. Shelley woke her up an hour later. Time to go. Elocution class was next on her schedule. Masha peeked inside the plastic shopping bag. There were the three pairs of jeans, folded on top of one another along with the skimpy tops, the dress, and the bras. She had to start the rewiring. She pulled on a pair of the jeans. Again, the feeling of stiff cloth between her legs felt bizarre. In the bathroom she leaned in to the mirror and lined her eyelids with black pencil, coated her lashes with mascara. Her eyes looked enormous, biblical. Shelley walked in, all bare legs and fluffy white hair, her orange platform shoes revealing bright red toenails.

"Sexy mama!" she exclaimed.

Doris van Hoff was dressed in solid beige, spectacled, and a little shaky—whether from age or a slight palsy, Masha could not tell. She had an elegant way of speaking, however. For eradicating accents, Nevsky claimed, Doris was the best in the business. Her people went back to Dutch New York. The only danger was, if you studied with her too long you could end up sounding like Cary Grant. And she had an intimate style. Right off the bat she positioned herself so close to Masha's chair that their knees were touching. Then she tilted her head back, causing her limpid eyes to grow huge behind the thick lenses.

"Repeat this in a natural way," said Doris carefully, her great magnified eyes fixed on Masha's mouth. "*I forgot to open the door for you.*" Masha repeated the phrase.

Doris sat back and patted Masha's knee. "It's going to take a bit of time, dear. But we'll get there."

Masha tried using Doris's sharp consonants to sever and flatten her singsong words. She rolled the glacial syllables across her tongue like marbles. It felt impossible to change the way she talked. Plus, she felt truly naked in her tight jeans and tank top. She kept moving behind a floral armchair to hide her crotch from Doris van Hoff, but the woman called her back again and again so she could look down Masha's throat while she talked.

A high buzzing noise took Masha's attention as she enunciated. Through the window she could see a large black boat, and a man wearing ear mufflers, passing something back and forth over its dusty flank. It was the big man she'd met the other day on the porch, the one with the woman's name. Leslie.

Once her elocution lesson was done, Masha walked through the cool dark hallway, feeling herself drawn toward the back of the house. She felt her nipples contract and twist beneath the thin bra, goose bumps rise on the flesh of her bare arms. She rubbed her hands along her shoulders, anxious to get outside, into the sun. She wanted to talk to the man, see what he thought of her jeans.

Leslie looked up from his work as the screen door slammed and she stepped off the porch. A cordial little wave, and he went back to his work. Masha laughed at herself for thinking she would make such a big impression just because she was wearing a pair of blue jeans and a sleeveless shirt. That was all these people wore! She walked over to the black boat and leaned back on it a few feet away from Leslie, the hull nearly hot against her back. Her heart sped up as she waited. At last he looked up at her again from under his baseball cap, his deep-set pale blue eyes focused intently on her blushing face.

"What's up, Masha?"

"Nothing," she said. "Just kind of bored."

"Want a job?" he asked. Her eyes widened.

"I don't mean employment, I mean somethin' to do," he said.

"Sure." There were bits of paint on the interior that needed to be sanded down by hand. He helped her into the boat. Her skin ached a little where he touched it.

"I'm going to have to strip her right down," he called up to her. "This boat is a disaster."

"Why?" asked Masha.

"The people that owned her didn't take care of her."

"I've never been on a boat," said Masha, taking hold of the wide Bakelite steering wheel, swinging it left and right.

"You gotta be kidding me," said Leslie. Masha took up her sandpaper. They worked for a while in silence. She liked watching the honey-colored wood peek out from under the shiny black paint. It made her forget her nakedness a little. She rubbed until her arm hurt. She stood up straight, the shame returning.

"I'll get a couple of my guys out here soon," said Leslie, taking off his cap and wiping his brow with his forearm. His face was coated in sweat. "They'll make the work go faster. But they all have jobs they need to finish."

"I'm thirsty," Masha said. "You want a soda? They have Coke in bottles in the fridge."

"I'd love a Coke in a bottle." Leslie smiled.

Masha climbed down the ladder unaided and hurried away, hopping up the steps to the house. She couldn't stand being this exposed anymore. Would it be too weird, she wondered, to come back wearing something else? She had a dress in her bag, to wear for class later. No, she couldn't change entirely. She ducked into the room she'd been working in with Doris, where she had left Shelley's hoodie flopped over the arm of the big chair, and tugged it on, zipping it with relief. Then she fetched the Cokes from the empty, staff-neatened kitchen.

What was Ross Coe up to with a beauty like that? Leslie wondered as he waited. Nothing savory, he guessed. The girl came back with the bottles, a black sweatshirt zipped up to the neck.

"Got cold in there?" he asked.

"Yeah," she said, handing him a bottle. She seemed so small beside him, he thought. Fragile. The little gap between her teeth as she took a sip, the shy, concave way she held herself, those big glittering obsidian eyes, her every sentence spoken like first steps—wobbly, hopeful, important: he found her touching, mysterious.

"How old are you?" he asked. "If you don't mind me asking."

"Twenty-one," she said.

"Don't worry, I'm not gonna card you," he said. A confused smile flitted across her face. A moment passed.

Helga Coe marched out of the house in a zebra swimsuit. She walked straight into the pool. They both watched her as she performed a perfect breaststroke, bony arms parting the water mechanically as she swam. A staff member, clad in chinos, darted from the house to the guesthouse carrying a stack of towels.

"What's your last name again?" Masha asked him.

"Senzatimore. It means 'fearless' in Italian. *Senza*, 'without.' *Timore*, 'fear.'"

"You don't look Italian."

"Italian-Irish. What about you?"

Her eyes seemed to lose focus, her face went slack. Then she looked up at him boldly, a challenge in her gaze.

"Guess," she said, raising her chin.

He squinted down at her. "Could be Sicilian . . . but no . . . I'm gonna go out on a limb and say Romanian."

"Romanian! You think I'm a gypsy?"

"Not with a name like White, I guess."

"White isn't my real name."

"What is?"

"I'm done with it, anyway." She leaned back on the boat, pressing the base of the bottle into her lean belly and gazing out at the pool and the sea beyond it. Her eyes, Leslie noticed, had taken on an oddly purple cast, like an oil slick. He wondered if she was a runaway.

"You're from the Tri-state area, anyway," said Leslie, "whatever your forebears."

"Four bears?"

"Forebears. Ancestors."

"Fancy."

"You know it."

"I'm hoping not to sound this way soon," she said, worrying a few pebbles with the tip of her ballet shoe.

"You sound fine to me," he said. "If you don't mind my asking, what's your connection to Ross Coe?"

"Derbhan Nevsky is my manager and Ross Coe is investing in his company. Mr. Coe's letting me and Shelley stay in one of his apartments for free till we can get acting work. Unless I don't get any in six months, in which case I think I'm being returned."

"Return to sender," he said, thinking the whole arrangement seemed creepy.

"The thing is," she went on, "I need to make some money. I left home in a rush, I paid almost everything I had for acting classes, and now I'm kind of broke. I don't like being so . . . in debt. It's like I'm a little kid."

Leslie nodded, thoughtful. A notion to protect the girl spiked in him suddenly, like a sharp pain.

"Are your parents okay with this arrangement?" he asked.

"They don't really know."

"I bet they're worried."

"I'll get in touch with them soon."

"I'll pay you minimum wage to work on the boat for a couple weeks," he offered, regretting it immediately. The last thing he needed was a beauty queen climbing all over the boat, getting in everybody's way.

"You will?"

"You probably wouldn't want to do this kind of work," he said.

"I like it," she said.

"I'm sure you'll be busy with . . . whatever it is you'll be doing. Auditions and whatnot."

"I guess I can only do a few hours a day."

"If you don't have time, no sweat."

"Okay," she said. "Thanks." She smiled, small dimples appearing high in her cheeks.

Driving home that evening, Leslie thought about the girl. She seemed both guileless and cunning, her flirtatiousness ill-fitting, tentative, as if she were playing a part. He had never seen anyone blush that much. Where had she come from? He would keep an eye on her as much as he could. Maybe invite her to the house, introduce her to Deirdre. Deirdre would take care of her.

That night, I gave Leslie this dream:

A house is burning. Inside, Leslie crawls through the black smoke, blinded, feeling along the wall, breathing air through his mask, hearing its rhythmic, steady hiss. He opens a door, feels his way across the room. He feels a bed. A foot. A belly. A breast. He lifts up the body and rushes to the window. In the light, he sees her: it's Masha. Her body is limp in his arms. Now he is on the grass outside, kneeling over her, breathing into her mouth. She opens her eyes.

I figured, when manipulating a spirit as upright as Leslie's, it's best to stick to the classics.

## 30

I flew through the golden whorls of dust lit up by the evening rays streaming across Leslie's backyard, passed over the pool: undulating molten silver. The guests cast distended purple shadows as they milled and talked and ate. A table laden with food stretched halfway across the lawn: barbecued chicken, pasta salad, hot dogs, arugula. I'd had my fill. Every few seconds the sizzling sound of an idiot mosquito hitting the zapper broke the placid burble of talk. Deaf little Stevie was meandering through the company, the pimply au pair holding his hand, crouching with what I suspected was feigned solicitude; she was leaving for Amsterdam in the morning. The boy's blond wispy hair was lit up by the sun. Eyes wide, lips parted, he seemed fascinated by the play of light on the pool.

Taking his eyes from his son, Leslie flipped a skewer of shrimp. He didn't want to overcook them. Tony, his buddy from the firehouse, was standing beside him watching the burgers, a spatula in his hand.

"Do they have to be hockey pucks?" he asked.

"That's the way you're supposed to cook 'em now," said Leslie.

Tony shook his head. "There's something wrong with a country when you can't serve a rare burger in your own home." Leslie chuckled.

Statuesque Deirdre, her Choctaw cheekbones casting shadows

on her jaw, was listening to Marcie Doyle, Dennis's wife. Marcie, a pharmacist, had cropped blond hair, and was moving her short arms with precise explanatory chops. Dennis the police officer was beside her, his face turned sideways as he bit into his third hot dog.

Leslie nodded in his direction. "He's gonna give himself a heart attack if he doesn't stop eating like that," he said.

"It's because all she gives him is fish," said Tony. "When he gets out of the house he's like a wild animal."

"Deirdre only wanted to serve chicken and shrimp," Leslie said.

"Dennis would have probably cried," said Tony, removing the charred burgers onto a plate with his spatula. Little Jenny, Bud's wife, walked by in her spritely, carefree way, hair in braids, the baby on her hip. She was looking puffed around the middle these days, Leslie noticed. He had a terrible feeling she might be pregnant again. He imagined the cost of his life ballooning. Bud the Buddhist loped up to him, the beads around his neck clicking as they swung.

"Dad, we need more beer up here," he said.

"Okay. You know where it is," said Leslie. Bud turned and walked into the house just as a baby-blue Mercedes crawled down the block. Leslie saw it from over the top of the fence.

Inside the car, Masha shifted in the leather seat. The new, viscous gloss on her lips made them feel heavy, a foreign presence. She could smell her own perfume. Shelley had dressed her up with new clothes they'd bought with Nevsky. She was trying out a different look. False eyelashes and everything. Nevsky called it "classic seductress." The dress was snug, but at least it went below the knees. Shelley had tamed her own hair into platinum waves, and was in a skimpy little sundress. She sat back in the seat, her knees splayed. She looked so at ease. Masha wished she could be like that. She felt stiff, self-conscious, as if she were wearing a face over her face. Surinder slowed to a stop, got out, and opened the door for them. There was Leslie, opening a gate to the backyard. As she got out of the car, his eyes changed. They looked hurt, or worried. Masha felt blood rush to her face. Nevsky trotted past her, beamed up at the big man.

"Mr. Senzatimore!" he croaked. "I hope you don't mind me turning up uninvited, but I generally try to keep an eye on the girls."

"You're welcome," said Leslie firmly. "Come on back." In the backyard a tall, strong-looking woman in jeans and cowboy boots approached them. Her eyes flicked over Masha's dress as she smiled slowly. Masha's throat tightened.

"Are you Masha or Shelley?" the woman asked in a low, warm voice.

"Masha."

"I'm Deirdre. Leslie's wife. Come on in, I'll get you both something to eat."

Leslie watched his wife lead the girls to the table where the food was laid out. Deirdre would sort Masha out, Leslie thought. Make sure she wasn't being hoodwinked. If there was a problem, Deirdre would draw it out of her. He spotted his mother-in-law, prancing across the lawn barefoot, a pair of high-heeled sandals dangling from one hand. She whooshed over to him and tossed her head. "Sorry we're late," she said. "Don was napping and I felt I should wait for him to wake up, make sure he wasn't dead."

"And is he?" asked Leslie.

"He's right there," she complained, pointing her finger at Derbhan Nevsky, who was talking in an animated way with a large tree. Don leaned out from behind it and slapped Nevsky's back. *Old friends*, Leslie thought. He began to regret the invitation.

I had pumped the dream of rescuing Masha through Leslie's head three nights in a row by now. A preoccupation with the girl was building. Leslie pulled a bottle of cold beer from the cooler and allowed himself a long look at his dream victim. She was listening to Deirdre and Shelley, or rather, observing them. She looked noncommittal. She was only on loan, her manner seemed to say. On loan for the evening, for this particular forty-five minutes. Soon she would return to the place she inhabited, some interior space. She was halfway there already. Leslie wondered what it was like inside Masha's head. He wondered what secret she carried around in her. Her mystery emanated from her. The other men felt it too. Tony drifted over to her and started talking. Dennis. She was a magnet. Leslie hung back. Masha looked over at him, though, through the others, and smiled. Her attention thrilled him. This pleasure was not what he had intended. This was not why he had invited her, not at all. He wished they would all just leave. What was Nevsky doing with Don? Leslie walked over to them, riled. Don was still leaning on the big tree.

"Talking business?" asked Leslie.

"Mr. Nevsky is just filling me in on the progress with his new company," said Don. "He's managing those two starlets over there. I'm considering a modest invesment, to start with."

Leslie looked down at Nevsky. He had a rodent face, he thought. A scuttler.

"I don't want to twist anybody's arm," said Nevsky. "Truth is, Ross Coe is bankrolling the enterprise. But there's room for a few individuals to come in on the ground floor, that's all." Don was nodding. Leslie wondered at this. As a bank officer, Don was a pessimist. This guy was obviously a huckster. Why was Don so mesmerized? Plus he had no money to throw around.

Deirdre came up behind Leslie and squeezed his waist. He put his hand on her wrist. "They're fine," she whispered in his ear.

"Who?" he asked, turning to face her.

"The girls. You were worried about Masha. I think she's got her head screwed on. They've got free room and board on spec, and a contract. If she doesn't get work, she'll go back home to her family."

"What kind of people is she from?" asked Leslie, pulling her away from Nevsky and Don.

Deirdre shrugged. "I don't know. She's cagey about that. Shelley's been around the block; she'll take care of her. You have to stop worrying about everybody, honey. The world keeps spinning, even when you don't hold it on your shoulders. Right?" she said to Stevie, who had put his arms around her knees. She picked him up and put him on her hip. Leslie watched Deirdre carry his boy back into the house, feeling a little clunk of hopelessness in his sternum. His poor son. As if in flight from the feeling, he walked over to Masha, who was standing alone now, a glass of Coke in her hand.

"You're gonna rot your teeth out with all that Coca-Cola," he said.

She smiled at him. "They're my teeth," she said.

"So far."

"Are you a strict dad?" she asked him.

"It's hard to be strict with Stevie. Did you meet my sons?"

"Yeah, and your grandchild. My father has five grandkids."

"How many kids in your family?"

"A lot." Her waist, cinched in by the silky material of the dress, seemed especially small this evening.

"You look different," Leslie said.

"I'm overdressed," said Masha.

"People don't dress up enough anymore," he said. "I got pictures of my parents out on a Saturday night with friends, they look like they're going to the opera." She looked up at him. His rough-hewn face was lit up nearly orange by the dying light. He seemed to have been carved out of rock. "Did you get something to eat?" he asked. "There's shrimp and salads . . ."

"Yes, your wife gave us loads of food."

"Deirdre's the best," said Leslie. Masha felt pinched out of Leslie's life by that statement. Her disappointment surprised her.

Hugh was going for a drink after class. Shelley and Masha were coming with him. Outside, blue dusk. Masha still half expected Miriam
to spring out of a bush and drag her home.

The bar was a hot, loud, jumpy place with ska playing on the
speakers. Shelley was shouting amicably to a guy in a porkpie hat. Hugh
inhabited the green leather booth, his long arms spanning the back
of it. He was sipping whiskey. Masha drained her glass of wine. The
alcohol made her feel fearless. She thought about Carol Cutrere,
from *Orpheus Descending*. Carol loved her liquor. She stayed out all
night driving up and down the Dixie Highway, hopping from one
drinking establishment to another, spending her family money till
she didn't know where she was. Carol was a feral, lost, disillisioned
person with very few positive attributes, yet Masha had come to love
her fiercely.

"I've never been drunk before," she said to no one in particular.

"Take it easy, girl. You'll make yourself sick," said Hugh, standing
up and sweeping a bowl of salted peanuts from the table beside them.
She took a few into her mouth.

"And you know what else?" she asked.

"What?"

"I've never kissed anyone before." The bar was so loud, she wasn't
sure he'd heard her. He slid his arms down from the back of the leather
bench and leaned in to her, taking her in with his wide eyes.

"I'm not like a normal girl from your world," Masha said.

"Are you saying that because you want me to kiss you?" he asked her.

She missed Eli, like a sudden cramp. And she could never have
him now. He was gone. Vanished. She shook her head.

"I was just telling you," she said.

Hugh leaned back in the booth. "Duly noted."

Afterward, he walked them both to the Coes' blue Mercedes,

parked outside the bar. Surinder Multani seemed to be deep in thought, leaning on the side door, his hazelnut-brown skin and spotless turban gleaming in the streetlight. When he saw them he smiled and opened the rear door.

"It's like you two are being kept by gangsters," Hugh said.

"Come with us to meet the Coes," said Shelley impulsively. "Come to dinner. Right?"

Hugh looked at Masha. "I wouldn't want to intrude," he said.

"Sure," Masha said. "Come."

The Coes were not displeased to see that the girls had brought an attractive visitor from acting class to join them at their favorite seafood restaurant. They adored other people. Shriveled, elegant Helga, her hair a shining helmet, teeth a dazzling bulwark of enamel, asked Hugh if he knew white wines. "When I was a girl, we had a villa with beautiful vineyards . . . ," she began, eyes drooping as she lost herself in the reverie. Whenever she pronounced *s* it sounded like a kettle was whistling in her mouth. Hugh, ever chivalrous, listened to tales of her prewar past in the Rhineland, downing his whiskey and asking for another. Meanwhile, Ross Coe concentrated on the women.

"So. Tell me about yourselves," he said. "Shelley. What do your parents do?"

"Well," said Shelley, gazing at the ceiling, "My mother is a massage therapist, she lives in Newport, Rhode Island. Which is where I grew up. And my father is an airline pilot. He lives in Delaware. I have a younger brother, he's still in college."

"And when did you know you wanted to be an actress?"

"I guess when I was sixteen, I was in a high school production and I realized that was just it for me. My ex-boyfriend—we moved to the city together, but we've kind of split up—he wanted to be a playwright, so . . ."

"Aw," said Helga. "What made you split?"

"Honey, that's personal," said Coe, patting his wife's spotted hand with his small one.

"Pardon me," said Helga, "I am always so sad to hear about broken love affairs."

"That's okay," said Shelley. "We were just . . . we've been together so long . . . we're too used to each other, I guess." Her eyes met Hugh's for a beat, Masha noticed. It hadn't occurred to her until now that there might be something between those two. "We're still good friends, though," Shelley added, shrugging.

"And Masha?" said Helga. "What is your story?"

"I'm . . . from Far Rockaway, in Queens," said Masha. There was a pause as her hosts waited for more, but there wasn't any.

"What nationality are your parents?" asked Helga. "You have such an amazing look."

Masha bit her lip. "Irish and . . . Romanian," she said. Shelley smiled.

"Ross, I was right! I knew it!" said Helga.

"That's a good one," said Hugh. His voice had thickened.

"Excuse me?" said Helga, turning to him.

"I mean," he said, fixing his glassy eyes on Masha, "Masha is a special person. She has a special power. Over . . ." He looked around the restaurant, as if for the end of his sentence. "People."

They let themselves into the free rental and switched on the lights. The air in the apartment felt cool. Shelley turned on the heat, plugged her iPod into the speakers, then went off to change. A gravelly female voice sang over a guitar. Hugh opened a bottle of wine, poured them all a glass. Masha took a sip and looked out the window at the passing lights. She had the sense that they were the last three people on earth.

"You talk less than any girl I've ever met," said Hugh, his elbows on the counter.

She turned to him. "Hm?"

"You're taciturn."

"Am I?"

"Yup."

"I don't know how to keep talking," she said. "I just . . . dry up."

"I'm the same," said Hugh. "And yet I hear the words come out of my mouth, regardless. I talk and talk, while within, I have often vacated." The expression on his fine, battered face was vulnerable, transparent. Looking into his murky eyes, she felt in him: yearning, sadness, and something else—his dark fate, perhaps, emanating from him. The intimacy was painful, claustrophobic.

"I'm tired," she said softly.

The next morning she got up and checked Shelley's room, as she always did. Hugh was asleep in Shelley's bed, his long, bare arm flopped over the side of the mattress, face buried in the pillow. Masha walked out into the living room, and there was Shelley, her hair a white spray around her face, curled up on the sofa, drinking a cup of tea. She grinned at Masha.

"Hugh is in love with you, you know," she said.

"What are you talking about?" said Masha, sitting beside her. "You just . . ."

"We slept in the same bed, is all," said Shelley, putting her lips against the warm cup. "I've known him a long time. He used to be in Bridget's class years ago, when I first came to New York. That's how I met Paul; they went to college together. Then Hugh started to get acting work and he left class. He moved to L.A. But . . . something happened to him out there, like, I don't know. One person said it was a car accident, and someone else said it had to do with drinking, but he had some kind of crisis and he came back to New York last year. And then he asked Paul and me to move in with him in his apartment. He pays most of the rent. But now he's sort of . . . different."

"Different how?" Masha asked.

"I don't know, like . . . quieter? He was reckless before, always getting into scrapes. Now . . . I don't know, he seems sort of folded into himself. A great guy, though."

Masha sat down beside her friend. "I don't think I'll ever get the hang of this," she said.

"Of what?"

"Of being like you. I don't know how to do it."

"You're fine," said Shelley. "Relax. That's what's great about you. You don't seem like anybody else. I'm all shiny and obvious, but you . . . you're a mystery."

Masha laughed softly, shaking her head.

That morning the three of them went out for breakfast. Masha ordered a cheeseburger. She hadn't planned to; she just blurted it out. She had never combined meat and dairy before in her life. She tasted the salty meat and cheese on the back of her tongue. It was delicious. I watched proudly as she ate up her guilt, consumed it like a little heart. That was the moment she knew she really wasn't going home.

## 31

Early one morning before dawn, I was woken by Le Jumeau's strident voice echoing in my room. I went to the window and stuck my head out, peering sleepily down into the courtyard. Two harnessed carriages stood on the cobblestones, along with an open cart laden with luggage. Le Jumeau looked up and saw me.

"Hurry up and pack, we're leaving in half an hour!"

"Where are we going?"

"To Villars, Le Naïf!" He used my new nickname, which had, unfortunately, stuck since the incident with the prostitutes, with exasperation, as if I should have known. Breathlessly, I rubbed my teeth with a scrap of linen, dressed, and packed my few things: aside from the livery I was wearing, I had a set of clothes I had bought second-hand with Solange, at the market in Les Halles. I ran downstairs. Le Jumeau had me climb on top of the tarp covering the luggage, to be sure none of the cases fell off. If it rained, he said in his usual mocking tone, I would get wet.

The cortège set off: inside the first carriage were the count and Le Jumeau. In the second were Solange, Clothilde, and Frechette, a hairdresser who was in charge of the count's wigs.

I had only been out of Paris once, as a boy, to visit Metz, and I barely remembered it. As we left the gates of the city, horses trotting into the countryside, all was white. Hard frost had sugared the leaves on the ground, the grass, the branches. The pink sky cast a rosy glow on this sparkling confection. Far off, a raft of purple clouds seemed thrice lanced. The brilliant wounds poured three shafts of golden light on the distant hills. A flock of black-faced sheep stared at us through a wash of mist. The wheel of my cart hit a stone with a pop. One sheep started, turned; the flock followed her in perfect sync, scampering off as one. I lay back on a soft leather case, bathing in the cool air. I had never breathed air as pure as this, never seen so much sky. I imagined falling off my luggage cart and careening, untethered, through the clouds.

In the past, reflexively, I would have thanked Hashem for the day. I felt my tongue tense to utter the silent prayer, but I relaxed it. The need had passed. I unwrapped my freedom, marveled at it like a gift.

At noon we stopped at the rim of a great valley. Le Jumeau and I set up a little table and chair on a hillock for the count. Clothilde presented him with a meat pie. I poured him a glass of wine. Solange, meanwhile, set out a cloth on lower ground for the servants to sit on. We sat in a jolly circle as Le Jumeau doled out thick slices of salami. It was the first pork I had ever had. It tasted salty and fat. I completed the sacrilege by chewing on a hunk of cheese forthwith.

"Gebeck!" the count called down. "Sing a song. Something your mother used to sing you." I shook my head, ashamed, but they all insisted. My cheeks burning, I stood up, sang out a quick Yiddish ditty, then sat down, mortified. The moment I'd finished, as the party was still clapping and hooting their amused approval, Solange stood up and sang out in a harsh, strange language. Strands of her dark hair came loose from her lace bonnet and whipped around her face. When her song was done, she smiled shyly at me, revealing her charmingly narrow, crooked teeth, and said:

"My mother is a Basque." What a gesture.

Later that afternoon, we passed over a humpbacked bridge into the tiny town of Villars. Barefoot children teemed from every cranny of the village to see the count's gleaming coat of arms. They had plenty of time to do so; our wide carriages could barely pass through the narrow streets of the town. We inched along like a royal procession. Men stood outside the shops, clutching their hats and bowing their heads in feudal deference to the lord of the village; women curtsied. When we finally reached the town square, the count's carriage came to a stop. Le Jumeau disembarked, followed by the little count, his habitual scarlet stockings vivid against the wet gray cobblestones. As the hushed townspeople looked on, my master mounted the steps to a bronze statue of Henri IV, faced the crowd, and made a brief, impromptu speech, coating his silly manner in a lordliness so overdone, it would have been perfect in a farce at the Comédie-Italienne. Fluttering his hands till the lace at his wrists shivered, exaggerating his lisp, he said something to the effect of being glad to return to the bosom of his true people. A pretty blond girl in peasant dress walked haltingly up to him and, trembling, laid a bouquet of wildflowers at his feet. Le Jumeau stepped forward, snatched up the bouquet, and handed it to the master, lest the count be seen to stoop and possibly split his pants in the process. At this, the townspeople piped up with a rousing folk song. It was fascinating, but I was uneasy, despite my disguise: a Jew was never safe in towns like these. If anything went wrong—if a child went missing or a rotting animal poisoned a well— these quaint types would lose no time in stringing up the first Hebrew they could find. That's what I had been told, at any rate.

Built in the fifteenth century, the Château de Villars was a turreted, moat-encircled palace. As we drove up, the staff of the château—over a hundred persons—filed out and stood waiting to greet the master. At the front of the crowd was a barrel-chested man with a proud, ruddy face, wearing a suit of stiff corduroy, his feet encased in a pair of muddy boots. He stood very erect and watched the approaching carriages like a guard dog whose master was returning after a long journey. When the count emerged, the proud man greeted him, then went straight to the next carriage, opening the door for Solange, whom he met with an intimacy I found most disconcerting. Le Jumeau whistled at me to get off my ass. I broke my trance and disembarked, grabbing some luggage. The count was greeting the waiting staff one by one when bodies parted to allow a slender, very beautiful woman to emerge. Flaxen-haired, with a profile so perfect it could have been carved out of ice, she stood looking at the dumpy count with a tense smile. This was the first I knew of the Comtesse de Villars. The count dove at her, kissing her hand. They walked arm in arm toward the château, but, after an exchange of a few words, the couple halted. The comtesse turned, scanning our party. Villars pointed me out. The elegant lady took several steps in my direction, fixing me with a curious, hostile stare. Then she turned, taking up her husband's arm once more, and they walked toward the castle.

It was my duty to unpack the count's things and put them away in his room. A high-handed little housemaid directed me in this undertaking. She couldn't have been older than fifteen, but she treated me as though I were the child, scolding me when I failed to find the glove drawer or installed the count's beloved ermine muff on the wrong shelf. Her harelip was my only consolation.

I was relieved when Le Jumeau entered, a fur coat over his arm. Small, dark, muscular, his britches inevitably snug, the valet exuded a brutish sexuality that had a universal effect on females. The housemaid giggled the moment he arrived.

"I didn't know there was a countess," I said.

"But of course," said Le Jumeau, handing the pelt to the blushing maid.

"She lives here?" I asked.

"Much of the time," he said, walking to the door and clicking his tongue at me. Like a dog, I followed him.

"Are there children?" I whispered as we hurried down the hall.

"No, Le Naïf." The satyr grinned at me, dark lips curling. His eyes were little black pits of mirth.

The guests began to arrive that afternoon. There were so many of them, I couldn't keep track of their names. The countess was issuing orders to the servants with imperious calm. I imagined her skin to be cold to the touch. She had a way of raising her chin, cocking her head, and narrowing her eyes as she listened. Yet, surprisingly, she could melt into laughter at some witticism on the part of her guests. This helpless hilarity caused her head to flop over on its stalk, her tense arms to dangle at her sides, the firm flesh of her bosom to be squeezed over the rigid bounds of her corset as she rocked with laughter—until she regained her composure and solidified into marble once more. I found her fascinating and repellent. At one point, to my alarm, she fixed me with her metallic gaze, her eyes the color of pewter.

"Tell the count there will be a game of whist with the Marquis and Marquise de Clermont-Tonnerre in the pink drawing room in half an hour; we would be most pleased if he could join us as a fourth. I believe he is in the library." I bowed, turned, and walked off blindly, anxious to remove myself. I got lost and increasingly panicked, speeding down a nightmare of hallways, entering door after door, running through rooms that looked familiar yet strange, bursting in on clusters of gleaming aristocrats in the act of playing cards, tinkling clavichords, or stealing kisses, until I wept with frustration. In the end, the count came upon *me*, in an intimate study adjoining the music room. He had been searching for his snuffbox. He laughed at my distress.

"Gebeck. Are you all right?" he asked. I wiped my eyes.

"I'm sorry, sir," I said, standing up. "I was lost."

"Well, now you've been found," he said with gentle mockery, as if to cheer up a child.

"Madame la Comtesse wanted you to know that she invites you to the pink drawing room to play a hand of whist with . . . with . . ."

"It doesn't matter with whom," said the count, thudding down despondently into a gilded chair and regarding his red stockings, one of which was wrinkling at the ankle. I knelt and straightened it for him, pulling it up tight about his calf.

"I wish I could change places with you, Gebeck, just for this one week." He sighed.

"You do, sir?" I asked.

"Most emphatically," he answered.

The next morning at first light, I dressed the sleepy count for his hunting expedition. Woolen undergarments, thick woolen britches, chemise, socks: my master stepped into them all dutifully, like a small boy being outfitted by his nurse.

"You are doing well, Gebeck," he said, as I did up the buttons on his waistcoat. "I am well pleased." I looked up from my task. The wide pores of the count's skin, his fleshy mouth, that hunk of a nose—without being conscious of it, I was constantly lending him other features that seemed to go together better.

"I'm glad, Monsieur le Comte," I said.

"I would like to give you something," said the count, his protruding eyes roving around the room. "Ah!" He grabbed the candelabrum at the center of his round table and handed it to me. "Here. It's quite a valuable piece. Belongs to my wife, but she'll never notice." I took the candelabrum in both hands. It was heavy. I examined the intricate porcelain work, the tiny cherubim gamboling on the base, the lifelike flowers winding around the candlesticks.

"Thank you very much," I said.

"Put it in your room, and then we must be off."

The party set off after breakfast: ten nobles, dressed in the finest woolens, carrying muskets and little kidskin bags over their shoulders, the servants following close behind. I was one of three *valets de chambre* to accompany his master. The others were both older men who looked as though the last thing on earth they wanted to be doing at this moment was traipsing through the woods.

The master chatted away to his guests as we walked through the tangle of woodland and into an open field. Solange's husband, DuBois, walked ahead of us, his back rigid, a clutch of hunting dogs sniffing at his heels. He was giving terse orders to the beaters, bent, stick-wielding men in tweed caps and baggy britches. At a word from DuBois, the beaters thrashed the bushes with their sticks, and a frightened bird blasted itself into the air, only to be shot at by ten muskets simultaneously. When a bird fell, DuBois sent a dog after it. I watched the man for hours as he stalked through the countryside, grimly providing pleasure for the count and his guests.

As the morning progressed, the poor count did not shoot well. His shots were wildly off the mark. All the other guests had at least a brace of partridge each in their hunting pouches. My master had one bird. Eventually his gay chatter petered out and he fell back from the group, dragging his musket dejectedly along the thawed ground. He didn't even bother to raise his gun when a spray of partridge erupted into the air in front of him. DuBois knew the count wasn't hitting anything, yet he continued marching along, ordering the beaters and the dogs about, and keeping a careful tally of each guest's kill in a small notebook. Cruelty nestled in the rectitude of the man's corduroy; I knew it. Poor Solange. At noon, the party disbanded. The count muttered something about work he needed to do and walked into the gardens, while the others returned to the château to dress for lunch. I followed the count, taking his musket from his limp fingers.

Dejected, he walked some distance without even acknowledging my presence, yet he expected me to follow him. I knew he needed me. He sat on a bench by one of the rectangular ponds, staring into the water listlessly. I stood by his side, watching him. After a long moment my young master's gaze quickened. He stiffened like a bird dog, staring into the pond, and stood up very quietly, gesturing urgently for me to hand him his gun. Aiming, I soon realized, at one of the large carp that lazed at the bottom of that shallow pool, he blasted it to pieces. Then he handed the gun back to me, saying, "I'll wear the chestnut silk for lunch." And off he tromped toward the castle, as the golden corpse of the bleeding fish tumbled up to the surface of the pool.

At lunch, as Le Jumeau and I joined the other servants bustling about bringing in new dishes and pouring wine, I noticed Monsieur Cabanis, the desiccated man I had met on my first morning out of prison, watching me gravely from his seat beside the countess. My service was, by now, impeccable. I was a natural mimic, and acted the part of a servant to perfection. Over the course of the meal the count sent me out for his snuff, and then again for his tobacco. Each time I returned, I felt Cabanis's eyes on me. The count, taking the requested object from my hands, seemed to be checking on the other man's reaction to my service. I was relieved when, at last, the guests stood up.

"Gebeck," said the count, "follow us please."

I followed the count and the shriveled Cabanis to the count's study, where they both sat down.

"May I bring you some brandy?" I asked.

"Later," said the count. "For now I want you to show Monsieur Cabanis some of what I have taught you. I am proud of my achievement." I looked over at Cabanis. His wig was very dark, and curled along the front, with two pointed braids trailing down his back. He seemed like a vain, serious person. From his inside jacket pocket he produced a sheet of paper, clamping it between the tips of his fore- and middle fingers.

"Please translate into French," he said, stretching his arm out and handing it to me. It was Latin. I recognized it as the work of the poet Virgil. I sat down and translated as best I could. This took me over half an hour, I believe. In all that time, neither man said a word. The only sound was the scratching of my quill on the paper.

"There are some words I do not recognize," I said.

Cabanis took the paper from me and read, then looked over at my master, nodding. He then asked me questions about Aristotle. Voltaire. Diderot. I did my best to answer. Then, he turned to my master. "And the habits, the rituals?"

"Gone. You have my word."

Cabanis thought this through for a few seconds. "The final act," he said. "Nothing until that is accomplished."

"In time," said the count. Then, turning to me, he said pleasantly, "Monsieur Cabanis has been kind enough to advise me on your education, stage by stage. He is a man of letters, far better qualified than I to devise a curriculum. But I insist that such a radical reorganization of a person's mind takes time. Now. Go on. Take the rest of the day for yourself."

I spent the afternoon in the kitchen, watching Solange add up the week's purchases in a large ledger, sipping coffee with milk.

"What's the matter, Johann?" she asked me. "You look so mopey."

"Is he good to you, your husband?"

"What kind of a question is that?"

"The personal kind," I said.

She pushed a plate of cakes toward me. "Eat," she said.

"Why is that your solution to everything?" I asked, piqued.

"It's not the solution to everything. Only to nosy little boys who say things they shouldn't."

"I can't help it if I care about you," I said. "I—I love you."

Solange looked at me, astonished at my clumsy outburst. I had the terrible feeling she might be about to laugh.

"Oh, sweet boy," she said.

"I am not a boy," I said. "Not that you care, or have ever asked, but I'm married. Was—married. I am a man."

"What happened to your wife?" she asked earnestly.

"I have no idea, and I don't care," I said. "I only mention her because you all insist on calling me Le Naïf and treating me like a child, when I was once the head of a household!"

"Do you want to go back, perhaps?"

"I couldn't go back if I wanted to," I snapped. "All I ask is, if I tell you I love you, treat me with the dignity I deserve."

"All right," she said. "I'm sorry. I cannot return your love, not because I could not love you, but because I am married."

"But look around you!" I said. "What does marriage have to do with anything? Look at the count!"

She shrugged and smiled. "It's not the same for us." She drew the ledger toward her and began writing in her tiny, flawless script. I bit into a cake resentfully, but I didn't leave her side.

A week later, the count had gone into the village with Le Jumeau.

I was in the library, up on the ladder, replacing some books on the highest shelf, a great distance from the floor, when the mirrored doors to the room opened and the countess walked in, shutting us in with a deliberate push.

"Madame la Comtesse," I called down, assuming she did not know I was there.

"Come down, Gebeck," she called up in her open-throated, sonorous voice. "I need to speak with you." Fearing I was in trouble, I traveled down what now seemed like an endless ladder, acutely aware of my baggy britches. Reaching the ground at last, I bowed. The Comtesse de Villars was ghostly in a bone-white dress with four black silk bows tied adamantly up the front. The slender silk bodice emerged from the wide frame of the skirt like the neck of a precious vase containing a single perfect white flower. Her mask of daubed skin was unlined, yet she did not seem young to me. Her cornsilk-blond, lightly powdered hair was bedizened with flashing black birds. Diamonds spangled at her ears.

"Madame?" I asked. She walked over to the library table, surveying the messy papers spread across it and touching the edge of a portfolio thoughtfully.

"Have you ever wondered why my husband went to all that trouble to hire you as his second valet?" she asked, a little curl, like a snail's tail, rising at one corner of her lips. "I mean, why you, and not a Frenchman, or someone not in prison, for that matter?"

"I have wondered, yes," I answered.

"He hired you because he needs a Jew. He needs a Jew because, to put it bluntly, he needs money."

"I don't understand, madame."

"He made a bet," she said, walking to the window and looking out at the endless lawn with her large, heavy-lidded eyes.

"A bet?" I asked.

"My husband is a compulsive gambler. Some years ago, he bet Monsieur Cabanis four hundred louis that he could change a Jew into a Frenchman in six months. Like most of us, Monsieur Cabanis believes that your people are too obstinate, too steeped in their own primitive, superstitious world, and, moreover, too vain, to truly become a part of our civilization. My husband insists that all people are essentially the same, that all customs are learned, that there is no such thing as inherent Jewishness. If a Jew can change, anyone can change, he says. But let me ask you something. Do you think, in biblical times, hawks ate pigeons, when they had the chance?"

"I'm sorry?"

"Have hawks always eaten pigeons?" she repeated.

"I suppose so," I answered.

"If hawks have always maintained the same character, it's absurd to think Jews will change theirs. Human nature does not change." Her deep-set large eyes were fixed, inhuman, as if made of gray glass. I peered through those glittering windows and glimpsed an intelligence so cold it stilled my breath.

"So you see, his interest in you is scientific as well as financial," she continued. "But the thing is—and here is the truly difficult element: the count will lose the bet unless you are baptized as a Christian within the next two months. What do you make of that?"

"Madame, why are you telling me this?" I asked.

"I just wanted to know how you would answer."

"I don't know what to say."

"You would do it? You would betray your faith to enrich him?"

Le Jumeau oozed into my room, slid onto my bed, and settled his stocking feet on my pillow. Two grimy middle toes protruded from the brown stockings like unearthed parsnips. I saw them through a blur of tears.

"What's the matter, Le Naïf?" asked the valet. "What are you doing pouting in your room?"

Weeping with rage, I told him about the bet. There was a pause as he let it sink in. Then he chuckled. "And that fat little bastard kept it to himself all this time," he mused.

"Would it have been better if he'd let you in on it?" I asked, folding my clothes jerkily and setting them into my small canvas satchel. "I don't care to be used as a performing monkey to enrich that cynic."

"Here's what I would do," said Le Jumeau. "Confront the count, and tell him you'll only go through with the baptism if you get a third of the money. No, say half, and you'll end up with a third."

"But I don't want to be baptized!" I said. "It's completely out of the question for us."

Le Jumeau sighed, rolling his eyes. "Come on, Gebeck. Do you truly believe in all your rules and regulations now? It seems to me you sank your teeth into that pork sausage pretty happily. I haven't heard any of your chanting lately either. For better or worse, the count freed you, he's educating you, and now you can earn a nice fat parcel if you just play along. Ah, forget it, you don't deserve my advice. I don't know why I bother. Go ahead. Pack up, get on the highway a penniless Hebrew, and see how the fates treat you." He folded his hands over his taut belly and closed his eyes.

I stomped over to where the count was surveying a new building project. He was having a small pyramid built at the end of a path in the woods. Six strong village men were setting the slanted stones. The count stood, plans in hand. The architect, a tall man with a pointy beard, gestured grandly at the useless edifice. Villars turned, and, seeing me, lit up.

"Le Naïf! Have a look at my pyramid."

"I need to speak with you privately, monsieur," I said breathlessly.

"Has something happened?"

"It's a private matter," I insisted.

The count handed the plans to the architect, who rolled them up in an exaggerated show of discretion.

"I'll be back," said the count. "Come. We'll walk through the park."

As we walked through the magnificently organized park of the château, I unburdened myself, my voice shaking. The count walked for a long while in silence, his hands behind his back, a frown on his wide, froggy mouth.

"It's not as simple as you make out, Gebeck," he said. "I need money, it's true, but there are other ways, easier ways, to get it. My wife has her own reasons to discredit me. I took you in because . . . I suppose I wanted to know if it was possible to . . . wash a Jew clean of his Jewishness. To make him simply a man. It's a debate that's all the rage, what to do about the Jews. How to make them more useful, less scheming, less 'a nation apart.' There are those who would love to ship you all to South America. I simply wanted to prove them wrong. That it's a question of education and habit. Do you see? My project is simply . . . ideas made flesh. Instead of writing a treatise. You are my theorem. As for the baptism, that is Cabanis's requirement. He's an ardent Catholic. If it were up to me, there would be no religion involved whatsoever. I detest it, as you know."

"Give me half," I proclaimed, "and I will do it."

"Half! Do you realize I am giving you a free Jesuit education, minus the beatings?"

"A quarter, then," I said.

"Very well," he said, chuckling. "I suppose there will always be a bit of the businessman about you, if you know what I mean."

"It was Le Jumeau's idea," I retorted. "*He* suggested a third!"

The count stamped his small foot in mock outrage. "That con artist! He's always looking for a way to fuck me up the ass."

A date was set with the parish priest.

———

The count, Solange, and Le Jumeau were in attendance as I stood bareheaded beside the baptismal font and became an apostate, swearing to the doddering priest that I believed Christ was Moshiach. I did not even bother to cross my fingers, as so many of my brethren had done when converting to save their own lives. I didn't deserve to cross my fingers; my life wasn't in danger. Try as I might to shrug the feeling off, I felt the Old Tyrant's eyes boring into me, his fury gathering. *"I am a jealous God,"* he liked to say in the old days. Didn't like competition. The old priest etched a wet cross on my forehead with his trembling digit: holy water trickled down the side of my nose, spread along the seam of my lips. It was done.

As my master and his valet looked on my conversion with a depth of cynicism difficult to find even in eighteenth-century France, I saw that Solange's eyes were brimming with tears. Afterward, as we left the village church, I asked her tenderly, "What is it, Solange?"

"You are in the house of God now," she whispered, her face glowing. "Whatever the reason for it, now you are safe." That's why she had helped the count find a Jew in the first place. If it were up to her, we'd all be converted.

I was paid within the week.

The holy day following my baptism, which was, unfortunately, Good Friday, Solange took me to afternoon Mass in the quaint country church where I had been baptized. We were celebrating the Passion of Christ. I sang out all the hymns and recited the special Easter prayers, one of which spoke eloquently about how the Jews had insisted Christ be killed.

And Pilate . . . said again unto the Jews, what will ye then that I shall do with him whom ye call the King of the Jews? And they cried out again, Crucify him. Then Pilate said unto them, Why, what evil has he done? And they cried out the more exceedingly, Crucify him.

The congregation joined in lustily whenever it was time to yell, "Crucify him!," playing the bloodthirsty Hebrews with passion. So did I. It was an awkward moment, but I got through it by pretending I was in a play.

The final ritual of my stay in the Château de Villars was a celebration in honor of the finished pyramid. There was to be an opening ceremony, followed by refreshments, music, and fireworks. The count invited the treasurer of the local *assemblée générale*, Lefèvre the architect, and various local bourgeois, who came dressed as if for a coronation. The countess was a disapproving cloud of black muslin, the stones at her neck flashing in the late pink light.

The count, dressed in his chestnut silk waistcoat and britches, his red stockings glowing, raised his double chin, readying himself for one of his speeches. He swayed slightly; I realized with alarm that he was drunk. The squat pyramid behind him had been wrapped with a cord of white ribbon tied in a sad little bow.

"Ladies and gentlemen, all of you gathered here, I am so happy to say that the wonderful work of our local stonemasons, as well as the superb architect Monsieur Lefèvre, has yielded this lovely edifice, an ancient shape with no purpose or use whatsoever but to perplex and entertain. And, in memory of the great people who were once enslaved by the Egyptians and yet came out of Egypt by divine intervention, according to our Bible, which so many of us here hold to be a historical document and not the product of feverish priestly imaginations—and in memory also of the character—or should I say man—revered, revered man, Jacob, also known as Israel, who, in our deepest past, wrestled with an angel of God . . ." By now the crowd, predisposed to enjoy the speech, was utterly lost and moving toward being insulted. Lefèvre cleared his throat.

"In honor of the great old biblical times," babbled the count, "when an eye was an eye and a man was a man and God ruled the world, I am naming this small building 'Jacob's Folly.' I shall have it etched in the lintel above the doorway. So that, for all time, as long as these stones stand, people passing will think of Jacob, and the past, and the Egyptians . . ." He looked at me and raised his glass. It was strange to hear myself called Jacob. I had nearly forgotten my name. The ribbon was severed. Champagne was poured. Fireworks ripped across the sky. The count disappeared and was found some hours later, passed out on a mossy rock.

## 32

Leslie kept working on the boat alone. Most days, Masha joined him, when she didn't have anything else to do. She found him reassuring. He couldn't admit it to himself, but the real reason he wasn't putting any other guys on the Coe job was: he needed to be near this girl. He could have stayed in the workshop—at least part of the time—and sent Segundo, or Pete, or Mike Diggis to do the initial work on *Sweet Helga*. But he made out to Vera that eccentric, deeply rich Mr. Coe wanted only Leslie on the job. Leslie implied this without actually stating it—a slanted lie. He couldn't help it. He needed to be near Masha.

I confess I had some input. In a metaphysical tour de force, I managed to funnel some old memories I had lying around—of Masha standing naked by the bathtub, for example—directly into Leslie's brain, ruining an afternoon of his work and causing him to nearly buckle with desire during one of their little tête-à-têtes over bottled Coca-Cola. But even without my help, Masha caused the very atmosphere around her to shift. You couldn't be near her and not sense the animal, alien power that drifted from her innocent body like perfume. Three weeks into my experiment, Leslie fell easy as a rotten tree pushed over by a toddler.

## 33

When we returned to Paris after my baptism, I hid my portion of the bet money, one hundred gold louis, in a dirty sack at the bottom of my linen chest. My employment continued as before, though the count no longer bothered to tutor me, now that he'd won the bet. A Christian man in a Christian country, with papers to prove it and money in my pocket, I moved through the world with new ease. Le Jumeau even had a degree of respect for me, and I no longer felt inferior to him.

In addition to my secretarial duties, I accompanied the count on some of his outings in Paris. He always sent me with messages to Mlle Giardina at the Comédie-Italienne or at her home, which was near the theater.

One morning, when I arrived at her apartment with a note from the count, she greeted me in a dressing gown the color of whipped cream, fastened by a flock of crisp blue-green ribbons just at the point where her décolleté became most interesting. Her honey-colored hair tumbling down her back, she led me through several rooms into an octagonal study. The eight paneled walls were painted with tableaux of wildlife: ducks, otters, a fox gamboling in the reeds were rendered in a playful, realistic style. The room was densely furnished with a

clavichord, a chaise longue, a small round library table with a few fo-
lios of plays spread out on it, and a charming little desk. I walked into
the room bewitched. Eventually my fluttering gaze settled on a small
inlaid music box decorated with enamel birds. Mlle Giardina saw me
looking at the box and opened it; a little tune piped up.

"Sit there," she said, indicating the chaise longue.

I perched at the end of it. Closing the music box, the little actress
sat down and placed her elbows on the table, folding her hands in a
neat cradle under her chin. The lace of her sleeves flopped back from
her arms like exhausted lily petals, revealing the firm pale flesh near
her elbows. Oil-starved flames struggled behind the tortoiseshell
sconces, conjuring copper strands from the coils of her hair. The
light on her full face was most flattering, which, I believe, was no
accident.

"Were you born in Italy?" I asked nervously.

"No. My father is Italian," she said. "Though I never met him."

"Fathers can be tiresome," I ventured.

"Or protective," she mused, sliding one slippered foot out from
under the creamy folds of her dressing gown like a gangster revealing
a tiny weapon sheathed in a silk holster. "My talent is the only thing
my father ever gave me," she added. "He was a singer."

"I would love to be able to sing," I said.

"I could teach you," she said. "If you have an ear."

She went to the clavichord and sat down. "Repeat after me," she
said, playing a tune, singing a string of notes. I did my best to mimic
the sounds she was making. She laughed, and let herself fall back a
bit, so that she was leaning against my side. I stood very still. Eventually our notes fell apart; the sweet tyrant led me back to the chaise
longue.

Kneeling, she unbuttoned my britches and gently peeled the cloth
away, as if unwrapping a delicate pastry. When she had uncovered me,
she took in a little gasp. I lay back on my elbows, nearly weeping with
shame at the long, wrinkled member with its bald head—the clue, I

knew, of my provenance. The traitorous fellow moved a little, as if shrugging insolently at my humiliation.

"Gebeck!" exclaimed Mademoiselle Giardina delightedly. "You're a Jew!" She leaned down and blew a little stream of warm air onto my sex in a matter-of-fact way, as if she were stoking a fire. Slowly my member inflated, staggering up into the air and weaving back and forth like a drunk. She marveled at it; I was filled with pride.

"Magic!" she whispered, darting out a pointy tongue to lick it.

From this point, all was delirium. When I was sent to deliver a message to Mademoiselle Giardina at her home, we paddled through each other's bodies with the crazed will of drowning souls, reaching our respective pleasures in record time, then parting, sweaty and disheveled. Occasionally, if the count was out for the evening, I was able to spend a part of the night in her apartments.

Yet, my favorite way of seeing Antonia was during the day, at the Comédie-Italienne. I loved everything about the place. The smell of burning wax wafting through the theater from the candle-making room; the pong of rabbit-skin glue sizing, boiling in great pots in the scenery department; the rich dusty red velvet of the seats, the red damask walls. This internal-organ color scheme made the place feel cozy as a womb; fallopian passages led to the stage, which I often walked across when unobserved. Each chair, every footstool of a set seemed haunted, special. I could feel the ghost of the play that had been uttered there last, I could hear the music sung by Antonia. A set was more than a real place to me. This was, perhaps, the closest thing I have ever felt to a true metaphysical frisson. It beat my sputtering attempts at religiosity with Cousin Gimpel, hands down.

Masha's meetings with the casting directors began, instigating a tumble of botched auditions for TV shows, a play, a couple of movies.

Masha was almost paralyzed by nervousness, embarrassed by her scanty clothing, and still uncertain of her accent, despite Doris van Hoff's palsied ministrations. Bridget Mooney coached her nearly every day now, traveling to the Coe manse by Surinder-mobile and sometimes spending the night (!) in the guesthouse with Nevsky. Looking a little less tightly wound these days, her blond coif loosely curled, the citadels of puff around her eyes powdered with care, Bridget lounged by the Coe pool and encouraged Masha to enjoy the power of her allure; it would be gone soon enough.

Masha was shedding her customs one by one. Eating what she fancied, shaking hands with male strangers, exposing her limbs, singing before menfolk, ignoring the Shabbos, neglecting to bless her food: all of this had happened. She began to wear her body as if it were a beautiful new dress.

Yet there were still times, as Masha woke in the morning, when she felt terror rush through her. She'd put her hand to her mouth, sure she had just done something awful, something unforgivable, and lay waiting to be punished. The only cure for this malaise was a trip to Shelley's room. Finding her friend asleep in bed, or reading, or sipping a cup of tea, reassured her. Shelley lived as though nothing were wrong with the way she lived.

Pearl sat at the edge of her bed, before dawn, staring sightlessly out the window. Every morning these days she was dredged urgently from sleep, as if by pulleys, only to remember that her daughter was gone. The last text she'd received was still saved on her phone: *I love you Mommy. Don't look for me. Will call soon. Masha.* There was no calling the police after that. Masha hadn't been abducted. She wasn't a minor. She had simply left.

The baby cried out from Estie's room. Tucking her long, soft hair into a terry-cloth turban, Pearl hurried down the hall. Quietly, she walked into the younger girls' room. Estie was asleep in her bed; Leah was standing up gripping the high bars of her crib, bouncing up and down. Pearl lifted her out. The plump, strong baby hugged her mother, burying her face in her neck. Pearl loved that feeling. She kissed Leah's cheek, setting her on her hip. The twins' alarm clock went off then, and Pearl, on her way down the stairs, whispered to the boys not to hit the snooze button. Mordecai could sleep for another hour if he needed to.

Pearl set out the breakfast things, warmed the baby's bottle, and sat down cradling Leah. Rocking back and forth, breathing in the scent of her baby's silky scalp, she prayed to Hashem to keep Masha safe. That was all she could do.

One Saturday, Leslie came by Masha's Victorian towing his old motorboat behind the truck. Deirdre was away with Stevie that weekend, visiting friends in the South. It was the first Saturday Leslie had had to himself in a long time, a fine, hot day.

He rang the buzzer at ten o'clock, as he had told Masha he might, if the weather was clear. Masha looked out the window, took in a sharp breath when she saw the wooden boat, so neat and pretty with its turqoise leather seats and polished wooden decks. She had forgotten Leslie's invitation.

Hugh was asleep on the couch. She woke him and Shelley, and the three of them filed out of the building and got into Leslie's big truck, the two girls in front, Hugh folded into the narrow backseat with Stevie's baseball bat, mitt, and other items.

It was embarrassing, Leslie thought, chauffering these three younger people for a day of recreation, his big hands turning the wheel as he barked out absurdly cheerful remarks. He felt like an idiot. He had expected Masha to emerge alone. Nothing to be done about it now. He drove to the marina, his chest imploded with disappointment. Masha was beside him in a long dress of fine cotton. He could feel the warmth of her thigh against his.

Once the boat was smacking the water, Masha seemed to come alive. She knelt at the bucking prow, hands clutching the rail, her dark mane whipping in the breeze, yelling at him to go faster, faster! The gusting wind, tearing at her loose white dress, churned a foaming wake of cloth toward him. Reflexively, he opened the throttle, as if to close the distance between them. She turned to him once, her face striped with strands of black hair, her mouth open, smiling, drinking the wind. The other two huddled together in the passenger bench, sleepy, looking out to sea. He drove them to a strip of beach on Fire Island that was almost always clean of people.

She lay on her belly, the orange bikini brilliant against her tanned skin, the golden hairs glistening on her back, one leg bent, the foot flexing and pointing idly toward the sky. Her scarlet-tipped hands clawed the hot sand, playing with it, her face toward him, half smashed into the towel he'd brought for her, one eye peeking through that river of blue-black hair.

"You got sunscreen on?" he asked her.

"No," she said.

"You better put some on. You'll get broiled." Shelley and Hugh were wading in the water down the beach, talking.

"Okay," said Masha, not moving. Leslie reached a big hand into his canvas bag and took out the tube of suncreen.

"You want me to do your back?" he asked. She nodded. He could feel muscle and ribs through the warm young skin. He was lost now. He didn't care anymore. He lay down on his belly beside her, his face close to hers. He looked into her night eyes. She stared back boldly. He wondered where the other two were. He could hear their voices growing fainter. Her hand was close to his, almost touching. He linked his pinkie with hers. She didn't move away, but looked at the twined fingers, curious. He drew the hand toward him, drew the girl toward him, her towel wrinkling in the sand, his big hand against the small of her back. She felt tiny. He could feel her breath on his face.

With a brief smile, she put a small palm against his chest, pressed him back. A spray of sand caught the light as she launched herself down the beach. Her bathing suit was a flicker of orange against the opal sea.

She waded out to Shelley and Hugh. The shadow from Shelley's straw hat made a polka-dot light pattern on her cheeks. Her body was like a young boy's, her chest flat, hips narrow.

"What's going on there?" she asked, nodding her head at Leslie.

"Nothin'," said Masha. She couldn't kiss him. His callused hand felt good against her skin. She could feel his desire and she liked it, but. What if she would only ever want Eli in all her life? What then? Reflexively, she turned to Hugh, who was already looking at her, his baggy trunks wet, hand shading his eyes. She couldn't make out his expression in the glare. Letting his arm fall, he turned, wading up to his slim waist in water, and dove into the sea. The two young women watched him cut through the water expertly with his long arms.

Shelley took Masha's hand and squeezed it. "Hugh's going back to L.A.," she said. "I hope he's gonna be okay."

Masha felt a pang of loss. Hugh had become part of her life with Shelley in the free rental. She wanted things to remain as they were. She looked at her friend. The quirky landscape of Shelley's face had become dear and essential to her: the soft, nearly weak chin, pert nose, surprised blue eyes, charming little overbite. Masha loved that face.

After a month of rejections, a casting director, a thin lady with the manner of a somnambulist, assessed Masha with greedy eyes.

"I have someone I want you to meet," she intoned.

The ensuing audition, for an off-off-Broadway musical: Masha walked onto a bare stage surrounded by empty bleachers. The director was a hunched man in a wheelchair with a wide torso and slender, hairless arms emerging from a short-sleeved Hawaiian shirt; the composer, a mournful-looking pale woman draped in a black shawl. They sat side by side in the front row of the empty theater. Coincidentally, each of them had a walleye; his right iris favored the right-hand corner, her left eye was frozen on the left. Masha couldn't tell if either of them was looking at her or not. I was reminded fondly of dear Cousin Gimpel, with his rolling eyeball that seemed trained on the heavenly spheres.

As Masha sang the song she'd prepared with the singing coach Nevsky had found her, under the grinding scrutiny of these two amblyopics, she was so frightened, she felt her chest, her innards being compressed by some invisible weight. Yet it was thrilling too, to expose herself this way. There she was, an observant Jewish girl, revealing her deepest nakedness to a bunch of strangers. I was euphoric. And they loved her! She got the part.

Titled *Charcot's Women*, the piece was about Dr. Jean-Martin Charcot, the famous nineteenth-century French neurologist, and the group of female hysterics he used to demonstrate his theories with. Medical students, fellow physicians—including Sigmund Freud— and curious members of the public used to cram themselves into the medical theater in the Salpêtrière Hospital in Paris to watch the bizarre act unfold. Every Tuesday Dr. Charcot would hypnotize his patients one by one and they would duly act out childhood traumas, have fits, suffer temporary paralysis—in a manner and order precisely reflecting Charcot's theories of hysteria. The question of suggestion, of how much of these acts were real symptoms brought out by hypnosis and how much were fabricated to please the great professor and keep up the women's star status, loomed large over the story.

Masha played a girl named Geneviève. It was a small part, but she got to do a lot of weeping and thrashing. The character had lost the power of speech through trauma and could only speak (or, in this case, sing) when under hypnosis. I worried that Masha's own mystery symptom, her ghost pains, would return to her and make it impossible to work, but they didn't. I came along on all the rehearsals. The theater was desperately impoverished, with bony benches rising up around a tiny stage more suitable for a flea circus than human drama. Rehearsals were like a visit to the madhouse, with twelve women of varying ages screaming and writhing, singing and shaking as the walleyed director wheeled himself around them all, muttering, and the composer sat in her seat, wrapped to the neck in shawls, drinking sloppy tea from a thermos and frantically scribbling notes onto a pad. I wished I could summon Antonia from whatever state *her* spirit was in, just so she could witness this chaos.

The musical opened to one brief, ironic review. Masha was singled out, however, and praised.

"Dunster is big news," Nevsky whispered to Masha in the deserted elevator as they enjoyed the silken ride up to the thirtieth floor. "A British director, just came off a hit called *My Way*. Dj'you see that?"

"No," said Masha.

"Course not. You never see anything," said Nevsky. "*Marauder* is a franchise. Three-film contract. And they want exotic—but not too exotic. I.e.—my interpretation—white. That's where I think we have the trump card. You're exotic. But you have to be hot when you go in there. You need to sear the seat. Dunster is known for his love scenes. You look amazing."

Masha was in a pair of Shelley's leatherette pants that fit her like skin, a red halter top, and four-inch heels bought at the mall in Patchogue. She looked like a hooker in a movie. When the elevator doors opened, Masha saw there were five or six girls dressed almost exactly like her, a jungle of lip gloss and hoop earrings and lashes, each one checking her out with fatalistic curiosity. When the assistant finally called her name, all the girls followed her with their eyes. Nevsky looked nervous and a little sad to be left behind. Doglike, Masha thought, looking back at him.

She wasn't as scared as she usually was. She had the whole scene mapped out; she had made a decision how to play every line. When she had done the scene three times with the casting director, who read with her, Johnny Dunster sat back in his chair looking at her, brow furrowed. He was a disheveled man with an English accent, prone to long silences followed by sudden movements and emphatic, stuttered requests. She looked back at him, motionless, waiting. After a long time, he said, "Thanks."

Five days later, she was called back.

"This is Carl," said Dunster when she walked in. "You're going to be reading together." Carl was blond and stocky, with smooth Germanic features, a pleasant, wide-open face. "So what I want you to do is," said Dunster, "sort of make out while you're doing the scene."

"What?" said Masha.

"Like, you're making out and talking. You know how that happens."

Masha looked at the young man, who put his hands in his pockets in a show of harmlessness.

"Just snog, make out, I need to see what that feels like."

Masha didn't move. She was trying to understand.

"It's a hot scene, I can't tell what it's like if I don't see a bit of the physical side," explained Dunster.

Carl, who had clearly been doing this all morning, and in fact still had a tiny smear of lipstick on his chin, sat down on the floor and looked up at her expectantly. She peered down at him from her chair as though he were a pool of freezing water she was expected to dive into. So this was going to be her first kiss, with this stand-in? She felt trapped. She couldn't leave; she couldn't blow this. She scoured her mind for details of love scenes from the movie she'd watched with Hugh. Taking a deep breath, she lowered herself onto the floor, crawled over to the fair young man, and kissed him. His mouth tasted like mint gum. Dunster shot up and pranced around them like a goat on its hind legs, calling out encouragement.

"Go on, hold the man! Grab his hair! Good. And again!"

Masha said her lines mid-ravish, her lips wet with the stranger's saliva. Jealous, unexpectedly horrified by Masha's defilement, I buzzed around them helplessly, floating in the air, a voiceless, futile housefly.

When she came to the end, Masha climbed back on her chair and wiped her mouth.

"Good," said Dunster. "Thanks, Masha." Masha stood up, trembling. She barely remembered any of the last three minutes. Confused, she mumbled something and left.

And after all that, she still didn't get the part.

One night, on his way home from work, Leslie veered suddenly off the LIE and drove into Manhattan. He knew Masha was in a play there. He looked the theater up on his phone. After the failed kiss on the beach, he had been too embarrassed to speak. He had just driven the three kids back to the Victorian, slinked off in his truck. The next few days he and Masha avoided one another at the Coe manse. But he needed to find a way back to her. He wasn't capable of forgetting about her, going back to his normal life. He was too far gone for that.

Standing in line to buy tickets to see the play, along with three other people, Leslie worried what Masha would think. He didn't want to seem like a stalker. Maybe he would just leave afterward. Wait a few days, tell her he had seen it with his wife. He bought his ticket and sat toward the back of the bleachers. Eventually the place filled up halfway, the lights went down, and the show began.

Dr. Charcot, a short man in a morning coat and bow tie, his dark hair slicked back neatly, walked onstage and sang a number explaining what was wrong with the first madwoman. A portly lady in a Victorian slip, her hair in disarray, wandered in, twitching. Charcot imitated her tics in a most entertaining manner as he explained her various syndromes. Then he hypnotized her. Deep in a trance, the woman proceeded to sing out a horrible experience of being run over by a cart, then had some kind of seizure. Once he woke her up, in came another one. This freak show went on for forty-five minutes, interspersed with snippets of Dr. Charcot's home life, where his wife kept singing to him that the women were all making it up to get attention. Leslie thought she had a point.

When Masha walked onstage, led by the nurse, Leslie was frightened for her. His palms were slick, his throat tightened. She didn't speak, but the way she looked around the room, played with the cross at her throat, hunched her shoulders, seemed sharp and real to him. The doctor explained that Geneviève had not spoken out of hypnosis for two years.

When she was hypnotized, Masha's eyes rolled back in her head and the harsh, unfamiliar sound of her singing voice sent shivers down Leslie's spine. It was dark, pure. The strange tension in her face, the way her hands curled up, her head falling back as she responded to the commands of the doctor—it all belonged to another woman. At one point, in order to demonstrate her hypnosis-induced catatonia, Charcot had the nurses balance her rigid body between two chairs. She was stiff as an ironing board. It was like she was channeling.

When the lights went down, he heard someone whisper, "That black-haired girl, the mute—she was incredible."

Leslie felt his face burn when he heard that.

Masha ambled across the stage. She felt emptied out, a staring husk. She was trying to piece together the evening's performance, but all she had to go by were a few scattered shards of the experience. This kind of amnesia was usual for her after a show. She was aware of her body onstage, but she felt it like an animal feels—the hairs rising on the back of her neck, chills up her spine, a rush of anger or shame. When she sang, she felt she was nothing but an open throat, a conduit for something that began beneath her feet and spouted into the atmosphere. Her everyday self disappeared. Masha had a bottomless appetite for this heady feeling of forgetfulness, of freedom. Night after night, she stalked oblivion. I knew what she meant. But I'll get to that later.

Masha was starving. She would get Surinder to stop for a slice of pizza on the way home. And a Coke. She heard someone call her name. She looked up. It was Leslie. She suddenly realized how lonely she'd been a minute earlier.

"Leslie!" she said.

"I had to come see you, didn't I?"

She smiled up at him from the stage. He walked down the bleachers.

"You were terrific," he said.

"Really?"

"You had me believing you were completely nuts. You want to grab a bite, or a drink?"

"Um, Surinder is waiting for me . . ."

"Give him the night off. I'll drive you home after," he said.

They stopped at a steakhouse on their way uptown.

"I'm always starving after the show," Masha said, filling her mouth with baked potato. "I'm gonna get fat."

"You're okay," said Leslie. "Oh, hey, I owe you something," he added, handing her the check he'd been carrying in his wallet. "It isn't much, but you earned it."

"Great," she said, taking it.

"You have a bank account, right?"

"Yeah."

"But you're employed now. You're on your way."

"Not necessarily. This kind of theater doesn't pay much and we close next week anyway. I don't know when I'll get another job."

"If you need to, you can always work for me in the office."

"Yeah?"

"If you need to. You can file. Vera always says she could use a little help."

"I'm trained for secretarial."

"There you go, then. Shall we head home? You must be tired after all that lunacy." Masha smiled. Leslie hated every avuncular quip that came out of his mouth. But he couldn't tell her what he felt. It would scare her away. And anyway, he had no business wanting what he wanted.

Driving along the LIE, they listened to the radio. A plaintive song. He parked in front of the Victorian house. She opened the door, hesitated.

"What?" he asked.

"Would you mind . . . just coming up with me and sort of walking around to make sure everything's okay? Shelley's in Manhattan with her boyfriend for the night. Once all the lights are on I'm fine. I just get nervous walking in alone."

"I don't blame you," he said.

The bare windows made the apartment seem a little sinister: street-lights blaring in, the place vulnerable to any Peeping Tom. She asked him to check her room, Shelley's room, inside every closet, behind the couch, in the bathroom, for attackers. It was touching. She was really scared.

"Anyone else moved into the building yet?" he asked as he pulled aside the shower curtain.

"Not till they finish the renovation," she said.

They returned to the kitchen.

"You want a glass of juice?" she asked, opening the refrigerator. "That's all we have."

"Sure," he said gently. He felt relaxed. Deirdre thought he was at the firehouse for the night. If anything went wrong at home, she would call his cell first.

He lifted his eyes from his juice and saw Masha looking at him.

"Is Shelley moving back to the city?" he asked.

"I'm not sure. She's back and forth. They were broken up and now they're sort of getting back together."

"But it freaks you out staying alone."

"I never even slept away from home until I moved in here," Masha said.

"Are you serious?"

"Yeah."

"Not even for sleepovers with your girlfriends?"

She shook her head.

"No wonder you're uneasy."

"I'm getting used to it, though," she said, pulling out her hair elastic, letting the heavy hair fall free around her face. "It hurts my scalp," she said, scrubbing at her head with her fingers.

"You're beautiful," he said.

"No."

"You know you are."

"There's all sorts of things wrong with me."

"There's nothing wrong with you."

"Yes, there is!" she insisted, smiling at him. "I'm bowlegged, and my ribs stick out. Look." She pulled off her dress and took three steps to the middle of the room. Leslie dashed to the wall and turned off the light immediately, lest anyone see her from outside. She wasn't wearing a bra. Folding in two, she slid off her underwear, standing up in the darkness. As his eyes adjusted, Leslie saw exactly the body I had imprinted in his brain all these weeks, glowing in a mix of light from the street and moon.

"Can you see me?" she asked.

"I can see you," he said quietly.

"See what I mean about the bowlegs?"

"You're perfect."

"You really think so?"

"Yes."

She walked back toward him, reached down and pulled on her dress again, the underwear.

"Masha," he said urgently, as if to catch hold of the moment.

She walked over to the wall and switched on the light, turned it up high. "I'm not scared anymore," she said, biting her lip. There was a pause as they looked at each other.

"Not scared of what anymore?"

"Being in the apartment alone." A moment slid by.

"You want me to go?" he asked.

"I should go to sleep. I'm sorry if. I just . . . can't, um . . ."

"It's okay," he said. He walked over to her, bent low, and kissed her on the cheek, weighing her heavy hair with his hands. Her skin was so soft, as soft as a child's, but her gaze was frankly impenetrable. What was she doing?

When Leslie left, Masha bolted the door and went straight to bed. I accompanied her, settling on the duvet.

---

She had loved Leslie's eyes on her skin. His gaze felt like sunshine. His hands, though, were too much. She could not transgress that far. Didn't want to. Shooing the thought away, my chaste girl stared out the window, her mind void, till her eyelids fluttered and sleep enveloped her.

Outside, Leslie sat in his truck, staring at the Victorian house. Masha's light was out now. He imagined the house on fire. He could rescue her then. He wanted to rescue her so bad.

## ∞ 34

The basement of the Hôtel de Bourgogne, where the Comédie-Italienne was housed, was a hive of storage chambers and scenery machines. On Sunday mornings before the matinee, or whenever we were both free, Antonia and I would wander from room to room down there, looking for a new place to secrete ourselves. There was one room filled entirely with fire equipment. Fires were so common in theaters, the Hôtel de Bourgogne had its own reservoir under the building, just in case. I have a precious memory of my girl reclining on a coiled sailcloth fire hose. As she arched her back, her small breasts emerged from that torrent of glinting hair like little white rocks in a streaming river. I dove in. She was tiny but fierce, with padded paws, sharp nails, biting teeth. She always fought me when we made love, made me find strength in my slender limbs.

One day I asked Antonia if the count was as good a lover as I. She laughed. "But don't you know?" she asked.

"Know what?"

"Villars is impotent, because of smallpox. Le Jumeau does all that for him."

"You mean . . ."

"They are a team," she said, smiling gaily and pulling me in for a kiss. I stood up, appalled.

"Since I met you, my love, I haven't allowed it," she said unconvincingly.

"But why—why can't he use me?"

"I have thought of that. I can't ask him, though, he would be suspicious. I promise you, most of the time it is not a matter of . . . His demands are not typical."

"I know," I said.

"I haven't set eyes on Le Jumeau for ever so long," she said breezily.

"How can you just sit there and smile at me like this is a normal situation?" I asked, banging my head against the wall. Once she had checked me for blood, she settled back on the bed, stroking my back.

"But why is one thing worse than another?" she asked blandly. "Your prick is part of you, and it works. Lucky you. His doesn't. I feel sorry for him, in a way."

I rubbed the growing welt on my forehead, trying to believe that Antonia avoided Le Jumeau entirely. It didn't work. I became tormented with jealousy, yet it only augmented my lust. I was permanently priapic, moving sluggishly through a thick soup of desire, barely seeing the world around me. The fact that I was betraying the count seemed irrelevant, separate. His relation to her was a convoluted business transaction. Mine was a bond of the flesh. In contrast to his paid evenings with Antonia, and, perhaps, Le Jumeau, I got mine for free; a *greluchon* was there to give pleasure. It was a courtesan's right to have her own lover. The fact that Antonia's *greluchon* was her patron's valet—this was problematic, perhaps, but I was past caring. It was her former paramour, Algrant, I worried about. Whenever I walked by his ticket window with the count, he smirked at the two of us so openly that I worried the count would take him to task for his insolence, and get an earful of truth in exchange. Luckily for me, as a rule the count arrived by the side entrance reserved for people with season boxes, so we avoided the ticket collector. The affair went on quite smoothly for several months.

One night during the interval, I was relaxing in Antonia's dressing room, my feet up by the hearth, having brought the count a bottle of champagne in his box where he was entertaining several friends, when there was a knock on the door. Antonia and I both rose and looked at one another. The count had told me he would not be visiting Mlle Giardina during the interval. Why was he banging on the door? Antonia stalled him, I hid behind a screen, Villars stalked in and said in a voice of terrible, whispery calm, "Mademoiselle, may I trouble you to ask if there is a male person here with you?"

"But monsieur," Antonia said, "I am about to go onstage!"

"I cannot leave until you answer my question," said the count.

"You can see there is no one here," said Antonia haughtily. "I did not realize that my every action was to be monitored by you."

"Please do not insult my love," said the count. "You have complete freedom apart from our time together. However, I have reason to believe that a man of mine is in this room, and that is a humiliation I cannot bear."

Antonia snorted. "That's a good one," she retorted. A merciful knock on the door warned Antonia she had a minute to get onstage.

"Please go, monsieur! This is the wrong time to twist my wits."

"Where is he?"

"Who?"

"Gebeck!"

Another knock. The door opened. The stage manager hissed that she was about to miss her cue. Antonia panicked and ran to the stage. Like a furious bear, my master ripped away the flimsy screen, revealing me. He was reaching for his pistol when I ducked and fled, following the natural path down the wing onto the stage, where Antonia stood blazing in the footlights, a look of astonishment on her face. I ran toward her. Her leading man stepped aside as I slid past him on the waxed floorboards, coming to a stop center stage. It was hot here, and all was saturated with unearthly light. I squinted into the shadowy, packed house: seats, carpets, walls upholstered in velvet and silk as red as an inflamed vulva, a thousand white faces staring up at me like rows of teeth. Paralyzed by this vision, I stood stock-still as waves of laughter bombarded me: the audience took me in my blue livery for a valet in the play! I became obscurely aware that my deft mistress was attempting to weave me into the plot line. Copping on at last, I was about to improvise a bit when a teapot resting on the table beside me exploded into shards. There were screams from the audience. I turned and saw the furious count reloading, stage left. I ran offstage right, jumping over all sorts of theatrical paraphernalia in my wild bid for life, clattered down the stairs, through the foyer, up another quick flight, and down a hall past the guard room, where members of the French Guard were deep in a game of cards and only noticed me once I had passed them. At last I reached the stage door, held open for my convenience by the grinning, slit-eyed ticket collector—architect, no doubt, of my ruin.

## 35

The night of *Charcot's Women*, Leslie shut his engine and lights off and coasted up to his house. It was past midnight; he didn't want to wake Deirdre. The lights in the parent trap next door were blazing, and he could hear exuberant big-band jazz trumpeting inside. Don and Libby were having one of their all-night sessions. Leslie was anxious to get inside before he was collared to umpire a fight. As he reached the door, he noticed the big orange tabby huddled on the windowsill, imploring him with a furrowed brow. The cat had been scrounging around the place for months.

"You again," Leslie said to him with a sigh. "Okay, I give up."

Leslie unlocked the door carefully, slinking into the kitchen, spooned some cat food into a plastic bowl, and set it outside. The big cat oozed heavily to the ground, prowled over to the bowl, and set to, its head bobbing up and down as it picked out chunks of meat and gnawed them, needle teeth exposed, eyes on Leslie. Leslie slipped back inside and shut the door.

"Do you have to rescue *everybody*?" Deirdre was standing, statuesque, in the kitchen.

Leslie walked to the sink and began to wash his hands. "I got sick of him looking so miserable," he said.

"So he's our cat now?" she asked, leaning against the counter.

"I just gave him some food, Deirdre."

"And that'll be you feeding him every day from now on, right?"

"I'm not saying we have to feed him every day."

"Once you start that, there's no end to it. You can't just feed an animal once."

"What are you talking about?"

"That cat is an aggressive animal. Our cats hate him, don't you realize that? He bullies them. He steals their food. And then you go and feed him—for what reason, your vanity? The only way to get away from a cat like that is to move."

He was drying his hands, looking down at the dishcloth. "You want to move?" he asked.

"Where would we go? We've got the whole frigging circus to drag along anyway."

"You mean your sons and your parents and your grandchild? That circus?"

"Oh, excuse me. Pardon me for not being perfect for two seconds. You weren't even on duty tonight, you faker."

"What are you talking about?"

"I called the firehouse. Tommy tried to cover for you once he figured out you'd lied to me, but it was too late. So where were you?"

"I went to a show."

"You went to a show?"

"Yeah." He was looking at her now, right in the face, and he didn't recognize her at all.

"What show?"

"It was called *Charcot's Women*. It was about a bunch of crazy females."

"Where was this?"

"In the city. Some tiny theater."

"With who?"

"Alone. I went alone. Okay? Masha White was in it. Remember her? She was okay." There was a silence then.

"Yes, I remember Masha White," Deirdre said slowly. "And this play went on till, what, midnight?"

"I gave her something to eat and drove her home."

"What's going on, Leslie?"

"What's going on is I went to see a friend in a show." He walked past her, brushing her shoulder. He continued through the kitchen and up the stairs, a block congealing in his chest.

Deirdre stood at the counter, frozen. Strangely, it was his feeding the orange cat that had her really steamed. It was such a thoughtless thing to do, masked as a kind thing. Mr. Rescue. Meanwhile, their marriage was dying. But the cat, the asshole cat that would have murdered them all for a dish of slimy meat, that cat gets saved. All she wanted to do was run, take the car keys and drive away to a place where no one knew her. She could drive to California, rent a cheap apartment, get a job, write her stories, eat cereal for dinner if she felt like it. The fact was, they didn't need her here. Leslie did all the things she could have done, better than she did: he knew how to be with Stevie, he had the patience. He managed her parents. He even cooked. She allowed herself to imagine a single day without her family. In her fantasy, she was driving home by sunset; she missed them all too much.

She walked into the bedroom. He was already in bed with the light off.

"Leslie?"

"You just woke me up."

"Are you leaving me?"

"I'm trying to go to sleep here."

"I'm asking if you're leaving us."

"I'm here."

"You know what I mean."

He lay there in silence, hating her, hating himself.

"What did you mean," he asked, "when you asked me if it was vanity that made me feed the cat?"

"I meant," she said, "that you like to get in the phone booth and put on the cape and tights."

"Is that all I am to you, some pathetic Joe who signs up to save people because he needs to feel big?"

"No," she said.

"So I guess that goes for all the volunteer guys, then, the whole system, fueled on vanity. You really are your father's daughter."

"What does that mean?"

"You're the big cynic, you figure it out."

The next morning, rain was battering the windowpanes. Leslie answered his cell phone at seven. It was Evie. Her car had broken down; she needed a ride to a job interview at a preschool. Deirdre was pretending to be asleep. Without hesitation, he got dressed and ran out of the house through the rain.

Leslie got to Evie's condo and parked, his engine idling. He didn't want to knock in case he had to meet another one of her men. At last Evie rushed out the door, locking it. She was wearing a zebra-print slicker and a pink miniskirt with high-heeled rubber boots, frosty pink lip gloss glinting. She did not look like preschool material. She hopped into the truck, reeking of fruity shampoo, and beamed at him with her overtanned, mildly booze-puffed face.

"Everything okay?" Leslie asked hoarsely, managing a smile.

"Yeah," said Evie. "Just need a ride, is all."

"Well," said Leslie, "here I am."

As Leslie drove through the swirling skirts of the hurricane currently, according to the radio, waltzing across the Atlantic, he felt the rain outside his truck to be a solid thing, a tangible continuity of water. There didn't seem to be individual raindrops anywhere. Headlights floated toward him, smeared and bleary as he moved along, his wipers beating frantic time, cutting ineffectual, temporary wedges out of liquid sheets that glided down the windshield like melted plastic. A red car popped up behind him, started flashing its lights, wanting him to go faster, even in this gale. Leslie slowed down instead. The radio was turned down low; barely audible frenetic guitar was mesmeric shoved down that deep. The hothead behind him was flashing desperately. Leslie slowed down to fifteen miles an hour, just to spite the guy. At last the road straightened out and the red car whooshed past him, the driver turning to glare as he passed. Leslie saluted. Chances were, the fire department would be cutting that moron out of his vehicle before too long.

The fuel light came on. Leslie pulled into the first station he saw. Infuriatingly, there was a line for every pump. He inched forward as the cars filled up and drove away. At last he was next. The emaciated woman pumping gas in front of him was clinging to an inverted umbrella, hair wet, staggering in the wind. The narrow protective roof over the tanks did nothing against this horizontal rain. Leslie pulled on his baseball cap and sighed. He was going to get soaked. The woman struggled into her car and drove off. Leslie pulled up to the tank and stared at the pumps lined up there: Regular, Plus, Premium. His hand on the door latch, he was stopped dead by a memory: Masha lying beside him in that orange bikini, black hair shimmering in the sun. He felt yearning flood him, then quicken like concrete. He couldn't move. The horn blasting behind him sent a thrill of fear through his belly. He looked in the rearview mirror. It was some jerk on his phone, some ass in a new Beemer, gesturing at him impatiently. Leslie whipped around in his seat and glared at the guy, who honked again. Climbing out of the truck, Leslie was drenched immediately. He strode up to the BMW, rain coursing down his neck, dripping from the brim of his cap. Leslie saw the man on the phone register his size as he approached him, but the guy didn't get off the phone, he just grimaced at Leslie with an expression of anger, impatience, and condescension, pointing to the gas pump with an open hand raised to the sky, a sort of jab, like, *Pump the gas, you idiot.* Leslie didn't realize he was going to get into the BMW until he was in it, soaking the leather seat. The man still had the phone glued to his ear.

"What are you doing?" he cried. The man was small, dark-haired. Smelled of aftershave. His green rain jacket looked brand-new. "You're ruining my seat!"

"Would you mind getting off the phone, please?" asked Leslie quietly.

"What was that?" asked the man.

"Get off the phone, please," said Leslie, touching a seam in the leather gearshift thoughtfully.

"Jeff, I have to get off, okay? I'll call you back in five," said the man. He shut off his phone but kept it in his hand.

"I need you to get out of my car now," the man said, his back against the door.

Leslie continued to fiddle with the taut leather gearshift. Beautifully made. "What's your name?" asked Leslie.

"My name."

"Yes."

"Richard Demos."

"Is that . . . what kind of name is that?"

"It's a Greek name." A tremor ran through one of Demos's eyelids.

"Well, Dick. You shouldn't honk at people. It's unpleasant." Demos shook his head, looking at his Rolex.

"I realize you're in a big hurry." Leslie sighed. He imagined reaching across the seat and grabbing Demos by the throat of his new rain jacket.

"That's right," said Demos.

"I'm just advising you not to be rude," said Leslie. "Your horn is really more of an emergency tool. To be used as a warning." Leslie locked eyes with Demos. The eyelid twitched again. The small man's fear was gratifying to Leslie; he couldn't help it.

"I take your point," said Demos in a tight voice. "Now can you pump your gas? Please?"

"Absolutely," said Leslie, getting out and leaving the car door open as he walked over to the gas pump, ignoring Demos's entreaties to close it. Through the window of his truck, on the narrow backseat, he saw Stevie's baseball bat. In his mind, he reached in and grabbed it, turned and walked, unhurried, up to the guy's car, and, with one expert swing, caved in his passenger window. Then he walked back to his car, threw the bat into the cab, shut it, and started prepaying for his gas, just like nothing had happened. Immersed in the fantasy, Leslie fitted the pump into the mouth of his tank, squeezed the lever, and squinted at Dick Demos, who was backing his Beemer up. Leslie watched him retreat with a level stare. Demos flipped him the bird.

Leslie ran up the back steps of the Coe house and knocked on the door. Mr. Cruz, the butler, opened it.

"Mr. Senzatimore," he said, smiling.

"Hi, there, Mr. Cruz. Masha said she wanted to work a couple hours on the boat—could you tell her I'm here?" His face was soaked.

"Masha and Shelley went into the city with Mr. Nevsky, they have auditions."

"Oh."

"Sorry. Masha didn't tell you?"

"She probably texted me. I haven't checked," he lied.

"They won't be back till tonight," said Cruz apologetically.

"No problem, I just thought she wanted the hours," said Leslie.

"Come in, get dry. Have coffee."

"Thanks, I'll get some later," said Leslie, trying to cover his disappointment. Cruz's sympathy for him was unbearable. He turned quickly, running through the rain to the garage, and yanked open the door, which yawned with a clatter.

The black boat hulked over him, a sulky presence in the gloom. He flipped on the lights. The hum of the fluorescents mingled with the dull drumming of rain on the shingled roof of the building. Since Stevie, sound meant more to Leslie. It made him feel guilty that he could hear what Stevie could not. At least he should appreciate it. He sat on a stool and listened, staring out the open garage door at veils of rain billowing over the lawn. He thought of her, in the city, high up in some skyscraper, raindrops zigzagging down the plate-glass windows. She was Being Noticed. Making an Impression, no doubt. The desperation that had been gathering around Leslie like a poison ground fog was drifting closer, rising. Soon he would be engulfed.

My old-fashioned fire rescue concoction stole into the hero's mind as he sat listening to the rain—but he embellished it: he imagined driving over to Masha's Victorian, saying he was there for a fire inspection. The workers let him into the basement. In his mind's eye, he saw himself taping open the lock on the basement door leading outside, then checking the back of the dryer for the gas pipe. That night, on duty at the firehouse, he crept into Masha's unlocked basement silently. On his knees, Leslie loosened the gas line feeding the dryer. He set a small fire in the laundry basket at his feet.

In his mind, Leslie drove to the edge of his district, five miles east, picked a random house, called 911 from a pay phone, reported a fire in that house, to divert the department. Sitting on the stool in Ross Coe's shed, Leslie's heart sped up: he saw himself ramming open Masha's front door, running through the smoke, up Masha's stairs, swinging open her door. He lifted her up, smashed open the window, held her face to the fresh air. Regaining conciousness, she opened her great, wet, black eyes and recognized him.

"Leslie," she whispered.

In Manhattan, high up in a glass building, Masha was staring at rivulets of rain weeping down the high window. She was auditioning for a musical film called *My Alchemy*. Bridget had gotten her the meeting.

An elfin person sat behind a desk before her. Masha was not sure if this person was male or female. The name didn't help: Rathgar Kennet. Masha was looking at the window to avoid staring at the director too hard.

"I came to your show as a last-minute notion," it said. The tight voice was high for a man, but low for a woman. "Because a friend of mine did the lighting design. I wasn't expecting to find such a powerful performer." Masha looked back at the androgynous person: lank blond hair fell over a pale forehead, piercing eyes seemed to pin her to her seat. It worried Masha that she found this person attractive. So—male?

"Where were you trained?" Rathgar asked, glancing at Masha's CV.

"The Bridget Mooney School of Acting," Masha said.

"Will you read for me, Masha? And then maybe sing a little?"

"Sure," Masha said. She held the script pages before her, turning to the reader, a dark form in a red sweater. Masha focused on him for the first time now, noticing a set of beautiful white teeth.

The emotion buried in the text surprised her. She didn't think it would make her so sad to read those words in front of someone.

"Good. Now. I'd like you to sing."

Masha had planned to sing a song from the Charcot musical for this audition. But when she took in her first breath, she realized she was going to sing K'vakoras, the exquisite Hebrew prayer she had sung in front of the men at her parents' Shabbat table, when she tore the napkin, all that time ago—when she was a child, it seemed. *Like a shepherd who seeks out his flock, passing the herd under his staff, so do You make pass by, and number, and take account of, and notice the spirit of every living being.* She disappeared into the song, losing herself gratefully in its dark, winding passages. There was a moment of silence when she went quiet.

"Beautiful," Rathgar pronounced. "I'm just at the beginning of the casting process for the film, Masha. So . . ."

Masha nodded, stood up. She was used to being told no by now. Expected it. "But whatever happens with this movie," Rathgar Kennet added, "I'm glad I found you."

## 36

Running from the Comédie-Italienne, the shots of the crazed count still echoing in my head, my lungs burning, I instinctively fled to my old neighborhood in the Jewish quarter.

I walked down the middle of my dark street. The moon shone on the wet cobblestones. An old lame peddler appeared from the shadows, his basket of rags strapped to his back. He gaped at me in my wig and livery. I tipped my hat, which seemed to frighten him. He hurried past me, limping up the street. I stopped at my parents' door. The street was silent. All good people were asleep. I thought with yearning of my old corner of the bed. Shlomo had it to himself now. I imagined sneaking in beside him. He would let out a bellow. I chose a dark doorway across the street, a few doors down, and waited for my father and brother to emerge for morning prayer. The night felt eternal. I kept dropping off, then waking with a start when my cheek felt cold, wet stone. I was so hungry. At last, at dawn, the Jews began their day. Men striding to prayer, women setting off with baskets of rags or used clothing. The door to my building opened, and my father, stout, glowering, officious, emerged, followed by the scarecrow-like Shlomo, whose gaze was always trained on his own feet. My father was explaining something to my brother, his arm waving.

Once they had walked up the block, I scurried into the building and up the stairs.

The door to our apartment was open. My mother was sewing below the back window when I stepped in. She didn't hear me. Buttery light softened her pointed features, made her look young. I stood very still, watching her, her head bent low to see the stitches. The room was bare; the furniture had been pushed to the walls, and an iron tub stood in the center of the floor, as it always was when there was a body to purify. As I have mentioned, my father was among those who prepared our dead. When someone found the body of a Jew, it was my father who was notified. The dead were washed, shrouded; then, the regime suffered us to bury them in cover of darkness, without fanfare, in silence.

"Who died?" I asked. My mother looked up. Nearsighted, she gasped at the liveried figure in a powdered wig standing there, incongruous as an apparition. Then, squinting, she stood. Her darned sock fell to the floor.

"Jacob . . ." It was almost a growl.

"Mother," I answered. She walked toward me, into shadow. Reddish pockets under her eyes made her look haggard. I opened my arms, expecting to embrace her, to drink in the scent I knew so well. Tears sprouted from her eyes as she approached me. A low moan escaped her lips. She walked up to me, looked me level in the eye, and hit me in the side of the head.

"You're supposed to be in jail! What happened? I've been going there for months! They told me you had been released, but I didn't believe them. I didn't believe you could disappear like this!"

"Please, Mother, can I sleep here for the day, while Father is out? I am very hungry and tired."

"Are you crazy?" she shrieked. "You're going back to your wife! Take off that ridiculous costume."

"I'm not going back to that maniac," I said.

"What kind of a man are you?" she whispered with frightening disdain, turning and opening the bread basket. She took a challah roll, cut it in two with a furious sawing motion, then hacked a thick slice of cured beef off a haunch hanging from the ceiling. Pressing the sandwich into my hand contemptuously, she drew me to her, kissing me hungrily all over my face, then pushed me away, tears running down her cheeks. I ate like an animal.

Just then we heard footsteps on the stairs. My ear was still hot from her slap as she shoved me into her bedroom. I heard shuffling, something being dragged along the floor. My father's stentorian voice boomed out a few orders. My mother came back into the bedroom carrying a bowl of stew, handed it to me furiously, and bolted us in.

"Who died?" I whispered between mouthfuls.

"Chayim," she answered.

"Chayim Levi?" I asked.

"Be quiet," she said, her eyes ferocious. She sat down in a chair opposite me and watched me eat. It was unnerving, but still I licked the plate clean. In the next room I heard the sound of water being poured over the body. The purification had begun. This could take ages, I knew, and it was making me thirsty. My mother would return me to Hodel, probably that afternoon. I would be yoking up my peddler's box by morning. I had to get out. I stood and walked to the door. My mother's exhausted eyes seemed to bulge from their sockets as she beseeched me silently to stay in the room. But what was there to lose? I unlocked the door and walked into the kitchen.

My father and Shlomo were standing on stools holding beakers of water. The tall, wasted body of Chayim the petty criminal was on a slanted board, held up by two strong men.

The board was propped inside a metal tub. My father was pouring a cascade of water over the naked dead man, washing his sins, the only things that had distinguished him, away. Poor Chayim, the rake. His jaw was tied shut with a strip of white muslin. In life, he had never shut up. He had loped around the neighborhood whenever he was in Paris to sell some gems or seed pearls, his coat flapping open, ragged slippers on his feet, his deep-set eyes glimmering with anarchic humor. It didn't seem fair to cleanse him like this without his permission. The water glided, shining, over the wasted flesh, gradually filling the metal tub. My serious brother stood at the ready with his beaker. The flow of water over the body must not be interrupted. My father looked up and clapped eyes on me. He took me in slowly, from head to toe. The flow of his beaker thinned. My father turned to Shlomo, who was now staring at me, and told him to begin pouring. When Shlomo began, my father got off his stool and turned his back to me, watching the proceedings. I could hear my mother sobbing in the next room. I thought about going in to her, but I couldn't bear to.

I was almost down the stairs when I heard her shouting my name. I turned. Her face swollen from weeping, she ran down the steps, stuffed a few coins into my hand, kissed me on the mouth, then ran back upstairs.

I spent a week in flophouses or sleeping in parks. I wrote to Solange, begging her to meet me at eight o'clock at night one evening, any evening, at a certain fountain in the Tuileries, with my earnings from the bet. Every night for two weeks I waited for her. I began to get to know the night life there. Once the sun set, figures moved silently, furtively, through the hedges. Fine carriages slowed and were approached by silken shadows. Figures alighted and were dropped off, flitting back into the darkness. A great deal of money was exchanged as I waited, hungry, for Solange. One night a well-dressed man sat beside me on the cool stone rim of the fountain. He wore a powdered wig. His face was very pale in the moonlight. He was looking at me intently from under long lashes. I said nothing.

"I've had a long night," he said. "But my rod is ready."

"Excuse me?" I asked.

"Let's go," he said, grabbing my hand. I looked at him stupidly.

"Are you deaf?" said the man. "I'll pay you thirty sous!" At that, a man with an enormous mustache, a rarity in those days, emerged from behind a neighboring shrub.

"You are both under arrest!" he pronounced. Beside him, an officer of the watch shook his leg, trying to get his circulation back after squatting in that bush for hours, I guessed. My companion on the bench turned to me with a withering look. "*Sale mouche*," he muttered, then rose to meet the inspector with great hauteur.

"I am the Marquis de Saumane, second cousin of the Duc de Condé," he said. "Do you still want to arrest me?"

The inspector was flustered and bowed his head. "In this case, monsieur, I will be happy with your pledge that you will no longer indulge in the Italian vice, at least not in such a public way. Our sovereign has made it clear he will not abide by it."

"What is your name?" asked the man.

"Inspector Marais. I act on the pleasure of the king."

"You are the famous Inspector Marais?" said the marquis, smiling. "I hear the king sits in bed with Mme de Pompadour and reads out your reports on the intimate habits of the noblesse. I hear that the royal consort finds it all very entertaining."

"The king wishes me to keep track of the nobles of Paris, and I do so. What he does with the information I give him is his own affair," said Marais, raising a low-slung chin. It was dark, but I imagined he was blushing. The marquis gave a little snort and walked off. Marais dismissed the officer with a shrug. The man walked off to find more scenes of Sodom, still limping slightly. Marais looked down at me.

"I really was just sitting here," I said.

"I know," said Marais.

"You're not going to arrest me?"

"No," said the inspector, sitting down beside me, his large behind drooping over the rounded rim of the fountain. He eyed my livery. "You are in service?"

"I was. I lost my job," I said.

"Well, that is fortuitous," Marais said, smoothing his mustache. "Because I have one for you."

So began my life as a honey trap, a "*mouche*," a fly to catch the spiders. Every night I reported to the Tuileries at nine o'clock, meeting up with my fellow informer, Georges, a desperate young runaway from the country with broad shoulders and stubby legs. Clearly, Marais was looking for two physical types. I was meant to attract the men who were looking for a slip of a thing. Georges could have killed his potential customers with his bare hands. Marais had given me money to buy a set of gentlemanly clothes to work in. I found a yellow silk jacket and britches at Les Halles. The job also came with a place to live: I roomed with Georges in a furniture-free rented room near the Tuileries. We shared a straw mattress on the floor.

Eventually Solange appeared one night, her back rigid, slender hands firmly jammed in a muff, despite the warm weather. She had been trying to find me for days, she said. My money was gone—and so was Le Jumeau. He had found my stash and fled with the well-padded cook. So that was that. Solange gave me a few sous, her mouth turned down with dismay. "Ah, Johann," she said. "What has become of you?" She took me for a prostitute. I didn't bother to set her straight. My current occupation was not much better than whoring.

For several months I worked for Inspector Marais. I was good at the flirting. I got reprobates of all types arrested, from chimney sweeps to men of the Church. For me it was a game, an act. Georges took it much too seriously. He felt ashamed of posing as a pederast, and often cried himself to sleep on our lumpy straw mattress. It was impossible, he explained to me, for him to return home. His father, a violent drunk, would almost certainly kill him.

One night, Marais and his policemen were nowhere to be seen and I had trapped a man ready to give me a fat sack of coins for my services. He offered to take me to his home—a rarity. I went. It did me no harm.

## 37

Leslie lay beside Deirdre as she slept, his chest tight with longing. His body was corrupted by need for the girl. There was no pure bit left in him, clean of her. He imagined an automobile turned over. She was in it, unconscious, blood on her face. No: screaming, awake, pleading with him. He held the Jaws of Life in his hand, a great pair of scissors to open the car like a can. And she, inside, soft and vulnerable as her carapace was removed, reached her trembling arms out to him. The charge of the scene was overwhelming to him. He stood, ruffling his hair and passing his hand over his face. He looked down at Deirdre sleeping. She seemed inanimate, alien. He had no way to reach her. He walked to the window. The moon was full, fading against the tender blue dawn sky. Down on the lawn the orange cat, the interloper, was stretching himself. The two Senzatimore cats stalked around him in a peculiar servile fashion, tails up. Two more felines emerged from the shadows. Several were skulking down the street. Leslie's lawn was filling up with cats. He stood and watched, incredulous. It was eerie. They all seemed to be swirling around the orange cat. Some were yowling. A fight broke out somewhere. He worried for his own cats. He should go out there and break this up.

He hurried downstairs in his slippers, pulling on his robe over his

T-shirt and pajama bottoms. He walked into the teeming yard, look-ing for his pets. "Trix! Patty!" It was impossible to tell them apart from the other animals in this half-light. The cats moved with savage delicacy from one point to another with no apparent cause. Why were they here? Leslie tried to shoo them away, kicking out with his feet, clapping his hands. The cats would skitter away a few feet, then close in again. Leslie walked to the center of his lawn and looked around him. Cats were sniffing, mewling, stretching, yawning. Unsettled, he waded through the furry tangle of them and onto the sidewalk. He felt repelled from the house. Turning, he walked off in his pajamas and robe, meandering down a few streets in his slippers, until he found himself in front of Dennis Doyle's house. Dennis's squad car was parked in the garage. The kitchen light was on behind the shades. A paunchy silhouette crossed the plate-glass window. Dennis. Les-lie walked up and knocked on the door. The birds were singing now. He could hear footsteps, shuffling. Dennis was arming himself, no doubt.

"Who is it?" he asked.

"Leslie."

Dennis opened the door. He was fully dressed in his tight uni-form, gun in holster. "What's up?" he asked, ready for an emergency.

"I have about sixty cats in my yard," said Leslie.

"Come again?"

"I couldn't sleep and I got up and looked out the window and there were all these cats," said Leslie. "I've never seen anything like it."

"What do you want me to do about it?"

"Nothing, I just thought you might want to see it."

"I'm okay," said Dennis, eyeing Leslie's pajamas. "You want to come in and have a cup of coffee? I don't have to leave for a few minutes."

"Sure," said Leslie. Dennis's kitchen was done up in aqua, one of Marcie's recent whims. Leslie sat at the gleaming table, his long legs splayed out.

"Why do you think that would happen—a convocation of cats like that?"

"No idea," said Dennis. "Animals are weird. They get signals . . ." There was a pause. "I'll take a look on my way out in the car," he said.

"It's a strange sight," said Leslie.

"Everything okay?" asked Dennis. Leslie took a sip of coffee and grimaced.

"What?" asked Dennis.

"It's like water."

"That's how I like it."

Leslie put the cup down. "You come over to my house, I'll make you a real cup of coffee."

"Invite me, I'll come over," Dennis said.

"I am inviting you."

"What—now? I have to go to work."

"When do you start?" Leslie asked.

"Five-thirty."

"I should leave you to it, then."

"How's Deirdre?" Dennis asked, a little too quickly. Dennis admired Deirdre. Always had.

"She's all right. It's hard with Stevie sometimes, but she's fine. Life continues." There was a silence between them. Leslie heard a car whoosh by. "How is it, with no kids?" he asked.

"What do you mean?" Dennis asked.

"I just wonder what it's like. As a couple."

"To be honest, for the marriage, I think it's good. Kids seem to get in the way of that. But . . . I think Marcie's sad about it sometimes. I hear you're working over at Ross Coe's."

"Yup. He has a Chris-Craft I'm refurbishing. Wants me to do it all there."

"I was called to his house a couple of times over the years, when I was stationed out in the Hamptons," said Dennis. "False alarms."

"It's a big paycheck," said Leslie.

"I can imagine."

Leslie stood up reluctantly. He didn't want to leave. Why did he feel the need to be near Dennis, of all people, when he found him so irritating?

Dennis was the last of the kids who had been playing in the cul-de-sac, the day Leslie's father died. Chuck Tolan was dead; the others had moved away. Dennis was the final witness. He and his parents had come by the house when they heard the news; Leslie could still see chubby, freckled little Dennis's embarrassed expression as he hovered near the doorway. To have your old man die was a tragedy; to have him hang himself was humiliating. Leslie resented Dennis for having been there. Yet it made him feel close to him, too, this shared horrible thing. Neither of them had ever mentioned it.

Back at the house, the cats were gone. Leslie called his own animals, but they were nowhere to be seen. It was as if the whole thing had never happened. When he returned to the bedroom, Stevie was sleeping in the center of the bed beside Deirdre, his skinny arms flung wide. Leslie gingerly climbed under the covers and gathered the boy to him, cuddling him, kissing his warm, soft cheek. Stevie snuggled in, resting one small hand on Leslie's shoulder. Without warning, Leslie's chest quickened, tears sprang to his eyes. He buried his face in Stevie's birdlike chest and sobbed. The boy stirred, but he didn't wake.

Deirdre heard her husband crying. She put her hand on his shoulder, but he huddled in toward Stevie. Sliding her hand down his arm, she lay still, her eyes on the ceiling. Something bad was happening to him. She didn't think it was just the girl.

An hour later, Stevie woke. Deirdre took him downstairs, then to school. When she came back home, Leslie was still in bed. His eyes were open. I was replaying the fire rescue of Masha over and over in

his mind. And words too, injected into his brain with the needle pre-
cision of a mosquito: *Get up. Go to her house. Tape open the door. Needs to
happen soon. In and out in fifteen minutes. Rescue her.*

"You want some coffee?" Deirdre asked him. He shook his
head, but his eyes stared out the window, vacant. She sat down on
the bed.

"What I said about you last night. It's not what I think. You know
that."

"It doesn't matter," he said. When she left the room, Leslie rose.
He walked over to Deirdre's purse and peered inside. A packet of
Marlboro Golds were nestled amongst the debris of everyday life. He
opened the pack and drew out one clean white cylinder.

Late that morning, Leslie drove to Masha's Victorian wearing his
navy fire department casual jacket and matching trousers. He knew
her schedule: she was at the Coes' at the moment, ironing out her accent with Doris van Hoff. Striding up to the front door, a clipboard
cradled in his massive arm, he knocked on the door. A worker, a short
young fellow with a scraggly blond beard, opened the door and let
him into the basement without question. The respect in the man's eyes
shamed Leslie, but he stayed his course. He felt he had been sup-
planted by something else, a story spooling out of him. It was almost
a relief to give in to it.

The basement was neater than he had imagined, swept clean and
bare but for the washer and dryer set against the back wall, and two
wicker laundry baskets tucked under a long table. Leslie walked over
to the dryer, shimmied it away from the wall a few inches, and checked
the gas feed pipe. He leaned down, took a small wrench from his
jacket pocket, and loosened the lead to the dryer. Then he tightened it
back up. He pushed the dryer back in place, walked over to the door
leading to the outside. He took a roll of silver duct tape from his
pocket, ripped a piece off with his teeth, and taped the door strike

open. Then he walked back up the stairs into the front hall of the house. He could hear the workers in the living room.

"Thanks," he called out to them.

That night, Leslie was on duty. He slept in the den, like always, in case his pager went off. Nothing strange about that. He stretched out on the couch and stared through the window. He told himself if he slept through the night, he would forget the whole thing.

## 38

It was July. A balmy evening, I remember, still quite light in the Tuileries. I had just turned nineteen. A small, sleek monkey on a long chain loped toward me and grabbed my hand. I was frightened at first, but the little fellow looked up at me kindly and chirped. He was wearing a blue jacket with gold buttons. His chain led to a colorful painted sign that I could not make out. A large man stood beside the sign. He had a big, ferocious head framed by a mane of hair.

"Turco!" he bellowed to the monkey. And then, seeing me, he beckoned. "Come! Free of charge!"

A crowd was gathering around players from various centuries: Henri IV, Eleanor of Aquitaine, some sort of Viking character, and others I did not recognize, ignorant as I was of most European history. Two fiddle players appeared in the circle and began to play a jaunty tune. I worked my way to the front of the crowd. The act began. I can only remember slivers of the action. The spoken part of the play consisted of bawdy rhyming couplets of varying quality, which, I suspected, the actors were largely making up on the spot. The crowd was roaring with laughter. Some people were weeping in hysterics. I didn't laugh, but I was intrigued. When the play ended, the man with the great leonine head, monkey on his shoulder, called out in a booming voice, "Our main show begins at eight o'clock in the Spectacle des Grands Danseurs, our brand-new theater, at the ramparts by the boulevard du Temple. You can't miss it. Come and bring your friends. Bring your wives. Your mistresses. This is a show that leaves the Comédie-Française looking like a bunch of anemics. We will show you real theater!"

When the crowd dispersed I approached the impresario.

"Monsieur," I said.

"What is it?" he asked brusquely.

"I would like to join your company. Do you have a job for me?" Jean-Baptiste Nicolet took me by the shoulders and looked down into my face, turning me this way and that.

"What can you do?"

"Anything."

"What are you called?" he asked.

"Le Naïf," I answered without thinking.

Nicolet frowned. "Come to the theater, we'll try you out. We need a fop."

I scuttled in the shadow of the mountainous Nicolet as the troupe straggled through the teeming streets, my hopes already pinned on his protection. Henri IV eyed me suspiciously from beneath his velvet toque, thumbs tucked into his vest. Eleanor of Aquitaine, a sallow lady of giant proportions, farted dolefully as she trudged past me, weighed down by her gilt robes. A rat-faced girl in a Hellenic costume rushed to my side, then turned and walked backward, scrutinizing me openly, her athletic arms swinging.

"But Nicolet!" she cried to the impresario. "He'd be perfect as the dying prince!" Then she confided to me, "Ours has been arrested."

Nicolet led us into the theater through a side door. The smell of melting wax, deeply familiar from my days of love with Antonia, gave me a false sense of homecoming. Impatiently, I pushed away the heavy ropes that sagged like vines from the ceiling, rushing to keep up with the maestro. Onstage, jugglers tossed painted balls back and forth; a man walked by on his hands. The monkey, Turco, hopped from Nicolet's shoulder and swung into the arms of a rather pretty girl, who kissed him on the lips, then pirouetted away. The members of the troupe scattered and disappeared into various crevices. I swiveled to face the house, and was disappointed by the barren long hall, with its tiers of utilitarian box seats surrounding a scuffed wooden floor. Nicolet roared out, "Taconet!" A small hunchbacked man with a shock of black hair appeared from behind a canvas backdrop of an ivy-covered ruin.

"Here's your new prince," said Nicolet, holding me by the back of the neck. Taconet took me in with hopeless, bored eyes. My yellow silk suit was stained, my wig frayed. "Do you think we can use him?" asked the impresario. Taconet shrugged.

"We'll try him once," rumbled Nicolet, pushing me away.

That very night, I was lolling in a bath chair, white paint on my face, dark circles smudged around my eyes. I was the tubercular Sardinian prince, married to the lusty princess of Naples, played by the rat-faced girl of that afternoon. Nicolet had rushed me into my costume while giving me a quick description of the plot. Around us, other players hurriedly did up buttons and crammed on wigs in the communal dressing room.

"But what are my lines?" I asked, as Nicolet smeared my cheeks with lead.

"You don't need to speak, you're dying. But, when she admits to her infidelity, make an indignant speech of a few lines . . ." He then stuffed me into my bath chair, turned, and walked off, preoccupied. Eleanor of Aquitaine, the giantess, now dressed as a nurse, burst into the dressing area, took up the handles of my invalid's chair, and wheeled me onto the stage, where a family of acrobats was somersaulting into the wings. In a panic, I let my head fall back and shut my eyes, deciding to affect semiconsciousness, thereby explaining my mutism.

Squinting, I could make out the audience below us, some rapt, others milling about, eating, and breaking into fights. As the melo-drama unfolded, I listened keenly for my cue, my mouth dry, breath short. At last the dreaded moment arrived: I heard the princess of Naples boasting to her handmaiden that she had been unfaithful—with my own brother! My cheeks burning with embarrassment, I roused myself, sat up in my chair, and gave my faithless wife a lashing I imag-ined my master might have given Antonia after my escape: "Is this how you repay my generosity? My trust? Lie down, sow, and traffic in the mud where you belong!" I cried, reaching a trembling hand out and pointing at the ground. The rat-faced girl seemed amazed by my liveli-ness. The crowd cheered and clapped. I felt a surge of joy rise up in me.

After the performance, Nicolet called me into his office. The mon-key was hunched on the maestro's desk, picking at a roll in near darkness. A scattering of crumbs had fallen over the wood like snow. One side of Nicolet's tortured head was thrown into relief by the warm light of a lone candle. The other side fell into pitch-darkness.

"Where have you come from?" he asked me, peeling an orange with his big fingers. The fruit glowed in its meager spill of light.

"I . . . I was in service. A valet," I answered.

"What led you here?"

"I was dismissed, some weeks ago. I have nothing else."

"Can I expect the police to come calling?"

"No—"

"Because I have had enough of that for one season."

"Nothing like that."

"Why were you dismissed from service?" The scowling half face floated in the dark like a planet.

"I became the *greluchon* of my master's mistress." For the first time, I saw Nicolet smile. He shook his head, severing a section of orange with a spray of juice and popping it into his mouth. The tantalizing smell of the fruit reached my nostrils. Chewing, he slid a few coins across the desk.

"Your first week's pay," he said, tossing the rest of the orange to the monkey.

And so began my career as the actor "Le Naïf." I became a member of the Spectacle des Grands Danseurs, receiving meager pay for my work in the *canevas*, brief plays in which the players made up almost all the lines. Really we were filler, storylets sandwiched between the strong men, jugglers, and acrobats who were the true stars of the Spectacle des Grands Danseurs. Our working process was simple: our resident bard, the hunchbacked Taconet, designed a canvas backdrop with a melodramatic flavor—a ruined temple in Athens, for example, or a canal in Amsterdam. Then he devised a plot, and a few lines for each character to spout at crucial moments. Apart from these flimsy anchors, the actors cooked up the whole play every night. It was terrifying and exhilarating, walking the tightrope without a net day after day. With my petite stature and guileless face, I was always cast as the innocent prince or the simpleton valet. Eventually I pasted on a beard and branched out to foreign emissaries, mistrels, and . . . Jews. I suggested casually one day that there might be a Jewish peddler in one of our *canevas* that took place in Amsterdam. Unsuspecting, Nicolet told me to invent a character. Chayim Levi was a comic triumph. I did him for years, dancing across the stage in a yarmulke and protective fringes.

With my earnings, I quickly saved enough money to rent a small flat on the rue de Grenelle. I even employed a flunky to make my bed and clean my house. I had no need of a cook, as I ate all my meals at my local inn or in the houses of friends. Apart from my meals and a few hours' sleep a night, I lived in the theater.

I began to enjoy a bit of a reputation. By practice and force of will I had eradicated my accent and sounded purely French. I became an expert at improvised cascades of righteous indignation. I used rage as fuel. I found it plentiful in myself; once I hit the first vein, there was enough to stoke my engine for an hour. I could also assume an air of wounded pathos. I could be funny. I had audiences howling. Gradually I became a second lead, the antagonist.

At last the lazy hunchback, Taconet, managed to write down an entire play on paper all by himself: a wretched melodrama called *Tears on Sunday*. For the first time, I was cast as the lead, a fragile young noble at the brink of suicide whose despair is interrupted when he falls in love with his coachman's daughter, but then the daughter marries someone of her own class and our noble shoots himself after all. The play was a huge hit with an audience ready to ditch the worship of reason for that of sentiment. Wishing to be in touch with the people's newly maudlin tastes, Louis XV commanded a private viewing of the play. Statuettes and engravings of me in swooning poses were sold on the street. Whenever I left the theater, fans engulfed me.

One evening, several well-known actors from the Comédie-Française came to see the play, and asked me to join the company. I had scaled the heights, albeit on the back of a donkey. And now I would be speaking the words of Molière! I walked straight over to the leonine Nicolet, my head high.

"Monsieur Nicolet!" I exclaimed. "I am happy to say I have been approached by the Comédie-Française to be a part of their illustrous company. As I am sure you understand, this is a chance I cannot forgo."

The impresario looked down at me with his predator's eyes, Turco perched on his shoulder eating a handful of nuts. He said nothing for a long moment. His silence made me uneasy. Eventually he turned and walked away.

The Comédie-Française was the most important theater in France. The actors owned the company, as well as being subsidized by the king. With my first pay, I employed a cook I could barely afford. I became short-tempered with those I felt were wasting my time, but not as short as the leading men were. It took me several more years to become a real bastard. I felt this was the behavior expected of me as a serious artist. At first it was an act, but gradually it became my personality.

About a year after my arrival at the Comédie-Française, a valet knocked at my door with an invitation. The Marquise de Maillé de Brézé requested my company at an "at-home" that evening. My landau was stuck for twenty minutes behind a line of other carriages as I waited for the other guests to disembark before the Hôtel de Maillé de Brézé, a spectacular residence blazing in candlelight. At last a footman opened my door, and I alighted.

Rose-Béatrice de Maillé de Brézé was more than twenty years my senior, a tall woman with long white arms and a teasing wit. She adored the theater, had many of the finest actors in her salon regularly. To be folded into her world was a coup. That evening I was entranced by the velvety soup, the plump quail, the melting meringues, the torrents of whipped cream, and the rivers of champagne that raged down the table. I simply opened my mouth and let it all stream in. By the time the marquise showed me her private theater, a gem equipped with every modern convenience, I felt as serenely pliant as an overfed lapdog. I could barely rise to the challenge of her carressing goodbye, and fell asleep in my coach on the way home. The next morning, I was invited to witness the marquise's toilette, to see her primp her wig, powder her face, tie her stays. I arrived late, having overslept and taken time to dress with care: my suit was white silk, with fine horizontal stripes of rabbit fur sewn onto the vest. I wore ivory hose, and the light, summer lace of my cravat was from Brussels. A maid showed me into the marquise's dressing room, where my splendid hostess was already seated, a cup of coffee in her hands, fine curls framing her face, her dressing gown a mountain range of violet brocade expanding around her in luxurious folds. I took a seat beside her, and dared to rest my elbow on her makeup cabinet, an ingenious little table with a built-in mirror and many drawers. It reminded me of the box I used to wear around my neck.

The Marquise de Maillé de Brézé was approaching fifty, yet her skin was very smooth, lined only around the mouth and eyes due to her tendency to smile. Her front teeth protruded slightly, giving her an involuntary little pout when she closed her lips, which I found quite charming. The principal signs of age on her face were along the jawline, which sagged slightly. But the near-constant animation of her features, so filled with intelligence and mercy, and her warm, steady brown eyes distracted from this flaw. The marquise was enchanting. I watched her play the little porcelain boxes of rouge, powder, and scent with nimble, expert fingers as she quizzed me on my impressions of the evening before.

"And the Comte de Brésaille? What did you think of him?" she asked me, winding her fluffy hair into a bun.

"I had the misfortune of being sat downwind of him," I answered.

She swiveled her head to look at me, delighted. "He has a terrible digestion, it's true."

"The worst, I'd say, in Paris."

She laughed joyfully, putting a hand on my arm as if to steady herself. "So you are as cruel in life as you are on the stage?"

"I am gentle. The plays are cruel."

"Le Naïf," she said, narrowing her eyes. "What is your Christian name?"

"Johann."

"I had an Austrian mother."

"Yes?"

"But the past is so boring," she exclaimed, waving her hand before her face and raising her frank, searching gaze to mine. "Isn't it, when there is so much to enjoy right now?" She didn't care where I was from. I was an artist; for her, I transcended class—and even, perhaps,

religion. This fact was still miraculous to me. In the days when I had
worn my peddler's box or borne a tray of pastries, this great lady
would not have acknowledged my presence. Now, not only did I exist,
but she was very slightly in awe of me. Not that I was her equal. She
wished from me only a little cruelty—understandable in a woman
who got everything she wanted—and much affection. I played the
game until she tired of it.

Thus began an affair marked by a complete lack of drama or posessive-
ness. Rose-Béatrice was incapable of jealousy. She simply wanted to
enjoy her life, and to help others enjoy theirs. I was glad to assist her
in her vocation, eating off the fat of her plentiful income, stretching
out in her creamy bed. Mad about plays, the marquise often assembled
little companies to play in her private theater. Though it was against
my contract, I often did so, on my night off. Private performances were
lucrative. Rose's husband, the old marquis, had his own mistress—an
actress from my company, in fact—so it was all quite cozy. Even after
our story had ended, the marquise had me star in her private productions, and allowed me to slip in and out of her shimmering world at
will. In my new guise, I saw quite a few of the nobles I once served at
the Hôtel de Villars when I was working for the count. None of them
recognized me. My one worry was that I would run into the count himself at one of Rose-Béatrice's gatherings, and he would try to shoot me
again. But I did not see him. I was not to find out why for some time.

When I was not scaling the social heights of Parisian society, I was
busy nosing its depths; when the curtain at the Comédie-Française
descended, I often took my carriage to the Tuileries. My wheels inching along the avenue, I peered out my window and watched the little
whores, male and female, bravely walking through the shadows, waiting to be snatched up and squeezed like lemons. This might have been
me, I often thought. I would have the coachman stop my carriage and
chat with a young boy or girl. Sometimes I picked up several, and we

made a merry party at my house. I was often robbed on these occasions. When in a hurry, I made do with the bushes. If I was flush, I would simply drive to one of various houses where my tastes were catered to. I didn't ask much: several girls and the use of a sitting room for an hour or two. In this blissful span I would create little erotic parties. Being the only male at these affairs, and surrounded by prostitutes, I was guaranteed a great amount of attention. Standing at a window, I could have a casual conversation with one lovely, a hand spanning her bosom, while another girl knelt at my feet, my battering ram down her throat. I could set up little stories between the girls. I could join in. I had an endless appetite for pleasure and work in those days. Each morning I woke feeling I could eat the world.

As an actor, I rose to the very top, playing Alceste in *Le Misanthrope*, which put me in a lousy mood. It was at this point that I ran into Blond Nathan. He had been to see the play, doubtless in order to steal from the patrons. I saw him first, skulking by the open stage door, his hands in his pockets, the edges of his protective fringes peeking out from under his vest. I considered turning tail, going out the front entrance to avoid him, but my desire to lord it over him was too great. I emerged.

"Jacob?"

"Not anymore," I said.

"Le Naïf. I knew it was you. I stood there for an hour watching the thing, thinking, *It's him! It's not him. It's him! It's not him.*" Nathan had changed little since we were teenagers. He was heavier, his hair was thinner, but he still had the two-tone teeth and the overbite, the big, innocent blue eyes. He kept looking at me, shaking his head, until he made himself laugh. He laughed and laughed until tears came to his eyes. I just stood there. "They all think you're back in prison, or dead. How in the world did you become an actor?" I looked at the friendly ne'er-do-well with contempt, wondering what he had lifted during tonight's performance and where he had stowed it.

"You sold me a stolen weapon, for starters," I said, smiling coldly.

"Sorry about that," said Nathan. "But how did that lead to this?"

"Come," I said, looking around us. I didn't want to be seen talking to him.

Back in my house, the disgruntled cook, woken to tend to my surprise guest, whipped us up a couple of omelets as Nathan admired my cozy rooms: freshly upholstered furniture, a large tapestry of a hunting scene, Oriental rugs, all purchased secondhand, gave off a feeling of quiet luxury. My many books spilled from the library into a glass case in the sitting room. A marble bust of Aphrodite, given to me by Rose-Béatrice, glowed on the mantelpiece. Nathan walked from one corner of the room to the other, examining everything while my flunky stoked the fire.

After we had eaten in the dining room in relative silence, we returned to the sitting room. Nathan drew his pipe from an inner pocket of his black jacket. I told him my story, omitting the baptism. He listened, shaking his head, staring into space, the smoke rising from his mouth in lazy wisps.

"You have a son," he said dreamily. At first I didn't understand him.

"That's impossible."

"How so?" he asked.

"No, I mean, I am surprised."

If the child was mine, he had been conceived when Hodel was unclean. Atheist that I was, I was not free from all the old superstitions. If anything, my years in the theater, a superstitious place if there ever was one, had strengthened them in me. The child Hodel bore was cursed, unclean, the product of sin. Of all the Torah's precepts I had been taught to observe in my early life, I now honored only one: a bloody quim filled me with repugnance bordering on horror.

"Hodel," said Nathan, "is dead. She went very strange after the child was born. Violent. She jumped into the Seine." My Hodel had returned to the river. Perhaps the river demon had never been expunged. What kind of child did she give birth to? "The child," continued Nathan, "is a fine, healthy boy, about ten years old now. He lives with the Mendels, of course. Madame Mendel is raising him as her own. She has called him Ethiop."

"Ethiop!" I exclaimed.

"An ugly name to guard against the evil eye," Nathan explained. I was quiet for a moment, imagining my son walking through the world with that name around his neck like a lodestone. What luck could find him now?

"Nathan," I said. "Will you do something for me? If you do, I will completely forgive you for what you did to me. The slate will be wiped clean."

"I can't see how I did anything so terrible, given the outcome," he said. "But tell me anyway."

"Tell my mother you had news of me, that I am well, living in Italy. That she should not worry anymore. Will you do that?"

"Yes, I will do that, Jacob," he said in an insolent singsong, a strained smile on his lips. "Tell me, within all of this, you still live as a Jew?"

"I live as a man," I said with a cool shrug. A long silence ensued. At last, Nathan stood up. Without saying goodbye, he left. I sat motionless until the sun came up. I had a son. I tried to imagine his face. I could not go back. It would have to be enough to know that when I died, I would not be extinguished.

## 39

Leslie woke up and checked the clock. Three a.m. He brushed his teeth in the downstairs bathroom, splashed water on his face. As he dried off with the towel, he looked at himself. What an exhausted-looking man, he thought. He went to the dryer, grabbed a few of his own T-shirts, shoving them into a plastic bag, then opened the front door as silently as he could, crept out to his truck, and felt for the fire gear he kept in the backseat. It was there. Deirdre's cigarette and lighter were in his glove compartment. He started the engine and pulled out, glancing at the clock on the dashboard: three-fifteen.

He got to Masha's minutes later, parked by the side of the building. The door to the basement was still taped open, as he had left it that morning. Once inside, he peeled the tape off the door strike, ran up the basement stairs, shut the door leading to the rest of the house. That would give him a few extra minutes before the fire spread. He walked across the basement, reached behind the dryer, and loosened the fitting with his wrench, jiggling the line until he could just hear the hiss of gas. It had to fill the room slowly if it was going to catch. Swiftly, he took the laundry from its plastic bag. He placed the clothes in one of the wicker baskets, kicked the basket over to the dryer, took the cigarette from his pocket, lit it with a trembling hand. The smoke made his throat clench. He dropped the lit butt into the laundry basket, knelt down on the floor, and blew till a little tongue of flame flared.

As he stoked the fire, his breath caught the plastic bag he'd brought the clothes in; moved it, ghostlike, a few inches across the floor.

I exulted. How good was my good man now? *All righteousness is a mask*, I thought. The only truth is the black mirth bubbling like pitch from the center of the earth. *Beauty is Truth*, I thought with a chuckle, having gleaned the phrase from a skin-care advertisement in one of Deirdre's magazines.

Having rigged the dryer, Leslie ran to his truck, drove the five miles to the end of his fire district, and picked a house. He figured he had a good twenty minutes before Masha was in any kind of trouble. Plenty of time. The phone booth receiver felt heavy in his gloved hand. He dialled 911. His hands were shaking. A woman's voice picked up immediately.

"There's smoke comin' out of the first-floor window in 48 Division Street," he said. It was a Cape house. He'd seen so many fires in this type of house.

"What is your name, please?"

"Bobik," he answered, hanging up and hurrying back into the truck. As he sped toward Masha's house, he heard his pager go off. "Calling all units. A called-in fire, 48 Division Street." The whole department would report to a called-in fire.

Turning onto Masha's street, Leslie saw smoke coming out of the first-floor window of her building. He stepped on the gas, passed the house, and made a quick U-turn so his truck would be facing the right way when he parked, as if he were on the way from his place. He called the fire dispatcher on his radio.

"It's Leslie. I got a structural fire on 155 Marine. By the boat club.

I was on the way to the other one, on Division. Be advised, I'm going in to investigate. I'm gonna be off the air for a few minutes." He had about ten minutes before the department caught up with him. He needed to get her out himself.

He reached behind him and grabbed the heavy jacket, the helmet. He stepped into the boots, pulled on the bunker pants. The smoke coming out the window was black. This fire was moving faster than it should.

He banged open the front door with his shoulder. Worried for my own safety (who knew how much smoke a little fly could take?), I decided to zip outside and witness the rescue in absentia: I nestled in the crook of a tree and inhabited Leslie, seeing what he saw—the first floor was clotted with black smoke. He could just make out the staircase. He had no air tank with him; if he didn't get up there fast, he'd be overcome. As he reached the first step, he looked down and saw that a wide square of the first floor was missing. The workers were putting in a new floor! He hadn't known. The fire in the basement would flash through the house now. He ran up the stairs. The hallway was gray. Masha's door was open. He could barely make out her bed. He radioed in: "I have located a victim on the second floor, three-four corner."

Masha woke, confused, logy, coughing. Leslie heaved her up, walked her down the stairs, crouching low. He had to get her out. He could hear the sirens now, faintly. They were on their way. It was pitch-black on the stairs. He felt his way along the wall. It seemed as though he was creeping down those blackened stairs forever. Her body was so heavy, slung over his shoulder. The heat and smoke were hellish. He thought he would pass out. At last he saw the open front door, a faint rectangle in the evil dark.

The trucks were on the lawn as he knelt at the doorway, set Masha down on the porch gently. She flopped like a rubber mannequin. She was barely conscious, but her eyes focused on him. She knew he was the one. There were men crawling by him, carrying a hose into the building. They would have the fire out out in minutes. Curious to see the firemen at work, I flew up to the second floor and peered in a window. I could see a fireman crawling up the stairs, the light on his helmet the only illumination as he felt his way through the darkness, looking for victims. I could have told him no one else was there. I looked into Shelley's room, to see what was left of it. A lick of light from one of the flashing trucks illuminated a hand. I stared in horror. Leslie and I had both assumed Shelley would be in the city, having gotten back together with her boyfriend. I dive-bombed down toward Leslie, screaming.

Unaware, Leslie walked to the ambulance where they had Masha on a stretcher, oxygen up to her face. The paramedic set him down on the bench and gave him some as well. I buzzed around his face frantically. He waved me away. I kept bashing myself against his mask, yelling into his mind, but he was deaf to me, swatted at me. Masha looked up at him.

"I was driving toward another fire," he explained to her. "I saw smoke coming out of your basement window." She nodded, then drew the mask from her face. Asked him:

"Did they get Shelley out?"

Leslie ripped the oxygen mask off his face and stood, suffocated by fear. He grabbed his helmet, tore actross the lawn, his eyes only on the blackened door of the house, running over crisscrossed hoses, through beams of colored light pulsing from the trucks. When he reached the door, Tony stepped out of the house and blocked Leslie's path. His fire hat was set far back on his head; sweat streamed down his face.

"What's up?" he asked Leslie.

"There's another victim up there."

"McCauley's got her," said Tony.

"Did she make it?" asked Leslie.

Tony unclipped his walkie-talkie from his vest pocket, legs spread wide. "Hey, Jim. Do you read me?" There was a pause. "Come in, Jim McCauley."

The walkie-talkie let out a hiss. "I'm comin' down."

"What's the status of the victim?"

"She's conscious. Looks like she burned her hand."

At this, Tony looked up at Leslie, his flat mouth turned down at the corners. "Okay, Les?"

"Okay," said Leslie.

Tony stepped to the side, away from the door, putting his hand on Leslie's arm. Leslie turned to face him. "The fire's out, Les," he said. "Nothin' left to do. You . . ."

"What?" Leslie said.

"Take a load off. You gotta stop worrying about everybody so much. You're just . . . too good a guy, sometimes."

Leslie crossed his lawn. The birds were chirping. The dawn was fine and clear. He walked into the open garage, unlocked the green metal cabinet in the back, and pulled the gun from behind the motor oil. He couldn't remember where the bullets were. He always hid them so carefully so Stevie wouldn't find them, now he couldn't remember where they were.

He walked into the silent house, sat down at the kitchen table, the handgun balanced on his long, splayed fingers. He looked around him, at his place, this kitchen he had built with his own hands. It seemed like a kitchen in a commercial now; nothing to do with him. What had happened? It all seemed like a dream, and now he had nearly murdered that girl. He would never see Masha again. He didn't even want to. The shame of what he had done was unbearable.

The solution to the problem was obvious. They say it runs in families. In all the world, Leslie thought himself the least likely to. Mr. Positive. Yet here he was, bowing his head to the symmetry. Where were the bullets? He didn't feel sad, only determined to remove himself. He still wondered at it, though, how he had been ruined so quickly. Maybe it had been coming on a long time.

For the first time, I wished I had left Leslie alone.

There was a shuffling on the stairs. Leslie felt afraid. He didn't want to see her. It was Stevie. Tiny blond boy. Leslie was holding the gun under the table. He shoved it into the loose pocket of his sweatpants.

Stevie signed: "There was a fire?"

"Yes," signed Leslie.

"Did you save anybody?"

"Yes."

Stevie walked over to him, climbed up on his big lap, put his head against Leslie's chest. In his toneless, too-loud voice, he proclaimed, "I wanna watch cartoons!"

"Is that why you came down here?" Leslie signed.

Stevie nodded. He slid off Leslie's lap and pulled at his hand. Leslie stood up, led, shuffling, into the living room. He slumped into the soft leather couch, pulling the boy up on his knee. Stevie switched on the TV. It was on mute. The bright colors on the screen flashed and whizzed and popped. Leslie took the remote and turned on the sound. He held the little boy very close and watched the cartoon, the empty gun in his pocket. Deirdre entered. She was wearing her fluffy peach robe. She sat beside Leslie, squeezed his limp fingers.

"I didn't hear the pager last night," she said.

He stared at the TV. A tear made its crooked way down the crags of his face. My poor man. He had fallen, crashed into pieces, and I got no pleasure from it, after all. Stevie watched the cartoon, nestled into Leslie's lap, oblivious.

"Did something happen?" Deirdre asked.

He turned to her. It was Deirdre's face again, her dear face. He tried to move his arm to touch her, but it felt too heavy.

"I need you to help me, Deirdre," he whispered.

"Of course I'll help you," she said, infused with sudden, startling gratitude for all she had not quite lost. Leslie stared into her, his eyes fierce, clear globes.

## 40

I went on with my life in the Comédie-Française. As to the boy playing somewhere in the Jewish quarter, my blood in his veins: I tried to think of Ethiop as a dream, fag end of the hallucination that was my life before I became a Frenchman. For the most part, I succeeded. Aside from a persistent cough, nasty reminder of damp nights spent trawling the Tuileries for sodomites, I remained one hundred percent carefree.

I had exchanged several letters with Solange over the years. She knew I had gone onstage. One morning she appeared at my door, her eyes glassy.

"The Comte de Villars has been arrested," she said. I brought her inside, struck by her solemn beauty. Her face was fuller now, and there were steel-gray streaks in her dark hair. I gave her a cup of tea, and she explained that the count had lost control of his finances. Le Jumeau having disappeared with my portion of the winnings from the bet, Villars seemed at a loss, adrift in his life, and began to gamble compulsively, mounting up huge debts. The countess was furious that he was spending her dowry. She called him a child, a lunatic. She began to work day and night to have him arrested. She wanted him to be judged insane. This was a solution of desperation among aristocratic families, for inveterate profligates: they were simply put into prisons and kept there. The families bypassed the regular judicial system by virtue of something called a *lettre de cachet*—a sealed letter from the king, demanding the arrest of the person in question. With a *lettre de cachet*, anyone could be disposed of, and released only at the pleasure of the king. Some noblemen incarcerated in this way were never released at all. Now the grand Comte de Villars was in prison at the Château de Vincennes, the holding pen for aristocrats! As my old nemesis, Inspector Buhot, once said, "Nobody can predict his own fate."

Solange became my housekeeper that afternoon, having unwrapped my porcelain candelabra, memento from the count, and set it proudly on my dining table. I could not afford to keep her as the count had done, but she was satisfied with the wage I offered. Going to the country to live with her husband did not seem to be an option she favored.

Immediately, my life improved. Solange thought of everything: menus to please my palate and ease my digestion; softer bedding to promote sleep; fragrant potted narcissus to create peace of mind and please the eye. She led the two servants with a firm but gentle hand. It was as if I had a wife, and yet I was completely free. Heaven.

I loved Solange. She swished through my house with her light step, her intent expression. I drew comfort from her orderly mind. I think Solange was really a secret nun. She had the private radiance of a truly spiritual being. She was sister, mother, friend to me; for kicks I had almost any actress in Paris, and a few society ladies besides. I was never short of company. I had become a cold person, filled with sour quips and unkind ironies. I was amusing, though. People feared me and were drawn to me because of it. I trusted only Solange, who knew my original self.

My lungs hadn't been right for years. One day, after a violent coughing spasm, I drew my handkerchief from my mouth and saw that it was stippled with blood. Instead of taking it easy, as Solange bade me, I took on more work, and stirred myself into a social whirl.

I invited groups of people I didn't particularly like over to my house and entertained them compulsively, never satisfied unless I had them weeping with laughter. The improvisatory skills I had learned at the Spectacle des Grands Danseurs never left me; in fact, I now had a need to speak in paragraphs. I plied my guests with the best drink, sending poor Solange down to the cellar for more and more champagne. Many of the actresses in those days were also courtesans, as Antonia had been; it wasn't uncommon to see a pair of nipples poking out from the top of a loosened bodice. After each such grotesque evening, when the guests had stayed till dawn and the rouge on the women's faces was smudged and formless, the false hair on their heads coming apart like old sofa stuffing, the men's faces gray, I was filled with sadness. Without even saying goodbye to the last of my guests, I would trudge up to my room and lie on my bed. Sometimes I wept without expression, my face a blank. Solange always came in at those times, brought me chamomile tea and some buttered bread. She sat on the chair beside my bed, doing needlepoint or reading a book. She listened if I wanted to talk, but mostly she was just present. Eventually I fell asleep.

The coughing seizures got worse and worse. There were sudden fevers. The theater doctor prescribed all sorts of remedies, including mustard plaster and being bled by leeches. For a time I thought I was getting better. I played Argan in *Le Malade imaginaire*, of all things, hoping not to expire on the stage like Molière himself. I felt myself growing stronger. Gripped by a sudden lust for extreme enjoyment, I held a dinner every night for a week, inviting all the most entertaining people I knew. Antonia herself made an appearance. It was a small world, ours; we were bound to run into each other. She was over thirty now, and no longer commanded the huge sums as a courtesan that she once had. But she was still a fine singer, spritely and fun, and loved a romp. I didn't mind that she knew of my origins. Many people did, by now, know I was a Jew. No one much cared in that society. Players were outcasts, in a way, just like Jews. So that made me a double outcast.

The morning of the final party, I had one of my fevers. I played onstage anyway, and came home slick with sweat. I thought half a bottle of champagne would raise my spirits, and it did, for a while, but by the time dinner was served I was shivering violently. I took to my bed, raising my glass to all present and commanding them to stay until dawn if they wished. Solange divided her time between the guests and me. She wished she could ask them all to go home, but I wouldn't let her.

She placed the count's candelabrum next to my bed. I stared at it, listening to the aggressive laughter downstairs, and remembered how as a child I had gazed at the Shabbos candles with such wonder. Now my eyes, drained of their credulity, stared, empty as two dry buckets, at the mesmerizing flames that crouched, reared up, and swayed from side to side in the breeze leaking through the loose windowpanes like six charmed snakes.

## 41

Masha's hand was sandwiched between her mother's palms as Pearl sat gazing out the hospital window. Masha stared at her mother's hands, waiting for time to pass so the drug they'd given her would kick in. The pain in her chest was deep, as though a spade were digging into her with every heartbeat. They had done all sorts of tests, but, again, they'd come up with nothing. Ghost pain, they said. Something was stalking her from the inside. She felt helpless. *How strange that Leslie was the one to rescue me*, she thought. She remembered seeing the massive figure coming at her through the smoke. She had thought she was about to be murdered. For the first time, Masha missed Leslie, and imagined him charging into this hospital room and taking her away with him. She would gladly go. She wanted him to come get her. The rescue had opened her up.

Pearl cleared her throat, shifted in her seat, but she didn't let go of Masha's hand. A muted knock at the open door, and Derbhan Nevsky tottered in, his skinny legs looking almost too frail to keep him up. He was carrying a bunch of flowers and a stuffed plastic bag.

"Masha," he whispered. His face had gone slack, deflated. Pearl looked up at him.

"I'm Derbhan Nevsky, Masha's personal manager," said Nevsky, bowing, the flowers behind his back. "I am so sorry about this." Nevsky slumped onto an orange plastic chair, his back curved.

"Is Shelley okay?" asked Masha.

"They've already released her."

"She was supposed to be in the city," she said. "She stayed 'cause I was scared."

"She's fine, though. Don't question it," said Pearl. "You'll drive yourself crazy."

"You mean I'm supposed to believe this all happened for a reason? It's in the plan?" Masha spoke in a hoarse whisper. "Please just leave me alone with that stuff, Mommy." Pearl let go of her daughter's hand, smoothed her skirt.

"The Coes are on their way to their boat in Greece," said Nevsky. "I think the best thing—and Mrs. Edelman, I'm sure you agree with me—is for Masha to go home. You need to recover."

He swung a full plastic bag onto the bed. "You left some clothes at the Coes', I thought you might like to have them," he said. "Plus your cell is in there."

Back in her own bed again, Masha stared down at the dish of melting chocolate ice cream, the only food she could get past her gullet without gagging. Pearl had brought it on a tray. Masha drank a spoonful of the sweet, cold soup at the bottom of the bowl, thought of Shelley, how she loved ice cream. She might be licking a cone now, out in the sunshine. Masha felt a great chasm opening up between her and her friend. The pain had led her back home. She would never live in the story machine now, nor be a part of that magic world. It occurred to her that she might not live very long.

Masha hadn't spoken since she got home. Pearl, Yehudis, Miriam, and the others came into the room many times a day, filled with worry and consolations. Masha sat, wordless, wild-haired, with dark circles around her great glittering eyes, her catatonia turning each family visit to awkward cajoling. She was beginning to frighten them. Her thoughts were muddled. Bundles of memory exploded in her mind and radiated outward. She stared into the still-fresh images, marveling at what had been her life such a short time ago: the view she had of the marina from her bathroom window as she brushed her teeth, boats bobbing in the glittering sea; her customary black chair in the now-charred free rental, where she would sit with her feet tucked under her every morning, planning her day with Shelley, filled with a sense of possibility, her destiny mounting; her bare limbs gliding through the Coe pool, the warmth on her face as she turned it toward the sun, eyes closed . . . and, though she tried to avoid it, there was another, darker recollection: a few hours after Nevsky left the hospital, the Coes had made a surprise visit. Shiny-faced Ross appeared bearing a huge bunch of roses in his manicured hands. Ancient Helga clacked in after him, tight beige trousers tucked into black boots, low-cut top revealing deep creases in her overbaked breastplate. She struck a pose of exaggerated sympathy, thin lips turned down in a clownish pout, head tilted to one side.

"Oh, my beauty!" she whined. "You poor thing."

Masha smiled up at them. "I thought you'd gone," she said, taking the cellophane-swaddled roses from Ross and holding them in her arms like a baby.

"We're on our way to the airport," said Ross.

"How could we leave without saying goodbye?" effused Helga. "You look so like a Klimt, with your marvelous eyes and your hair . . ."

Coe drew a photograph from his inside blazer pocket. "We're going to have Leslie keep working on *Sweet Helga* while we're gone," said Coe, handing her an image of the black boat. Masha looked at the photograph. In it, she was standing at the prow of *Sweet Helga* in a T-shirt and shorts, an electric sander in her hand. Leslie was beside her, had his ear mufflers on. "Thought you'd like a picture of her, you did so much work on that boat."

"Thanks," said Masha. The picture seemed as though it had been taken a long time ago. Two people, high up on a big boat, fuzzy with overexposure, nearly pulverized by light. She felt like weeping. It was then that Pearl walked into the room, her wig neat and shining, stockings thick, sleeves long. Helga turned—saw Pearl—froze. I watched as a blush boiled up under Helga's skin, mottling her chest, her neck, climbing up to her cheeks. Her capped smile appeared swiftly, bravely. I couldn't tell if it was panic or embarrassment that was affecting her so deeply. Masha witnessed the sanguine tide rising beneath the epidermis of Helga Coe. Her dark night eyes traveled to her mother. She knew these people wouldn't help her anymore.

"I'm Pearl Edelman," Pearl said. "Masha's mother."

"Of course," said Helga, almost to herself.

"Pleased to meet you, Mrs. Edelman," said Ross, putting out his hand, which fell back to his side, untouched. "Ross and Helga Coe. We simply adore your daughter."

Pearl regarded the pair of them. "Good to meet you," she said, then began to fold Masha's things, as if to leave them to their privacy. The Coes left with cheery haste.

Neither Pearl nor Masha spoke of the Coes, once they were alone. I crept along the edge of Masha's breakfast tray, wondering. Some horror had been acknowledged by Helga's blush, some vile thing released. I didn't know what it was yet, but it terrified me.

After a week at home, Masha woke to find that the pain had receded from her chest like a noxious tide. She propped up her head on her fist and cast a hostile glance around the room: her sisters' tidy beds, the bare desk, each pencil in place, a row of dolls they had once shared crammed on the shelf above the radiator.

The plastic bag of Masha's clothes lay crumpled on the floor beside her. Masha reached out for it, leaning over in bed to peer at her things: a pair of jeans, a dress, shorts, a couple of tank tops. Shelley's favorite orange platform shoes had somehow been added to the pile. Masha took out each item and spread it on her bed. Hungrily, she dressed herself in the tight jeans, a tank top, the shoes. Masha thought of her shining friend, wobbling along in these heels, her coltlike legs skinny and strong, shock of blond fluff pinned down with girlish pink clasps. Masha was brushing her hair for the first time in days when Estie walked in.

"Oh, what are you—what are you wearing, Mashie!"

"I'm alone in my room," said Masha. "I get to wear what I want."

Estie walked over to Masha's bed and sat down at the end of it, pulling the covers over her bony knees. "They talk about you all the time, you know," she said.

"I bet," said Masha.

"Yehudis feels bad."

"Why?" asked Masha.

"Because of Eli," said Estie. "Oh! Can I have one?" she was holding up a bag of purple hard candy she'd found under the blanket.

"Sure," said Masha. "What about Eli?"

"That he's taking out Yehudis," said Estie, sucking on the sweet. "But Mommy says if it's *beshert*, it's *beshert*, and she shouldn't worry so much. I think they're gonna get married."

Masha just sat for a long time. She was amazed by how much she could cry. No sobbing; just silent, unstemmed tears that dripped down her face. Yehudis rushed in and wept too, when she realized that Estie had told her. She sat beside her sister, held her hand.

"It's okay," said Masha. "You should marry him. I couldn't have made him happy. I don't think I'm that kind of person. I don't know why."

"Of course you are," said Yehudis. "When you meet the right person it'll all work out."

Masha shook her head. "I wish I could get out of here," she whispered. She had no money. She didn't know anyone outside. It was finished with the Coes; Nevsky had disappeared.

She began walking around the house in her skimpy clothes. Mordecai wouldn't even look at her. The younger children stared; Suri and the twins avoided her, embarrassed. Miriam told her she could at least have the consideration to dress modestly while in her parents' house. "Why must you insult us?" she asked. Masha didn't answer; she couldn't, really. Her mind was a blank. She could not do more than what she was doing: haunt the house, her mind clogged, her legs and arms moving mechanically. She knew one thing: if she put on her old clothes, if she covered up again, then it would be a sign that she was ready to die. She ate in her room, lay in bed all day. Pearl looked in on her daughter every fifteen minutes or so. She insisted the door be kept open at all times.

I despaired of my plan. The ruin of Leslie Senzatimore had brought me no joy, as it turned out. And here was Masha, on suicide watch. My meager powers were not enough to rectify the situation. I began to hope someone would swat me and put an end to my misery when Pearl's sister, Rivkah, came to visit from Baltimore.

Rivkah was plump, bustling. She wore a bobbed brown wig. Glasses. She ate the modest late-morning snack Pearl served up with gusto, and spoiled the youngest children with books and sweets. Then she lifted a large blue folder from her satchel.

"I know you have a million things to do before sundown, and I promise I'll help you," she said, beaming at her sister. "But I can't wait anymore, I have to show you this."

"What is it?" asked Pearl.

"The family tree!"

"You finished it?"

"Can you believe it? Ten years it took me! Don't worry about spilling coffee on it, this is just a copy," she said, spreading out the laminated page for inspection. "Now, look. The pink squares are direct relations. The blues are indirect. You know we originally came from

Poland. Well, boy do I have a surprise for you!" The page was a maze of lines connecting pink and blue rectangles. Each rectangle contained a name, a place and date of birth, and death. The print was tiny.

"Look how far back that goes," murmured Pearl, tracing her finger from her own name, with its impressive eleven offspring written below it, up and up, to people born in the seventeenth century. "Sixteen ninety-two!"

"Yes. There are still a few names outstanding. We already knew about Grandpa Max coming here through Portugal, but look. Look at this. In Poland. See? He's not a direct relative, but he is a relative." A shiny red fingernail was pointing at a name. Curious, I hovered over it. I read: *b. 1732. d. 1780. Gimpel Cerf.* It couldn't be. Cousin Gimpel? I landed on the name, only to be shooed away by Rivkah.

"He was a maggid. A wandering holy man. A tzaddik. He was the disciple of the Rav Dov Ber, who was of course a disciple of the Ba'al Shem Tov!"

"No . . . ," Pearl whispered. I landed on the table with a thud. Was I *related* to these people? Tears came to my eyes and I looked up to heaven. This would really be too much.

"We have a true tzaddik in our family," Rivkah continued. "And not just any tzaddik—one of the originals! Now try marrying off your girls, they'll go like hot cakes!"

"Rivkah!" Pearl laughed. "That's a little shtetl for me."

"Say what you like, you know it's a nightmare getting them all married, and everybody loves a tzaddik in the family," said Rivkah.

"I have to admit, you're right," said Pearl, checking her watch. "Oh, I need to get to the store, it's so late!" They fled, leaving the baby in the care of Trina, the housekeeper. The family tree was left exposed on the coffee table. I flew over to Gimpel Cerf's name and landed on it. As my filament-thin legs trod across the characters, I had a strange sensation: images were being drawn up into my brain, as if through the pads on my feet. I could see Mezritch. The men in their high fur hats, their black caftans, the women, hair covered, aprons soiled, walking through the streets, their children hanging off their arms. I smelled the woodsmoke pouring from the chimney pots, heard the sound of the droshky cabs clopping along the streets, and the loud, vehement people calling to one another in Yiddish. I saw Cousin Gimpel, that dear friend, his wandering iris floating aimlessly, his other fixed before him as he walked to prayer. He looked older than I remembered, and so intent. Gone was his bumbling manner, his foolish smile. This was a wise man, a man who knew the holy names, the Book of Creation. He had hid his power from all of us. Why? I wondered. Out of modesty? An unwillingness to face what he really was? I would never know. Filled with curiosity, I took off and buzzed over to where my own name might be. After a long search I found it. Jacob Cerf. Married to Hodel Mendel. Issue: Ethiop. Ethiop married Hannah and they begat Jacob, Sarah, Abraham, and Scheindl. I hovered over the name of my son, afraid to land, and yet wanting so much to see his face. In the end, of course, I alighted.

I found myself in a tailor's shop. Pigeonhole cubbies filled with every color of thread and ribbon lined the walls. A large glass window framed a well-heeled populace bustling outside. The women wore the waists of their dresses very high now, just below the breasts. They didn't wear wigs, but charming little knots of hair at the base of their necks. How I wished I could try my luck with those beauties. Now my gaze shifted. I saw a young man seated in a fine black suit, a yarmulke on his head, his pale face bent over his work. My son had my light eyes and a quick, foxlike expression, the dark brows and swarthy skin of Mme Mendel. He was sewing a gentleman's waistcoat with great intensity. The silk was pale green as new leaves. Ethiop's work was fine, precise. I stayed with him for several hours. He only looked up from his task when a customer walked into the shop. The man was tall, wearing a pair of tight-fitting vanilla-colored woolen britches and a short navy jacket. To my surprise, he referred to Ethiop as "citizen." *Had the Jews become citizens of France?* I wondered, incredulous. My son deftly took the man's measurements, made notes of his desires for a new jacket, and nodded without a hint of servile groveling when the man left. I was impressed.

At noon a large dark girl in a matron's bonnet swished in. She had a covered basket dangling over her arm. Ethiop peeked under the cloth with a smile, anticipating his lunch. This was clearly his wife. She was pregnant. With my grandchild! I could have wept. After that, greedy for more of my lineage, I walked the generations, each name streaming its secrets fluidly through my sensitive feet, flooding my eyes. We were a prosperous, fecund family. By 1900, my heirs had moved out of the cramped Jewish quarter, into a newly built neighborhood, with paved wide boulevards and freshly planted trees. They lived bourgeois Parisian lives. Ethiop's tailoring business was passed down from father to son all the way to a boy named Max, who eschewed tailoring to become a professor of French literature at the Sorbonne in 1935. Max's last name was Levi, but he was my direct descendant. I saw him very clearly as I traversed the letters of his name: dark-haired, honey-eyed, with a narrow jaw and a somewhat pointy chin, he looked like the Jewish intellectual he was.

## 42

PARIS, SEPTEMBER, 1941

Max chopped the onion fine. Behind him, oil smoked in a pan. He swiveled around, turned down the gas, slid the onions off the chopping board with a frayed wooden spoon, watched them sizzle and brown. He was making his wife, Suzielle, her favorite dish, even though he had just discovered she was having an affair with a mutual friend of theirs. The compulsion to please her in this way was odd, and he wondered at it.

Max had a lot of time to cook these days. One year earlier, shortly after the German invasion, he had been fired from his professorship at the university in a general culling of Jews from the teaching professions. Now, with the occupation, as a Jew he was banned from:

public swimming pools
restaurants
cafés
theaters
cinemas
concerts

music halls

markets

museums

libraries

public exhibitions

historical monuments

sporting events, and

parks.

He could only shop between five in the afternoon and seven at night, when all the good food, rationed already, had been bought up. He had been lucky to find the carp. His parents and sister were already in Cuba. Max had elected to stay in Paris, in part out of loyalty to his wife, in part because he didn't believe he would be harmed by the French police. They were rounding up the refugees, not the old, established families. His mother was nearly hysterical when he put his parents and sister on a train to Lisbon, their port of embarcation. She wanted her only son with her, and she distrusted Suzielle. Mme Levi had taken the liberty of obtaining a coveted French exit visa for Max, as well as Spanish and Portuguese transit visas. She begged him to get to Lisbon as fast as he could, as the visas would expire in three months. Max did not yet have an entry visa to Cuba, or the United States, or Mexico, but his mother had applied for all of them on his behalf. Instinctively, he had put off discussing his mother's escape plans with his wife.

Suzielle smoked as she ate, as she always did, her fine, plucked eyebrows arched over a pair of upturned green eyes. A sharply drawn mouth, thin nose, hennaed hair made her look a bit like a circus performer, though she was a clerk in a bookstore. That's how he'd met her—over a copy of Baudelaire. Max didn't touch his food as he watched his wife dispatch hers efficiently, her garnet-colored nails flashing as she bent over the plate to snatch another bite of fish, chewing rapidly.

"Your carp is wonderful, as always," she pronounced emphatically.
"*À la juive*," he said.

"The best recipe in the world," she said, finishing the last bite. She took a long, final drag of her Gauloise, stamped it out in the remains of the sauce, and stretched, smoke streaming from her nose.

"I worked so long today," she said.

"It must be difficult, being employed," he said.

"Oof," she exclaimed, rising with her plate and sweeping up his. "You didn't eat," she noticed, walking leisurely to the sink, overturning a plastic tub, and humming as she turned on the tap.

"What a picture," Max said, looking at her.

"What? I always do the dishes when you cook!"

"Yes," he said. "You are a marvel."

"Why are you so sarcastic today? Did something happen?"

"Nothing special. A couple of French policemen came by."

"What did they want?"

"They confiscated my bicycle."

"Why?"

"Jews aren't allowed to have bicycles anymore, apparently. They were quite embarrassed. German orders, you know how it is. Also—radios." Suzielle swiveled around to where the radio normally stood.

"But that was *my* radio!"

"I know! The injustice of it. I told them. They did say that in mixed marriages the confiscation of property becomes very tricky." Suzielle dried her hands hastily on a tea towel and grabbed her coat from the hook.

"Where are you going?" asked Max.

"To the police! You aren't some Pole who just got off the train! You are a Frenchman! Your family goes back to the eighteenth century, in Paris! They can't just steal your belongings."

"But that's the thing—they can, Suzielle. That's what I realized—only today, because I'm an idiot. They can. I've been a fool all this time, staying here, thinking I was safe because I am a French citizen with Balzac in my head, better than the poor Eastern refugees gushing into Paris, with their beards and their caftans. But as it turns out, for them I am only a Jew, whatever my education and attire."

"For the Germans . . ."

"It was a French policeman who took my bicycle. It'll be a French policeman who knocks on my door when it's time to put me on a train."

Suzielle stood, solemn, her dance-hall legs turned outward, arms dangling at her sides. "You blame me," she said.

"Not for this, no. Why would I?"

"Then for what?" she asked.

"My dear Suzielle. I prefer not to."

Still, she went to the police.

When she returned, embarrassed yet triumphant, with her radio but no bicycle, Max had departed. He left no note, but the dishes were washed.


CONEY ISLAND, 1943


Max lay on the double bed staring up at the lumbering ceiling fan, sweat trickling from his temples. His cotton shirt clung to him. Hot as Paris could be, it was nothing compared to August in New York. This was pure swamp heat; paved nature, asserting her rights. The crazy rattle of a roller-coaster drifted through the wall, accompanied by dispassionate screams. He tried not to think of the real screaming going on across the Atlantic.

Max had been lucky to find this place. A couple he'd met while stalled for a month in Lisbon waiting for a boat to New York had given him the lead. His new landlady, Lydia Schwartz, had a weakness for refugees. She rented him her largest seafront room for a nominal sum.

Every morning, after his breakfast of black coffee and a slice of rye bread, Max took a stroll along the Coney Island boardwalk. The morning pleasure seekers stood in line for the Ferris wheel, roller coaster, ice-cream cones with unsmiling, even dour patience, as if waiting to buy sardines. As the sun climbed there were flocks of them. These people took their frivolity very seriously, Max noticed. Only when they were terrified on one of the rides did they bare their teeth in a smile, their mouths open and shrieking in high-pitched, automated bursts. It was all so far from what he had come from in Europe, he found it impossible to comprehend. The Coney Island images he saw every day simply lay in his brain undigested, like a wad of chewing gum stuck in a kid's intestine: Salamandar Boy eating a sandwich in his tank, little flipper hands gripping the bread as the bearded lady chatted to him, smoking; floating bouquets of balloons struggling against their tethers in the breeze; fluffy domes of light blue and pink and yellow spun sugar, the tender colors trembling against the crumbling gray woodwork of the amusement park, with its long traditions of ritual excess. People descending pell-mell in chutes, whipped around in teacups, yelping in the House of Horrors. A painted face high as a hill, its open mouth a gateway to hours of fun in Luna Park. At night, winking lights, swirling pinwheels of light, comets of light. Faces hungry for pleasure, eyes straining to see what's next, what's new. Carnival without end. All this while nobody knew where all those people in Paris were being taken in the trains. To the East. And none of them ever came back. The trains in France had never run so punctually as when there were Jews in them. Maybe there was a full boxcar pulling out of Drancy at this instant. How was it possible, as a ten-foot-high custard cone cast a shadow on Max's bronzed face, as a thousand half-naked people were swarming into the Atlantic for their morning dip, as the dark-skinned man squirting mustard on his hot dog smiled without malice and asked if he wanted onions?

Poring over the job listings in the newspaper, Max did not see any openings for professors of French literature. He realized with a shock just how unqualified he was for any kind of practical work. He had given himself over entirely to a life of the mind. He could not plumb a drain, build a chair, sew a jacket, lay bricks. He barely spoke English. He had no driver's license. Finally, the doe-eyed Mrs. Schwartz set him up with a cousin of hers who owned a carpet remnant store on Flatbush Avenue. His days were spent heaving rolls of wall-to-wall carpeting from shelves to the floor and back to the shelves again. Eventually he was promoted to sales. The women loved his accent. He sold a deep-pile taupe remnant to the mother of a quiet dark-haired girl named Maxine, of all things. Just twenty, she stood at the back of the shop as he spoke to her mother. Now and then he caught her observing him and she smiled very slightly. Three days later she returned, ostensibly to buy a welcome mat. Max asked her to dinner. At one point during the meal he made her laugh; she flopped her head back and howled. That laugh was what made him fall in love with her. His instinct was correct: Maxine was passionate, loyal, vivid, and hardheaded. Once his divorce from Suzielle came through (hurried along by a French bureaucracy eager to split mixed couples), he proposed. Max and Maxine.

After the war, as the attempt began to scrape Nazi pus from the rotting abdomen of Europe, Max, with the help of Maxine, opened a carpet business in Flatbush. His refinement lent the place class. Maxine's practical streak kept it in the black. Within a few years the couple had opened a store in Manhattan that also sold high-end rugs from Turkey and Morocco. By this time Max and Maxine had three children: Sam, David, and Dinah. Once they could afford it, Max moved the family to the Upper West Side. He became a member of the Metropolitan Opera, sent his children to private schools, took courses at Columbia to satisfy his intellect. A total believer in assimiliation, he put up a Christmas tree along with the menorah. Sam became a doctor, David a journalist.

It was Dinah who strayed back to her roots. She met an Orthodox girl from Brooklyn on a camping trip with the 92nd Street Y. The two corresponded, and Dinah went to spend the weekend with her new friend. Without Max or Maxine realizing it, Dinah was gradually falling in love with Judaism. She majored in Jewish studies at Brandeis, and started dressing more and more modestly. Maxine, a straight talker, asked her if she was planning on becoming a nun. Dinah responded passionately that she had had enough of Max and Maxine's indifference to their religion. She didn't understand how they could simply throw away five thousand years of tradition, an incomparable history of suffering and resilience. She made a break with the family, married an Orthodox yeshiva student from Long Island, started what she hoped would be an enormous family, and cut her parents off.

Over the years, the rift was sutured together but never healed completely: Max simply couldn't understand why, when the feast of American Possibility was laid before her, his only daughter decided to leave it untouched and eat gefilte fish instead. Dinah covered her dark hair in a wig, grew her skirts below the knee, and sent her children to be educated in religious schools that gave short shrift to secular studies. This was what Max could never forgive: his grandchildren would grow up ignorant of the great European culture that was their birthright. Yet, Dinah contended, they would lead deeply spiritual lives, live according to the word of G-d, and anyway, who needed more than the Torah, the Talmud, all the commentaries, and, for the boys if they got that far, the Zohar? There was a world of knowledge in those books; it took a lifetime to understand half of them. What was so wonderful about secular materialism?

Dinah was fertile as well as obstinate: she gave birth to seven children, the youngest of whom was Pearl. So, all in all, I had spawned twelve generations. Fuck you, Hitler! What a deity. To think that I, sybaritic stage strutter, libertine valet, son abandoner, police informant, and apostate, should end up as patriarch to a vast tribe of Israelites . . . These were my *children*.

As the news sank in, I began to play the part: crossing Pearl's coffee table, I affected a grandfatherly shuffle, my wings tucked officiously behind my back as I inspected my descendants. I saw myself with a well-tended white beard, a neat paunch, green slippers, and—a yarmulke. Yes: overwhelmed by the strange, intransigent beauty of our way of life, the indestructible story line of our people, joy and terror mingled in me, building into awe as I contemplated the fate of the Jews. I was vanquished. The Old Man had concocted a logic so deep and so wide I could not but drown laughing at the folly of my own life. The care he'd taken! Honing each detail until it sparkled. Only love could fuel such dedication to a single, humble being. Could it be he lavished equal attention on *every soul*?

An alternate cosmology presented itself to me as I stood there trembling: before Creation, when Hashem was nothing but a perfect mind, something funny occurred to him. Like a baby letting out his first guffaw, he cracked himself up, burst out laughing, and exploded into the physical world.

*I submit*, I thought feverishly. *You triumph. Not only do You exist, You are everything. You are good, You made evil. There is nothing but You in all the universe. I was a fool to think I was raising Masha up, bringing Leslie down. It was all You!* But he wasn't done with me yet. My religious ecstasy had taken me so far from awareness of my own body that I had flown into the kitchen without knowing it. And there was Masha, formerly the object of my lust, now my great- (times five) granddaughter, wearing a pair of horrifyingly skimpy shorts and platform shoes, hunched over the cold stove, eating from the cholent pot—from the stew meant for the coming Shabbat—*with her fingers*, just as Hodel did when she was possessed! The girl turned then and looked in my direction, checking the doorway, her eyes the eerie multicolors of oil on a black pond. Her lips had gravy on them. Her snarled hair hung down, half covering her face. The river demon. That's what she was. "*The iniquity of the sons shall be visited on the third and fourth generations.*" Well, he went further than that in my case.

This thing had survived nearly three hundred years. The creature's cell phone vibrated in the pocket of her shorts and she flipped it open, turning toward the stove to hide it. I flew behind her and read over her shoulder:

*open your front door*

## 43

Masha opened the door. It was Derbhan Nevsky, his clothes blazing white, hopping from one foot to the other.

"I've been trying to reach you since yesterday," he whispered, exasperated.

"It's Shabbos," Masha said, leaning her hip on the doorsill. The sight of Nevsky irritated her.

"You're not going back to that, are you? This is not the time," he said, looking up and down the street.

"I just didn't think of turning on the phone till now," she said, shrugging. "What do you want to tell me?"

"You got the part," he announced. "In the Rathgar Kennet musical—*My Alchemy*. You got it."

"What? I thought that was all over."

"It was. They cast a girl, got her out there, and she didn't work out. Kennet fired her, reviewed all the audition tapes. Now they want *you*. We gotta get you to Mexico."

"When?"

"Now. Shooting started September first. There's a fitting scheduled for tomorrow morning." Behind Nevsky, mute threads of far-off lightning glimmered in the sky. Nevsky swiveled around to see what she was looking at.

Masha stomped upstairs screaming with excitement, broadcasting the headline of her triumph and imminent departure through every room in the house. Rueful, jealous, proud, I watched her take off, a blur of limbs ascending. That was my path she was taking. Hovering sadly in the air, I saw myself reflected in her, purified, my debasements burned away, my talent deepened. Our shared fate was hers to complete. My girl was going to be glorious!

Masha rushed into her room, opened the closet, and removed a small light-blue child's suitcase, the only one she owned. Flipping the clasps and opening it onto the bed, a thought came to her. It didn't matter how long she had. She would just eat up whatever time she had left, grab it with both her hands, consume it, and apologize to no one. That's what she would do.

Pearl invited the small, nervous agent man into the kitchen, gave him a cup of coffee and a blintze. She sat down beside him, feeling a strange kind of relief mixed with mourning. She knew that Masha had to go. In a way, she even wanted her to. That was the worst of it.

"Will they take care of her?" she asked him.

"Take care of her! She'll be treated like a queen. I'll make sure of it. This director may be a genius, by the way."

"But . . . what happened to the other girl, the one they chose first?" asked Pearl.

"She wasn't Masha. That was her problem. This is Masha's part. Sometimes things have a way of aligning themselves," said Nevsky mysteriously, pressing the edge of his fork into the blintze. "These are spectacular, Mrs. Edelman," he said, chewing rapidly.

"Thank you," said Pearl. Nevsky looked up at her solemn face and winced. It was so unpleasant being face-to-face with open pain.

"Masha can't help being what she is, any more than that fly can turn himself into a ladybug," he said, pointing a leathery finger in my direction. In the process of performing my morning ablutions in a droplet of water, I rubbed my forepaws together in prayerful assent.

Her attention drawn to me, Pearl stared down for a long moment. I knew this was the end. I didn't move. I was ready. Nevsky watched, his loaded fork poised midair, as my progeny raised her hand. The canopy of her palm stiffened above me. I spread my legs wide, lying prostrate on the table, and prepared for my execution.

*Please, El Shaddai, Creator of all things, listen to me!* I cried in desperation. *I got it all wrong! I frittered away my life in sin, You gave me a chance to return, and what do I do? I mess it up again, thinking only how to hurt You, ruin people's lives. But now I swear I've learned my lesson. I beg You: let me be born as a man again. I promise to be good next time!*

As Pearl's killing hand descended, I heard a dark sound, a kind of cosmic drumroll, clustering, echoing, tumbling—down from a mirthful sky.

*Acknowledgments*

I would like to thank Max McGuinness, whose dogged research helped me penetrate some of the mysteries of life among eighteenth-century Jews, and whose knowledge of the French Enlightenment was crucial to my own understanding; Suri Weingott, who welcomed me into her home, allowing me a view of her family life, its rituals and traditions; Rabbi Ellen Lippmann, Rabbi Scott Fox, Shulamit Kadosh, and Julia Bolus, for their advice and expertise; Gene Spiotta, for opening up the world of fire rescue and the culture of volunteering, as well as being an inspirational figure; Jane Spiotta, for her hospitality and the tours of Patchogue; Peggy Gormley, for the hours inside the eruv in Far Rockaway; my agent, Sarah Chalfant, for her early enthusiasm and constancy; my editor, Jonathan Galassi; my dear Daniel, Gabriel, Ronan, and Cashel, who have helped shape this book, each in his own way.